NOW, CONJURERS

NOW, CONJURERS

FREDDIE KÖLSCH

UNION
SQUARE
& CO.

NEW YORK

UNION
SQUARE
& CO.
NEW YORK

ISBN 978-1-4549-5159-9 (hardcover)
ISBN 978-1-4549-5161-2 (e-book)
ISBN 978-1-4549-5160-5 (paperback)

Library of Congress Cataloging-in-Publication Data

Names: Kölsch, Freddie, author.
Title: Now, conjurers / by Freddie Kölsch.
Description: New York, New York : Union Square & Co., 2024. | Audience:
 Ages 14-18. | Summary: "Following the murder of their leader and friend,
 a tight-knit coven of queer teens takes on a wish-granting demon lurking
 in their town"-- Provided by publisher.
Identifiers: LCCN 2023029201 (print) | LCCN 2023029202 (ebook) | ISBN
 9781454951599 (hardcover) | ISBN 9781454951605 (trade paperback) | ISBN
 9781454951612 (epub)
Subjects: CYAC: Witches--Fiction. | Supernatural--Fiction. | LGBTQ+
 people--Fiction. | Horror stories. | BISAC: YOUNG ADULT FICTION / Horror
 | YOUNG ADULT FICTION / Paranormal, Occult & Supernatural | LCGFT:
 Paranormal fiction. | Horror fiction. | Romance fiction. | Novels.
Classification: LCC PZ7.1.K67566 No 2024 (print) | LCC PZ7.1.K67566
 (ebook) | DDC [Fic]--dc23
LC record available at https://lccn.loc.gov/2023029201
LC ebook record available at https://lccn.loc.gov/2023029202

For information about custom editions, special sales, and premium purchases,
please contact specialsales@unionsquareandco.com.

Printed in the United States of America

2 4 6 8 10 9 7 5 3 1

unionsquareandco.com

Cover and interior design by Liam Donnelly

This one is for Katharine Lynn
Miyajima Hochswender.

After a while, crocodile.

CHAPTER ONE

Sunday, November 21, 1999

Bastion's corpse was found in the thin woods at the edge of Stepwood Cemetery, covered in bite marks, by the biggest dickbag at Regional No. 9 High School. Cameron Winship, a junior and our school's only notable track-and-field star, was taking his bleach-blond bowl cut out for a morning run when he literally stumbled across my boyfriend's dead body.

Or so we thought at the time. Actually, at the time I wasn't thinking at all, because North Coven had planned a ritual for eleven o'clock sharp, and the four of us had walked up to the crime scene about ten minutes after the cops and the first responders.

Cameron never went for a run without his $900 Nokia, which further illustrated what a total dickbag he was, but it came in handy when he discovered the cadaver of his murdered classmate. I think he was in a shock blanket when we walked out of the woods and tried to understand what we were seeing. I'm actually sure he was, sitting there like a wounded deer and tearfully

1

talking to a cop, but I only noticed Cameron for a second before I started screaming.

They hadn't covered Bastion up yet, and so I got a last look at him before he was loaded into a body bag, only to see that the fingers had been chewed off on both of his hands. His handsome face, with the white patch of vitiligo over the left eye, looked like it had been pushed through a lawn mower. Blood congealed over holes in his black jeans where something had *eaten* at him, chunk of flesh by chunk of flesh. So yeah, I screamed. I started screaming his name and then Dove started yelling and pushing her way through the people working, which made sense, because he was her *baby brother*, even if he was like a foot taller than her.

It was so obviously a murder that they didn't want us contaminating the scene, if you follow me. I ran after her, trying to shove through the cops and EMTs and whoevers to get to Bastion, and when someone grabbed Dove in a way I felt (in my shock-induced freak-out) was too rough, I will admit that I started throwing my fists around, which is how it happened that three grown men had to pin me to the freezing November graveyard ground on the day I saw Bastion for the last time.

I mean, for the second-to-last time.

Later, when I'd been given "something to calm me down," and Drea and Brandy had gone home with their respective moms, and Dove and Bastion's parents had gotten the worst news of their lives, my older brother picked me up from the emergency clinic that was the closest thing North Dana had to a real hospital.

"Dad's coming back from Boston right now," Nic told me.

Like I cared at that moment. As far as my dad knew, Bastion was just my friend from my weird little witch group, not my first boyfriend and my true love and the most fascinating person to ever walk the earth.

"From the . . . Is he at the car show?" I asked. I felt like I was talking through a wad of cotton.

I don't remember if Nic answered me, though, because the sedatives finally kicked in around then, and I faded into nightmares. I dreamed I was at the auto show my dad had gone to . . . but in that long gray room every dim spotlight lit a shining antique hearse, and from behind each silver grille of each black car I could hear Bastion crying out for me.

"*Nesbit,*" he called, faint and pleading. "*Nesbit, you have the power now. Not* just *you—it's for all five of you, of course—but* **you** *have the dreams—*"

"Bastion!" I screamed, terrified for him even in my sleep. "Bastion! Where are you?!"

"*No—please stop him, why won't you stop him? Nesbit, I revoked the token, you have the power now . . . no, no, oh help oh god oh please he's killing me—*"

And in my dream, I clawed fruitlessly at the front of each car in turn until the skin on my hands tore and Bastion's terrified entreaties turned into agonized, wordless shrieks. As something I couldn't see ate him alive. When I woke up it was Monday afternoon, and I had pressed my nails so hard into my hands that I had eight bloody half-moon marks on the flesh of my palms.

After a minute of staring at my hands, I flipped my left hand over to look at the little tattoos that ornamented each of my fingers.

A heart for Dove.

A sword for Bastion.

An eye for Brandy.

A mouth for Drea.

And finally, on my thumb, a little miniature hand, index finger pointing skyward, like you sometimes see on the top of old gravestones.

My most meaningful tattoos. North Coven, united.

Never to be united again.

"Bastion."

I said his name out loud. Once. Just one time, like I was talking to him.

Then I went out to the kitchen and started my life without him. If you can believe it, things only got worse from there.

CHAPTER TWO

Friday, November 26,
& Saturday, November 27, 1999

The wake was held at the Attias' rambling colonial mansion on Friday night. I didn't want to talk about the wake with Dad or Nic, so I lied and said I was going to skip it entirely and take a long calming drive around the reservoir.

I did head to the wake, though, and made it as far as the Osiris statue that guarded the long front porch before I felt sick to my stomach. I put my Walkman on and listened to the entirety of *Cause for Alarm* while I hid on one of the garden benches scattered throughout the huge yard, watching people come and go from behind a shield of holly bushes. I tried to make myself go in. I would stand in the line of mourners and shake hands with the family of the dead boy I had kissed less than a week before. I would say the right things. Be sad but not so sad that it was *embarrassing* for everyone else. I would try to act normal. Any second now I would get up.

The people came and went, and I stayed still. In a world where Bastion wasn't dead, North Coven would be heading over to the Micenmachers' Y2K party tonight. But the party had been canceled, out of respect for the murdered quarterback.

Every breath I exhaled in the freezing air looked like a tiny phantom, and I watched the foggy air dissipate and thought about the first time I ever met Bastion, how it seemed like I'd been waiting to meet him forever without knowing it.

I restarted the CD at the same time that the holly bushes crinkled and Dove appeared, with Drea and Brandy behind her. It was funny—they wore black from head to toe every day, so their wake clothing just looked like business as usual. Brandy was blotchy from crying, but everything else seemed normal.

"Hiding?" Dove asked. Her eyes were dry, but she looked like she hadn't slept in days. School had only been a two-day week before Thanksgiving break, and I had stayed home Monday and Tuesday, unable to handle the thought of sitting through a weepy memorial service for Bastion on the gym bleachers. So it was the first time the four of us had been face-to-face since the day we'd seen Bastion's body, and I saw a terrible feeling reflected back at me in the faces of my three best friends. *Haunted.* We all looked haunted.

"Yeah," I said. "I don't think I can go in there. And see your parents and . . . everyone."

Brandy sat down next to me, tucking her long black skirt around her for maximum heat retention.

"But what if his killer shows up?" Drea countered, sitting on my other side. "He could be anybody here."

Dove stayed standing and pulled out one of her extra-skinny, extra-long menthol cigarettes. Her prized red S.T. Dupont lighter appeared from her pocket like magic, flamed into the air, and vanished again. Drea reached out for a drag, and I watched the shapes the cigarette smoke made in the air and thought about ghosts.

"If he does, we won't know it," Brandy said. "He'll just seem like anybody else."

We all knew enough about murder statistics to assume the killer was a man. Murders, serial killers, violent crimes, conspiracies: these things were basically Drea's greatest passion in life, and she had educated the rest of the us extensively. Her VCR played taped-off-the-network episodes of *The X-Files* and *Unsolved Mysteries* in an endless alternating loop.

"The coroner's office confirmed it was a murder," Dove said when I looked at her questioningly. "They thought animal attack for a little while, they said, because of the . . . intensity of the wounds."

Dove's mouth was set in a grim line. Her eyes were the same honey-brown color as Bastion's, and for a second, I had to glance down at my lap and realign myself to this awful new world instead of just getting lost in the *unreality* of it.

If I went inside right then, I thought, Bastion would be waiting for me, and everything would be normal. We could have dinner with his folks and then go for a drive around the Quabbin Reservoir. I would give him another lesson on parallel parking, the only thing I'd ever seen Bastion actually suck at, and then I'd park in a secluded spot and we would make out while the windows on my aging Hyundai fogged up and the stars came out.

If only you would just be okay, I begged, silently. *I would even let you pick the music tonight. Even if it was that droning classical crap with harps. Anything. I would hardly even tease you about it, Bastion. You can forget about our last fight, too. I'll never bring it up again. Just don't be dead.*

"Bastion told me you guys had a fight," Dove said, in the mind-reader way that she has sometimes.

"Yeah," I admitted, embarrassed by how choked up I sounded. "We did. About the 'I love you' thing."

"You *know* he can't!" Dove snapped, almost viciously. "Christ, Nez, like you don't know he has problems—" She cut herself off, her anger vanishing as quickly as it'd appeared. "*Had* problems," she amended, taking a long drag from her skinny cigarette.

Brandy started to cry, and Drea reached an arm behind me to grab her shoulder.

"We have to figure out who did this before the cops," Dove said, throwing the end of her menthol onto the ground and crushing it out with one heavy stomp of her boot. "I want to kill whoever it was. Find him. End him. If the cops get him, he'll just go to jail."

"I do, too," Drea said, and even Brandy nodded through her tears. They all looked at me, waiting for my answer.

I thought about it. Even if we somehow managed to figure anything out, Bastion wouldn't have wanted us to exact vigilante justice. Off the football field, he was a pacifist. He disliked violence, bullying, and general cruelty in all forms, which was part of what had made him clash with Cameron Winship's group so frequently.

"They tore him apart, Nez," Dove said when I was quiet for a beat too long. "Somebody ate my little brother's tongue and his heart. *Chewed* on him."

"Jesus. Stop," I said, holding up a hand. But Dove was relentless.

"They did it with their hands and teeth. Anna freaked out when they told her it was gonna have to be a closed-casket funeral because his body was so . . . wrecked. We can't ever tell Wren or Robin or Lark what happened because they're too little and it will, like, damage them forever. I . . . can't live in a world where we don't *find* this bastard. Please. Help me."

"Dove—"

"Please. We *have* to."

They were all my best friends, but Dove was my *best* best friend, and she had never asked for anything this important before. Still, it wasn't her asking that decided me. I was remembering the way Bastion's hands, his fingers gnawed to nothing, were curled into his chest. Like he had been trying to protect himself from something even as it consumed him.

"Fine," I said. "We can investigate. I don't know if I want to kill him . . . *them*, or whatever. I might want to turn him in. *If* we find him."

"Let's decide that when we find him," Drea said.

"If we *can* find them," Brandy said, her voice still a little teary. "It seems like not a . . . natural killing, doesn't it? Monstrous. An inhuman murderer. With the . . . *wounds* being so severe."

That idea sent an icy bolt of fright down my spine. My forearms broke out in goose bumps. Drea looked equally creeped out.

Bastion had been eaten alive. Now that Brandy had said it aloud, it couldn't be unsaid. The grim possibility of other magic—magic beyond our own—filled the silence around us with an ominous feeling. Until Dove dismissed it.

"No way," she said. "We've been practicing together for years and the only supernatural things I've ever seen in the Near-Depths—or anywhere else—are *us*."

I didn't know if I entirely agreed with her. But I was not in the mood to think about monsters.

"I'll help you investigate," I said. "We'll all do it together. Then, *if* we find the murderer, we can figure out what kind of justice we want to exact, okay?"

"Agreed," Drea said.

"Agreed," Brandy said.

"Agreed," Dove said, with a look that did nothing to convince me she wouldn't try to kill the guy who killed Bastion the instant we had a name.

"We should meet tomorrow," Brandy whispered. "After the . . . after. And do a spell. For answers."

None of us voiced our doubts about whether a spell would even work with only four members of the coven. We didn't have to say it. I couldn't imagine our magic working without Bastion to lead us.

"It's just like the other murder," Dove said, after a beat of silence while I hunted around in my jacket for my box cutter. I'd worn a black sweater to look decent, just in case I actually attended the wake, but I only had one jacket: my dad's cast-off black work one with the shoulder patches and Dickies tag, the

Nuñez Auto Body logo my brother had designed for him stitched on the back in red.

"What other murder?" I asked, finding the blade in my inside left pocket. "The body you guys found when you were kids?"

"That was like nine years ago," Drea said, sitting forward. "You think it's the same killer?"

"Most definitely," Dove said, pulling up her sleeve. "The way we found that lady, the Jane Doe, it was . . . it was the same, and it was like twenty yards from where Bastion was. You know. *Found*. I'll tell you about it tomorrow."

"We're not going to be allowed to go back to Stepwood after *two* murders," Brandy said, pulling off her fancy gloves.

"So we'll make something up," Drea said, and I nodded in agreement. "It's not like they're going to ban us from hanging out."

"We'll be okay if we're all together," I said. "They might do a town curfew or something. They never caught the guy who killed your Jane Doe, did they?"

"No. No, they did not," Dove said. I understood a little better why she was so vehement about us investigating. The idea of someone doing that to Bastion and getting away with it sat in my stomach like a stone.

"Nexus?" Brandy asked, and I pushed the button on my box cutter. The razor slid out with a satisfying *schnnk*, and I held the blade aloft in the direction of the North Star.

Nexus. Bastion's word for a pact made by the coven, to be used only for the most important business.

"Nexus, my nulligravida," I said. That was Bastion-speak for *time to make an oath, bitches*. Making fun of his way of talking was easily one of our favorite pastimes when he was alive, but without him there to look unfazed by our teasing, it fell flat.

Brandy let out a shaky breath, and I cut a capital N lightly into the skin above the bone of her left wrist before she could start crying again. I waited until I saw a few tiny beads of blood appear on the cut to move on to Dove, then Drea. Finally, I handed the blade to Brandy so she could do mine. Bloodwork was rare, and any cuts we made on ourselves in the name of North Coven usually faded entirely after we completed the ritual associated with them. All of our lingering scars were from other, non-magic-related crap.

"Tomorrow at eight we investigate," I said, and kissed the N on Brandy's wrist.

"Tomorrow at eight we investigate," Brandy echoed, and kissed Dove's wrist. Dove repeated this to Drea, and Drea then kissed my wrist, and the pact was sealed. I felt no thrum of power, no sudden hush in the air, nothing like before.

"It will work," Dove said, acknowledging the fact that *nothing* seemed to be happening, no matter how defiantly. "It has to."

"I hope so," Drea said, and the three of them trudged back up the stone path to the grief-stricken Attia household.

I retreated to my car, slammed the bright-orange door (custom-painted by yours truly), and drove home. I wanted to listen to *Cause for Alarm* again because it felt like a night to blast music until I couldn't think anymore, but I fat-fingered the panel when I was putting the disc into the (custom-installed by yours truly) CD player and ended up slapping the FM button. The radio blared to life and filled my car with thunderous classical music. It was still tuned to WJIN, the Northampton public access station that played three hours of orchestral pieces every Friday night. The station Bastion always put on when he got into the Hyundai for a date night after his football games. Just like he had a week ago, when he was still alive, grinning his broad, handsome grin and declaring *Now, this is music, Nesbit!*, or something equally pompous. I thought about our last date. Couldn't bring myself to change the station. It felt like a betrayal somehow. I couldn't bring myself to go home just then either, so I ended up taking a drive around the reservoir after all, and I didn't head home until the guy who ran the classical bloc passed the radio-program torch to two college girls doing a show that consisted of spoken-word poetry read over a background of acid house music.

At home, I slept badly and woke up around noon the following day to the sound of my brother using the table saw directly behind my bedroom wall. Lately, Nic spent weekends working on our eternally under-construction "back deck," a project I liked way less than his spring and summer weekend project, when he'd been apprenticing at Black Thistle Tattoo over in Gardner. Throughout my entire summer vacation, he had spent weekends honing his craft on my skin. By the beginning of junior year, I had more tattoos—ranging in skill level as he got better, from *extremely badly done* to *very cool*—on my body than any other student at Regional 9. Now that Nic was a real tattoo artist and did it for work, he was way less inclined to ink me in his free time, so my Bad Brains sleeve had been in unfinished limbo for three months.

Dad was working at his shop on the lot to the left of our house, and when I went outside with my coffee, I could hear him talking to Manny and Erik in the pauses where Nic turned the saw off. Rich people came from all around central Massachu-setts to have my dad fix their old cars, and rich people didn't work weekends (if they worked at all), so Dad's weekend was Monday and Tuesday. It was a relief that he wasn't in the house. Dad had been hovering in an overprotective way since Bastion was murdered, asking me lots of prying questions, coming up with new rules to restrict my freedom and *keep me safe* that I planned on ignoring, and even calling Mom and sticking me on the phone with her so that we "could have a long talk." He'd actu-ally said I could take another week off from school after Thanks-giving break if I needed to, an unprecedented allowance in the Nuñez household.

Outside it was cold and bright. The sky was a solid blanket of light gray clouds. Nic was plugging the sander into an extension cord, but he stopped when he saw me.

"Dad wants me to take you to the funeral," Nic said. "When is it?"

"Three. I don't need you to come. I'm picking up Drea and Brandy on the way, we planned it days ago."

"Tough titties," Nic said, taking his cigarette-replacement toothpick out of his mouth and flicking it at me. I dodged it and gave him the finger.

"I'm serious, Nic, it's private and we're hanging out later," I said. Nic produced another one of his gross, I-quit-smoking-this-year toothpicks and popped it between his teeth.

"Don't care. Dad said I have to."

I stomped back inside as loudly as I could manage with only socks on, dumped the dregs of my coffee in the sink, and went to the closet-sized third bedroom of our little ranch. When Nic had decided to assert his independence as an adult and "moved out" into the Winnebago in the driveway, we'd converted his old room into a workout space, but mostly I was the only one who used it to work out while Dad used it to expand his hoard of spare tools and junk. There was a boom box plugged in next to my weight bench, and I shoved a stack of *Hemmings Motor News* magazines off the top and turned it on.

I heard the screen door slam and a minute later Nic was in front of me, chewing his toothpick like he hadn't eaten a decent breakfast.

"Nez, come on," he half-yelled over the opening of "Victim in Pain." "Dad's just worried."

"Yeah, well, he should be," I snapped. "There's a murderer in North Dana. Since there are only like two thousand people who live here, we have a good chance of knowing the bastard."

"He's worried about *you.*"

"I'm fine."

"Dude. It was your boyfriend who got—"

"Dad doesn't know that." *Shut up*, I added silently. Normally I didn't pick fights with Nic, especially over meaningless crap like who drove where, but I needed to be alone with the coven so we could do what we had sworn to do.

"I know," Nic said, but his forehead was wrinkled with concern. "I think he's worried you're going to kill yourself."

"I'm not going to kill myself," I said, feeling incredibly indignant. "That's projection or something. He's worried about that because you OD'd."

"Aaaand I've been clean for fourteen months," Nic said. "He's probably also worried that whoever targeted Bastion is going to target you. Dad's not *completely* up his own ass, Nez. He definitely suspects your little Wiccan group is 'unique.'"

I loaded weights onto the barbell so I didn't have to look at Nic's stupid worried face. *Unique* probably meant *gay*, which infuriated me. Bastion insisted we were safe, for reasons he'd only barely elaborated on, but I lived in the real world. In the real world, national headlines from the last year included an obviously gay kid getting tortured and left to die, tied to a fence in Wyoming like the world's saddest scarecrow. Despite the obvious parallels, I hadn't thought that Bastion could have been the victim of *that* kind of crime until the very moment that Nic brought it up, and the sudden chill I felt made me rack my weights before I dropped them on the floor. Bastion had always seemed so unconcerned, so above it all, so certain of our untouchability. It was easy to get sucked into his worldview. Still—what if?

But: Dove's Jane Doe, nine years before. Same spot, same circumstances.

"I'm pretty sure it's not about that. Seriously. But we'll stay together, in a group, I promise. We're just going to Drea's house. Her mom will be around all night. And I need therapeutic alone time with my friends," I said, trying my most serious voice. It worked, kind of.

"I have to go with you, but we can take your car. You can drop me at home right after, okay?"

"Fine. Great," I said, deliberately.

Then I spent an hour working out, trying to get lost in my music. And, of course, trying very, very hard not to think about the thing that hung around in every room I entered, just at the corner of my eye. A formless thing, but almost tangible, pushed to the edge of the space I occupied. If I focused too much on that thing, it slid closer to me, syrupy and hard to escape, like grief.

But worse. I had grieved for my grandfather and my dog. I'd even grieved when my folks got divorced, dumb as that may sound. This, however, was tainted by the viciousness of Bastion's death. It felt filthy and . . . inhuman. Somehow it stained Bastion's whole life, throwing a gauzy veil of shit over all the bright parts of his existence.

Obviously, I had no idea at that point that I was right about the inhuman thing. As far as I understood the world, there *were* witches. And spells that worked. But no monsters—never even a hint of one.

So I didn't think about monsters. I thought that I was just processing my grief in the way people do when a loved one is violently murdered.

I showered and Nic emerged from the Winnebago looking like he usually did, except in a suit. We drove in silence to the Woodland Estates trailer park and pulled up to the purple double-wide with the moon and star ornaments hanging out front. Brandy and Drea were waiting in the living room with Drea's mom.

"Hi, Jamie," I said, nodding at Drea's mom, who was surrounded by tissues and bleary-eyed on the couch. Agent Scully the tabby rubbed against my legs in greeting, leaving hair in her wake.

"Hi, Ms. Pearson," said Nic, who thought that Drea's mom was extremely hot. Hotness I can't speak to, but she was definitely my favorite out of the other members of North Coven's parents, the only one we could tell almost everything to, and the only one we had ever consulted for a spell.

"Hey, boys," Jamie said, and burst into tears.

"Mom," Drea said in the tone of someone who was currently being tortured in hell. "Please. Stop. Brandy will start again if you keep crying."

"We should go," I said.

"Are you coming, Ms. Pearson?" Nic asked with more than a glimmer of hope.

"I'm sorry, honey, I've got to work second shift," Jamie said. "But I'll be thinking about all of you. I'm so sorry. Please tell Anna and Youssef I send my love."

"I will," Nic promised.

I held my breath, waiting for Nic to realize that Drea's mom was not, in fact, going to be around when we met tonight. But he either didn't notice or didn't care, probably because she had called him *honey*.

Nobody spoke on the way to the funeral. Nic fidgeted with his toothpick next to me, and when I glanced in the rearview mirror, I could see Brandy and Drea holding hands tightly in the back seat. It made my heart twist, not just out of envy or wistfulness, but out of fear for the stability of our circle. Bastion had said that two sets of people in relationships, with Dove taking the fifth and central role as a free agent (*Free Space Slut*, Dove called it), seemed to be particularly effective. Where would we be without that efficacy? Lost in a place where we couldn't locate the murderer? What if everything went back to how it had been before?

I thought about Nic's miraculously easy sobriety right after his overdose in the summer of 1998. He had no idea how we had assisted with that. How it remained, to me, the most important spell we had ever done. What if without our stable coven he started to use again?

"Nez," Nic said.

"What?"

"You drove right by the funeral home."

"Right. Just looking for parking," I said, to cover the fact that I had been completely zoned out.

Luckily for my pride, I was correct: everywhere immediately outside of Ashby's Funeral Parlor was completely packed with cars. Cars overflowed from the funeral home's lot, and people had parked all the way up and down Main Street, slowing traffic to a crawl in North Dana's tiny downtown. The houses of all the rich people in North Dana (there weren't a ton of wealthy people in our town, but, except for the Micenmachers, the families that had money all lived right on Main) looked like they had been converted into miniature car parks. I could see the Attia house from our vantage point and Mayor Winship's family walking down to the service from their white Victorian house. Cameron walked behind his parents, looking almost as freaked out as the day he'd found Bastion's body.

I tried to enjoy Cameron's obvious misery as I locked the car. I had never hated him with Dove's passion, or with the passion of Cameron's reciprocal hatred for both Dove *and* Bastion. There was a lot of contempt being traded back and forth between our two friend groups, and very little of it belonged to me. But Cameron was still a bullying dickbag, and I still, in some illogical way, blamed him for Bastion's death—like if nobody had found his body, there wouldn't have been a murder at all.

North Coven had not even discussed the possibility that Cameron could be the murderer, and I kind of doubted it would ever seriously come up. Cameron was a star at Regional 9 when it came to track, but his speed seemed to fail him on the football field, and he just couldn't do . . . enough of whatever it is football players are supposed to do to make the varsity squad. He kept trying out for some kind of receiver-position thing every year and not getting it, and the only thing I found dumber than playing football was repeatedly trying to play it when you clearly sucked at it. Cameron was all mouth and no guts. The idea of him managing to devour Bastion alive was too stupid to even be considered. Bastion was six feet three by the time junior year started, and the one time I'd seen Cameron actually try to fight him, Bastion had lifted the asshole up and held him against a locker until Cameron literally exhausted himself.

Maybe it was a premonition that made me focus on Cameron Winship and his parents as we walked in a sad little group up to the funeral parlor entrance. The funeral director took our names and our coats and asked us to sign a register, which Brandy dutifully did first, handing the veiled vintage black hat (which she had rescued from the Salvation Army up in Gardner and lovingly restored) to Drea while she signed her name in perfect loops.

Mayor Winship stood behind us. I want to tell you that he looked just like an aged-up Cameron, but it wouldn't be true: the mayor was way taller and broader, with thick gray-white hair and a kindly smile that didn't go all the way to his eyes. Cameron had three older brothers who lived in ritzy metro areas around the country and had high-paying jobs, skinny wives, and advanced degrees from Ivy League schools. The brothers (Chase, Christopher, and

Calvin, if I'm remembering right) all looked way more like Mayor Winship than Cameron did, right down to the fake smiles. I only knew about them because their old pictures were enshrined in the football section of the giant sports trophy altar that dominated a whole wall of Regional 9's cafeteria, and it gave me a weird pleasure when we ate lunch to see Bastion's many, many trophies filling up the section and edging out the Winship boys.

Bastion was already getting talked to by recruiters for major football colleges by the time he was a sophomore, and he gave every single one a really nice speech about how he had no interest in going pro because he wanted to become a poet like his mom, or an FBI agent so he could see the aliens at Area 51 up close, or move to Kuala Lumpur and explore the expatriate community there. Always something different.

"Why do you play at all?" I asked him once, when he was cramming himself into my car after letting down another scout. "If you're so, like, indifferent to it?"

"Now, that's an interesting question," Bastion said, cranking the Hyundai's passenger seat back as far as it could go. "Not at all motivated by your distaste for organized sports, I imagine."

"Not at all," I answered, straight-faced.

"Nebulous physical benefits aside—I think I would probably risk less traumatic brain injuries if I simply took up jogging—I do it to keep my mind sharp."

I snorted. "You can just tell me if you like it. I'm not going to judge you. Any more than I do already."

Bastion turned, as much as the seat belt would allow him, to face me. I navigated out of Regional 9's student parking, feeling the intensity of his look—having Bastion focus *all* of his enormous personality on me was still a little distracting at that point—and debating between making him buy me fries at Hazy Dee's or just finding a spot in the woods around the Quabbin Reservoir where we could feel each other up without interruption.

"Nesbit, I mean it," Bastion said, rolling my name out like we were in a dark bedroom. I glanced over to see that he was giving me his best come-hither face, which was only saved from complete dweebery by how chiseled his cheekbones were.

"Nesbit, have I told you how much I enjoy your name? Nesbit, have I mentioned how I delight in the cheat of using your very attractive name to initiate my sentences? Nesbit, have I expounded upon the benefits of your name for my tongue?"

"Literally a million times," I said, trying hard not to laugh. He stuck his tongue in my ear and I faked swerving the car. "Cut it out, Big-Time Romance."

"Never," Bastion said, dramatically clutching his chest like a lovelorn actress in an old movie. His huge forearm glanced off of me harmlessly as I made my choice and pulled onto Redwick Road. Quabbin it was.

"How the hell does football keep your mind sharp?" I asked, curious about what fantastical crap he was going to spin out to prove his point. Bastion started jiggling his left leg when he saw the direction I was heading in.

"Now I'm afraid you've instilled some kind of Pavlovian response in me about Redwick Road," he said, noticing me noticing his wiggly leg. "Nesbit makes a left, and his boyfriend gets an erection."

I tried to remain cool in the face of that admission, but I felt my face turn red. "I exist to classically condition Your Enormous

Majesty until you're nothing but a walking boner. Glad to know it's working."

Bastion laughed, slapping my thigh in delight. I'll never know, now that he's dead, but I like to think that was part of why he liked me so much. I could always keep up with him. I took total pleasure in messing with him. I felt like I had been waiting for someone like Bastion to talk to for my entire life. I . . . I hope he felt the same way, no matter how awfully, ultimately alone he was in the bargain none of us knew he had made.

Bastion could get kind of prudish sometimes, especially after doing something as overtly weird as referring to his own erect dick in the third person, and he changed the subject back to the intellectually stimulating aspects of football without me having to ask again.

"Normative thinking about sports comes with the assumption that athletes are idiots," Bastion said, clearing his throat. "No matter how often the *players* might be dullards, the *games* are not. Nearly every war game, whether it's a logic-based one like chess or a game of psychology and chance, like football, involves creating multiple threats. Nurturing as Coach Thornton is, he's not too great at crafting the hundreds of plays that we must have available to make it through a game. No, he mostly borrows famous strategies . . . or leaves it to the QB, who, in addition to working on the playbook, gets to decide what strategy best fits what's happening on the ground in real time."

"You despise Coach Thornton," I reminded him. I was debating which of the many gates that led to the trails all around the reservoir would be the most abandoned on a weekday evening.

"Needed a word. *Nurturing* was supposed to be imbued with lots of sarcasm so you'd take the opposite meaning."

"I see where this is going," I said, pulling into the dusty lot that marked the entrance to Gate 43 of the Quabbin. Gloriously deserted. "You're a mastermind."

"No," Bastion said. "Not nearly good enough. N-n-n-n-n-n—"

I had just parked and looked over at him when he made that weird stuttering sound, totally freaked out, thinking for a second that he was choking. I only saw Bastion "neatly fail to meet his own verbosity," as he called it, or "get stuck," as the rest of us called it, a few times.

He always insisted that he didn't have OCD, that his tics were *physical obligations*, not mental compulsions, and that it was frankly messed up for us to compare his issues to the struggles of people with real psychiatric disorders. I assumed that this was totally untrue and that Bastion had just steamrolled everyone in his life into accepting his version of reality, like he did with everything, refusing to budge until the world seemed to bend to his will. Bastion only "got stuck" when he was trying to express something very important, so important that he lapsed. That he forgot to start a sentence with the letter *N*.

"Hey," I said, grabbing his hands, which he had balled into shaking fists. "Hey. Big Fun. You're okay. What's up?"

"Nesbit, I'm fine," Bastion said, clearly embarrassed. But his eyes were watery and the smile he gave me was weak. "Now I'm fine."

"What did you want to say?" I asked carefully. "You can think about it if you want."

"No, I was just going to say I'm not a mastermind. Not yet. Not at all. Nevertheless, football comes in handy if you ever need to hone your skills in the area of 'strategizing how to fight something when you cannot anticipate what it will do next.'"

What a weird choice of words that was. I wish I had given more thought to it when Bastion was alive, but at the time all I could understand was that he was sad. It never occurred to me that the thing he was talking about fighting wasn't just a metaphor for trauma or mental illness.

I mean, it never occurred to me until Cameron Winship started beginning every sentence with N. But that came later.

CHAPTER THREE

Thursday, October 30, 1997

In 1997, I moved to North Dana and started my freshman year of high school as a stranger in a strange land. I spent about two months of that school year as "the new kid" before I befriended the coven. Or I should say, before they decided to befriend *me*.

The beginning of my first year at Regional was a busy but lonely time. In the evenings, I helped my dad clean up the new-to-us auto shop. Even though the ranch house trended toward being crappy, it wasn't nearly as small or depressing as our old apartment in New Haven. Dad and I fixed up the body shop and Nic fixed up the house and salvaged what he could from the junked cars Grandpop Salvador had left moldering on the lot. Nic was doing better for a while after we moved, but eventually he made new scummy friends and his addiction came creeping back.

I went through the motions at Regional 9. It was a big school in the middle of nowhere with a lot of poor people and farmers around, and a decent number of rich families that wanted to live hidden in the New England countryside. It had two major buildings, connected by one depressing fluorescent-green hallway: the regular high school and the Vocational Agriculture building.

If you haven't gone to a school with a Vo-Ag program, you wouldn't know how the semi-division of schools kind of . . . creates a social hierarchy.

Aggies—which is what they were unfortunately called by the other students—basically go to a tech school for most of the week, studying things like marine technology or environmental science, with the idea that they're going to work in those fields when they graduate. A lot of poor kids in the backwoods do this, and so do horse girls, future farmers . . . you get the idea. The Aggies are seen as lesser-than, or something, kind of like hicks.

Yours truly was, of course, enrolled in the Vocational Agriculture program. Listen, I had less than zero intention of becoming a farmer, but they offered an Agricultural Mechanics program that taught everything I already had an aptitude for: engines, woodworking, welding, machining, stuff like that. I liked it. My days were spent on projects like deconstructing tractor engines, getting cleaned up, and then heading back to English class or whatever in the main building of Regional. So it didn't seem weird to me that I had hardly any contact with the members of North Coven, or anyone from the main part of Regional, for my first few months.

I didn't have close friends at first, but the family business and exploring the Quabbin Reservoir kept me occupied.

So the Quabbin is definitely not what you'd imagine when I say "a reservoir." It supplies water to all of Boston, and it is massive: forty miles across, twenty miles wide. And that's *just* the water. The whole place is ringed with protected forest. There are like fifty "gates" (dirt parking lots with numerical, faded wooden signs nailed into trees) that open to two hundred miles of overgrown roads where you can get onto that protected land and take a walk in the woods.

Or to put it another way—it takes almost an hour to drive from North Dana, on the northeast side, down to Rabbitville, on the southwest, and that whole time you are driving along the Quabbin.

The weirdest part, though, is that when the state *made* the reservoir, back in the 1930s, they evacuated and flooded four towns to do it. The ruins of those towns are lost under all that Quabbin water. I'll get into that more later, because it's going to matter. But for now, all you need to know is that there was plenty of nature to explore.

And I found out that I liked spending time in all that nature. The darkness of the forests. The old buildings crumbling into ruin in the middle of sleepy fields. This place, so different from where I grew up, seemed like it had been forgotten by time. It was exotic to me, and beautiful. I was already working on my orange Hyundai, but I was still too young to drive it alone, so I biked everywhere. I was tight enough with the other kids in my mechanics classes, and Coach Silva kept trying to get me to go in for the wrestling team (not in a million years). I wasn't incredibly fulfilled or anything, but I was doing pretty okay.

In the middle of all that, I kept seeing these three goth girls around. To me, they were the most interesting of all the students at my new school.

The ringleader was definitely Dove, the tiny troublemaking sophomore in her big boots. Dove violated the dress code almost every day, teetering through the halls on chunky platform boots paired with skimpy black dresses and striped thigh-highs. And when you violated the dress code at Regional, you were stuffed into an oversized and hideously ugly old blue and highlighter-yellow school shirt from before the school had changed their team colors to black and silver.

The Punishment Shirt said *QUABBIN MONSTERS!* in big bubble letters on the front and had Sad Sam, the Quabbin's own Bigfoot, silkscreened in all his hairy glory on the back.

So Dove was always memorable: small girl, giant boots, *QUABBIN MONSTERS!* muumuu.

The one I heard *talking* most often was Drea, a chubby freshman considered "cute but weird" who dyed her long, blond hair dark and wore the same black hoodie and JNCO jeans combo every day no matter the weather. Drea had cherubic features. Wide, light-colored eyes. Blond eyebrows and eyelashes that clashed with her dyed hair. Silver rings covering her pudgy fingers. She didn't exude an attitude like Dove or standoffishness like Brandy. Drea seemed sweet and extroverted and happy to talk to literally *anyone.*

Drea did Regional's morning announcements, chatted up various cliques in the lunchroom (mostly about aliens and government conspiracies), and had asked me in passing to help her "break into her locker" once before suddenly remembering the combination. When she wasn't with the two other girls, she could be spotted in the hall after the bells had rung, running late to class. Or painting her nails black in the commons area. Or emerging from detention.

I could also tell (you can usually tell, if you didn't grow up wealthy) that Drea was poor and Dove was rich. Or at least that

Drea was *kind of* poor and Dove was *kind of* rich. Brandy, the third member of their group, altered her own clothes—and wore so much vintage stuff—that it was hard to know for sure. But I guessed she was somewhere in the middle.

Brandy was the definition of unapproachable—unsmiling, stern, always perfectly composed. For the (many) boys who might have liked to ask her out, Brandy was stratospherically out of reach.

Brandy was tall and solemn and estimated by the other dudes to be the hottest girl at Regional. Her looks were compared to Naomi Campbell, which wasn't, like, particularly accurate, except maybe for the runway-level-pretty part. But I figured that a lot of the kids at Regional were just comparing her to the only famous Black model they could think of.

Brandy's beauty garnered a lot of gross and pathetically hopeful comments from the other Aggie guys in my Vocational Agriculture program . . . but she kept everyone except for Drea and Dove at arm's length. The rumor mill said that this was because Brandy was crazy religious. Deeply Christian but following some obscure culty Baptist branch that was totally unknown in rural Massachusetts. Her clothes, goth as they were, supported that argument. No Punishment Shirt required. Brandy was always buttoned-up, always in black, always in long skirts. Always dressed like a Victorian in deepest mourning. The look was cool, regardless of the reason behind it.

I *also* noticed Bastion coming and going, the football player who was bigger but younger than all the other varsity players. I saw Bastion with almost *everyone*, including the aforementioned girls a few times at lunch, or sitting out in one of the fields. Bastion leaving the auditorium where the band rehearsed. Bastion sitting cross-legged in the janitor's hallway, deep in conversation with a stoned-looking girl who totally didn't travel in the sports crowd. Bastion trying to articulate some impassioned point to Mrs. Sloe after AP Physics—standing with a teacher casually, so it looked like two adults conversing. Bastion in a black T-shirt, jogging past the glass walls of the greenhouse at the end of the Vo-Ag building with his teammates.

I didn't like him, didn't know him. But I noticed him. I dismissed him as a hyper-extroverted jock in terms of personality: definitely dull, probably homophobic.

I mean, I did say my intuition isn't perfect.

As far as looks, though, he was really, really hard to ignore. Handsome and unusual. The patch of white vitiligo over his left eye looked like a little starburst and turned one-third of his dark eyebrow a pale blond. Kids might have teased him about it if he wasn't so terrifyingly big and so astoundingly popular. His hair was dark brown and curled a bit over his forehead. He always wore a thin gold chain around his neck, but whatever was on it invariably fell under his shirts, so I assumed it was a crucifix. Brandy had a cross, a big silver one that she always wore over her ultra-covered-up blouses.

The day I talked to Bastion for the first time was October 30 of my freshman year. But it was Dove I talked to first.

I had a routine by October: Nic would pick me up around five so I could take some time after school and use the dingy "exercise room" that was really just a narrow hallway behind the gym. This was pre-Nic's Big Winnebago Adulthood Move, so I was without a weight room at home, and North Dana was pretty lacking in the gym scene. I liked to work out alone because I'm gay and I didn't want any guys catching wind of it in school. They probably wouldn't have, since I don't, like, *ogle* hot dudes or anything, but I was pretty paranoid. I always used a shower stall to change before and after gym, too, while everyone else got naked together in the main part of the boys' locker room.

In the exercise room, after school, I was safe from scrutiny. It was just me . . . and the guy I mentally called "my gym buddy," at least until I learned his name. Although we were not really *buddies*.

This kid, another freshman, was the only other person who worked out at the same time I did, though I assumed it was for other reasons than being closeted. He was constantly trying to bulk up, but he was so skinny-lanky that he really was made for running, not football.

We rarely spoke, but I got kind of used to his presence. And while I was getting used to his presence, other information about him (about everything and everyone at my new school, really) trickled in.

I hadn't gotten his name—we had zero classes together—but I saw him in the halls sometimes with his friends. He was the kind of kid who hung out with all the other future Ivy Leaguers in a tight little knot of shitty superiority. These Massachusetts rich kids were a variation on a theme, echoing dickbags I'd known back in Connecticut. They spent summers on Cape Cod, stuffed kids into lockers, and terrorized the nerds, but only when they wouldn't get caught. *Future politicians*, I thought.

My gym buddy was cute—I had to admit that—but it was a whole preppy *thing*. He was tanned and blond and always dressed in polo shirts, cable-knit sweaters, brand-new Tommy Hilfiger jeans, tragically unironic cowrie shell necklaces, stuff like that. I mean, when I saw him around school. Not in the exercise room.

But there was something else about him. We didn't read *Walden* until junior year (at least, we didn't read it until junior year in the "average intelligence" English class), but in the book Thoreau has this famous quote: "The mass of men lead lives of quiet desperation." I think Thoreau was talking about all the people who didn't do what they wanted with their adulthoods. But that phrase—*quiet desperation*—is a great phrase.

By October 1997, after only about five weeks of us working out at roughly the same time, I'd had to save my buddy twice when he added too much weight onto his bar. For context (I'm not bragging here, it's just that working out has been a hobby of mine forever), I would consider myself pretty muscular. Even as a freshman. Part of the reason Coach Silva had begged me to join the wrestling team from basically the first time I set foot in Regional.

Gym Buddy was taller than me but significantly less strong, and he kept trying to bench-press an amount of weight that was near the upper limit of what *I* could manage. And I wouldn't have tried it without a spotter.

He exuded an air of *quiet desperation* when he came to work out. Never once did I get the sense that he was doing it for enjoyment, like I did.

On October 30, 1997, I was on my third set of reps at the seated overhead press when I heard a lilting girl's voice at the door. I couldn't place it until I looked up and saw that it was Miss Goth

Sophomore Year, decked out in her normal hideous-shirt-and-cool-boots combo.

"I know you screwed up my cross-examination on purpose, Winship," Dove said. "Faking an asthma attack is ridiculous even for *you*."

"It's not my fault that you suck so badly as a prosecutor that it makes me wheeze," Gym Buddy (surname *Winship*, apparently) said smoothly. He set down the free weight he had been using with a nasty little smile.

So they were talking about Mock Trial, a thing I had absolutely no knowledge of beyond the fact of its existence. I tried to tune them out and focus on my reps.

"You don't *have* asthma, you slimy puke! You literally run track!" Dove said, stomping one huge boot and then taking a step into the exercise room.

"My flare-ups are managed with medication," Gym Buddy said primly, but his smirk stayed the same.

"You're just mad that I ruled at the last meet, and you want to screw up my practice! You're such a transparent asshole," Dove said. "You're glass, Cameron. Do it again and I'll—"

"What? Get your brother to beat me up?" Gym Buddy (full name *Cameron Winship*, as I'd just learned, although with these Massachusetts yuppies I guess *Winship Cameron* was just as possible a name) said.

Now *Cameron* stood up, not waiting for Dove to answer him. He was still talking smack about her supposed brother. "I thought the big moron was a pacifist."

"I don't need my brother to beat you up, you wad," Dove said. "Also, not a moron. He's got twice your brains."

"Not able to talk, though, what a shame," Cameron said, with fake sympathy. "I'm sure if he *could* speak properly, he'd be a wonderful defense lawyer."

"I can handle you myself," Dove reiterated, grimly. "And I will, if you don't stop ruining my trial. Or spewing about my brother."

"Oh, I'm terrified," Cameron said.

They circled each other—just a little bit, but enough to make me really pay attention.

"Don't screw me up again or I'll kick your ass," Dove said, in a much lower tone.

"Right," Cameron said, with a little fake laugh that set my teeth on edge. "Sure. I'm scared. Are you going to punch me out, you stupid bitch?"

"Okay, stop," I said, crossing the room before I even realized I was on my feet. It looked like they were potentially about to start trading blows. "That's enough," I continued, when I was standing between them. "Dick-measuring contest is over. You win," I added, pointing at Dove.

She looked like she still might lunge for Winship, who loomed behind me with his nasty expression.

"Stay out of it, Nesbit," Cameron said, and I paused for a moment, surprised that he knew my name.

I realized that this was a situation where I was picking a side. And—though I didn't know her at all, and Cameron was my gym buddy—I picked Dove's side. The hatred in Cameron's voice when he said *you stupid bitch* had made my mind up almost automatically.

"I'm not going to just hang around while this girl beats the crap out of you," I answered, without turning around. That broke the rage that had gathered over Dove's features. She looked right at me like she was seeing me standing there for the first time and laughed. Behind me, Cameron started to make an indignant sound, but I was already kind of guiding Dove back to the door.

"Take a walk with me," I said, putting on my best "relaxed" voice. "He's so not worth it."

"Anytime you want a free shot!" Cameron yelled from behind us, and Dove started to turn around. I shook my head.

"Don't dignify it," I advised. "Guy like that? Asthma faker? Hit him one time and he'll be suing your family for his overblown hospital bills."

"God, he so would," Dove said, and the moment of crisis passed. I realized I'd left my threadbare red Toad's Place sweatshirt, a souvenir from my mom's bartending job, in the workout room and let it stay there. I didn't want to go back for round two.

"You're Dove, right?" I said.

"You're Nesbit Nuñez, Hot Aggie at Large," Dove replied. "Right? Freshman?"

"Right and right," I said, embarrassed by the Hot Aggie thing. I liked this girl and didn't want to have to dodge some crush she had on me.

"You're blushing," Dove said, and rolled her eyes. "Relax, killer. It's not *my* nickname for you."

"Cool," I said, trying to seem nonchalant instead of relieved.

"I'm actually into older dudes," Dove clarified. "Not younger."

"How *much* older?" I asked.

"Not too old. Like seniors," Dove said, taking out her lighter and cigarettes. "I'm not into pedophiles, either."

"Seniors? Like sixty-five and up?" I asked, and Dove let out another sharp laugh.

"I always see you around and you seem cool," she said. "I like the earring and the fingerless gloves. Very Billy Idol."

"Oh, gross," I said, because it was actually distressing to have my look compared to musicians I hated. "You don't like Billy Idol, do you?"

"Loooooove him," Dove said. "But only because of his style; his music isn't really my thing. My current faves are Patti Smith, L7, Strawberry Switchblade, Tom Waits, Jack Off Jill, Hole, Concrete Blonde, Malice Mizer, obviously Nick Cave—"

"Eclectic," I said. We were not going to be jamming out to anything we mutually enjoyed anytime soon.

"But I'm actually mostly obsessed with Type O Negative right now."

"Marginally better," I allowed. "Peter Steele is—"

"The hottest man to ever live? Have you seen his nudie pics?"

"He's okay," I said, frowning. It made me a little uneasy how she seemed to think I might have rifled through *Playgirl* at our local bookstore to check out a famous guy's dick (I had, but not Peter Steele's). The implication that she knew something about my sexuality was freaky. Was it obvious? Or was she that perceptive? Or did we just . . . understand each other?

We stopped at her locker, where Dove stripped off the giant *QUABBIN MONSTERS!* shirt and threw it into a balled-up pile of identical shirts. Her coat was shiny black vinyl with a belt, and she disappeared into it when she put it on, just the way the shirt had consumed her. I found her totally charming: so much force of personality in such a strange little person. Later, when I knew her better, I could list a hundred ways she and Bastion were completely different and a hundred ways they were just alike.

Dove grabbed an armful of books and a tiny black backpack. "I gotta roll out, Drea's mom is taking us to Stepwood. You want to come?"

"My brother's picking me up," I said, but even as I said it, I realized I *did* want to hang out with her. "What's Stepwood?"

"Stepwood Cemetery. I can come in your car and direct you, my mom will pick us up at Drea's later, it's like five minutes from there."

"Cool," I said. We stopped at my locker, and I grabbed my coat and bag. The Toad's Place sweatshirt was definitely headed for the cavernous, reeking lost and found by the school nurse's office. "Yeah, my brother will take us there."

"Cool," Dove said, and it felt good. It felt . . . companionable.

We walked together through the long concourse lined with student art and out into the rainy October dusk. Dove waved, and I saw Drea and Brandy, the two girls she was always with, getting into a junky Cadillac Cimarron by the curb.

"Yo, I'm bringing someone," Dove announced. "I'm going to go with his ride. Nesbit, Drea. Brandy, Nesbit."

"Hot Aggie at Large? You're a good sister," Drea said. I stared at her, kind of bewildered, and then Brandy held one hand out.

"Nice to meet you," Brandy said. Her tone was as formal as her vintage clothing. Up close, she was even more perfect-looking. Her box braids were twined at the back of her neck in an old-fashioned updo that made her look like a Victorian painting of a ghost.

I shook her cold hand. "Same to you. Hope you don't mind if I come."

Brandy gave Dove an odd look that almost made me back out.

"It's fine, we'll do some vetting on him at the cemetery," Dove said, and Drea nodded. Brandy visibly relaxed.

"Nearly lost track of time in the library," a strident voice called out, and I turned to see Bastion jogging up behind us. He stopped short when he saw me.

"Bastion, Nesbit," Dove said in the same businesslike tone she had used with the girls when introducing us. "Nesbit, this is my brother. Bastion, you can come with us in Nez's ride to Stepwood."

"Nesbit," Bastion said. He smiled widely at me, and his huge hand wrapped around mine. He did *not* call me Hot Aggie at Large, though I was about as surprised as if he had.

"*You're* Dove's brother? Dove, I thought Cameron said your brother was a pacifist who couldn't talk."

"Nesbit, you shouldn't listen to anything Cameron Winship says, particularly during an interaction with my hot-tempered elder sibling," Bastion said, looking grave. But there was a twinkle of humor in his eyes. "Nary a word comes out of his mouth that isn't steeped in gossip and untruths. Nasty kid, but half-right in this case. Naturally I would say my inclination is toward the pacifistic, but unfortunately for everyone, I am *highly* verbose."

"He can talk. A lot," Dove said flatly, and Drea snorted a laugh and jumped in the Cadillac.

"See you guys in ten!" Drea yelled, and Brandy got in with an awkward little wave goodbye.

"Nesbit Nuñez is the perfect name, incidentally," Bastion said. Up close he was a little overwhelming. His height and the broadness of his shoulders, his handsome, smiling face—but most of all his *energy*—drew all of my attention.

"Why?" I asked as Nic rolled up in his wheezing, tiny 1987 Mazda. It had almost no back seat, and Bastion stared at it doubtfully.

"The *N*'s," Dove informed me.

"Oh, you like alliteration?" I asked, throwing open the passenger door. "You'll love this. Nicolas Neptune Nuñez, meet Bastion and Dove—"

"Attia," Dove supplied. I pushed down the passenger seat so she could climb into the back.

"Bastion and Dove Attia. I'm hanging out with them at a cemetery. Dove can direct you."

Nic seemed to take this in stride. "Rad. Hi, guys. Nez, I told you not to tell people my middle name."

"Nice to meet you, Nicolas," Bastion said, extending his giant hand. Nic switched his cigarette from one hand to the other to shake (this was before the toothpick era), and Dove took that as an invitation to light up one of her long-ass menthols.

"Our parents were, like, teen hippies when they had Nic," I explained to the Attia siblings. I followed Dove into the back, leaving Bastion to squash himself into the passenger seat, which was kind of funny and kind of attractive to behold.

"He got off way easier," Nic said, as Bastion managed to slam the door shut.

"Why? Is his middle name something less awesome than Neptune?" Dove asked, reaching forward to flick ashes out of Nic's open window.

"It's North," I said. "So only marginally less weird. Nesbit North Nuñez."

Bastion made a delighted sound. "Novel, alliterative, lovely. Nesbit, your parents have excellent taste. Nicely done."

He wasn't being sarcastic in any way that I could detect. Not that I had fantasized about talking to Bastion super often, but this . . . was nothing like I had imagined his personality to be. He was a completely earnest freak.

My brother took the road through the rapidly darkening pine-and-birch woods that surrounded the cemetery just as the rain started to let up. By the time we climbed out of his car, it was only drizzling. Chilly vapor hung in the chillier air, and any clots of fog that formed in the little valleys around old graves were blown apart by the intermittent gusts of late-autumn wind. An old man with a white beard, who looked like one of those weathered hikers you see trekking the entire Appalachian Trail, meandered past the graveyard gates with a walking stick and a soft-eyed, off-the-leash beagle.

"Be home by eleven or Dad will lose it," Nic said. "Later. Have fun with your Mischief Night stuff that you're so totally *not* doing."

"Nicolas, adieu!" Bastion said. Nic gave me an *Is this guy for real?* look through the windshield and waved goodbye before peeling away.

"Your brother is so hot," Dove said.

"Yuck, dude," I protested. "Also, he's *six* years older than me. He's twenty-one! I thought you didn't want to be the underage victim in a pedophilic relationship."

"I would one hundred percent let him take advantage of my underdeveloped mind and body. He is a magma-hot volcano of molten hippie wet-dream sex. That *hair*, ugh! God!"

"Now, Dove, that is vile," Bastion said, throwing his hands up in theatrical disgust. "Nasty. Nic seems like a pleasant guy who keeps age-appropriate company. Nice day, Mr. T!" he added, waving at the old man who was leaving the cemetery with his dog.

"Yeah, the cold rain and fog just make it extra lovely. Sounds like something a person who doesn't live outside would say, kiddo!" the old guy answered, raising his walking stick in a hello-goodbye gesture.

Bastion laughed and waved goodbye.

I want to tell you now: remember that old guy. That old guy is very important, actually, to everything that happened.

So: before it was destroyed forever on November 27, 1999, Stepwood Cemetery didn't have anything in the way of a caretaker. Once upon a time it had been the family cemetery for Northcott House—the big old mansion that was connected to it by a trail called Magnolia Path—but over the decades it had basically become a public park without the benefit of public landscaping.

It was old, but not as old as the burial grounds full of Puritan bones that Massachusetts towns put in the effort to keep from disintegrating completely. The other members of North Coven said that as kids they were all warned away from the hilly slopes and toppled graves. The walking paths that meandered southwest through the mossy graveyard and toward the forest around the Quabbin were made by junkies and vagrants, adults said. Our coven never met any homeless junkies there except for Old Tet, the guy Bastion greeted at the gate, who was harmless and—as you might have guessed from me repeatedly mentioning it—pretty old. Even Tet rarely hung out around Stepwood. Other places in town were more convenient, if not more welcoming.

Stepwood impressed me immediately that first October night. It felt forbidding from the moment you came up to the gates. Thirty-foot-high pillars of dull, mossy stone, each topped with a squat lump that might have once been a carved funeral urn, connected by a circular garland of iron. Iron fencing, equally as high, splayed away from the gate and into the forest that encroached on the edges of North Dana. It was ominously off-kilter—like an old oil painting by someone who sucked at perspective, where everything was just slightly askew.

It was probably intuition that made me feel that way. I mean *a little* intuition, not a strong intuition. I liked the cemetery for the otherworldly creepy vibe. I was glad that these kids were cool and weird, and that they had invited me to what was obviously their private hangout spot. I was honestly enamored with the gloom of the place. If I had better intuition, I would have known to stay away from it.

"Noted and dear friends," Bastion said as we reached Brandy and Drea. Brandy was wearing Drea's hoodie draped over her shoulders, but Drea seemed not to care about the cold. "North Coven, hail."

"Hail, coven," Drea said.

"Hail, coven," Brandy whispered, and her voice broke a little. Bastion wrapped his arms around her and hugged her tightly, bent in half to avoid lifting her off the ground. When they broke apart, she had tears on her face. Brandy didn't seem like the kind of girl who allowed hugging under normal circumstances, and I again got the feeling that I had stumbled into (or actually been invited into) something complex that was in the middle of happening . . . and was probably none of my business.

"No tears, my dear friend. Nexus will end the terrible things that she does to you," Bastion said, taking Brandy's hand. I looked at Dove for some kind of explanation as to what the hell we were getting into—this was not shaping up to be some typical toilet-papery Mischief Night shenanigans—but she just nodded and motioned for me to follow them up the hill.

You know something? Thinking about it now, that memory really kills me. Bastion being so comforting like that, suddenly so serious and kind, made sense since his friend was obviously in terrible distress. But none of us knew what he was getting ready to do. How much it cost him. The way he handled it, with no hint of fear, with nothing but concern for other people, while all the time he knew that he would pay the price.

Bastion. Bastion deconstructing himself bit by bit, trading things he needed just to save us. I miss him.

In a line, we walked up the crest of one of the weird little hills and plunged into an area where the woods intermingled with the graves. Here, Stepwood shook some of the pauper's field vibe it had and gave way to actual mausoleums for named individuals.

"Who was that guy you were talking to?" I asked, glancing over at Bastion.

"Nice fellow called Old Tet. Not too many years ago he had a career as a well-regarded local historian, before he got lost at the bottom of a bottle," Bastion said, looking a little bit thoughtful and sad about it, like he actually cared for the random old dude.

"Old Tet?"

"Nomenclature is a little *off*, for sure," Bastion said, falling back in line and stepping beside me. "Nobody in North Dana is particularly sensitive to the indignities visited upon the homeless, least of all a mildly insulting nickname."

"That's not really the right way to use *nomenclature*," I said, wondering how he would react if I gave him a hard time. It actually was an acceptable way to use the word, but I had an urge to mess with him. This jock. Was the "earnest and kind" act really an act? "But I guess you knew that; you seem pretty smart. Then again, if you have to start every sentence with N, you—"

"Navigate within the linguistic boundaries!" Bastion said, seeming pleased. "Nesbit, you catch on quickly. Normally it takes people a while to—"

"Do you have a disorder? Is it like a school project, an experiment? Are you just being a wiseass?" I pressed, and to my surprise, Bastion blushed. I was suddenly aware of how close I'd gotten to him. And how much I was grilling him. Something about this guy brought out the urge in me to get a little closer, ruffle his feathers.

"No. No. Necessity, it's pure necessity. Nesbit, I hope you don't find it to be—"

"Okay," Dove said, loud enough to interrupt us. "North Coven, we are here to make a Nexus into reality. I brought Nez along because I have a feeling about him. I think he has . . . intuition. Maybe more, maybe our kind of abilities too. But this is Brandy's show. Brandy, we can interview him and see if he's a fit. If you aren't digging it we release him. All good?"

"Yes, that's fine," Brandy said, and Drea nodded.

We'd stopped at a faded sandstone grave in the classical panel style, Greek-looking pillars supporting its sides. The only writing legible was at the center, where it said *Dearest* in weathered grooves. Directly behind it was what appeared to be the last mausoleum of Stepwood before the woods took over completely: a big marble job with double brass doors and a first and last name carved above them. *Northcott Faire.*

"Nexus-fulfillment time, my nulligravidas," Bastion said, walking toward the Northcott mausoleum. "Nesbit, I'll have to come up with a word for you that isn't bastardized Latin for 'woman who hasn't been pregnant.'"

"And probably for Dove, soon enough," Drea said, snickering. Dove jabbed her in the shoulder.

"Quiet, please," Dove said. "Like you and Brandy wouldn't have three kids and ten abortions under your belt by now if you were a straight couple."

I think my mouth dropped open. I'll admit now that I was a little repressed. For example, I would never *ever* talk about my sexuality so openly, and Dove basically blabbing that these girls were a couple was really kind of shocking to hear.

Brandy seemed to agree with me, covering her eyes with her hands in clear mortification.

"Dove," she said in a voice of total exasperation. "I swear sometimes you're actually *incapable* of thinking before you—"

"Now, I'll just be a moment . . . ," Bastion said, not paying attention to the girls. He reached under his sweater while he spoke and pulled out the gold chain that I'd assumed had a cross on it. It was a surprisingly *long* chain, with fine links that looked like snake scales and bounced back little flecks of gloom from the overcast sky. At the end wasn't a cross, but a key. A big antique-looking skeleton key in a similar gold color. Bastion unhesitatingly slipped the key into the lock on the large brass double doors of the Northcott Faire mausoleum and opened the door, disappearing inside.

"Um, you can get into the mausoleums here?" I asked, surprised for the second time that minute.

"Just that one," Dove said. "It's empty inside, no cool skeletons or anything. We keep our coven stuff in it."

Drea kicked a bunch of branches and pine needles aside to reveal a makeshift firepit hidden directly between the Dearest grave and the Northcott mausoleum. It already had a pile of sticks sitting in it, though I figured they had to be wet from the misty weather. Dove tossed Drea the Dupont lighter, and Drea pulled a smudge stick out of the hoodie that was draped around Brandy's shoulders.

Brandy faced me, looking drawn but determined. "What do you make of all this, Nesbit?"

"Um, I think . . ." I squared my shoulders, trying not to be too nervous or too flippant. This felt important. "I think you guys are all witches and this is my witch job interview. It's clear you've been doing this for a while; you seem organized. I think whatever you're doing today is related to you specifically, something to help you. Maybe Dove feels like you need extra manpower. I think you all maybe watched *The Craft* too many times, but I'm down to try it."

That actually got a smile out of Brandy. Drea laughed out loud from where she was crouched by the firepit.

"I'm Nancy, I'm Nancy!" Dove declared, pulling a weird face.

"You so wish," Drea said.

"Do you believe in magic? In the power to direct the flow of fate via ritual and intention?" Brandy asked. I did not for a second think that she would be fooled by a lie.

"No," I said. "But I believe in intuition. I have it, sometimes, like Dove said. Just a little bit."

"What's your favorite movie?" Drea asked, slouching over to us. Fragrant sage smoke curled away from the firepit.

"Is that relevant?" Brandy asked her, but Drea smirked and forcibly wiggled Brandy's shoulders.

"Sure is, Grand Inquisitor. Gotta know if Nez is a man of taste."

"*Alien*," I said easily. "I'm into Giger's art big-time."

"Oh, good choice," Dove said. "Mine is *Akira*."

"Anime? Between that and Billy Idol, I just don't know if we can be friends," I said. Dove snorted at me, rolling her eyes.

"Mine is *Fire in the Sky*, it's one hundred percent true real-life alien stuff," Drea said very seriously. "Brandy likes the BBC version of *Pride and Prejudice*, but we don't hold that against her, since her mom doesn't allow TV, and her pop-culture knowledge is verrrrrry limited. Bastion's is *The Neverending Story* because he's a giant toddler."

"That kid movie with the dragon?" I asked, kind of charmed by the information.

"Aw, it's only because the main character is named *Bastian* Balthazar Bux," Dove said. "He was nuts over the book as a kid, too. Mom read it to him in the original German. *Die unendliche Geschichte!*"

"What do you think?" Drea asked Brandy.

"I think we can trust him," Brandy said. "Nesbit, do you want to become a part of North Coven?"

"I do," I said.

"Excellent," Drea said. "All you need to know for today is that Brandy's mother is into some seriously schizoid religious shit. Think the mom in *Carrie* and you're on the right track. It's kind of a challenge to get out here to do rituals."

"We've fabricated an entire Bible study club at Regional to pull it off," Brandy said.

"Yeah. We want to give Brandy a little room to, um, grow. So we're going to divert some of her mom's energy to better, like, behaviors," Dove said. "You follow all that?"

"I'm sorry about your mom," I told Brandy, who closed her eyes for a second.

"Three and a half more years," Brandy said after a pause. "Then I can be free."

"This is going to work," Drea murmured, and kissed Brandy on the cheek.

Bastion emerged from the Northcott mausoleum and locked it up. The key on the gold chain disappeared back under his sweater, and he marched over and dumped a handful of dried sticks on top of the smoking fire. The fire crackled into more vibrant life immediately. Then he handed Drea a spool of narrow green ribbon, which she took in her left hand.

Bastion pulled a piece of bright pink-red chalk from his pocket. "Now we make our mark."

Dove grabbed my hand and tugged me forward, so the five of us were standing in a ring around the smoking firepit. Bastion traced our shapes loosely with the chalk, marking out a rough sunburst of five points rather than the witchy circle I expected. When he stood up inside the outline, the girls all looked at him.

"North Coven, we stand together," Bastion said. Behind him, the last fragments of light faded from the cloudy sky.

"Northcott Faire before us. Nearest grave behind us," Bastion went on, gesturing toward the Dearest grave. "Necropolis around us. Nexus compels us."

"Nexus compels us," echoed the girls. Each of them tugged or rolled up their sleeves, revealing bright-red N's slashed into their wrists. I definitely got a weird, culty vibe for a minute, but I was too intrigued to back out.

"Name your places and name yourselves and *Nous* will hear our voice like bells," Bastion said. *His* voice rang out like a bell through the old cemetery, and he seemed to really slide into a groove. I wondered if, skeptic that I was, I would ever be able to get into this very loose (actually totally made-up) version of Wicca with the same abandon my new acquaintances did. I didn't have to wait very long.

"North Coven, I am your heart," Dove said, to my left. "I feel the wrong and right of things. I, Dove Attia, bring my love."

"North Coven, I am your eyes," Brandy said, seamlessly beginning as Dove fell silent. "I see the truth and parse the lies. I, Brandy Jackson, use my sight."

It was fully dark now. The last hint of gloomy drizzled-over sun was gone, and I felt electricity building in the air. The hair on my arms stood up under my jacket, and I worried absently that we might get caught in a lightning storm.

"North Coven, I am your freaking *voice!*" Drea shouted, flipping her dyed-black Wednesday Addams hair over her shoulders, and Dove laughed. "I run my mouth tirelessly for you witches. I, Andrea Pearson, say all that's unsaid."

"North Coven, I am your will-be-done," Bastion said. I waited for him to give his name, but he was silent. Then I realized everyone was looking at me.

"You go," Dove said, nudging me with one giant boot.

"North Coven . . . I am . . ." I paused, hesitant. Then suddenly the wind gusted again, covering us in fragrant smoke, and I felt the electricity in the air move through me, a wave of sparks that opened my mouth and compelled me to speak.

"North Coven, I am your hands!" I yelled, forgetting to feel stupid about my own enthusiasm. The words came from my lips like they had been pulled out of the night around us. "I build and tear apart! I, Nesbit Nuñez, give you all that I can create!"

The smoldering fire jumped up on my last words, blazing suddenly hot and five feet high, a true pillar of flames. The bared N-shaped cuts on the wrists of the others glowed with the same luminosity as the fire. It felt like *magic*, like a moment from a movie where something was about to really happen. I clapped my hands in delight and whooped.

"Jesus Christ! Did you see that?" I asked, grinning. I was met by a total lack of surprise from the other four.

"We're going to make a believer out of this one, I think," Drea said in a comically warbling voice.

"North Coven, we gather here the evening before Samhain with the sun gone down. Near to the many universes we speak. Nullify our destinies and allow us to begin anew," Bastion said. "Nomographers of the new reality, present your gifts."

"The first letter that you ever wrote me, from sixth grade," Drea said, stepping forward. She produced a worn and folded piece of notebook paper and kissed it, then tossed it into the fire with her free hand. "So your love and those you love can be free from suspicious eyes."

Brandy nodded silently, holding one hand to her chest. I could see the glint of tears in her eyes reflected in the firelight.

"My mom's shawl from when I was a baby," Dove said, rummaging in her discarded backpack.

"No way," Bastion said. "Not the Hermès one, she loves that thing, didn't she nurse you while wearing that?"

You know something funny? Sad-funny, not *funny*-funny. *That*, that meaningless sentence, was the last time Bastion ever said *love* while he was alive. It's weird how unimportant stuff can become the most important stuff when you have context. You'll understand better in a little while what I mean.

"Gross. And yes. It has to be *meaningful*, dork."

"Now, honestly, Dove, I am aware—I co-authored this ritual."

Dove gathered a lengthy fringed ball of cloth from her tiny backpack and threw it into the fire without hesitation. "So that your mother can know her love for you as Anna does for us. With kindness and understanding."

It seemed like the shawl was too big to be consumed quickly by the fire, but the moment it touched the flames it turned to ash and was borne upward on a gust of wind.

"Jesus Christ," I said again, unable to totally contain my amazement. "This really is happening. Like magic."

"Just like it," Drea said.

"I give my Bible," Brandy said in a quiet voice. "Given to me by my mother. To be free of the fasting, the prayer, the punishments, I offer the only gift my mother has ever bestowed upon me."

I had nothing to offer. For a minute I thought about my abandoned sweatshirt, a gift from my often disappointing—but hardly ever malicious—mom. I would have given it up to my new friends just to see that fire trick again.

"I have no gift," I said, but in the reflected firelight I noticed Bastion nodding approvingly, like I had talked at the right time. "But I have a wish. My mother isn't great, but she's never unkind. I hope . . . I hope you have that. Freedom from cruelty."

"*Nous*, we implore you," Bastion said. "Never-ending fabric that knits the universe. Now reshape yourself in the heart of India Allstoe Jackson."

"Now reshape our lives," Brandy said, and stepped *into* the fire.

"Hey! Wait, *don't!*" I shouted, grabbing at her.

Brandy didn't fight my clutching hands on her shoulders, but instead of dragging her out of the flames, I was pulled in—it felt like my body had been magnetized to the center of the inferno. And as I was dragged into the bonfire that had somehow sprung out of the tiny firepit, I realized that nothing hurt. Nothing burned. The flames licked around us like leaves on the breeze, brushing gently against the cuffs of my pants and the ends of my hair without singeing me. I expected Brandy's long skirt to go up like kindling, but as we stood together in the center of the fire, all was cool and quiet. Brandy regarded me stoically, and I removed my hands from her shoulders.

"Sorry," I said, feeling awkward. The firepit seemed like it had expanded, stretching out far enough that Brandy and I could stand together in the eye of the flames. "I just thought . . ."

"No self-immolation on the menu tonight, Nesbit," Bastion said, and hooked an arm around my chest, breaking the magnetic force that held me in the fire with his sheer strength. He pulled me out and let me go, and I felt my skin tingle where his arm had pressed against me.

The fire was glowing a bright violet white. Brandy stood in the center, all but obscured by the rushing pillar of flames, as composed as Joan of Arc.

I looked up, blinking against the sage-scented smoke that billowed around us. The rain clouds had melted away, and beyond the black frame of the trees, there were a thousand times as many stars in the sky as I had ever seen before. The arm of the Milky Way transposed against itself a hundred times, our own galaxy arcing away from us over and over again.

"Within the Near-Depths, at this place between universes, where infinite outcomes are possible, we restring the loom of fate," Drea said. She took the spool of green ribbon and tossed it in the air.

I held my breath when the spool didn't come crashing back to the earth. It hovered in the starlit air, unwinding yards upon yards of ribbon of its own accord.

"Holy *shit*," I muttered, staring at the ribbon as it moved, and Bastion caught my eye and winked.

The ribbon spun out and wrapped around Dove's chest once, the spool bobbing in the air like it was directed by invisible hands. Then it encircled Drea's throat, making her the perfect image of the girl in that old scary story everyone read as a kid. The ribbon looped around Bastion's head like an emperor's circlet, resting lightly over the starburst birthmark on his brow, and then the spool spun toward the fire. I watched, transfixed, as Brandy closed her eyes before the ribbon lightly covered them.

The ribbon had almost run out, and the spool with the last length of it dropped out of the fire directly into my hands. We were all connected. I held the spool, turning it over and over in amazement as it bound the coven together.

"Eyes. Hands. Voice. Will. Heart," Dove said, and Drea picked up the chant. After a minute I followed suit, getting into the rhythm of it.

"Eyes. Hands. Voice. Will. Heart," we said, and I could see Brandy mouthing the words sightlessly from within the fire. She looked like a blindfolded saint.

Bastion murmured a counterpoint to our chant as we spoke. "Never-ending fabric that shapes the universe."

"Eyes. Hands. Voice. Will. Heart."

"Now reknit our fate."

"Eyes. Hands. Voice. Will. Heart."

"Now remake the world."

"Now remake the world," Dove said.

"Now remake the world," Drea and I said. It all flowed so naturally that I could hit every beat.

I think I was made for this, I thought. I felt something light in my chest, like happiness but more charged. My hands buzzed with energy. *I think I was made to be here, with these people.*

"NOW, CONJURERS!" Bastion said, raising his voice to a shout. It echoed off the trees, sent back to us a dozen times amplified by the place Drea called the Near-Depths, and suddenly the spool of ribbon in my hands crackled with the same electricity

55

that infused the air, and my hand clenched around it, and I was borne up, up—

The ribbon lifted me like I was as insubstantial as paper. The tips of my boots dragged against the earth before leaving it entirely. I looked over at Dove and Drea, likewise suspended. It didn't look like Drea was being choked by the ribbon—more like it was a guiding line that helped her become airborne. Dove and Bastion were similarly elevated. In the air, the four of us gazed down at Brandy with the hundredfold light of the stars shining back on the gleaming column of fire. She stayed alone on the earth, ribbon over her eyes, blind to our levitation.

"Oh, god," I said, looking at Bastion. My chest felt so light that I thought I could drift upward forever. "It feels so—"

I don't think I ever got to finish that thought, because suddenly the white-violet flames around Brandy became catastrophically bright and I had to close my eyes against the brilliance. There was a whiteness against my lids that blanked out everything, and I heard the electric hum in the air go silent all at once. I felt my feet touch the earth again. When I opened my eyes, everyone was back on the ground.

Drea's green ribbon was respooled and resting innocuously in her left hand. The fire had gone out, and Brandy was stepping out of the firepit, looking as dazed as I felt.

Drea let out a wild cheer and grabbed Brandy by the shoulders, pulling her in for a kiss that made me avert my eyes in embarrassment.

A patter of raindrops fell onto my forehead, and I glanced up. The clouds were back, like the multiplied starscape that had shone overhead moments before had never been.

"It worked, that really freaking worked!" Dove said, doing a delighted little spin in her platform boots.

"No duh," Drea said, leaning back but keeping her hands on Brandy's shoulders.

"I really hope so," Brandy said. "I guess we'll see soon enough. I'm out very late."

"Nearly positive it worked," Bastion affirmed, scuffing at the chalk outline with his feet. "Nice result, very promising."

"Nice?" I exclaimed, finding my voice "*Nice?* Do you guys normally float through the air and . . . and make magic fires and send yourselves to some kind of starry alternate multiverse and . . . insane crap like that? Jesus!"

"Nesbit, did you think we were just inviting you up here to practice make-believe?" Bastion asked. His tone was light and innocent, but I could tell he was teasing me. "Not the case. No, we're dealing with serious issues like parental abuse. North Coven won't settle for a few ineffectual feel-good chants when the lives of our members are involved."

"I think he believes us now," Drea said, smirking. "Right, Nez?"

"Unless you slipped me some peyote or something," I said, "I would be an idiot not to."

I looked at my hands and thought about the spool resting in them, the electricity coursing through me. My feet leaving the ground. It felt so *right* that I had been close to crying.

"I think I've been waiting to meet you all," I said. It made me feel kind of exposed to say that out loud, but it was true. After what they had all shown me, I wanted to be honest with them.

"Nothing we've done has ever been quite that spectacular before. I think we've been waiting for you," Brandy said. "I see it."

"I feel it," Dove added.

"It's true and I'll say it," Drea said, making it into a vow.

"Nesbit, I *know* it," Bastion said, with finality. "Now you guys should get back to Drea's."

"You're not coming?" Dove asked.

"Need to clean things up and get my run in," Bastion said, taking the ribbon from Drea. "Nice night to jog home."

Dove nodded, and Drea led us through the misty woods toward the trailer park. As we left, I turned back for a moment and saw Bastion, key in hand, about to enter the Northcott Faire mausoleum. I didn't think anything of it. I didn't wonder why Bastion hadn't given his name during the spell. I didn't dwell on the fact that he didn't offer a gift. Most stupidly, I never asked what *Nous*—which I had misheard as *noose*—was. Not even the tiniest pang of my flawed intuition warned me about what was to come.

I did, however, check the gross lost and found at Regional for my Toad's Place sweatshirt the next day. But I didn't find it anywhere. By then it was a moot point because that hoodie was red and Dove had told me that North Coven wore all black every single day, a guideline that was pretty easy for me to comply with.

I resigned myself to never seeing that sweatshirt again. And I didn't . . . at least not for another two years.

CHAPTER FOUR

Saturday, November 27, 1999

I'm avoiding talking about the funeral.

I couldn't bring myself to sign the register, just like I couldn't go to the wake or change the radio station in my car. Instead, I passed the pen from Drea to Nic and walked into the large main room, which was shut off from the bleak outdoors by heavy curtains. The place was packed, and as I made my way over to the reserved row behind the Attias, I passed almost everyone I knew from North Dana. There was the football team, all in uniform, a gesture Bastion would have probably found both stupid and touching. He was sentimental like that. Behind them were the cheerleaders, also done up in their Regional 9 black and silver, and in the middle sat Kim Palmer, who had approached Bastion at lunch eight weeks before to see if he would take her to the homecoming dance. I was sitting with him when she asked. As he let Kim down in the kindest possible way, he reached under the table and squeezed my hand, unseen.

Kim was crying, and her mascara streaked down her cheeks. I felt weirdly bad for her. Just then it seemed like a much worse fate to never have gotten to spend time with Bastion than it did to be me.

The funeral was not what you would call typical even before Mayor Winship dropped dead in the middle of it. The Attias didn't really do anything normally, and they retained that quality even when one of their kids died. There was no minister or anything since Bastion's folks were what Mrs. Attia called "luminously agnostic." It started with Mrs. Attia's best friend, a poet who was slightly less well known than she was, reading a poem he had written for her seventeen years before, to commemorate Bastion's birth. I stared at the glossy white coffin, covered in tiger lilies, that hid Bastion's destroyed body. Drea sat next to me with her head in her hands, and Nic sat on my other side, looking vaguely into the distance.

Next, Dove stood up and dragged out a CD player from behind a funeral wreath.

"For my little brother. Who was murdered," she announced to the room, and pressed play. She made the entire assembled group listen to all three minutes and forty-nine seconds of "Earth Died Screaming" by Tom Waits while she faced the crowd, silent and expressionless. Then she re-hid the CD player and wordlessly returned to her seat.

Lark and Wren, the five-year-old twins, got up and showed a collage that they had made, with the Prof patiently helping them explain how each glued-on piece related back to their dead brother. Robin was ten and shy—I don't think I ever heard more than two words out of the kid in all my time hanging out at their house—and she stayed sitting down with Mrs. Attia.

"It's the art show from hell," Drea whispered to me, and, as messed up as this sounds, I almost started laughing. Brandy gave us a sharp look from the end of the row.

Finally, one of the Prof's brothers, who had flown in from Cairo, rose to give a eulogy. You could hear people shift in their seats: now it was serious business time, when things got extremely sad. I could feel the collective energy of a hundred-plus people getting ready to cry. I still didn't feel any tears prick my eyes, like the part of me that cried had been taken away in a body bag the day that we had seen Bastion's corpse in the back of Stepwood.

The Prof was a short and skinny dude, but his brother was handsome and tall and had a deep voice. Looking at Bastion's uncle was like seeing into the future Bastion would never have.

The room got very silent as Uncle Somebody cleared his throat, and I heard Mayor Winship whisper sharply in the row behind us: "Put that *away*." Then a rustling. I guessed that it was Cameron-dickbag-Winship checking his stupid Nokia, and, as I found out much later, I was right.

"Well," said the Prof's brother, looking out over the assem-blage. "I suppose none of us wants to be here. Personally, this is the worst event I've ever had the sorrow of attending."

"He's talking about the Tom Waits," Drea whispered to me, and I elbowed her. Ahead of us, Dove craned her head slightly to the left, giving off the eerie impression that she'd heard us and was going to take revenge when she could.

"But while we're here, I would like to talk about the most remarkable young man I've ever known. In my conversation with Youssef and Anna about giving the eulogy, they maintained that they wanted nothing florid. Just the facts. So I will tell you the facts."

The uncle went on in the quiet room. "Those of you who know me are aware that I come to visit my brother in the summer of every second or third year. The summer that Bastion was nine, he beat me at chess for the first time. The summer he was twelve, he wanted to discuss the most promising avenues for creating universal access to clean water in third-world countries. Bastion, he was . . . noble, if I can ascribe such a quality to a teenager without being, as Anna would say, florid. I do believe that all of you here would agree with me."

I could see people kind of gently nodding in the corner of my peripheral vision, and it annoyed me. Bastion *was* kind and noble and also—occasionally—insufferably egotistical. It bothered me how people didn't want to admit that those qualities could coexist inside a person. If they wallpapered over Bastion's memory like this, his flaws smoothed into something perfectly presentable, then it was as good as forgetting him completely.

"The last time we spoke, Bastion told me of his great passion for A. E. Housman. He had an affinity for poetry, doubtlessly inherited from his mother. He— Sir? Are you well? Sir?"

For a second my brain couldn't track this wild new twist in the eulogy. Then I heard the gasps of other people in the room. *Then* I heard something in the row directly behind me, and as I turned to look, all two-hundred-something pounds of Mayor Winship crashed down onto my back.

I fell to the side, sliding mostly off the bench as the mayor's weight bore down on me. His big skull pressed against my ear, and he breathed shallowly through his mouth, making a low word-less sound about a centimeter from my neck. For a second I thought that he was drooling on me and then realized that Mayor Winship was completely soaked in sweat. And *heavy*, totally deadweight.

Drea let out a little shriek next to me as she was shoved side-ways into Brandy. Nic grabbed my arm and pulled me aside and up, leaving Cameron's dad lying prone on the bench. Uncle Some-body, who turned out to be a doctor, jumped over the row his family was sitting in and pushed us back, ordering the Prof to call 911.

I backed up as Mayor Winship's eyes rolled up into his head. As I got the hell out of the way, I inadvertently locked my gaze with Cameron's. His mother was holding his left arm and scream-ing, but Cameron made no sound. He just looked back at me with eyes so wide that I could see the whites all the way around.

Bastion's uncle started CPR. The ambulance came. The funeral attendees pushed back to the sides of the room and watched, but Mayor Winship was long gone by the time the first EMT got to him. Later they would say it was sudden cardiac arrest, that he had been dead within three minutes.

I took a second to press my hands against the lid of Bastion's casket while everyone else clustered around the edges of the room.

"Hey," I whispered. "Bet you're pissed that somebody stole your thunder on your Big Day."

It felt less final than *Goodbye* or *I love you*. When I talked like that, I could almost imagine that he was still alive.

Then the funeral director started ushering everyone out. The art show from hell was over.

Dove finally got away from the extended-family gathering at her house after seven. She met us at Hazy Dee's, where we had been stretching out our coffees and fries (ice water only for Brandy) since unloading Nic hours earlier. She walked in smelling like she had been smoking two cigarettes at once while mainlining whiskey, which was plausible since the Attia family was not super buttoned-up about their liquor cabinet.

"Hail, coven," Dove said, sliding into the booth, which had tartan print cushions to go with the tartan print wallpaper. Hazy Dee's was eighty percent tartan and twenty percent psychedelia. There was a Jefferson Starship poster tacked to the ceiling above our booth. There was also a vintage map of Scotland tacked on the wall next to our booth. Overall a very confused but very distinct atmosphere.

"Hail four-fifths of the coven," Drea said, unenthusiastically stabbing a fry end into a smear of mustard.

"Oh, wow, really? I forgot my brother was dead for a second there," Dove said, taking Drea's coffee and polishing it off.

I watched them, wondering if the banter was going to ramp up into a full-blown spat. Sometimes Dove's indomitable will ran up against Drea's inexhaustible spirit and created major friction. The last big argument between them (that I knew about) had been in July of 1998, when Dove had tried—probably way too forcefully—to give Drea cash for some bills that Drea's mom was falling behind on.

Dove called me after Drea flipped out on her. I still remember the phone call and how Dove's voice sounded small and embarrassed on the other end. Dove was really upset . . . not upset like after Bastion died, of course, but still upset in a way she rarely allowed anyone to see.

Dove confided in me sometimes about the things she felt kind of *naive* about—she never showed that part of herself to Brandy or Drea or Bastion. She had to be the Big Kid of our group, even more intensely when it came to her own little brother. Maybe it was because I hadn't grown up with them. Maybe because she knew I had a different perspective from her. Maybe because of the *best* best friends thing. In return I always gave her my uncensored opinion.

So, Dove apologized to Drea after I told her she was in the wrong . . . but god knows how freaking long that battle of wills would have gone on otherwise.

But this night was not a night for arguing. Drea waved a hand in immediate surrender.

"I know, I know," she said. "I'm sorry Mayor Winship died all over his funeral."

"Confidentially? Dad is upset about it, but Mom is *pissed*," Dove said, with the first actual smile I'd seen from her since Bastion's death. "She got pretty drunk at the after-funeral party and started telling everyone that it was in super-poor taste to drop dead like that."

Drea snickered, and Brandy shook her head. "Poor Cameron. It was extremely bad."

"I wish it had been Cameron, actually," Dove replied. She tried to grab my coffee, but I held it out of her reach.

"I'm also in mourning. Buy your own."

"I think the mayor is worse than Cameron," Brandy said. "He's a complete creep. Even my mother thinks so."

"Takes one to know one," Drea said, and nobody disagreed. Brandy's mom had dialed back her behavior dramatically after the spell we'd cast on her freshman year. But the lifetime of abuse before that had marked Brandy forever, in everything from the way she glanced around quickly when we entered a room to her always-quiet speaking voice. Those things hadn't changed just because we had used our magic to change Mrs. Jackson.

"What was with the music thing?" I asked. "That was pretty bizarre. Even for you."

"Tom Waits is a genius," Dove deflected, standing up.

"It was a spell," Brandy said, "wasn't it?"

"Yeah," Dove admitted, as the rest of us got ready to leave Hazy Dee's. "I charged the CD player with a ritual of revelation. I thought it worked. It was supposed to skip if I laid eyes on the murderer while I was standing up there."

"But it didn't, so either it didn't work or he didn't come," Drea said, completing the thought. "Right?"

"I feel like none of our magic is working," Brandy said. "I keep thinking that somehow Bastion was doing all of it, and just letting us come along for the ride because he liked us."

"Not possible," Dove said. "Spellcasting was my idea, to begin with. When I got sick."

Dove hardly ever talked about her cancer, but I knew from Bastion that she had been diagnosed with leukemia at eleven and had been in complete remission since she was twelve. Her recovery had been thorough and fast, and the Attia siblings always credited their first spellwork as the reason.

I set out my portion of the cash, then counted everyone else's to make sure they left a decent tip for Dolores, who was both Hazy

Dee's owner and one half of the entire waitstaff. Before my mom met Ted Thoroughgood and went to New York to have do-over kids with him, she'd bartended at Toad's Place in New Haven for as long as I could remember.

Three years before Bastion's funeral I was given the choice of living with Mom and her new husband, who was in the start-up phase of his recycled sandal company, or moving to Absolutely Nowhere, Massachusetts, to help my dad and brother take over my recently dead grandpa's auto shop. It was a strangely easy choice. I didn't want to live away from Nic, who (correctly, I think) blamed Mom for the divorce. Dad had already been a mechanic for my whole life and had spent many hours teaching me his line of work. Some of my most important little-kid memories are of my dad's calloused and oil-stained hands guiding my own tiny ones through the motions of repair. I was fascinated by his job as a kid and always begged to hang out with him while he worked. He let me, and as I got older, it became evident that I had a knack for it. So I was an easy sell on the idea of helping at the shop.

I still spent a few weeks in the city with Mom, Ted, and my little half sisters every summer, mostly to take in the superior music scene of NYC and hit as many shows as I could sneak into.

"Just because you got better doesn't mean it hasn't all been something Bastion was doing," Brandy persisted when we'd all climbed into the Hyundai. I drove toward the trailer park, where we could park at Drea's and walk through the woods into the back of Stepwood without being seen.

Drea pulled her grungy CD binder out of Brandy's purple L.L.Bean backpack and flipped through it. She tried to hand a

Massive Attack album (*Mezzanine*, I think) to Dove to put into the CD player, and I blocked her hand.

"No. Leave the radio," I said.

"This music sucks," Drea whined.

"Too bad."

"I know my brother was born with a strong personality or whatever," Dove said, dismissing the music debate. "But there's no way he did all of the things we worked on in the coven. Visiting the Near-Depths? Levitation? Making candles burst into flame? Summoning winds? Changing traffic lights?"

"The traffic lights thing is debatable," Drea said. "Traffic lights have a way of changing even *without* magic."

"Mother never hits me, and she never makes me pray," Brandy said quietly. "No punishments. Nothing."

I glanced in the rearview and saw Drea put an arm around Brandy's shoulders.

"Nic hasn't used any drugs since we did the spell," I added. "I mean, he still smokes tons of weed. But that's it."

"John paid Mom all the back child support *and* Mom got a raise," Drea said. "We own the trailer now."

"And I don't have cancer," Dove said with finality. "How the hell would Bastion manage all that?"

"Coincidence?" I said, to play devil's advocate. "Nic got clean because he OD'd and it scared him. You got better because you had chemo. John paid the child support because he didn't want to get in trouble with the law. Raises happen."

"And Mrs. Jackson? Abusive religious wackos don't just change without, like, therapy or meds," Dove countered. "How are you going to explain Brandy's mom? Or the *timing* of everything?

Was our routine breaking of the laws of physics part of Bastion's master plan?"

"I think it was the spells," I said. "And obviously the . . . Near-Depths visits and the floating and stuff . . . I mean, it's clear that our rituals are doing *something*. I'm just pointing out that the *end* results can mostly be explained."

"I think we need a fifth," Drea said. "It doesn't work without a fifth. The Nexus symbol on my skin doesn't feel like anything but a cut. It's seven-fifty. It should be tingling to remind us we have to fulfill our magic obligation soon. You guys feel anything?"

"No," I said.

"Nothing," Brandy said.

"Me either," Dove said. "But it isn't because we need a fifth. Bastion and I did our first spell with just the two of us. Nesbit didn't even start until like two years ago."

"Again, Bastion is the only missing link," Brandy said.

We all contemplated this for a moment. I could feel Dove's tension in the seat beside me. She wasn't prepared to accept that we might be incapable of using magic to catch Bastion's killer. (*Especially*—as Brandy had pointed out the night of the wake—if the killer also had something supernatural going on.) Then again, neither was I.

"Turn left up there," Dove said, and I shook my head.

"I'm going to Drea's so we can sneak into the cemetery from the back," I said.

"Nope. Stepwood is crawling with the fuzz," Dove said. "The cops are patrolling it to see if the murderer comes back to the scene of the crime. We're going to the county coroner's office, at the town hall building."

"What?" I asked, confused by this turn of events. I made the left, though.

"I let that slimelord Dave Fitch get to third base with me so that he'd agree to help us with the break-in," Dove said. "We can look at the Jane Doe that Bastion and I found when we were kids. And Bastion's file."

"Wait. But we made a Nexus," I protested. "We have to—"

"We made a Nexus to *investigate*," Dove said, "and we're about to."

Nobody else seemed to be surprised.

"You guys knew about this?" I said. "Brandy? You're okay with this?"

"I'm not," Brandy said. "But Dove is eighteen, so she can let the slimelord town hall intern feel her up if she wants."

"Finger-bang, actually," Dove clarified.

"Oh, gross," Drea said. "Ugh."

"I meant with breaking in!" I said. "I can't believe you guys didn't tell me the plan."

"Nez . . . ," Drea said. It was clear that she was weighing her words instead of running her mouth, which made me feel really weird.

"What?" I asked, almost snapping.

"It's just clear that you haven't been handling this very well," Brandy said in her gentlest tone of voice.

"Park over here. The cameras don't reach there," Dove instructed, and I maneuvered into a dusty lot across the street from the plaza. The little postal office was dark, as was the town hall, with only two yellow streetlights to show that anything official ever happened here. The flag had been taken down in deference to the windy night, but I knew tomorrow it would fly at half-mast for our freshly deceased mayor.

"So?" I asked, turning off the car. I felt defensive. Had I really seemed that *off* to them? "None of us are doing well. Bastion's dead."

"Yeah, and we're all shocked. And grieving," Dove said. "And he's my favorite brother who I loved more than this whole shitty world. But that's different from being *in* love. I know people talk smack about high-school relationships, but you guys were in love. Real love."

"No, we weren't," I said, surprised at how bitter I sounded. "Our last fight was about—"

"He couldn't *say* it," Dove said. "Not even to me or Mom or anyone. But he showed it all the time."

"I'm fine," I said, through my teeth.

"Dude. You literally didn't even blink when Mayor Winship *died* on you at the funeral," Drea said. "You're totally out to lunch. I respect that"—she added, as Brandy made a noise of protest—"I do. But we didn't feel like you were up to planning a crime with us."

"Great," I said. I felt excluded, but mostly I felt numb. Just like I had all week. Maybe they had a point.

"You can stay in the car if you want," Dove offered, squeezing my arm for a second.

"I'm coming," I said firmly.

"Okay, well, we have like twenty minutes before he shows up," Dove said. "Let me tell you guys about the Jane Doe."

Bastion would never talk about it. Ever since I'd known the Attias, "that day" when they'd discovered a dead woman in the woods behind Stepwood Cemetery had only been alluded to . . . which had always struck me as weird, because finding a dead body is *exactly* the kind of thing Dove should have been super eager to tell us about.

"You guys have never heard this either?"

Brandy shook her head.

"No, only what Mom told me," Drea said. "Which wasn't much because it totally freaked her out. She used to be all interested in Stepwood, too, and spend time in there back when she was pregnant with me. Probably why I love scary shit like unsolved murders. And then when the murder happened, it was like less than a mile from our house."

"Okay," Dove said. "I haven't told anyone about this but like the cops and a child therapist Mom made us go to. Ever."

This is what she told us . . .

CHAPTER FIVE

Saturday, July 11, 1992
& Saturday, November 27, 1999

The long-ago day when Bastion and Dove Attia stumbled upon the dead body in Stepwood Cemetery was preceded by a slow-moving thunderstorm that had lulled North Dana into a humid sleep for two days. When it broke, it was a perfect Saturday: a hot yellow sun dominated the chalky-blue sky. Bugs buzzed. Anna Attia's two oldest children had no activities for once. Not that Dove was much of an "activities" kid, but Bastion, even at nine, was a major joiner. He liked acting and swimming and hiking and sports, all manner of sports. He liked book clubs, even the grown-up one his mom's real-life author friends had at her house where they all got wine-drunk and made jokes about books like Pale Fire and Finnegans Wake. Actually, he especially liked that one, and would creep downstairs long after bed to listen to Anna and her clever clique poke drunken fun at their literary heroes.

Dove's illness was the only cloud that hung over the perfect sky of the Attia family's summer day, until they found the dead girl. The type of leukemia that Dove had been diagnosed with had a high survival rate, but she was still sick and pale and bald from her treatment, and there was still a possibility . . . however slim the excellent doctors made it seem . . . that she could die. But that day Dove was feeling well enough to want to tag along while her mom took Polaroids of old gravestones for her new poetry collection. And where Dove went, Bastion invariably followed. Robin, just a toddler, had stayed with Youssef in the garden, and Anna packed up the other two and drove to Stepwood.

Anna loved the strange graves at Stepwood and went there often before the day the corpse of the woman was discovered, even though it was considered a bit shabby and derelict by most townies. After that, she stayed away and forbade her kids from going, a rule that wasn't relaxed for several years.

Once they got to the cemetery, Anna meandered around near the gates. She was nearly five months pregnant and tired more quickly than was usual for her. Dove and Bastion wanted to walk in the woods by the old mausoleums near the back and look for fairy rings: toadstool circles that heralded magic and danger, a legend that fascinated Bastion. He called them "portals to Phantasien," after the fantasy world in his favorite book and was convinced he could get to the land of stories if he hopped into the right one.

Dove, already deep into things like The Crone's Book of Words, was too old for fairy tales but definitely the right age to embrace earth magic. She and her brother wandered off while Anna took pictures, and Anna was relieved that her daughter was feeling up to—

"Wait, wait," I said, holding up a hand. Dove was a decent storyteller, even if she didn't quite have Drea's *Voice*, and we'd all been listening raptly while we waited for slimelord-Dave-the-finger-banging-intern to arrive. Now I made her pause with my interruption. "Your mom was almost five months pregnant? That doesn't add up. The twins are too young."

"She had a late miscarriage like two weeks later," Dove said, frowning. "I remember she and Dad cried over it a bunch of times and I was mad that they were sadder about their stupid unborn kid than they were about *me* possibly dying."

"That's totally messed up," Drea said. "You were a little sociopath."

"*Drea*," Brandy said exasperatedly.

"I was eleven! At eleven, all kids are self-centered little sociopaths!" Dove said. "I'm just being honest. Obviously, I feel bad about it in *retrospect*. Well, all kids are sociopaths except for Bastion. I was fine like a day after we found Janey D., but he was . . . never the same. Like all his weird behaviors and compulsions started after that. Anyway, you guys are *messing* up my storytelling flow," Dove said, glaring into the back seat.

"No, keep going," I said. "You said the Jane Doe looked the same as Bastion."

"Was killed the same way," Dove corrected.

Dove and Bastion ran through the trees at the back of Stepwood Cemetery, passing the Dearest grave, with the old columns, and the Northcott Faire mausoleum. Bastion was a thoughtful kid, and every time Dove got out of breath, he would jog backward to her with a worried expression on his face.

"You okay?" Bastion asked.

"Yeah," Dove said, annoyed by his concern. "What's that smell?"

The smell of rot washed over the siblings from the line of pine trees behind the final mausoleum.

"I see something," Bastion said. "A dead deer, maybe."

Bastion was sensitive about dead things, often crying over squirrels crushed by cars and bugs that didn't make it. But Dove was fascinated by corpses and bones and urged him on toward the overwhelming stench of decay and the shape between the trees.

It was only when they were within a few yards of the body that Dove stopped, grabbing her little brother by the shoulder.

"Wait here," Dove said. "Stay right here. I need to go get Mom."

It was a woman, lying on the ground. She was dressed in tattered brown silk. What manner of outfit it had once been was unrecognizable, as was her face. She looked like she had been chewed on. The only thing left intact was a gold necklace that fell to her navel, neatly gleaming against her destroyed torso in the summer sunlight. Her hands were held up against her chest as if to defend herself. Her long hair made a matted halo on the mossy earth. Deep divots of flesh were missing from her legs and chest and face, and each wound was filled with maggots that spilled out onto the rest of her body. Dove saw a bare breast with the nipple eaten off rising from the dead woman's chest like a chalice of decay.

Then she took off through the trees as quickly as her diminished legs would carry her, screaming for her mother.

"I have one big regret in my whole life," Dove said. "Just one so far. I left Bastion alone with the dead woman for . . . maybe ten minutes while I went to get Mom. In my mind I was worried we would like, I don't know, *lose* the body or something. I was a stupid kid. But that ten minutes . . . he was always different after it."

"From PTSD?" I asked.

"Yeah, was it the trauma of it?" Drea asked.

"I don't know. I still have no idea. Anna and Youssef stuffed us into therapy immediately," Dove said. "My yuppie self-help-loving pseudo-hippie folks, I mean they did *everything*. Bastion seemed okay for a little bit. Then he started with 'N's have to begin every sentence' one day. Maybe six months after we found the body. It wasn't just the speaking; it was everything and it was freaking overnight. Speaking, writing, reciting, *anything*. It was hard for the little guy, too. He would get stuck all the time and choke on his words. He literally had to write an N at the beginning of math equation answers on his homework or he couldn't solve them. It took him forever to get good at working around all of his shit, and I *know* it was still a struggle for him. Then the next year he told us he couldn't dream anymore."

"He told me that, too," I said. "He said, '*Nesbit, I dream about dreaming. Nevertheless, I can't dream.*' I always remember it."

That was definitely too much depressing talk for Brandy, who put her face in her hands and started crying again.

"It's okay," Drea whispered, rubbing her shoulders. "Hey, it's okay."

"It's not," Brandy said, through her tears.

"No, it's not," Drea said, immediately reversing her position. "It's actually so totally screwed. Why did one of my best friends never get to . . . speak correctly or say his *own name* or tell anybody *I love you* or dream or . . . like a ton of other things?"

"He was so good, too," Dove said, and now she had actual tears in her eyes. I was shocked by it, and doubly shocked that I still felt unable to cry, not even at the sight of my best friend and the toughest person I knew almost weeping. "Such a good kid. My baby brother. I just don't know how he can be *dead*—"

Dove put her hands over her mouth and cried silently for a minute, no more. That night my car was a miserable place filled with miserable people, and it hurt more because we had all been so happy once. It hurt because—even if time healed our pain—it would never be quite that way again.

Then Dove straightened up like it had never happened and checked her eyeliner in the mirror. It was smudged to hell, but she didn't bother trying to fix it.

"There's one more thing," Dove said. "He swore me to secrecy, you know, because it could have been considered interfering with a murder investigation. But I *had* to cover it up. It was the only thing Bastion ever did in his life that was . . . well, bad."

"What was it?" Drea asked, leaning forward.

"He took her necklace."

"Her necklace?" Brandy asked.

"The key," I said, in a moment of realization. "The key to the Northcott Faire mausoleum."

"Yeah, but there was nothing in there!" Dove said. "That's why we've been using it for coven stuff for years. You guys have all been in it—it's just an empty mausoleum. Nothing in it could have identified her. The Northcott family owned the house that the Micenmachers live in now. Stepwood was *their* cemetery . . . but they've all been dead for a hundred years!"

"I thought that some of the graves in Stepwood belonged to the Northcott family, and others were presumed to be relocated graves from when they flooded Dana and all the other towns out to make the Quabbin Reservoir," Brandy said, still a little shaky. "That's why it's so unusual looking."

"That's the line in the local history books," Drea said. "But even those relocated graves would be from the 1930s at the latest. There isn't anyone in Stepwood with living relatives that the Jane Doe could've been connected to."

"How did he even know the key opened that mausoleum?" I asked. To me, it was somehow the most important question.

"Well, obviously we snuck back to Stepwood a million times from Drea's house even after Mom told us we could never go there again," Dove said. "And by high school, everyone had kind of agreed that the killer was—ha ha—not going to strike again, so our folks had minimal problems with us hanging out there."

"Yeah," I said. "But how did he know that the key on this random murder victim's necklace unlocked *that* mausoleum?"

Dove opened her mouth and closed it. "I don't know," she admitted after a moment of silence.

"Maybe he just tried the nearest keyhole to where the body was found," Brandy suggested. But I could tell even she was unconvinced by her own logical deduction.

"This is why we're breaking into the coroner's office," I said. "The necklace wasn't on him, was it?"

Dove shook her head. "Nope. He wore that chain under his clothes day and night for more than seven years. Youssef and Anna never even saw it, I don't think, because he was crafty like that. And I need to know if they confiscated it post-mortem. I have a *feeling* that we need that key. This case may end up getting turned over to the FBI or something for all we know, especially with a second victim in the same place."

"They normally don't have jurisdiction—" Drea started to tell us about criminal proceedings, her favorite thing besides conspiracy theories and aliens, but we were interrupted by Dave Fitch rapping on the passenger-side window. He was wearing a knit cap like a particularly greasy cat burglar.

"Let's go," I said, and nodded at Dove. She put on a fake smile for Dave, and we went out into the night.

CHAPTER SIX

Saturday, November 27, 1999

Slimelord Dave was clearly infatuated with Dove, which was true of about ten guys at any given time. True to his greasy word, he disabled the keypad alarms on the side entrance of the town hall and directed us to the county coroner's office. He even stood guard outside the building while we committed our crime.

North Dana and the other tiny towns in our county had no actual morgue for dead bodies, except for the basement rooms of the local funeral homes. Logically, the real desk-job office was where we needed to go to find written information. The girls had come well prepared. Brandy's purple backpack produced flashlights to go around, and Dove's little digital camera was on hand for documentation. They even brought me bobby pins and paper clips in case lockpicking was needed—I was a kid when my dad first taught me how to pick the wafer lock on an "*I lost the keys*" car door, and my interest had only expanded from there—and, as it turned out, lockpicking *was* needed.

"If we're on security cameras or something, we're screwed," Drea whispered, as I picked the lock on the office door of Thorla P. Davis, Coroner.

"Not if they don't check the footage," Dove said. "Which they won't if they don't know anything happened."

The lock popped and I guided the office door open. Inside the office, it looked like a bomb had gone off: stacks of filing cabinets sat in the middle of the room, and the desk was pushed up against the wall. A document scanner and a fax machine sat next to a blue iMac. Files crowded the desk in haphazard piles.

"They're in the middle of digitizing all these files," Brandy said, examining the chaos with the beam of her flashlight. "Good timing on our part."

"Bet they didn't expect a murder to happen during their project," Drea said. Dove was already prying open the *D–F* drawer on one of the cabinets.

"Gimme a Doe," Dove said. "Nope, no, no, no—"

"Bastion's report is over here," Drea said from the desk. "Front and center."

"Be careful," Brandy said. "Put everything back the way it was."

Drea nodded and opened to the first page. "Nez, light. The flash might not do it."

I had been standing uselessly in the middle of the room while they did everything. Drea's words broke me out of my stupor, and I shone a flashlight over her shoulder while she snapped pictures.

Snap. A list of personal items. *Snap.* A diagram of wound patterns. *Snap.* Interviews with friends and family and witnesses.

Cameron Winship's name flashed by. *Snap snap snap.* Picture after picture of Bastion's half-eaten body.

I closed my eyes as Drea took more pictures.

"Got her," Dove announced. "Brandy, hand me the bag, I'm taking this whole file."

"Don't you think the coroner will miss it?"

"That's a good point," Dove said. "I specifically mentioned this case in my statement. They'll go looking for it at some point. Drea, come over here and take pictures of this entire thing."

Then my hands started to ache out of nowhere, and I opened my eyes. Drea finished with Bastion's file and started photographing Jane Doe's. The girls were clearly keyed up, high on adrenaline from our espionage adventure. But I, the numb dummy that I was lately, had felt nothing much in the way of either excitement or fear until that very moment. Something was *wrong*, my hands told me. "Guys. Do you feel that?"

"I heard something," Drea whispered, shutting the file. "Like a voice. Shut up, everyone. Lights out."

We all flicked our flashlights off and got very still. In the dark, I just barely made out Brandy glancing around—like she saw someone hiding in the shadows. We were being watched. The hair on my arms stood up.

Dove leaned toward me very slowly and whispered. "There is someone here. We have to go."

That slinking inhuman feeling I had been feeling since Bastion's murder was back and suddenly amplified by a million. It was beyond the fear of being caught by some town employee. We crept like we were underwater, away from whatever lurked in the dark.

Out the door we went with our gathered information. Brandy led us, a stately specter haunting the dim hall, which was lit only by emergency lights. I checked the lock on Thorla P. Davis's office door, made sure that it was still functional, and relocked it from the inside. Then I stepped out, inching the door shut behind me.

Inside the office, something chuckled in the dark.

"I'm imagining that," I said, under my breath. The sound made me think of rotting silk curtains drawn over shuttered windows. It was like nothing I had ever heard before.

Then I swung the door closed and marched after the others as quickly and quietly as I could.

Once we were out in the night (Dove gave Dave a kiss that I could tell, but he could not, meant *goodbye forever* before we parted ways) the feeling of being secretly observed vanished. We piled into the car, and I sped away on a backroads route that veered in and out of Quabbin Reservoir territory.

"Take me home," Dove said from my left. "They'll check on me tonight before they go to bed. Anna's been doing that." *Since Bastion died*, she didn't say.

"I'll go through the pictures and take notes tonight," Drea said. "I'm working one to six tomorrow. Come by after Jay leaves at three and we can go over it."

"Did you feel something weird in there?" I asked.

Drea and Dove seemed like they were going to deny the overpowering feeling of creepiness, of being watched, that had come over us in the dark of the coroner's office. Drea shrugged (a quiet Drea was usually a *lying by omission* Drea), and Dove legitimately shook her head *no* as she reached up to mess with my radio.

"I don't think so," Dove said, and Drea nodded. I batted her hand away and turned down Bastion's favorite radio station.

"Are you kidding?" Brandy asked from the back seat. "Of course we felt something. Or . . . I *saw* something. Like a shape in the corner. It . . . This isn't possible, but it looked like it was something so large it had to *crouch* to fit in the room. But it wasn't distinguishable from the shadows even with my light on it. That sounds bizarre, and it is. I would certainly have written it off if—"

"If I hadn't bugged out about it," I said. I strongly disliked the image of some massive crouching thing watching us in the dark.

"Okay, fine," Drea acquiesced. "I heard something weird. I think it was just, like, mass hysteria."

"Yes," Dove agreed, firmly. "We need to focus on finding the killer."

"Drea. You heard something weird like what?" I asked.

"Like laughter," Drea said, after a second of hesitation. "Like low, quiet laughter."

Her words were like cold fingers brushing my neck in an empty room. Dove didn't have a comeback, either. We drove quietly for a few minutes, nobody sure where this incident left us.

I dropped Dove off in front of her house, which was all lit up and still filled with mourners who were close to the family. Probably drinking and crying and reminiscing. It made me feel hollow. These were the people who made up Bastion's life. They had known him longer than I had or ever would. But I didn't believe anybody really knew Bastion like I did. Like Dove said, love was different. Even if Bastion had never said it.

The route from their houses to mine meant that I dropped Brandy off last at her immaculately restored Carpenter Gothic house, which to me always looked—appropriately, considering her mom—like some depressingly austere church in a forgotten Midwestern town. When we were alone in the car, she climbed into the front seat and looked out the window as I drove.

"Something is going on," Brandy said after a minute where everything was silent except for the low weeping of the old-timey saxophone that WJIN was airing on their station.

"I agree," I said.

"It's more than a murder, Nez."

"I agree with that, too."

"It's beyond just a serial killer. The *key* to the mausoleum? The key Bastion was so obsessed with, that he never took off, was from a corpse he found? The corpse of a person who died in the exact same way he did?"

"And the way we all picked up on that . . . whatever it was tonight," I said. "I sensed it in my hands because I'm the Hands. Drea heard it because she's the Voice."

"Dove *felt* it because she's the Heart, and I *saw* something because I'm the Eyes," Brandy said, perfectly finishing my thought. "That occurred to me too," she added.

"It's something magical," I said. Listen, if I had heard myself saying this in 1997 before I met North Coven, I would be convinced that future junior-year me had completely lost his mind. But I'd seen too much and done too much since then to dwell in the bliss of total skepticism.

"It's something very bad," Brandy said, her usually serious voice getting even more serious. "I don't think we can avoid it. But Dove wants a murderer to catch, and I'm afraid that it won't be so simple."

"Catching a murderer isn't, like, super simple," I pointed out.

"Whatever is happening may be significantly more complex," Brandy countered. I agreed with her, honestly. It was starting to make me feel kind of paranoid, which was the first emotion I had really felt besides fear for a week now. It was not a super-warm welcome back to the world of emotion.

"Dove doesn't think it's something supernatural," I pointed out as my car chugged along through the darkness. "She says we've never encountered anything magical beyond *ourselves*. And Drea's kind of aboard the denial train, too."

"Drea's just scared. She'll see reason soon enough. And Dove . . . she truly doesn't want to admit it," Brandy said. "I don't know why. But I know that *I saw something* just now. And I know that the way in which Bastion was killed was not *normal*, even for a . . . particularly grisly murder."

I glanced over at the cross that Brandy always wore—what little of it I could see in the dark, anyway—before putting my eyes back on the road.

"You think it's the Devil?" I asked.

"I don't think the Devil exists," Brandy replied.

"But you think God exists," I pointed out. Despite everything, Brandy still believed in some kind of divine creator. Drea likened it to Agent Scully on *The X-Files*, who was both a devout Catholic and a hardcore skeptic. Contradictions existed within even the most logical-seeming people all the time.

"Believing that our universe was made by something greater than ourselves, something beyond our understanding, is one thing," Brandy said. "I see the Lord at work in our world. There's a push and pull of . . . these forces of good and evil around us all the time. In the magic we do. In the Near-Depths. In the entropy of our universe, in every human being, in art and . . . in *everything*. But I don't believe in some red-handed devil with a pitchfork and a throne of darkness."

"Me either," I said. I didn't believe the universe was made by anything in particular. Definitely not by someone's idea of God. But I agreed with Brandy that we were passing out of the bounds of our experience right now, dealing with something we had never dealt with before.

Something *bad*.

I dropped Brandy off and went home to find Dad and Nic waiting for me. We didn't talk about anything, which was great. Instead, we all ate reheated paella and watched a rerun of the NASCAR Winston Cup, which I had missed when it originally aired on account of that being the same day my boyfriend was murdered. I fell asleep on the couch under a pile of unfolded-but-clean laundry. And that was the end of November 27.

Now if you're paying really close attention, you might be wondering how Stepwood Cemetery could have been "destroyed forever" on November 27, 1999. I already told you everything about November 27, right? And I didn't mention anything about cemetery destruction.

So. I promise to tell you about that later. It will all make sense in the end.

CHAPTER SEVEN

Sunday, November 28, 1999

Sometime in the early-morning hours after (four-fifths of) North Coven did our first-ever stint of breaking and entering, I had a nightmare.

I was walking through an abandoned traveling carnival, the old kind from black-and-white movies. The surroundings were black-and-white, too, just like a vintage photograph. The only color in that place was the flat dark red of the sky.

I passed through a midway where not a living thing moved. Nothing made a sound but old bits of paper and crumbling hay under my feet, crunching in a muted way as I walked. It seemed labyrinthine, an eternal fair, and yet my feet kept me moving with that strange unwilling momentum that sometimes happens in bad dreams. I passed a glassblowing tent (10 CENTS, the painted sign said) and rows of empty wheeled cages that probably held animals once but now held only dustings of ancient hay. I was pushed inexorably past endless ranks of fortune-telling wagons with faded cloth pieces or filthy carpets covering narrow entrances. A sign for *Wolfson's Freak Show*, a tattered island of connected striped tents, came up in my view and disappeared behind me. The rusting bulks of Ferris wheels (too big to be as old as they looked—too big, it seemed, to exist at all) loomed on the horizon. Impossibly elaborate carousels, one after another, each totally different, framed my field of vision as I walked.

The eeriest part of the haunted place were the human figures—I thought of them as *false attendants*—that littered the midway. They were cutouts of people that stood behind the old popcorn stands and moldering pop-gun games. Each one was smiling brightly, people of all ages and in all styles of clothing. Every figure was exquisitely rendered in faded monochrome paint. They almost seemed ready to help me if I approached their particular booth, but perspective showed me that they were only wooden silhouettes, insubstantial and unreal. The painted people all had an arm raised, as if in greeting or welcome, until I realized they were all pointing to signs that were nailed to their booths.

A drawn girl of no more than ten in an elaborately detailed antique nightgown smiled from beside a fanciful wheeled building called *Mandy's Menagerie*. One of the frescoed panels of the building proclaimed *Worthy of your patronage!* in a swirling hand-lettered script. Mandy, if that was indeed who the little girl was meant to be, pointed up at another sign suspended on the wall of the menagerie building that was brief enough for me to read it as I passed by:

Fancy	*Fare*
I don't like it! I wish to take the necklace off!	*Revocation of the token.* *Granted.*

That was all it said. The sign was innocuous and painted in the same colorless way as everything else in the carnival world. But the letters in the *Fare* column were drawn in searing red, more vivid than the dark red sky, so luminous that they hurt to look at.

Something about the sign, and the way the illustrated little girl smiled as she pointed at it, forever and ever, made my hands tingle. My unease in the dreamworld bled and blurred into the edges of real fright.

From somewhere far ahead, I heard two voices in conversation. The words were distant, and the speakers invisible, but I could hear every word perfectly, like I had tuned in to a radio broadcast.

"No, I know we *did* something! Not for the first time we traveled together to the Near-Depths of all universes, even the place *you* come from. New person came tonight. Now we are stronger than ever before. Nous, our abilities—"

That was Bastion. Then another voice came in reply. It cut him off with a chuckle that made me picture a curtain of rotting silk falling against a derelict hallway window.

The same laughter I had heard in the darkness at the town hall.

"Are impressive. Yes, my clever one. But they are not impressive enough to remake the destinies of your world. Your aim to change a human being has not succeeded . . . and tonight your frightened friend

will go home late to a mother who has discovered her ruse and the letters from her love."

The voice of the second speaker was the most beautiful thing I had ever heard, at first. But as I listened, I realized it was terribly *wrong* somehow, full of decay, like it was vibrating out of sync with my hearing. The sound of it made my growing fear bloom sickly into true terror. For the first time, I tried to actively fight against the machinations of the dreamworld. I grabbed at the wooden counter of a cotton candy stand, trying to stop myself from inexorably moving forward. It didn't work. I was pulled away from the countertop, pushed toward the voices. And all the time they went on talking.

"No," said Bastion. His defiant tone was wavering. "No. Nous, I *will not* believe it!"

The sickly sweet voice of the *thing* went on speaking. *"India Jackson will strike her only daughter twice with that unpleasant crucifix taken from the nave of the old Obland Church, the one she keeps hanging in her spartan foyer. In the skull, of course, where poor disturbed India has always been convinced the Devil lives. She will not mean for the blows to cause such . . . catastrophic damage. But it will be enough to ruin your little friend forever. Brandy will die fourteen years from now in a long-term care facility. Unless . . ."*

"No, no, *no* . . . ," Bastion said, but the conviction had gone out of his tone.

"You know I cannot lie, dear heart. Was it not I who showed you the path of magic? You and your little friends. Maybe the new one with talented hands will become something special to you. Life is full of marvels. Now tell me. **What is your fancy?***"*

I was dragged into a clearing, a central point in the maze of the carnival. Here was the big top, a round tent that went on and on, striped black and white, and at its highest points topped with flags that seemed to touch the burned-out sky. A straw-lined path led into the darkness of the tent. A hand-lettered sign outside cheerily announced: *Fortunes Told and Fates Changed Within! See Mr. Nous! The One Who Knows!*

"Nous, I wish to keep Brandy safe from her mother, tonight and forever," Bastion said, shakily. "Now tell me my fare."

The thing started to answer, but suddenly the black and white and red swirled around me and faded. I felt myself pulled backward and out, swimming up through my nightmare and into my bed. I woke up gasping and found my sheets soaked in sweat. My hands ached unbearably, an itching tingling under the skin that I could not determine the cause of.

"Nez?" my dad asked. He was standing in the kitchen, at the midpoint between his bedroom and the living room couch I had passed out on. He sounded like he was still asleep. "You okay?"

"Dad, go away, I'm fine," I said.

"You were yelling in your sleep."

"I'm fine," I said, and I was. I tucked myself under the pile of unfolded-but-clean laundry and fell right back to sleep. I didn't understand the significance of my nightmare yet. I only thought about how Bastion was dead, and how it hurt so deeply, and how my dreams were going to be troubled because my waking life was troubled too.

Bastion, I'm sorry for missing your signs. I'm sorry that it took me so long.

But nobody really believes in dreams.

CHAPTER EIGHT

Sunday, November 28, 1999

I woke up after eleven in the morning, still on the couch, to Nic freaking out over burning his breakfast of Toaster Strudels. I had been building a bookshelf in my spare time, thinking I would give it to Drea for her birthday (the double-wide needed help holding her ever-expanding library), but my creative energy, even for something as basic as woodworking, was nonexistent. Instead, I helped in my dad's shop. That was something I was so practiced at that I could turn my whole brain off. The work at the shop that day was comforting and boring—it was a big day for replacing brake pads and rotating tires and changing oil and not much else. When I was done, I washed my grimy hands with the special soap Dad always kept in the garage, cleaned under my nails, and swapped out my "at work" gloves for my "it's cold outside" gloves, which were the same kind of gloves but cleaner. Then it was time to head to Drea's job.

The mundane day didn't really erase my feeling of paranoia. I didn't feel like I was being actively watched, but I didn't feel like I was totally safe, either. The carnival nightmare had only added to my fear that we had drawn the awareness of something big and fathomless in the coroner's office the night before . . . and now I had to keep very quiet to avoid being caught. I mean, on a metaphysical level.

I consider myself a pretty direct person, but I've gotten acquainted with all kinds of metaphysical ideas from my time in the coven. The starry place—the Near-Depths—that would sometimes reveal itself to us during a spell was, in our own theorizing, something like a corridor of the multiverse. I'd taken part in exercises that defied physics. But it had always been fascinating. Beautiful. Meaningful. Never *unclean*, like this felt.

What if there was a flip side to the good we had done and the marvelous things we had seen? Something vast and slinking underneath it all. A mirrored hell for the heaven we had made together.

Bastion would've had answers, questions, theories. But I had nothing except anxiety.

Dove had her mom's car for once and said she would bring Brandy, so I was the first one to show up at Drea's job. Galactic Video was the last shop on the left in the North Dana Common, which sounds like a park or something, but was actually just a grimy strip mall away from the manicured center of town. One-third of the strip mall sat eternally empty, with just Galactic Video, Twelve Fingers Skate Shop, Quabbin Liquors, and Village Pizza occupying the depressing space.

I liked Galactic Video, and since some of us had started driving we would visit Drea often when she put in time there on nights and weekends. Drea clearly enjoyed her job. It gave her spending cash, literally all of which she blew on UFO and true crime stuff (she had shown off her brand-new MUFON membership card to us like a month before) and it also gave her six free video rentals a week. The rentals were mostly reserved for date nights with Brandy, but it did mean we sometimes got first dibs on the good new releases.

Jay, the manager, was a total dickbag who only liked *auteur cinema* and gave Drea a hard time for letting us hang out. I waited until I saw him leave before going into the video store.

The little line of bells on the door rang as I walked in. Drea was blasting Mazzy Star from behind the counter and waved to me briefly before going back to checking a stack of returns from the dropbox.

"*Practical Magic* DVD thrown into a *Pleasantville* VHS case," Drea announced, as I came over to her. "Broken in half. People are so dumb. Like, look at it or something."

Drea had *Gremlins* playing on the wall of televisions at the back of the shop, and I glanced at it and then wandered around for a minute, looking at the tons of tapes and the newly released-on-DVD titles that lined the recessed walls. I gravitated toward the action section, where the galaxy-themed carpet gave way to creaky blue-painted floorboards.

"You want candy?" Drea called, and I walked back over to help myself to a bag of Sour Patch Kids from the snacks that dominated the front counter.

"Did you find anything?" I asked, and Drea nodded, tearing open a box of malted milk balls.

"Mm-hmm. A lot. I've got it here."

Drea was an awesome researcher, I need to give her credit for that. Years of obsessing over missing persons cases and Roswell had given her a private eye's attention to detail, which is why she had taken the lead on the project.

Before Drea could elaborate further, the bells on the door chimed again and Brandy and Dove walked in. Dove was still a good two inches shorter than Brandy, even in her platform boots, and she peered over the counter at Drea.

"It's freezing out," Dove said. Brandy rested her arms on the counter and Drea leaned forward to kiss her hello, very sweetly.

"Hey, babe," Drea said. "I have to mind the shop, but I wrote everything down. You guys want to take it out back?"

"Ugh, I said it was freezing!" Dove protested.

"Yeah, but you can't look at it in the Red Room," Drea said, referring to the little roped-off closet that housed all of Galactic Video's rentable pornography. "You're not supposed to be in there. And the last two hours are when all the pervs come in. Take this and go out back, I made a ton of notes."

Dove grabbed the notebook and stomped toward the glowing EXIT sign at the back of the store. I followed her, while Brandy and Drea had a brief exchange I couldn't hear.

The back of the North Dana Common was actually the best part. At least, it was the best part in the summer. The paved lot stopped at the rear of the building, so the back was just a narrow dirt track lined with dumpsters for each of the respective businesses that still survived there. Sometimes Tony and Meg would come out from Village Pizza all kitchen-sweaty and give us leftovers while we hung out. Johnny and the other guys who worked at Twelve Fingers had put a little ramp out for skateboarding, and they would be back there pretty often trying out new decks. Behind the dirt road, the wilderness encroached on the little plaza, a hill of wildflowers and sumac bushes that went up at a sharp angle into pine woods. And situated directly behind Galactic Video was what Drea called "the employee lounge"—an old green vinyl couch and three plastic lounge chairs from the eighties that were becoming one with the brambly hill. When Bastion was alive, he avoided the plastic beach chairs, which creaked ominously under his weight, so we would usually sit pressed together on the couch.

I picked a lounge chair and let the girls take the couch, not wanting to be reminded of how it had felt to have Bastion beside me any more than I already was.

Once we were actually outside, Dove didn't seem to mind the cold, but Brandy had snagged Drea's hoodie and wrapped herself in it with a shiver.

"Here we go," Dove said, flopping down on the couch and lighting a cigarette. She held up the notebook with her free hand. "Brandy, do the honors?"

"The mausoleum key isn't listed in Jane Doe's list of personal effects," Brandy said, pulling out several pages of paper in Drea's signature green-penned, loopy scrawl. "Obviously. But Drea says here that it isn't listed in Bastion's, either."

"What made him grab that key? Did he ever tell you?" I asked, looking at Dove.

"No idea. He just begged me to keep it secret," Dove said.

"He never stole anything. He even paid for candy when Drea gave it to us," I said. "Even though Drea gets free candy. Which is insane."

Dove nodded. "That was the only time he ever, like *ever*, did anything like that."

"So someone else has the key now," I said.

"Cameron found him first," Brandy pointed out. "What if there's a . . . compulsory aspect to passing the key?"

"That makes more sense than Cameron Winship having the balls to take anything off of a dead body," I said, digging out the last of the green Sour Patch Kids.

"Listen, I don't know if this is a magic thing," Dove said, putting up her hands. "Chill out. Maybe the murderer left the key on his last victim, our Jane Doe, and then took it back when he murdered Bastion."

Brandy and I exchanged a *look* over the top of Dove's head. That look said that *I* was going to have to deal with it, which, fair. I'd always been decent at getting the Attias to see reason when they wound themselves up.

"Dove . . . ," I said, in a tone that probably sounded a little too *nice*. Dove immediately gave me a sharp and focused glare.

"What?" Dove said.

"Why, um, *exactly* are you so sure that there's no supernatural aspect to Bastion's death?" I asked. "Speaking as one literal *spellcasting witch* to another. While we investigate a murder where the victim was literally *eaten*."

"Dahmer was a biter," Dove said defensively. But I could tell she was bullshitting. Brandy took the weakness in Dove's voice as a cue to press our advantage.

"The Jane Doe had no dental records they could pull or anything. Because something ate her face, teeth and all," Brandy said, eyes scanning Drea's pages. "I'm not paraphrasing. The report said the . . . *bites* taken out of the victim were hard to identify at first because they seemed to be too large to come from a human. But they were bites from a human-shaped mouth."

"A huge, enormous guy came along and ate them," I said flatly, and set the rest of my candy aside, feeling sick. "Dove. You think this sounds like a normal serial killer?"

"It *can't* be something supernatural, okay?" Dove said, sitting up very straight. Her hands were up in a *stop* gesture. "It just can't."

"Why?" I asked again. Gently.

Dove visibly gave up. Her shoulders slumped. When she answered me, she was almost whispering.

"Because I don't know how to do this without you guys. I made you swear to help. But if it's some kind of fucking *monster*, some other witch, some supernatural evil, I—I can't risk you guys being involved. It's too dangerous. I got all of you involved in witchcraft to begin with. If I made us *targets* for something, I can't lose you guys. Not after Bastion. I . . . I love you all more than anything. I—"

Brandy immediately wrapped her arms around Dove. "It's okay," she said.

Dove was not a hugger. One of the reasons that she was my *best* best friend, and I was hers, was because we both had similar attitudes when it came to . . . well, the whole idea of mushiness and gooeyness and lots of demonstrations of love. It was funny, because Dove was loud and passionate, Dove was our Heart— but she basically showed 90 percent of her affection through teasing and the other 10 percent through the occasional fortifying arm squeeze. She didn't (normally) cry. She didn't have long talks about her emotions. Which was great by me. We *got* each other that way.

But right now was a totally different situation. And Dove was accepting Brandy's hug without complaint.

"I know the thought of losing us is scary," Brandy said. "But we are as involved as you are. That's not your decision. It's not your responsibility. And what happened to Bastion was not your fault."

Dove looked over at me as Brandy spoke, her mouth in a flat line but her eyes wide and shining behind her little sunglasses. Like she was looking to me for affirmation of the things Brandy was saying. I nodded, to show my profound agreement. It hadn't occurred to me that Dove felt like she was responsible for the rest of us, now. But I guess it was that older sibling thing. Nic had it too—like he would sometimes take responsibility for stuff I was dealing with that wasn't even his *business*. It was infuriating, but it kind of made me feel looked out for.

"I know, I know," Dove grumbled, extricating herself from Brandy's arms. "I'm not a little kid. You don't have to baby me."

"So are you ready to talk supernatural horrors beyond our comprehension?" I asked, trying for joviality and totally failing.

"I guess so," Dove said. "It does kind of seem supernatural."

"No duh," I said, and dodged her when she tried to flick the side of my head.

"Here's the strangest part," Brandy said, back to business and flipping to a heavily underlined page where Drea's writing became larger and more urgent. "From the reports. Drea says that both victims had trace amounts of straw and hay on their hair and clothing. The origin of the straw could not be determined in the case of the Jane Doe, because the straw was sent out to a forensic botanist and never arrived."

"They lost the evidence?" Dove asked.

"They received something. It wasn't straw, though. The bag showed up empty," Brandy said, her eyes moving down the page.

"How does an empty bag help?" Dove asked.

"It's the fact that the straw was found both times," I said. "It's weird because I think in Bastion's case there wasn't time to move his body to another location and then kill him and move him back to the exact spot we were going to meet him on time."

"Okay. What did they say about the straw in Bastion's case?" Dove asked.

"No results yet that Drea could see," Brandy said, skimming. "Or even a receipt from the botanist. Did you know about the writing on her arm, Dove?"

"No. What writing?"

"It was thought that she did it to herself because it was in marker, and she had matching ink on her right hand. She wrote on her left arm: *'Its starless maw and boundless lust. The Stepwood Specter was discussed. I'm sorry, J. I love you.'* That's all."

"Who's J? The killer?" I asked.

"God, probably. Since there are like ten thousand guys named John in every square mile," Dove said.

"No writing on Bastion, right?"

"None," Brandy said. "It makes me think that somehow Jane Doe knew she was going to be killed before she *was* killed and left a message for someone."

"How has nobody connected these cases yet?" I asked.

Brandy shook her head. "No idea."

"Thorla P. Davis isn't the same coroner from back then," Dove said. "I think they *have* connected the cases, though, right? I mean the current murder victim literally found the last murder victim. Mom and I both brought it up in our statements."

"I find it odd, though," Brandy said. "The fact that this case was just sitting in a filing cabinet. If I were the coroner, I'd have it out next to Bastion's file."

"Maybe it's been digitized," Dove countered. "Or maybe it's the influence of some of those supernatural horrors."

I zoned out on their conversation for a minute as they debated and pored through Drea's notes. I was thinking about supernatural horrors. About my nightmare carnival and the straw that had covered the midway in my dream.

Bastion pleading. The buzzing, silky voice of the second speaker. *Now tell me.* **What is your fancy?**

"Nez?" Dove asked, and I snapped back to the present.

"I think we need that key," I said. "If we can't find it, we'll have to break into the Northcott Faire mausoleum by ourselves."

We had all seen the mausoleum before, unremarkable and empty. But now something could be different. Brandy and Dove nodded.

"Dove, you should go through Bastion's room," Brandy said. I was surprised. Brandy wasn't normally the person to suggest prying, no more than Bastion was the sort of person to steal. But desperate times made strangers of us all, I guess.

"I know where he kept some of his private stuff," Dove agreed. "Probably just flowery letters to Nez. The police have been through most of it, but I'll check again."

"I'll get my dad's lockpicking stuff," I said. "We can go after school tomorrow."

The sun was low on the horizon despite it being barely four in the afternoon. I watched the sky turn dark purple and wondered how on earth all of these threads fit together in a way that might solve Bastion's murder—in a way that might ever give us any resolution at all.

CHAPTER NINE

~~Monday, November 29, 1999~~

It took me a while to notice how the world had changed.

I got up on Monday for school, showered and put on clean clothes, drove myself to Regional, arrived slightly late, and worked through two hours of Vo-Ag classes without any idea that something world-altering had happened. I mean, nobody around me could have pointed it out, either. I wasn't exactly starting conversations about Bastion with my classmates. I could barely even focus on my work. Being back in school felt so weird, like I was going through the motions on a ship that had long since wrecked on the ocean floor and was now populated entirely by ghosts. Of all the phantom crew, carrying out their daily duties, I was the only one aware that we were no longer alive. That we weren't on the water, but miles underneath it. Where there had once been endless stars there was now only the blackness of the deep-sea trenches, vague monsters lurking in the dark above us.

Enough boat analogies. I think the only one lost at sea was me, really. I didn't notice that the ugly paper turkeys were still adorning the halls, either—or, I did, but I just kind of glazed over when I looked at them.

Right before I was released back into the general population for World History, the intercom system crackled, signaling the day's announcements. Everyone in the garage where we held the hands-on mechanics classes spared it a glance before continuing cleanup. Announcements happened every day before lunch, and a limited roster of students rotated the responsibility of reading them. Drea was one of the designated student announcers, so it wasn't surprising when I heard her start to speak.

"No, that's not the right date," Drea said, her voice a little distorted by the intercom. "These aren't the right notes. It's the twenty-ninth."

Then the intercom system clicked off again.

"The twenty-ninth? What is she smoking?" said Rob Malone, a chill dude who spent most of his time on photography.

"It *is* the twenty-ninth," I said, confused. "What are *you* smoking, Rob?"

"Marijuana, mostly," Rob said. "But it's the twenty-second."

The intercom system came alive again. "I don't know what kind of crap you're pulling on me, but I'm *not reading this bullshit!*" Drea said. She was almost shouting.

"Holy Monday-morning meltdown," Greg Auberson said. There was some interest being sparked around the room. Drea had sounded pretty unhinged during her last message.

"I don't know why anyone would do the announcements any-ways," Rob said. "Public speaking makes me want to die."

I tuned him out and grabbed my binder. Drea was doing announcements from down in the AV room. It was probably just some kind of misunderstanding. She probably wasn't *really* as upset as she'd sounded over the intercom. Still, I walked pretty fast through the hall that connected the Vo-Ag building to the rest of Regional. Then I kind of ran down the stairs to the basement level that housed all the audiovisual and art rooms. Just to make sure.

There was a crowd gathered in the back of the hall. I realized that my intuition had been right as I skidded up to the gathered kids, who were watching the adults forcibly remove Drea from the doorway of the AV classroom. Drea, unathletic and tangled up in her own hoodie, was *flailing* away from Mrs. Bledsoe, who was saying something in a soothing tone of voice.

"It's not a big deal," Mrs. Bledsoe said. "It's just a misunderstanding, Andrea—"

"I KNOW WHAT DAY IT IS! I KNOW WHO MY FRIEND WAS! YOU GUYS AREN'T GOING TO FOOL ME WITH YOUR COVER-UP MKULTRA CIA FBI MEN IN BLACK FAKE DATE AND TIME CONSPIRACY BULLSHIT!" Drea yelled.

"Drea!" I called, from back a little ways in the crowd. "What's wrong?"

"I think you just need to lie down for a few minutes, Andrea," Mrs. Bledsoe said, and Drea pulled away from her with force.

"No *way*, dude!" Drea yelled—but in the act of pulling away and shouting, she lost her balance, and slammed directly into the AV room doorframe. She tried to right herself as she banged her shoulder—it looked pretty painful—but she slipped sharply to the side, hitting her nose directly on the metal door handle. There was a groan of commiseration from the gathered students, instead of laughter. (Drea was the most well-liked member of the four-remaining-fifths of North Coven, for sure). Blood sprayed, and Drea fell backward, landing against the legs of Madison Hames and Gary Castaletti, two baffled-looking AV kids who had appeared at the door of the classroom.

"OH, CRAP! Are you okay?" I shouted, trying to force my way toward Drea. But the adults were faster. Bledsoe and Mr. Morgans flew in to lift Drea up.

"Time for a little trip to the nurse," Mr. Morgans said. "Maybe we can calm down there."

"You fubkink LYINK BASTARDS!!!" Drea howled as the teachers pulled her away. "FUBK YOUUUUU!!!"

"I don't know what she was *talking* about," Madison Hames said to Ms. Perga (ceramics teacher, looked like a blue heron) as Drea was led away. The confusion shot through Madison's voice sounded genuine. "She got mad when we gave her the announcements. She kept saying we'd given her the wrong day, even though I just checked them. Then she was talking about some guy, and how Thanksgiving *happened* already—"

"Drea—" I grabbed at her hoodie as the teachers marched her past me.

"Find Brandy and Dub," Drea said through her swollen nose, which would have been funny if she hadn't been so bloody and freaked-out-looking.

"You will do no such thing, Mr. Nuñez," Ms. Perga said. "Everyone! Please head to your next class. The bell has already rung."

I stared at the drops of blood on the ground by the AV room door. Drea never made a scene like this. Never. She could be outspoken. But Drea was not the kind of person who had actual bona fide public meltdowns. And Drea *liked* doing the morning announcements. For her to be losing her shit in such a dramatic way? I couldn't even imagine what had provoked her.

Brandy came up next to me, so quiet that I didn't realize she was there until she started talking. "Is she all right?"

"I think she might have broken her nose," I answered. In public, away from the trusted sanctuary of the coven, Brandy didn't give much away emotionally. But I could read the signs. The V-shape of worry on her flawless forehead was the equivalent of a less repressed person shrieking and rending their garments. Brandy was never quite as demonstrative as Drea, except, I gathered, in the letters they exchanged (and probably in private). But their love was maybe the most powerful thing I had ever known. Once, I had thought that Bastion and I would be like that someday. Once, I had believed that we were *that* connected. Until our last fight, that is.

"Why?" Brandy asked in a perfectly calm voice that nonetheless made me think that the entire AV class was about to get a metric ton of curses put on it.

"I don't know," I answered. "But it sounds like . . . Drea thinks there's some conspiracy about today's announcements? For some reason?"

"*Damn* it," Brandy said, which shocked me again. *Damn* was Brandy's ultimate swear, her holy grail. I had only heard it from her like two times before, ever. "I was trying to get a chance to talk to all of you before . . ."

"Before *what*?" I asked. The alarm I had felt so acutely as we snuck out of the town hall the night before last was back, making my palms sweaty.

"Watch," Brandy said, and stopped Dylan Everett as he walked by. He slowed immediately when she leaned toward him, obviously eager to talk to the school's most beautiful closeted lesbian.

"Dylan," Brandy said, almost sweetly. "What is the date today?"

"Uh, the twenty-second? Of November?" Dylan said, like it was a trick.

"It's the twenty-ninth—" I started to say, but Brandy shook her head minutely. *Listen.*

"No, it's the twenty-second," Dylan said. "Short week before Thanksgiving break, remember?" He paused now, looking between me and Brandy. He decided to go for it despite my proximity, and smiled at Brandy, leaning in a little. "Are you going to the game tonight?"

"No," Brandy said shortly. "But if I was going to . . . who would the quarterback be?"

"Uhhh?? Cameron. Winship. Cameron's our QB," Dylan said.

Dylan was on the football team with Bastion. He knew who his quarterback was. He knew the quarterback was dead. He knew there had been no game on November 22 on account of the quarterback's brutal murder. And he knew that Thanksgiving was *last week*. I was not amused by any of this and was about to inform Dylan of that fact with a few choice words (my fists) when I suddenly remembered what Madison Hames had said and stopped cold.

She was talking about some guy, and how Thanksgiving happened *already—*

"What do you think about Bastion Attia?" Brandy asked, looking straight at me while Dylan answered.

"Um. Never heard of the guy," Dylan said. I honestly believed he was too dumb to lie that convincingly, and I felt cold all over in the face of his simple, clueless honesty.

Brandy led me away without so much as a parting glance for Dylan.

"Do you see?" Brandy asked. "Or should I repeat that with a teacher? I've run through it with about twenty people, staff included, since first period. Nobody knows who Bastion is. Everybody thinks the past week never happened. Except for us. Provided you know what I'm talking about, of course," she added, sudden anxiety lacing her voice.

I nodded. "I'm with you."

"Oh, thank the Lord," Brandy said, some of the tension in the straight line of her shoulders easing. "I was very worried that I was losing my grip on reality." *Like my mother*, she didn't say, but I heard it as clear as day.

"You're not," I said. "But I don't think everyone else is, either. This is that thing we were talking about. Supernatural horrors beyond our comprehension, remember?"

"We need Dove," Brandy said, and started briskly up the stairs. I followed her.

While we walked, I pulled up my gloves and checked my hands, just to make sure. The sword tattoo on the ring finger of my left hand, for Bastion—the *will* of North Coven—was still there. The *N* cut from our Nexus hadn't disappeared, which was weird. A Nexus-mark normally vanished after being fulfilled.

We had investigated. But the Nexus hadn't tingled like usual, so something was up with that, too. But that was a very little issue in the face of . . . reality falling apart around us.

I'm just the Hands, I thought nonsensically. *What can I do?*

I'm not a leader. I never have been. In the theater of life, I'm a grip. Dressed in black and moving things around where the audience can't see.

And it's not that I think my foot soldier qualities are worthless, you know? But the girls had proven themselves with all these wellsprings of bravery and ingenuity and resolve in the week after Bastion had died, and I . . .

I looked at Brandy, who I absolutely knew would rather be curled into a ball and crying somewhere, as she led me through the halls with perfect poise and confidence. The world was falling apart, and she was strong and brave. I loved her dearly then (well, always, but I felt it so *strongly* for a minute) for being so unyielding as reality rearranged itself around us like a melting candle.

Brandy was perfectly right, of course, marching us straight toward the Round Theater. As we approached the theater, Dove, backpack in hand like she had just arrived at school, popped the side door open and gestured like she had planned to meet us. But I knew she hadn't. It was just that bond—Brandy *saw* where to go, and Dove *felt* that we were coming.

And my hands tingled. Which was pretty useless.

"Get in here," Dove hissed, and we slipped into the darkness with her.

CHAPTER TEN

Monday, November 22, 1999

North Coven had a ton of secret meeting places at Regional.

The Round Theater was my favorite part of the school—architecturally, anyway. I like weird architecture a lot, and almost no part of Regional made sense with any other part of Regional. And of all the weird additions, the Round Theater was aesthetically the weirdest. It had definitely been added on in the seventies. Inside, it was a circular auditorium with stadium seating and wooden slatted walls that were supposed to look artistic, an orange-brown color scheme, and a ton of recessed lights in an odd sunset color spectrum. It was the school's main auditorium before the remodel in 1991, which I had looked up because I was curious about all the mismatched architecture.

In the last thirtyish years, the school's student body had gotten much larger, and now the Round Theater was too small for much of anything besides the sex-ed presentation everyone suffered through in tenth grade and the elective Shakespeare Study.

Otherwise, it sat empty, and if some days it happened to be locked, well . . . I had no issue picking the lock.

Evidently, it had been unlocked already on that Monday. Dove flipped the lights on their lowest setting as we came in, so the empty space was suffused with a yellow ocher tint, and the ceiling, when I looked up at it, looked like it was dotted with little dying stars.

"You guys know what's going on?" Dove asked us, her eyes wild. "Please tell me you know what's going on!"

"Bastion," Brandy said, and Dove sank down onto the floor to sit in front of the first row of chairs, all but falling over.

Dove was crazy-upset, bad enough to seriously freak me out. She wore no makeup, which made her look even tinier and younger than she normally did, and her big gold-brown eyes sat above blue hollows that slashed down her face. She was still in her signature sleepwear: black sun-and-moon sweatpants and her threadbare 3XL *Live through This* T-shirt, with her jacket hastily flung over it. Her face was puffy from crying, her little red-tinted sunglasses missing, her hair sticking up. She looked like a lost kid at an airport. It made my stomach twist, not just in feeling bad for her, but with the awful realization that whatever the hell was happening, it was also happening in the Attia household. Dove did not go out in public without her look firmly pulled together, not even for her favorite brother's funeral. So whatever was happening right now was . . . worse than that.

"His room," Dove said, gesturing aimlessly with her hands like a woman in a dream. "It's a study for my mom. His room is *gone*. The pictures are all different. He's *gone*. I went to his gravesite, and IT ISN'T THERE! IT ISN'T THERE!"

"Hey, hey, hey," I said and grabbed at one of her shaking hands. "Hey. Hey, Dove Bar." Dove didn't respond for a second, looking at my hand holding hers like I was touching her from across the universe on some alien planet.

"This is still a murder investigation," Brandy said, and that seemed to partially summon Dove back to reality. Her gaze focused slightly. "It's just gotten more complex."

Now that it was just (three-fourths of) the coven, Brandy had taken off the game face she always wore in the halls of Regional. Her voice shook.

"This isn't just murder," I said, in agreement. "This is magic. Let's, like, review quickly."

"It's the twenty-second," Brandy said, going along with me. "No one except for the four of us seems to know that the last week ever happened."

"Nobody remembers Bastion was killed, or that he ever existed, I think," I said, looking at Dove for corroboration, trying to get her back in the real world. Dove nodded slowly.

"And Cameron Winship," Brandy said, her tone getting colder, "is evidently the quarterback of the football team."

"What," Dove said flatly.

"Cameron Winship is the quarterback of the Quabbin Monsters," I said. "So sayeth Dylan Everett, who I am pretty sure is too stupid to lie."

"I had sex with Dylan like four months ago," Dove said, still sounding a little messed up. "He is way too stupid. He couldn't even work a freaking condom. Very pretty dick, though."

Then Dove cracked a smile. Awareness came back into her eyes instead of just blank panic.

"Oh, thank god," I said, smiling back. "You're still a huge slut in this timeline." Relief coursed through me, making me feel lightheaded. We could not afford Dove having a nervous breakdown right now.

"Every timeline," Dove said, leaning back on her elbows and taking a huge breath. For a minute she stared at the starry ceiling of the Round Theater. Then she sat back up. "We need to go right now. We need to find and interrogate the utter shit out of Cameron and . . . go try to break into the mausoleum and then we need to do a Nexus and—"

"I want to go check on Drea," Brandy said, and when Brandy said something *that* firmly, we listened.

Dove and I hung around in the concourse until Brandy exited the main office and reported back to us that Drea was on a two-day suspension for swearing at multiple teachers (over the intercom, no less), and her mom was coming to get her.

"Let's ditch," I decided. "I want to try picking the mausoleum lock. And we can grab Drea after Jamie drops her off."

"I agree. I can't work like this," Brandy said, which was the first time literally ever that I'd heard her admit she was not feeling up to school.

"I'm not even officially here," Dove said. "But I have Mom's car. Can we get it later, though, Nez? You bring me back? I don't think I can . . . drive any more right now."

"Yeah, of course," I said hastily, trying not to look as disturbed as I felt by Dove's admission of weakness.

We snuck to the front doors without being spotted and slipped outside to make our getaway in my Hyundai. As we rounded the back of the building toward the junior and senior parking lot, we passed the combo soccer field and track where gym class was normally held until it got too cold.

Technically it was too cold just then, but since it was a holiday week, Coach Silva had let everyone come outside to play stupid games with the giant parachute. It was definitely an activity aimed more at middle schoolers, but on special occasions we would all get into it, feeling like little kids again.

I saw Dove scan the group of juniors playing with the parachute as we walked. It went up and down as the class moved in unison, dicking around with some balls on it or something, and one upward flick revealed a shock of bleached hair, the brightest thing in the gloomy landscape. Cameron, standing under a blue panel farthest away from the path to the student parking.

"I'm going to get him," Dove said, under her breath. Then she walked away from us really quickly, arms stiff at her sides.

Brandy looked at me. I looked at Brandy. Then we followed Dove.

CHAPTER ELEVEN

**Thursday, October 23, 1997
& Thursday, September 24, 1998**

Even though he was a total asshole, I was never able to entirely despise Cameron Winship the way Dove did. It had started way back in freshman year—back when Cameron was my nameless Gym Buddy, working out in quiet desperation.

I mentioned that by October, I'd had to save him two times when he'd tried to bench too much weight. That was when I first really started to worry about the desperation Gym Buddy exuded during his after-school workouts. But it wasn't until a week before I did my first spell with North Coven that I was concerned enough to bring it up to *him*.

That afternoon was the *third* time that Gym Buddy tried to bench-press way too much. He'd had to kind of breathlessly say, "Hey, you, could I get some help over here?" and I had gone over and stopped him from crushing himself with the weights (again).

"You know you don't have to push yourself so hard, right?" I asked, after I had probably saved his life for the third time. "It's more fun if you do what you can and just build it up gradually."

"I'm not here for fun," Gym Buddy said, sitting up from the bench. He was still breathing hard as he took a long swig of water and a big bite of those stale-ish granola bars that have a spot in every high school vending machine. It looked painful, like he was stuffing his face in the hopes that muscles would just pop up all over his lean body during the course of this workout session.

"Listen . . . I'm new here, so maybe—" *So maybe there's some context I'm missing about why you're in here trying to crush yourself to death*, I was going to say, but Gym Buddy cut me off before I could finish.

"I know. I've been in school with a lot of these people since we were kindergartners. When someone transfers here it's like headline news," he said.

"Right," I said. "Anyways. Like I was saying . . . I mean, I see your jersey. You're already on the track team, yeah? Why are you beating the shit out of yourself in here every day?"

"Need to make the football team," Gym Buddy said. "I did the late summer tryouts. Didn't make it. Now I'm getting ready for January."

I didn't think anybody really *needed* to make the football team. It wasn't like the football team was going to donate this preppy dude's sick relative a kidney if he made it on or something. But he said *need* like it was a real need, and not a want.

"Why?" I asked. "Football sucks."

Gym Buddy's face kind of closed off to me then, and he sounded a little bit pissed when he answered. "Well, everyone in *my* family plays football. My dad and all three of my brothers played in college."

"Sorry. I'm not trying to insult your family. But I'm sure they'll understand if you have an aptitude for something else, right?"

"I don't *want* an aptitude for something else. I want to play football," Gym Buddy said. His vehemence surprised me. Usually he was so quiet during our workouts . . . but now I could see the preppy dickbag version of him that I'd glimpsed in the school halls.

Normally, I would have gotten annoyed by this point, and matched my tone to his tone, which was angry and kind of sarcastic. But something stopped me. It was something about his expression. And it was the thing underneath the tone of his voice . . . a stubbornness, maybe, like he knew I had a point but couldn't admit it. A little bit of *quiet desperation*.

"Okay, okay," I said, putting my hands up in what I hoped was a "truce" gesture. "It's your business."

Then I went back across the room and sat down at the seated overhead press.

"I'm sorry I asked for your *help*," Gym Buddy said, from across the room. He sounded kind of petulant. "I won't do it again."

"You should definitely ask me for help if you need it," I said. "It would suck if you just died over there. Then my gym buddy would be a rotting corpse."

That got a short little laugh out of him. The tension of our whole awkward conversation kind of broke.

Silence reigned for a few minutes while we returned to our respective exercises. But then Gym Buddy cleared his throat.

"Can I ask you something?"

"Uh-huh," I said, not pausing my reps. I was listening, though.

"You really don't care about football at all?" he asked.

"I don't care about *any* organized sports at all," I said. It was true. I've just never been drawn to that kind of thing.

"Oh," Gym Buddy said. When I looked over at him, he was staring at me with this weird expression on his face. Like he was confused, but with a flavor of something else mixed in.

Things went back to normal between us in the days after that. Minimal conversation. I did have to save him from his own over-ambitious lifting again, but I didn't give him a hard time about it.

One more thing I observed during this time: my gym buddy trying to instigate arguments with Bastion at school. I didn't know the exact issue there, but it was clear that he really hated Bastion. After our football conversation, I assumed that some kind of sports-related jealousy played a role. I had a theory, based on what little I'd witnessed: that Gym Buddy—who had made the track team but couldn't make the football team—felt like he had been cheated, somehow, by Bastion's very existence. In any other school, in any place in the world without a Bastion Attia (which was probably *every* other place in the world), this preppy dude would have been the natural pick for the top of the high school (freshman) food chain. But at Regional he was hopelessly outclassed by someone larger than life.

I even felt a little bad for him. It wasn't that yuppie overachievers like him didn't *deserve* to get shown up (they did), but . . . I felt like Gym Buddy was under some kind of pressure that made him act that way. The quiet desperation that drove him to the exercise room after school, where nobody but me could see him struggle. The stubbornness that kept him coming back.

I didn't know if it was pressure he put on himself or pressure from somebody else. But it was pressure all the same, and endless pressure has a way of warping people.

Of course, a week after our one and only conversation, I sided with Dove over Cameron and never looked back. Cameron's asshole behavior over the years only solidified my opinion that I'd made the right choice. But I remembered his quiet desperation, and . . . it kept me from hating him entirely, even as he constantly harassed the coven.

This lack of complete hatred on my part got carried through sophomore year because of a single thing, one moment in time where he didn't screw me and Bastion over the way he could have if he'd wanted to.

I never got why a bully like Cameron, who obviously loved dumping on the most vulnerable members of Regional 9, would stay quiet about something that could be so damaging to us. But to tell you about it, I should tell you a little bit about the school musical of my sophomore year.

It was obvious that Bastion wished he could be in the musical. To me, anyway. *Why* anyone would want to be in a school play was beyond me, but by tenth grade I knew Bastion well enough to see the ways that he gave it away. Bastion never talked about being frustrated with his limitations, not ever. But he betrayed himself a little . . . if you knew how to watch for it. And musicals at Regional were like hard mode for Bastion's self-imposed Zen Master act.

Typically, our school put on two plays a year. Mrs. Vallese (drama teacher, control freak) did a fall production that started auditions as soon as school got back from summer vacation, always a big musical. In spring, the drama department put on another more traditional play: sometimes Shakespeare, sometimes something sadder and more modern like Tennessee Williams.

Guess what I hate? Musicals. Cerebral stage plays. Shakespeare. The soul-destroying horror of acting onstage in front of an audience. The drama that drama geeks create in their clique. And most of all, being forced to attend school theater.

Guess what the Attia siblings loved?

Actually, Dove seemed indifferent to the actual *content* of any kind of play but liked the limelight. She was good at it, too, not like *pro*-good but definitely good enough within the limited talent pool to usually get a big role. In the fall of 1998, we were doing this musical monstrosity called *Oliver!* (yes, with the exclamation point and everything). It was a musical based on a Charles Dickens book, with one ear-shattering, dry-heave-inducing song after another and a huge cast of extras.

"I love attention and costumes," Dove said simply, when I protested her wasting her precious lifeforce on *Oliver!* the musical. "This has both. I'm doing it."

Mrs. Vallese liked Dove already, and Dove got the role of Nancy—a big part, evidently— which prompted a whole new/old round of jokes from Drea about *The Craft*.

Drea was a ham by nature and was friendly with most of the drama kids already. She also had an incredible singing voice. But she got cast as an extra because Mrs. Vallese was a dickbag who only cast skinny, rich kids in the big roles.

Brandy said she would rather die in a fire than be involved in a play. She stuck to that, to my endless admiration.

And I was there. But only because Vo-Ag kids did all the set design and grunt work for plays like this. Remember that "in the theater of life, I'm a grip" thing I said a while back? Yeah. I was a grip for stupid *Oliver!*, doing set design and scene changes for extra credit.

Did I like it? I mean, I liked the set construction parts, and I needed the extra credit to bring my grades up. But we had to be there for dress rehearsals, and it was so, I mean *so* incredibly boring. The same cue eleven times. The same song and dance number six times in a row. The only fun thing about it was that Cameron Winship always did the plays too (no surprise there, he loved attention even more than Dove, and with *way* less self-awareness about it), and had been cast as Dove's love interest for this one. The palpable hatred between them made for a pretty entertaining watch.

And last but never least, Bastion. That was his first year as QB, and Coach Thornton had expressly forbidden any other teacher from messing with his precious prodigy's extracurricular schedule during football season . . . but Bastion couldn't have been in a play even if he wanted to. There were no plays where every line of dialogue started with the letter *N*.

He would still hang around the auditorium before football practice, though, under the pretense of killing time. Once I caught him backstage as Dove and Cameron did a scene together. He was semi-hidden in the third layer of stage draperies, right before the backdrop. I ducked into the red velvet folds of the curtain and let it fall around us, creating a miniature round room that stretched up thirty feet toward the ceiling.

"Hiding out, Big Hollywood?" I asked quietly, enshrouding myself next to him.

"Not hiding, Nesbit," Bastion said, making an airy gesture with one hand. The other hand he slipped around my waist, pulling me close to him. "Naturally I want to bask in the glow of my sister's enthralling abilities in the realm of performing arts."

"Bullshit," I said. "You wish you were up there with her."

"Nesbit, I am aghast at the accusation!" Bastion stage-whispered. "Now, I'll have you know that I am not a Lionel Bart fan. No, honestly, I find this to be a rather tepid adaptation, even by the standards of British-originated 1960s musicals."

"This has to be the one way you're a gay stereotype, huh?" I asked. "The worst way. The musical theater way."

"Nesbit, I'll remind you that I am gay in other ways," Bastion said. He looked down at me from his tenth-grade height, already even taller than when I had first met him. "Not-insignificant other ways," he added, and leaned over to kiss me.

I kissed him back, reaching up to cup the square part of his jaw and pull him down. His mouth was soft, and he still kissed me with a hint of caution, that early in our relationship—like he was worried about overstepping some boundary, or doing it wrong. It wasn't wrong, though . . . almost too *right*, if you know what I mean. Good enough that I didn't trust myself to stay alert. Bastion always insisted we were *safe* from gay-bashers, but Bastion (in more ways than I understood at the time) lived in a fantasy world. I couldn't afford to lose myself with fifty people around and only some stage curtains for secrecy.

"Hold your horses, Big Fun," I said. I stepped back for a little measure of protection against how attracted to him I was. "Making out is an off-campus activity only."

"Nnn-Nesbit, it was my mistake," Bastion said, shaking his head. It was cute—he was just a little bit red-faced. "Notably, I find our new relationship sustaining. Novel, really, and breathtaking. Naturally, I want as much of your lips as I can get."

"I'll get you a locket with my picture in it so you can be sustained by the memory of my lips during football practice."

Bastion laughed, elbowing me a little. I put my arm around his waist as he had done to me, holding on to him in our hiding spot. "Never more curious about your brain than when you leap to conclusions so deftly," Bastion said, after a few minutes with no sound but Dove, Cameron, and a kid named Charlie running their lines in the distance.

"Because I know you want to be in the play?" I asked, glancing over to find him watching me intently. "You're obvious."

"Nesbit . . . *how*?" Bastion asked, and his voice was so . . . he sounded so *sad* and so frustrated that I did a double take. His face didn't give away the depth of emotion I heard in his voice. He only looked wistful.

I shrugged, but actually gave it a second and tried to really consider my answer. This was clearly important to him, for whatever reason.

"Um. Well, I already know you can sing." This was true. I'd heard Bastion "Na na na na na" along with dozens of songs and classical pieces in his perfect baritone voice.

Bastion nodded slightly, looking a tiny bit pleased with the praise.

"And I am, like, extremely certain you can act. You're not scared of a crowd. You like being the star and you like performing in coven rituals. But I know you want to do more than that."

Bastion nodded again, and then I realized he was scrubbing his wrists together, his habit when he was anxious or lost in thought.

"Nesbit . . ."

"Yeah?" I asked, worried. For a minute, before, he'd sounded so *upset*. "I'm not talking shit on you, Large Marge. I like what a Renaissance man you are. Part of your charm."

"No. No, I don't ever think I'll be able to articulate it," Bastion said, almost wonderingly. He didn't sound sad at all anymore, and I wondered if I had imagined it.

"Articulate what?"

Bastion leaned in toward me, smiling.

"Nesbit, it feels . . . so good to be seen by you. Not just observed but understood. Need you to understand."

"I understand, you egomaniac," I whispered. Our faces were very close together, and I kissed him again, to show him how well I understood.

So basically, I broke my own rule about discretion and was pretty intensely making out with Bastion behind the curtains. The only sound besides our breathing was the ambient but distant noise of Dove running her lines up front. Not the most erotic soundtrack, but in sophomore year we didn't have a ton of privacy to fool around.

I do know exactly what happened next, even though I was very busy at the time: remember the insane amount of repetition that goes into these lame musicals. I could recite the stage directions for this Dove-and-Cameron scene by heart.

"What I say, Bill. I'm not going. Why can't you leave the boy alone? He won't do you no harm," Dove said, hamming up her fake accent to the max. "Why can't you leave him where he is, where he'll get the chance of a decent life?"

"You'll get him back 'ere, my girl . . . unless you want to feel my hands on your throat!" Cameron barked, in an annoyingly good British accent, from downstage left. He approached the center of the stage and pushed Dove onto a stool.

"Ow, you moron!" Dove shrieked, breaking character completely. "I know you're doing it that hard on purpose, you absolute puke!"

Side note: he definitely was.

"Mrs. Vallese," Cameron said immediately, in his most "I'm a prissy dickbag" tone. "I'm not trying to injure her. The stage directions say to shove her onto the stool *roughly*. If she's going to take it personally—"

We had sort of stopped kissing to listen to the brewing fight. Bastion, in the tradition of all siblings everywhere when there's nothing *actually* bad happening to a complaining brother or sister, listened for another second and then rolled his eyes at me. I shrugged. Bastion laughed against the top of my head and leaned back down for another kiss.

But something *did* happen, even if it was only Mrs. Vallese telling everyone to take five minutes and chill out, and I missed it because I was very busy being turned on. I didn't notice that a time-out had been called, and I didn't hear Cameron's footsteps as he stormed backstage. I didn't notice anything until he whipped the curtains open, revealing me locked in a pretty damn heated embrace with Bastion.

I'm not sure what Cameron was expecting to see, actually. I don't think he even realized anyone was *in* the curtains. My guess is that he was just flinging them aside dramatically to express his irritation as he walked through because he was annoying like that.

For a second, nobody said anything. Cameron stopped short, gaping at us, and I disentangled myself from Bastion as quickly as I possibly could.

"Nice afternoon, Winship," Bastion said amiably, like Cameron hadn't just caught us being gay.

Cameron stared at us with his mouth open. His face had gone totally white under his fading summer-on-Cape-Cod tan, and as I watched, his cheeks flushed a bright crimson. I was scared, man. I was so scared that he was going to start screaming slurs at us and alert everyone in the entire auditorium to my hidden sexuality. I was scared for myself . . . and I was scared for Bastion. For his status on the football team, which he insisted he didn't care about. For what he would do when he was faced with all the terrible social repercussions that he was always so insistent North Coven was *safe* from.

Even if I had been oblivious to the real dangers of being outed, I had seen at least one firsthand example of how bad a forced exit from the closet could be. All the way back from my childhood in New Haven.

I was in fourth grade—and Nic was in eleventh—when a kid in Nic's grade, Devon something, had been ratted out by a guy he made a pass at during a party. It didn't go well for Devon. In fact, a few of the dudes at the very same high school party where

Devon had tried unsuccessfully to get with the object of his affections had been quite *surprised* when they learned of Devon's secret sexuality . . . and took pains to let him know how very surprised they were. Devon's folks were not too pleased, either.

And by that, I mean that by the time Devon finally got out of the hospital, all of his belongings—which his dad dumped on the sidewalk when he found out his son was "like that"—had been scavenged through by New Havenites.

So Devon went out into the world alone, with nothing at all except for a rearranged face. Among the kids in our district the story of his *transgressions* became as powerful as any urban legend. It was such big news that Devon's little brother, who was in *my* grade, in a completely different school, got picked on and called a homo for like three years.

Devon's uncertain (but likely shitty) fate was there, not said out loud but definitely *there*, in Nic's stupid worried eyes whenever he talked to me about this stuff. And it was there in my throat like bile when Cameron caught us making out.

It was the most afraid I could remember being. We teetered for an endless few seconds on the grace of a graceless guy, while my heart pounded.

But Cameron just stayed quiet for a minute, as if Bastion hadn't even spoken. His eyes wandered slowly over us like he was trying to focus on a city hidden under the water. Then he stared right at me.

"Cameron," I said anxiously, aiming for a threatening tone. I was willing to beat the crap out of him to protect our secret if necessary. "Don't you dare—"

"I didn't . . . mean to, uh, I. See . . . you later, Nesbit," Cameron said. He said it stiffly, the way you'd address an acquaintance if you were talking to each other at a formal dinner party. Then he turned sharply to the left and walked away, as quickly as he had stormed in.

"Fuck, fuck, FUCK!" I said, grabbing my head. "Fuck! We are so fucked! That dickbag is going to blab to half the school before first period tomorrow!"

"No, he won't," Bastion said, with total assurance. "Nesbit, calm down. Nexus has been made against these sorts of dangers."

"Oh, Jesus Christ," I said. "Bastion. I don't think even the most powerful Nexus can stop *homophobia* from existing in the world."

"No, probably not," Bastion allowed. "Nevertheless, I believe that it will be enough to prevent Cameron Winship from speaking about our indiscretion." He kissed me again, on the forehead, and I ducked backward and stared at him, slack-jawed, totally taken aback by his lack of concern.

"Jesus. You have to be kidding."

"No need to address me via messianic shorthand," Bastion said, and literally *winked*, like the cheeseball that he was. "Now I must run. Negligible amounts of lateness to practice still result in heavy punishments from dear Coach Thornton."

Bastion sailed away like the world's least-concerned jolly giant, and I spent the entire night in an agony of anxiety, waiting for the hammer of Cameron's gossip to fall on us. Not just us, either. I was afraid the scrutiny that would inevitably come with us being outed could somehow endanger Brandy and Drea.

I didn't know how I would live with myself if *our* stupid carelessness made *their* lives worse.

"Did we do a spell to keep people from getting outed as gay or bisexual or whatever?" I asked Drea as soon as I saw her. I was trying to keep the fear out of my voice.

"Um. I never did one," Drea said. "Kind of a rad idea, though."

"We've never done anything like that, and also you're totally screwed. Cameron will tell *everybody*. The two of you are complete dumbasses," Dove said, in response to the same question. "We'll just have to be a united front, say he's making it up to mess with Bastion. Everyone knows he's jealous of Bastion."

Dove was not comforting. I could tell from how annoyed she was that she was worried, too.

Brandy I didn't even ask. I knew she'd be even more scared than I was.

But, as you've probably already guessed, Bastion was right. Cameron never said anything. Sometimes I caught him staring when Bastion and I walked through the halls, but that was it. It was a scare that ultimately made me much stricter about not fooling around during school, but a scare was all it was.

But I couldn't *entirely* attribute it to magic, either. It was hard for me to believe in the Nexus that kept us safe from prejudice, mostly because nobody else in the coven knew anything about it.

So I guess I chalked it up to Cameron Winship, being, well, not as much of a complete and utter dickbag as I'd always thought he was. I secretly forgave him a little for his generally crappy personality. I still didn't like him. He was still a first-class bully. Seeing him *lose* at whatever arbitrary pissing contests he set with Bastion and anyone else he perceived as a threat was still, like, pretty excellent. But. But he never kicked us out of the closet when he definitely could have.

I thought Cameron stayed quiet because he wasn't as horrible as he seemed to be. Bastion thought Cameron stayed quiet because of a Nexus—a mystery Nexus that no one else in North Coven had anything to do with casting.

We were both convinced that we were right. But, interestingly enough, we were both *wrong*.

CHAPTER TWELVE

Monday, November 22, 1999

"YOU LITTLE FUCKING PUKE!" Dove screamed, darting around the far side of the parachute. Coach Silva, who had been obviously zoning out, whipped his head around as I ran by, following Dove. Brandy had come as far as the top of the hill, but no farther. She stayed up there, too cautious to fight, but too loyal (as the Eyes of North Coven) to stop watching.

The other kids under the parachute looked at us like we had gone insane. Well, they mostly looked at Dove, as she surged through the center of their circle in a blur of boots, beelining directly toward an oblivious Cameron Winship, who was laughing at something Kim Palmer was saying to him.

"Winship, you utter slime," Dove said, and then leaned forward and *shoved* him, like really hard. But Cameron didn't rock backward. He didn't move at all, skinny as he was, but stood as if he was made of stone under Dove's onslaught.

"Now, now, um, what did I do to *you*?" Cameron asked, raising his eyebrows in what looked like genuine confusion.

"You're the quarterback? *You? You* wish, you freaking *wish*!" Dove said. When her fists seemed to do nothing to Cameron, she reached up and grabbed at the parachute overhead, pulling it down onto both of them.

Kim Palmer and I were summarily freed from the parachute as it engulfed Dove and Cameron and looked at each other in the gray morning light.

"What the hell is going on! Attia! Winship!" Coach Silva barked, struggling to walk over the roiling parachute as kids scattered.

"Can you please tell your crazy friend to leave my boyfriend *alone*?" Kim asked, looking at me with a pretty legit freaked-out expression.

"Cameron's your boyfriend now?" I asked, almost laughing. "But you always liked Bastion. Oh, right, but I guess you don't know who that is."

"Bastion?" Kim asked. For a second . . . I gotta give her credit here, because she was actually the only person who had this reaction: for a second, Kim looked like she *almost* remembered something. Maybe her crush on Bastion had been that sincere. Or maybe . . . maybe Kim had a little bit of the gift, the way the four remaining fifths of North Coven did. I didn't know either way. But for a second she paused, hesitating. Then she shook her head. "I don't know any Bastion."

"What did you do to my brother?!" Dove shrieked, as Coach Silva pried her out from under the parachute. She looked like a cartoon dust devil, arms and legs flying in the air in her effort to get back to (attempting) a beatdown of Cameron.

"Attia, what the hell has gotten into you?" Coach Silva asked, holding her off the ground as she struggled. "Calm down! Immediately!"

Then Cameron came crawling out from under the parachute with his shiny blond hair all messed up.

"He *KILLED HIM*! He killed my brother and he *took his place*!" Dove howled, struggling in Coach Silva's grip.

I liked Coach Silva, generally—he was certainly a much cooler guy than the football coach, Bastion's much-despised Coach Thornton—but I did not like seeing a grown adult man grappling with my best friend in such a fashion.

"Put her down, Coach," I said, kind of quietly. Coach Silva knew that I could hold my own if things got physical. I felt him looking at me, even as I kept my gaze on Cameron.

"She has a valid complaint," I added, glaring at Winship as he dusted off his stupid track pants.

"I'm going to let you go," Coach Silva said to Dove. "But you can't go after him again. Between this and Pearson's meltdown during the announcements, you and your little buddies are *really* stirring the pot. Whatever you're all snorting, huffing, smoking, or injecting, it has to stop. I don't want fights breaking out over some imaginary bones you think people are picking with you."

"He *knows what he did*," Dove growled, pointing one accusatory finger at Cameron.

"No idea what you're talking about, Attia!" Cameron said, throwing his hands up.

"Go stand over there, Winship," Coach Silva barked, pointing at a random spot on the grass. "The rest of you! Back inside!"

The class kind of slowly shuffled away, obviously hoping to see another fight. Kim Palmer left last, glancing back at Cameron over her shoulder. Brandy stayed put on the hill, meeting my eyes when I looked up at her.

"Okay," Coach Silva said, letting go of Dove. "Winship. Attia. You want to tell me what's going on?"

Cameron came forward looking nasty as hell, with grass on his clothes and his mouth fixed in a sneer.

"It's simple, Coach," Dove said, with suddenly perfect composure. "Cameron took something from us. He took it and he is pretending it belongs to *him*. But it doesn't at all belong to him. I feel that I am owed an explanation on why he has done this."

"Hmm. Very opaque. Not making me confident that you're not talking about drugs," Coach Silva said. "Winship, what do you say to these accusations?"

"N-no. No. No, I don't know what she's talking about!" Cameron said, defensively. Something had been *bothering* me every time Cameron spoke, and now I zeroed in on him as he talked.

"You do know!" Dove shouted.

"No, I said I *didn't*!"

"You're a liar and probably a MURDERER!"

"Not a murderer! Not a liar! Now leave me alone!" Cameron yelled, and a little switch inside of my head just . . . flipped. I walked right up in front of Coach Silva and Dove, faced Cameron, squared my shoulders, and punched him directly in the stomach.

And holy crap, it *hurt*. Cameron felt like a triple-reinforced wall of solid muscle, nothing like he looked. He felt as solid as, for example, Bastion. Cameron huffed out air, shocked but not really wounded. It suddenly made sense why Dove couldn't get a reaction from him when she was throwing her fists around. But I was unfazed. I swung again and punched him directly in the mouth. This time Cameron staggered back, a bloody lip evident over his perfect white teeth.

"What the *hell*, Nuñez!" Coach Silva said.

"Don't you *dare*," I said, taking a step forward. I got chest-to-chest with Cameron and looked straight up into his watering eyes. Cameron seemed shocked, one hand coming up to his bleeding mouth. I grabbed his hand, twisting his wrist.

"Don't you dare make fun of how he talked, you worthless piece of *garbage*," I said. I hadn't really ever completely hated Cameron before, but I hated him deeply at that moment.

"N-not doing . . . that . . . ," Cameron whispered, barely fighting my grip on his hand. "Nesbit—"

"More teachers are coming," Brandy announced from her vantage point. "We need to go." Coach Silva was on me, grabbing my arm, but I ripped myself out of his grasp and took off with Dove. We ran all the way to the Hyundai.

CHAPTER THIRTEEN

Monday, November 22, 1999

"There's no way he killed Bastion," Brandy said. "But it does seem like he has, possibly, taken Bastion's place."

"He knows something," Dove said. "Ugh. He isn't going to admit it so easily, though."

"He's *talking* like Bastion," I added, gripping the steering wheel tightly. Even thinking about it filled me with rage. I drove faster than was strictly necessary toward Stepwood, ready to take out my anger on the lock of the Northcott Faire mausoleum.

I let Dove chain-smoke in my car, which was normally strictly forbidden, but I ignored my own rule because of the way it seemed to make her hands shake less.

At one point I turned on the radio, realized it was no longer set to WJIN, and immediately switched it off. Was it really possible that every little thing about Bastion's existence had been erased, down to the station he had picked in my car? Except for our memories of him?

Well, you wanted to grieve privately, didn't you? I asked myself, feeling my throat get tight with self-loathing. *You wanted to be away from everyone mourning and fawning and acting like he was some saint, right? You couldn't stand the fact that other people could even dare to grieve for him. You wanted to be alone with your precious sadness because you knew him best.*

"Be careful what you wish for," I said, and was surprised to find that I had spoken out loud.

After a beat, Dove answered me in a voice that sounded like she was reciting: "No longer able to wish for anything—and in the second, all wishes for power and greatness would die within him."

I glanced to the side, confused at Dove's weirdly uttered response.

"What are you quoting?" Brandy asked from the back seat.

"Bastion's favorite book. You guys never read *The Neverending Story*, did you?"

"I saw the movie," I said, only getting more confused. "As a kid, like once, and then . . . Bastion made me watch it when we had our movie marathon night while the rest of you went to homecoming. It was . . . definitely for kids. The horse dying part was rough, though."

We had spent the night of the last homecoming dance in Nic's Winnebago while he was gone, staying over at his (latest) girlfriend's place. I had honestly expected that the movie marathon was code for *sex*, but Bastion had legitimately brought over a box full of his favorite tapes and insisted we watch all of *The Neverending Story*.

However, Bastion was as horny as I was, so we did end up getting it on for the entirety of Bastion's taped-directly-off-the-television recording of the 1961 Burgess Meredith version of *Waiting for Godot* before passing out at like four in the morning.

"It was weird that he liked *The Neverending Story* so much," I said. "Bastion was so into his pretentious stuff. It was sweet that he was still obsessed with this one kiddie thing; at least I thought so."

"It *was* weird. But it made more sense if you knew the book. The movie isn't as deep as the book," Dove said. "The book is like twice as long of a story, and the second half is all about the main character—"

"Bastian," I said, because I'd teased Bastion about the name thing when we'd watched the movie.

"Yeah, all about Bastian losing himself. The more wishes he makes with that magic necklace, the more he loses himself. Bastion was obsessed with it, he used to quote it all the time. Even after he stopped . . . talking normally, he used to say that part I just said, right from where he could make it start with an *N*. You saying 'be careful what you wish for' just made me think of it."

"What happens to him in the book? Bastian?" I asked.

"I don't remember," Dove said. Then, as we rolled through the gates of Stepwood, she tugged at the sleeve of my jacket urgently. "Wait, Nez, cops. The fuzz is patrolling, remember? We have to go in through Woodland Estates. Go to Drea's."

"They're not patrolling," Brandy said.

Because Bastion had never been murdered. Because as far as the people of North Dana were concerned, Bastion had never existed to be murdered in the first place. We all sat silently with that fact before I cut the engine and grabbed my dad's lockpicking stuff, which I had swiped that morning when the world still (as far as I knew) had at least a little order and reason left in it. I tossed my keys to Dove and walked away from the car before they were even out of it.

"I'm opening the Northcott Faire mausoleum," I called over my shoulder. "I'm opening it *now*."

The weather was cold and bright, exactly like it had been the last time we lived through this Monday, and that really, really agitated me. I walked faster, and faster, until the girls were way behind me. By the time the bulk of Northcott Faire came into view, I was almost sprinting.

I came up to the front of the mausoleum, ready to force the doors open by any means necessary. Screw the key. This place was a piece of the puzzle, and I was going to get inside and see something. Something different from the empty storage space we had always used it as. There had to be *something* there.

I put my hand to the place where the lock normally was and found no lock. Nothing. There was no keyhole. There was nothing but seamless uninterrupted brass. Not even a line down the middle to show where the two doors opened. It was solid.

"No," I said, out loud. "No, no, no, come on."

There *had* to be something. It was a trick of the light or my mind. I went by feel, tossing the lockpick kit and my mechanic's gloves aside so I could touch every square centimeter of the place where the doors were supposed to be.

"No, no, there *has* to be a door," I said, squatting down to run my hands all the way to where the stone met the earth. "There's ALWAYS been a door. There has to be a door, there has to be—"

I stood back up. It felt like I was at war. Invisible things dropped onto my shoulders from the sky.

Bastion's chewed-off fingers. The blank look on Dylan Everett's face when Brandy said his name. Cameron saying *No, no, no.* The mayor falling over on me as he breathed his last breath at Bastion's funeral. The way Bastion would kiss me slowly and then lean back and look away like he didn't want to own up to how much he felt. Our last fight. The buzzing voice of the thing in the carnival tent, and Bastion answering it.

What is your fancy?

What is my fare?

It was all too intense. If I could just open the door, something would make sense again. If there would only *be* a door here where a door had always existed before.

"Let me in, GODDAMN YOU LET ME IN, JESUS CHRIST," I shouted, finally giving in and pounding my fists as hard as I could against the unyielding brass front of the mausoleum. My knuckles split and started to bleed, but I kept hitting, willing something to give.

"Let me in, let me in, just be a door, just *please*, please be a door again," I said. "Please, please, please."

I wasn't shouting anymore. My voice felt cracked and broken, and I realized that somewhere along the way I had started to cry. Funny. I had thought a lot about how I couldn't seem to cry after Bastion died, and when I finally did, I didn't even realize it was happening until it was almost over.

"Please," I said again. I didn't know what I was asking for. My face felt hot, and I rested my forehead against the cold brass.

For a minute I thought I heard something from inside—like carnival music. Or laughter. But then it was gone, and I couldn't be sure that I had heard anything at all.

I lifted my head and turned around. Brandy and Dove were standing by the Dearest grave, looking at me with what I can only call "a lot of concern."

"Nez, are you . . . all right?" Brandy asked.

"No," I admitted.

I walked away from the mausoleum and put my gloves back on over my abused hands. The three of us stood together by the Dearest grave. Dove grabbed my left hand and squeezed it.

"Ow," I said, and then Brandy leaned in against my other side, and rested her head on my shoulder.

"I love you guys," I said.

"And we love you," Brandy said, simply.

"Guys! Guys!" yelled a congested voice from the woods, and Drea burst through the treeline, her nose covered by a thick piece of gauze and a long strip of medical tape.

Brandy turned from studying my face with concern and ran to Drea. They caught on to each other while their bodies were still in motion, and then held on.

"Don't *you* disappear from history," I heard Brandy murmur, carefully touching Drea's face.

"God, it hurts so bad, I was nuts to freak out like that, I *know* I'm clumsy," Drea said, leaning into the touch. After a second she looked up, grabbed Brandy's hand, and strode over to us.

"Dub," she said authoritatively, which made Dove snort. "Is it the same at your house?"

Dove nodded.

Drea nodded back. "I told my mom eberything."

"What did Jamie say?" I asked, rubbing my left hand through my glove. The un-door of the Northcott Faire mausoleum had little smears of my knuckle-blood on it.

"She doesn't remember anything about Bastion, anything at all. Or about last week. She remembers the Jane Doe murder. I don't know if she actually, like, beliebes me or not," Drea said, blowing a strand of hair away from her face. "She gabe me an eight-pack of Capri Sun before she went back to work and told me to 'take a few days to relax,' since I gained like an extra week of life."

"Very funny," Dove said. "At least she listened. I've seen too many movies to even try telling my folks. We'll all end up institutionalized or something if we talk about this."

"At least then you can realize your destiny of being Nancy from *The Craft*," Drea pointed out.

"Not funny," Dove said, though her mouth twitched a little. "Drea, I think we have to try the Vision Thing."

"Big Fun said he thought that ritual was 'Not remotely ethical,'" I objected. I actually winced after I said it. It felt weird to call Bastion by a nickname after he was buried. Unburied. Whatever.

Dove looked back at me over her shoulder. Drea started leading us through the woods toward the trailer park, her hand still tangled with Brandy's.

"It's different now. I'm not doing it to spy on Hersh," Dove said, and turned away—but not so quickly that I couldn't see her starting to blush.

The bathroom in Drea's house was entirely pastel pink and seafoam green. We stuffed ourselves into it while Drea ransacked her desk and bureau. Dove turned the faucet, and I watched the seafoam bathtub fill with water from where I sat on the precariously small Formica countertop.

"You got the candles and stuff?" Dove called down the little hall.

"Got eberything," Drea said, shoving her way in. She sat down at the edge of the tub while Brandy took the toilet for a chair and tossed a bundle of red taper candles to Dove.

"Nez, pull the curtains," Drea commanded, and I got up to cut the room off from the gray daylight while Dove melted the bottoms of the taper candles and stuck them upright around the corners of the tub. Drea shuffled through notebooks until she found the Vision Thing papers.

When the candles were all lit, we killed the lights and Drea motioned for us to come closer. We jammed ourselves against the rim of the full tub and stared into the settling water.

"Nexus?" I asked, getting out my knife.

"No. Not this time," Dove said, with authority. "Everything we've ever done with Bastion was to remake reality. To conjure up solutions to our problems. I don't want any more *adjustments* to reality right now. This time we're trying something different. We're not conjurers. We're magical detectives doing a little bit of spying. We're *seeing* reality."

Once again, I remembered the voice of the thing from my nightmare: *But they are not impressive enough to remake the destinies of your world.*

"Okay," I said. "Let's do it."

Drea cleared her congested sinuses with a wheezy snort, and we got down to business.

CHAPTER FOURTEEN

Monday, November 22, 1999

The Vision Thing was originally conceptualized as a way for Dove to learn more about her greatest and only love. Tell me you're not surprised that Dove has a person she could call her "greatest and only love." Personally, I was *extremely* surprised when I found out.

Yeah, our coven was lucky when it came to finding love, I guess: even Dove, the Woman Who Walked Alone, the Slut Lord, even Dove in all her cynicism had a person she adored above all others. They weren't exactly together or anything, but I think they both kind of liked it that way. At least for the time being.

Anyways, the guy was named Herschel Micenmacher, he was Dove's age, he kind of attended our school, and he was the weirdest kid I've ever met.

Herschel was like scarily smart and mostly took college classes. He came to our school only for English, the one subject where he wasn't brilliant. He and Dove had some kind of mystifying connection, and it was the only thing I had ever seen her get insecure about—thus the creation of the Vision Thing.

We'd never ended up *using* it (I doubt Bastion's protests would have really stopped Dove if she'd wanted to do it) because Dove and Herschel had some conversation that she'd never revealed the contents of to us, and "worked it out." They still weren't together, as far as I could tell, but whatever had been discussed the year before seemed to make Dove way more relaxed about the Herschel issue.

She continued fooling around with anyone who caught her eye, and Herschel continued . . . pursuing his hobbies, I guess, which included things like atmospheric science, astrophysics, and collecting bugs. I actually don't even know when or if they hung out at all, and I knew *more* about their non-relationship than anyone else in the coven. And I still knew basically nothing. But they had a blurry-detailed *thing* for sure.

Anyway: back to the bathroom of Drea's double-wide.

Drea lined us up to her satisfaction, all pressed together sitting next to the lip of the bathtub in the candlelit gloom. Wax dripped from the red candles onto the rim of the green tub. The water looked dark with the lights off and the curtains drawn, like the flickering flames were bouncing off of an impossibly deep pool. Dove bound all of our left wrists together with a spool of green ribbon. I sat at one end, tied to Brandy, while Drea squeezed several packs of Capri Sun into a pitcher and added a bunch of stinky herbs.

"Hold still," Dove said, while Drea swirled the pitcher around. "Hold still, I need your left hand."

"I'm holding still!" Drea said, not holding still at all.

"Are you putting *drugs* in that potion?" Brandy asked, wrinkling her nose.

"Just a teeeensy bit of magic mushrooms," Drea said, getting louder as Brandy started to protest. "It's negligible! Brandy, chill, we need it for this ritual."

"I'm not doing it," Brandy said. "Where did you even get that?"

"From Bronwyn, her dad grows them . . . Listen, you habe to do the drugs for the ritual," Drea said, not allowing herself to be deterred. "Gibe into peer pressure just this once. For Bastion."

"Fine," Brandy said. I knew that she would have been way harder to convince if not for these extraordinary circumstances. Brandy was not a big fan of mind-altering substances. "But I swear on the Lord, Drea, if I have a bad trip and claw my eyes out, I will end your life. I will do it."

"I swear on the Lord, I swear on the Lord," Drea mimicked in a prissy (and stuffed-up) voice until Brandy pinched her side. "Relax, babe. It's a microscopic amount of psilocybin. You are not going to claw your eyes out."

"I'd better not," Brandy said ominously.

"Last thing," Drea said, lighting a smudge stick. She held the pitcher out. "Eberyone spit in here. Then we drink until it's done, passing it left to right. One sip at a time. Oh, and pass with your bound hands. Eberybody got that?"

Brandy shook her head *no*. The spitting had obviously shaken her weak resolve. "I'm not drinking hallucinogenic saliva juice."

"I will," I said, which had some significance, I think, because I pretty much never touched drugs. No drugs, no booze, no smoking, nothing. Especially with my brother as an example of how much addiction sucked. But above my concerns was my commitment to North Coven.

I know that sounds crazy or screwed up. But don't forget—I'm talking about *magic* that *works*. I hadn't said so (I didn't want to seem like an easy sell), but I'd been committed from the first spell. From the minute I knew we could do extraordinary things together. From just about the second my feet had left solid ground for the first time. I would do whatever was necessary to fix this broken world, the way we had fixed my brother and Brandy's mom.

Dove caught my eye as I spit into the pitcher and mouthed *thank you*. Dove then hawked a totally disgusting loogie on her spit-turn, making Brandy gag.

But Brandy spit too, because her heart was with North Coven, just like mine. And Drea spit, and then we passed the Capri Sun mix from hell back and forth, drinking it by the light of the flames.

"This is insane," Drea said. "The parts about the *will* of the coven are gone from my spell. Not erased. It looks like I neber wrote them at all. But I remember writing them."

"He's been obliterated," Brandy said, so solemnly that we were all silent for a minute.

"Dub, think about what you want to know," Drea instructed when the pitcher was half-empty. I sipped again and passed the pitcher back down as Drea smoothed the lined notebook paper. "We get one bision only, one answer to a question. If we mess up, we get precisely squat. If this works, it'll only work once for a calendar year. It has to be something that is happening. Or has happened. The Bision Thing is not for future-gazing, just for learning."

"You guys wrote this spell. Why did you put an 'only works once a year' clause into it? Just to make life harder?" I asked.

"It wasn't me," Drea said, smiling a little bit evilly. "*Some*body was worried that they might abuse the Bision Thing. Use it to check in on what sweet little Herschel was doing too often."

"Shut *up*, Drea," Dove said, looking a little flustered.

"Aw, Dove Bar and Herschel's Kiss," I said.

"Those nicknames that you love to come up with, Nez? Not cute. Not cute at all," Dove said, drawing her left hand across her throat in a murderous motion. Our connected left hands bobbed up with hers.

"Watch it!" Drea said. "I think they're cute, Nez."

"I think they're cute, too," I said, serenely. "Just not as cute as sweet little ol' darling ol' weird-as-hell Herschel."

"I hate you both," Dove muttered. "Can we get down to business, please?"

She was so serious about her romantic feelings, probably the only romantic feelings she'd ever really had. It made me think painfully of Bastion.

Drea took another sip, making a face at the bitter taste of the herbs and fungi, and began to recite as we passed the pitcher back and forth.

> "With our bound hands,
> Our strong enchantments,
> Our sharp eyes,
> Our cunning hearts.
>
> With our one boice,
> Our darkened altar,

Our strong bonds,
Our better selbes.

With your kind blessing,
Your one exception,
Your many worlds,
Your sacred bisions."

The chant sounded weird without *N* to start off every sentence. It was Drea's narrative leading us, not Bastion's, and I felt oddly like I was betraying him. But my feelings didn't matter, because by the third repetition of the chant, there was a scent of ozone and a wind blowing through the closed bathroom.

"Hold that last sip in your mouths!" Dove said, raising her voice above the wind as Drea chanted. "Then spit it into the tub when I do."

The wind kicked up, and the seafoam-flowery curtains flew back and forth as Drea repeated her chant again and again. The candles showed no sign of extinguishing, though they bent against the moving air. Then, suddenly, they all flickered out at once, leaving us in the dimness. The conjured wind dissipated as quickly as it had blown in.

Dove took this as a signal to spit into the tub, and we followed suit, Drea swigging the dregs of the pitcher and spitting up a decent amount of nose blood. Brandy wrinkled her nose disgustedly, but the water swallowed up our spit like a dark hallway and smoothed out flawlessly.

"Look," Drea said. The water was black, incredibly deep looking, and pinpricked with flamelight, even though all the candles had gone out. I peered into the starry pool as Dove requested her vision, feeling my hands buzz with the electric current that ran through the air.

"Show me my brother's killer," Dove said. "At the minute—the exact *minute*—they decided to murder him."

I stared into the tub for a minute while nothing happened. I heard Drea breathe out a wheezy sigh of disappointment.

"Not working," she said, but Brandy held her unbound hand to Drea's mouth.

"Shh," Brandy said. "Wait."

Suddenly there was a crash from somewhere in the mobile home.

"Shit!" Drea yelled, and tried to scramble to her feet, dragging all of us with her as the green ribbon pulled taut. Drea bashed into the door as Brandy fell against her legs. I braced myself so I didn't get pulled over.

"Stop pulling, stupid!" Dove told Drea, but then another tremendous *crash* came from the house itself—this time from under us, like the trailer was lifting up off its foundations.

"What—" Brandy said, but she never got the chance to say anything else. Because suddenly, the *room* tilted.

Gravity shifted and we were all thrown back into the wall—which was suddenly the floor—that had the sink and vanity mirror on it. My head clanked hard against the mirror without shattering it, and the girls fell to either side of me, as toilet brush and bath mat and hand towels and still-hot, dripping red candles rained over us. The door of the tiny bathroom closet slid open above us and showered down bottled water that Drea's mom had been paranoidly hoarding up for when Y2K ravaged the earth on New Year's Eve.

"Ow! Ahhhh, what the HELL!!!" Drea shouted as a plastic bottle hit her in the face. Brandy was making a low whimpering sound of terror. Dove pointed as the hurricane of crap subsided, gesturing toward the tub.

"Look!" Dove commanded. The bathtub, which was suspended sideways over us, now a fixture of the wall, hadn't overflowed. Instead, the black water swelled out of it in a huge bubble of candlelit darkness. As we stared at it, awestruck and freaked-out, it rippled.

"Oh no," Brandy said quietly, and then the bubble ruptured. A tidal wave of inky blackness careened toward us, and I tried to cover Dove's head as Drea grabbed for Brandy. The water crashed down at tsunami force over all of us, rocking the tilted bathroom like an earthquake. For a minute, everything went utterly dark and liquidy, and I thought we were going to drown. But as the water surrounded us, I blinked against it, and we were . . . somewhere else.

We were in the Near-Depths, suspended in layered starlight, still bound by our green ribbon.

"Oh, thank the Lord," Brandy said. "I thought we were done for."

"Kind of dramatic, though," Drea said, and then the stars blinked out, and we were in the carnival from my nightmare.

CHAPTER FIFTEEN

Late July or Early August 1992

I had seen pictures of Bastion as a little kid before in the Attias's house, but I wouldn't have recognized him so quickly in real life if it weren't for the star-shaped mark of vitiligo over his left eye. Pictures are weird that way—they can be hard to connect to reality. The starburst mark, though, was unmistakable, and once I saw it, everything fell into place.

It was like watching a movie. One wall of an invisible room showed us the vision of the black-and-white carnival under the red sky—and the wall rippled at the edges like a pool of water. Old hay littered the floor beneath our feet, bleeding in from the rippling wall, but when we (still bound together) tried to advance into the world, it stayed two-dimensional in front of us. Our movie screen followed the little boy, who turned back anxiously to look behind himself every few minutes without seeing us, his silent audience. I could see that it was Bastion then, as he turned around to scrutinize whatever was behind him. We couldn't see what he saw. Only where he went.

He walked through the carnival that had occupied the most vivid nightmare of my whole life with his shoulders squared and the mausoleum key gleaming around his neck. He passed the painted people at their dusty tents and their rotting games, and our vision passed them, too, in silence. The red sky gave everything a rosy glow, but it was neither pretty nor comforting. It looked like something from long after the end of the world.

"Where is *this*?" Dove asked.

"I've seen this place. Once. In a dream," I answered.

Then little Bastion came to the cleared-out space at the center of the fairgrounds. The Big Top tent, as vast as it had been in my nightmare, loomed over him, reducing him to pinprick-size. He was a moving point far away against a striped canvas labyrinth. I read the hand-painted sign, remembering it as I read: *Fortunes Told and Fates Changed Within! See Mr. Nous! The One Who Knows!*

I was dragged forward again, like in my dream, but this time with the rest of the coven. We were only watchers: not *in* there like I'd been in my nightmare. But still, my skin prickled with anxiety and my palms were sweaty. I felt that forgotten fear again. That slow *creep* of unease as fairground trash rustled and the canvas of ancient tents fluttered.

Little Bastion seemed to hesitate for a second—it was actually kind of hard to tell what was happening with him facing away from our vantage point—and then pushed aside one striped tent flap and walked into the Big Top.

Inside the tent, he passed underneath old bleachers and into the center ring. The scale of the place was *massive*. For a second, the picture window through which we viewed the world tilted upward, showing us a ceiling so high above that it was almost lost in darkness. Nobody sat on the many benches. No ringmaster appeared as tiny Bastion walked through the grayscale world.

"Where *is* he?" Dove hissed, not taking her eyes away from the wall. "I've never been here. How could his murder be connected with *this*? He's like ten!"

Bastion walked on, to the most distant corner of the tent. There the black-and-white world melted into shadow, and as we grew closer, I saw that it was a curtained-off wall of the darkest velvet. Gleaming black rope pulls hung from either side. It reminded me of stage curtains before a show begins, but different . . . somehow ominous.

"This is gibing me a *really* bad feeling," Drea said. Brandy and Dove nodded without speaking. Something was about to happen. Over the curtained wall (so weird, it seemed like there was *depth* to it, even though only the tent wall should have been behind it) was a hand-lettered sign that read *Novelties!* in a looping, cheery script.

"Mr. Nous?" Bastion said, in a little voice. His child voice surprised me, but not as much as hearing him speak without starting his sentences with an *N*.

"Mr. Nous?" Bastion said again. "I've come with a fancy. Please tell me my fare."

Then the sound came: a *sliding* along the floor. A rustling. Or a *slithering*. Like something unfathomably huge was crawling toward us through long grass. It came from the picture, but also from around us in the Near-Depths of the room we had summoned with the Vision Thing. It was omnipresent enough that

Brandy startled, flinching, and we all turned to look behind us. But there was nothing in the darkness. And when I turned back, something had changed.

There were arms peeking out of the split in the black curtains.

Arms in red gloves that went all the way up and vanished into the velvety darkness. Two impossibly long arms . . . with hands hanging down, just slightly outstretched. Red-gloved fingers. Nails like knives. Hands twice the length of any human hand.

"Ahhhh!!!" Drea said (summarizing my feelings perfectly, I want to add). She pointed at the red-gloved arms with one shaking index finger. "What the—"

"Back so soon, my clever one?"

And there it was. The oozing sound of the voice from my nightmare. I forced my gaze away from the arms that gestured through the flaps of the black curtain, away from little Bastion's silhouetted back, and watched my friends. They reacted to the voice the same way I had, at first—it was bliss that bled into horror. A shiver that became a shudder.

But Bastion stood without moving on the screen, and when he spoke again his tiny voice was steady.

"I was stupid not to trust myself," Bastion said. "About what you are. My sister *is* better. But I have to . . . to think about what I did all of the time. My mother was sad when she had the miscarriage. You . . . make people do evil, don't you?"

He took a step forward, toward the red hands that looked poised to snatch him into the darkness behind the curtain. I halfway reached out—to try to stop him, I guess—before I realized it was useless and put my shaking hands at my sides.

"I **did** *offer you a choice, clever one,*" the thing called Mr. Nous said, amusement clearly coming through in its voice. *"Your unborn brother's life . . . or your eyes . . . for your sister's health."*

"Yes," Bastion agreed. "I made a mistake then. I was afraid to be blind. But now I'm afraid that I made an awful mistake by finding the key to begin with."

"You could always take it off."

"I know what happens if I do," Bastion countered. I glanced to the side, at the horrified faces of my friends, and felt something start to slide into place in my mind. Something bad. Mr. Nous chuckled from the darkness behind the curtains, and it was the same laughter I'd heard the night we broke into the coroner's office.

Whatever Bastion had been involved in . . . we were in it too. With this thing. *This* was the supernatural horror beyond human comprehension. It had been watching us.

"So then you need not make use of my talents if they upset you so. You know the Nine Rules. One fancy a year is all I require," Mr. Nous said, in a tone that was definitely meant to be placating. It was as if a thousand wasps learned to speak English in chorus, and when they spoke it was with syrupy condescension. I was not placated. It was clear Bastion wasn't, either.

"I know your rules! And I *will* only use one wish a year after this, just you bet!" Bastion said, raising his baby voice almost to a shout. "You call me 'clever' like it's a joke. Like all these other people you got were just *fun* for you to have. But not me. I'm going to starve you. I'm going to keep you from—from amusing yourself. And when I die someday, I'm going to make it so nobody else ever finds the key!"

The laughter came from beyond the curtains again. Mr. Nous's long hands tilted up toward the ceiling in a gesture of helplessness. *"What can I do against such a will?"* it said, no less amused than before. Then suddenly, the voice it used got much sterner. *"Your fancy, then, clever one."*

"I fancy a world where—as long as I have the key—nobody else can pay my fare but me," Bastion said, so perfectly that I just knew he had practiced saying it before coming to the dark midway.

I felt a tug on the green ribbon that bound my left wrist to the others and saw that Brandy had raised her hands to her face in a silent gesture of terror. Drea stared straight ahead with her brows furrowed above her bandaged nose. Dove took in the scene raptly, like she was learning the secrets of the universe.

Then Mr. Nous spoke—but not in the falsely friendly way it had before. Its voice was much colder now, stripped of all the previous buzzing amusement. The red-gloved arms drew in slightly and remained perfectly still.

"You must know, my clever one—and you are clever—that life brings many trials. And trials bring further fancies and further fares. The price for my talents can be steep. To pay it all yourself will be . . . difficult."

"I know that," Bastion said. "I'm not afraid. And as long as I live, you won't be able to hurt anyone but me. I hope it drives you *crazy*. That is my fancy. What is my fare?"

"You will regret this," Mr. Nous said warningly. Its left hand pointed straight at Bastion like an accusation. *"It will destroy your life."*

"I'm going to destroy *your* life, Mr. Nous," Bastion said. Now his voice shook a little. "What is my fare?"

"Perhaps we should let the ones watching us decide," Mr. Nous said. It seemed to have recovered its joviality from before, but the curtains shook around the red arms, and a cloud of fine dust fell from the distant ceiling of the tent.

"There isn't anyone watching us," Bastion said confidently. "Now you're stalling."

*"Indeed they **are** watching,"* Mr. Nous said, and the long red hands drew a gestural frame in the air. *"Your dearest friends . . . your darling sister . . . your truest love. And you are dead. I will have eaten your heart, you know, if you follow through with this."*

Brandy flinched back, and Drea started to shout something, but Dove grabbed them both.

"Stop. Wait," I whispered, and Dove nodded. I tried to stay calm. But I was afraid. Terrified. Confused. How could this thing—this monster from the past—be *perceiving* us?

"My fare," Bastion said one more time.

The thing behind the curtains sighed in a way that made the very darkness around us creak and rock. *"Very well. My clever one. If you insist. Your name or your voice."*

Bastion turned around suddenly, facing us, and I could finally see his face. If my heart had not already been broken the day we found him dead, I think it would have broken then. He was so tiny that I felt protective of him just like an adult would, and even though he had sounded so certain, I could see how his baby face twisted up in misery. He scrubbed his wrists together. Tears fell from his eyes and dripped down his chin.

"*You don't **have** to do this,*" Mr. Nous said.

"I know you won't give me another chance," Bastion whispered. For a second, he looked right at me without seeing me. Then he nodded to the air, set his jaw, and turned back around.

"Mr. Nous, I agree. I give you my name," the boy said. As he said it, a spark of vivid red light shot through the air between his body and Nous's outstretched fingertips. The red hands moved through the air in a razor-sharp dance. Then the light vanished, blowing away the falling dust in the circus tent with it.

"*You will see how kind I am,*" Mr. Nous said, flexing its palms toward the boy who'd lost his name. "*Though you doubt my intentions. I will even let you choose your new name, my clever one.*" Then one hand vanished into the curtain and reappeared, quick as a striking snake, with a piece of crimson chalk. "*Write it down.*"

Our view followed as he took the chalk. I heard Brandy gasp when his tiny kid hand touched the red glove, but nothing happened. The boy with no name knelt and wrote carefully on the dusty earth. I knew what I would see when he stood back up:

BASTION

was inscribed in red on the ground.

"He's my favorite character. But I think I spelled it wrong," Bastion said doubtfully, and only then did he have a name in my mind again. For a second it had been blotted out entirely, without me even realizing it.

"*Bastion. This is my gift to you. I have given you this name, clever one,*" Mr. Nous said. "*And you may never give it to anyone else. Do you understand?*"

"Yes," Bastion said. "But I—"

But we never got to know what Bastion was about to say, because the Near-Depths around us rippled and then *ripped*, tearing into a thousand strands of darkness that flew away, revealing the pink-and-green bathroom we had left. And Drea's mom was standing in the doorway, screaming.

CHAPTER SIXTEEN

Saturday, April 10, 1999

The conversation that led to the confrontation that led to Bastion's death—at least in *my* opinion—happened way back in April. It was a very warm Saturday, the kind of spring day that is a perfect preview of summer, and I had zero things to do at all except play guinea pig to Nic's tattoo gun. We sat in full sunlight on the unfinished back porch while he worked on the line art I had requested for my hands. I remember that Nic was playing *The Very Best of Cream* on repeat while he practiced and that neither of us spoke much. The pain on my fingers as he inked the marks I had requested to symbolize the coven felt like . . . like the only sensation tethering me to the earth. The forest all around our house smelled of mud and growing things. When the tracks switched, I could hear the ambient noise of Dad working in the auto shop on the next lot. I had nothing much on my mind except for the next coven meeting, so when Drea and Dove showed up just as Nic finished inking the heart (for Dove) on my left pinkie finger, it felt like I had summoned them.

"Whattup," Nic said, with a wave.

"Hey, Nicolas," Dove said, waving a little and definitely using her "flirty" voice. I made a *gag me* face at her when Nic looked away.

"I thought you two were going into Amherst to buy yourselves more pentagram necklaces or something," I said, but despite my teasing, I was happy to see them.

"That was a cover. Actually," Dove said, pointing toward the driveway, "can we talk to you about something?"

"You need to let me wrap that up," Nic said. "Don't take off."

"We won't be long," Dove said, winking at Nic. It was gross. Luckily, Nic seemed oblivious to Dove's come-ons.

"White Room" started playing for what felt like the millionth time that day, and we walked away from the boom box as a trio, leaving Nic behind. I glanced at Dove, who looked neutral behind her little red-tinted sunglasses. Drea, however, looked nervous as hell. She did not have much in the way of a poker face.

Dove opened the door of her mom's car, and I got in on the passenger side, looking between the two of them with suspicion.

"What's going on?" I asked, and Drea pulled out the thick black notebook that served as North Coven's grimoire.

"We need to talk about something. A spell we want to do," Dove said, staring me right in the face. "Just the three of us."

"Why just the three of us?" I asked. "What's with the top-secret act?"

"He's not gonna go for this," Drea said, almost involuntarily. I looked back at her, feeling a little bit alarmed.

"Nez," Dove said, in a placating tone. It was so unlike her to be placating that my alarm increased exponentially.

"Just stop trying to like, prep me for whatever you want to tell me, and just *tell* me," I said, and Drea handed me the grimoire, held open to a new page filled with her green-penned scrawl.

"This," Drea said. "This is what we're trying to talk about."

Things Bastion Attia Cannot Do, said the title. I felt uncomfortable immediately. "Guys . . ."

"Just read it," Dove said, her big Attia eyes staring me down. "Please."

I looked back at the page.

Things Bastion Attia Cannot Do (That we know of, so far)

1. Speak without an N to begin every sentence.

2. Say "I love you."

3. Dream.

4. Say his own name, introduce himself, give his name in any way.

5. Cry.

6. Apologize.

7. Give gifts.

8. Accept gifts.

9. Admit that he has obsessive-compulsive disorder.

Proposal: Execute a ritual to free Bastion from his compulsions. If not successful, create a secondary spell to allow Bastion to come to terms with the fact that he has compulsions.

The details of the spell went on to the next page, but I stopped reading to look up at them.

"What does Bastion think about this?" I asked.

"You know what he thinks," Dove said. "He thinks he doesn't have OCD. He literally will not even entertain the idea. He stopped all the meds and therapy my folks made him do right before high school."

"So you didn't tell him," I concluded, handing the notebook back to Drea.

"I know it's kind of uncool to go behind his back," Drea said. "But he . . . I mean, you can like, see how he suffers with it, right? Nez. You know. He won't do anything about it. So we need to help him."

"And what did Brandy say?" I asked, staring Drea down until her cheeks turned pink.

"I didn't tell her," Drea admitted. "She would never go for this."

"She's a stick-in-the-mud," Dove said.

"She's right! I am not casting a spell on my boyfriend to change him!"

"We did a spell when I had leukemia," Dove said defensively.

"Leukemia is not a psychiatric disorder! You're talking about literally changing his brain without his consent." I was appalled. I was mad at them. They both looked ashamed, too. Like they knew what they were doing was slimy, but they thought the end justified the means.

"We did that already," Drea said. "With Brandy's mom."

"Okay. If Bastion someday has children and then starts beating and starving them because he thinks God is telling him they're evil, I will consider casting secret spells on him," I said. I sounded angry and sarcastic to my own ears. But I was *pissed*. What if they went through with this spell and were somehow successful? What if they changed some integral part of Bastion?

"I've seen him living with this for so many years," Dove started, but I was in no mood to listen to her spinning out one of her speeches.

"I don't care what you've seen," I said. "I care about what he feels. He *is* living with it. It isn't up to us to change his mind."

"Dude. Doesn't it bother you?" Drea asked. "It bothers me. Bastion is a *genius*. He could do anything he wanted, if he could do anything he wanted."

"That's true for everybody. It's not more tragic that he has limitations just because he's *so smart*," I countered.

"Sometimes I feel like you don't even *care* about his problems," Dove said harshly.

"I'm not gonna go for this, Dove Bar, I don't give two shits what way you try to spin it," I snapped, and Dove looked away.

"Fine," she said. "We'll do it without you."

"It's not going to work without me," I said, with an assurance I didn't feel. But they seemed to agree. Dove looked down at her hands. Drea cleared her throat uncomfortably.

"Isn't there anything we can say to make you change your mind?" Drea asked, in a tiny voice. She was sad when she spoke. She was guilty. And I believed that *she* believed this was the best way to help Bastion. Drea, our Voice, always was the most persuasive of all of us, and it was her actual *sincerity* that made her persuasive. That one sentence, and all the emotion inside of it, compelled me more than Dove's speeches ever could.

I almost softened for a second. Not on the idea of doing the spell—I would never do that—but in my anger at them. I could see that they loved him. That they thought it was a way to help him. But it didn't make the idea any less terrible.

"No. He won't change his mind," Dove said, scrutinizing my face with an up-and-down glance that was highly reminiscent of her brother.

"I gotta go," I said. I hate serious arguments, and having one with two of my favorite people in the whole world had just completely sucked the life out of me.

"Nez—" Drea said, but I was already up and out and slamming the car door behind me.

Our interactions were pretty strained for a week or so after that. But eventually, things went back to normal. I don't think Dove and Drea ever quite came around to my way of thinking, but we all moved on. And if the two of them tried to cast a spell by themselves, it clearly hadn't worked.

I never told Bastion about it. Maybe that was a mistake, but ultimately . . . well, ultimately, it wouldn't have changed anything.

But I thought about it, you know? I thought about the list of *Things Bastion Attia Cannot Do (That we know of, so far)*. It got into my head a little. Maybe a lot. Enough that it festered, enough that I noticed when Bastion didn't cry, even when he clearly wanted to. When he didn't give me a present on my birthday and requested that I not get him anything for his. When he didn't apologize for his mistakes.

I thought about it. Eventually, probably when I had thought *too long* about it, I said something about it . . . and that's how the last fight I ever had with Bastion came about. It wasn't just the *last* fight—it was our first fight. Our only fight.

But I'll tell you about that later.

CHAPTER SEVENTEEN

Monday, November 22, 1999

"What the *hell* are you guys doing? The . . . My Y2K water, my . . . The sink . . . What the hell, guys?" Jamie yelled, holding her hands to her face. "What the hell happened?"

"MOM! I thought you were working!" Drea shouted back, at equal volume.

"I WAS! I traded shifts with Chet because I was *worried* about you! Starting fights and telling me some person you know *disappeared from the universe*!"

"He's not 'some person I know'! He's Bastion! Bastion! Dub's brother! I'be been friends with him since I was two years old!"

Jamie had Drea when she was sixteen, I think, and the fact that she was younger than the rest of our parents—and sane, unlike Brandy's mom—meant that she would listen to us a little more readily than other adults. She was into palmistry and tarot, enough that we had even asked for her advice with certain spells before. But her cool factor did not stop her from absolutely losing her mind when she came home and saw how we had trashed the shit out of her bathroom.

Brandy, who had an understandable panic response when people's parents yelled, started scrambling to pick up the scattered red candles. In her fearful effort to move quickly, she totally forgot about the green ribbon binding us together and dragged all of us to our feet. Jamie stared at the spectacle, clearly too bewildered to yell anymore.

"We're sorry," I said, while Dove burned the ribbon off our wrists with her Dupont lighter. "We'll clean it up."

"Very sorry," Brandy murmured, keeping her head down.

Jamie sighed and took her hands away from her face. "Brandy, I'm sorry for shouting, honey. I just . . . when I came back, it—it couldn't have been—it looked like there was nobody in the bathroom for a minute. I thought we were robbed and Andrea was kidnapped or something."

"We weren't in the bathroom," Drea said. "We were in the Bision Thing, trying to figure out who killed Bastion. And erased him."

"We just got back," I added. I knew it sounded insane, but I felt obligated to corroborate Drea's (true) story. Jamie raked her hands once through her long blond hair.

"Okay. Okay. I'm going to make some coffee. You guys clean this up. Then I want you to sit down and tell me exactly what you think is happening."

"It IS happening!" Drea said, but I touched her shoulder to get her to shut up.

"Okay. Thank you," I said.

We put stuff away in silence. I didn't know about the girls, but I was too shocked to talk. I wasn't entirely sure how to understand what I had seen inside the Vision Thing.

Jamie had a pot of coffee and a box of donuts waiting for us in the kitchen when we were done. We crowded around the tiny linoleum table to the faint sound of the wind chimes clanging outside, and Drea told her mom everything we knew.

It was a pretty damn harrowing story if I do say so myself. And it took a while to tell. Nobody was crying, not even Brandy. Nobody was screaming. We chimed in as we needed to, like when I described to everyone—for the very first time—my carnival dream, or when Dove talked about finding Jane Doe.

"I know you found that poor murdered woman," Jamie said. "But as far as *I* know, it was just you, Dove."

"No. It was never just me," Dove said. "Jamie, you have to believe that we wouldn't make this up."

Jamie didn't say if she believed us or not. Dove was fiery and loving and passionate and *also*, sometimes, a bullshit artist.

Bastion told me once that he was certain Dove's powers of obfuscation had started when she got sick. She would lie about feeling all right in her desperation to not be left out of "doing cool stuff" with family and friends. She would act like she felt fine. She was good at it, too, for an eleven-year-old. But there's something funny-sad about it, you know? Not just about the situation, but about Bastion relaying it to me with so much compassion for his big sister and the behaviors that stemmed from her juvenile brush with death. Because Dove might have been the *first* Attia kid to be able to hide whatever was secretly hurting her by sheer force of will . . . but I think that Bastion was the all-time champion.

But the rest of us (especially Brandy) were pretty honest. Even more honest with Jamie, who never made us feel like we needed to hide our hobbies or our sexualities. So I think she trusted us, mostly. I could tell she was actually *listening* to our story, at least.

When we were finished telling Jamie about what we had seen in the Vision Thing, she got up and poured herself another cup of coffee. Agent Scully had crawled into my lap and fallen asleep to her own purring at some point, and I scratched her with my non-donut-eating hand, appreciating the comfort.

"I don't understand," Jamie said, sitting down again. "Bastion sold his soul to the Fae? Brandy, is this true?"

Jamie knew Brandy wouldn't lie, and Brandy answered with the weight of that expectation in her voice.

"Yes. I think it was a demon," Brandy said. So much for her assertion that the Devil didn't exist. "It's all true."

"A demon or a djinn," Drea said. "An ebil genie. A cosmic trabeler. A monster."

"Mr. Nous," Dove said, flatly. Her eyes were wide and far away. "What the fuck, Bastion. I could have just gone through chemo like other people."

"His name wasn't even Bastion," I said. I was thinking about how Bastion had never given his name: Never introduced himself to someone that I'd seen. Never given it during a coven ritual.

"He gave that thing his voice," Dove said. "Later on."

"What else did he gibe it?" Drea asked.

"At least everything on the list," I said.

"The list?" Brandy asked.

"It was evil, and he fought it. So it killed him and ate him the second it could," Dove muttered. "He must have screwed up somehow—"

"We have to find it and destroy it," I said. Not that I *wanted* to face Mr. Nous. But I was firmly in Dove's vengeance-murder camp now. Pacifism was not going to get us anywhere with whatever waited beyond the black velvet curtains.

"I don't want to be anywhere *near* some ebil monster-thing that eats people and libes on bad wishes!" Drea said.

"We're *already* near it," Brandy said. "It can *see* us."

"Do you remember his real name?" I asked Dove. It had always seemed weird to me that the Attias followed their hippie bird-naming scheme with all their other kids, but not with Bastion. Now it made sense.

Dove shook her head. "It *took* his name, Nez. You get it? As far as I know, his name was *always* Bastion."

I thought about the day that Bastion had talked about fighting an opponent whose next move was a mystery to him and felt like screaming, or throwing myself down on the kitchen floor and refusing to ever get up. I had failed him. Utterly and in every way.

Clearly, Dove was feeling guilty, too, because she rested her elbows on the table, her chin in her hands, and looked downward.

"He did exposure therapy and took medications and like a billion other things for OCD and he told Anna and Youssef none of it would work," Dove said shakily. "Because he didn't have OCD. And he was right. But he did everything they asked until he went to high school, he did everything they wanted for . . . years . . . a-a-and he was always . . . so . . . *sweet* about it—"

"Hey," I said, and touched her thin shoulders. That collapsed whatever bit of resolve Dove had left, and she started to cry. This was like the second time I had ever seen Dove cry, and it felt absolutely no less terrible and weird than the first time.

"*I* thought he had OCD, Nez," Dove said, rubbing at her face. "I wanted to do that stupid spell! I'm a terrible sister, an utter slime, a terrible, terrible sister. I was supposed to protect him."

"I came *up* with the spell," Drea said, sniffling. "I suck equally as bad."

"What spell?" Brandy asked sharply.

"Don't worry, they didn't cast it," I said, meeting Brandy's eyes. Then I turned my attention back to Dove. "I thought he had OCD too. I fought with him about it right before he died."

"I mean," Jamie said, "you guys don't need to beat yourselves up about this. It seems like OCD would be more likely than an evil entity that lived under Stepwood . . . though . . ."

"Though what?" Drea asked.

"I'm not saying I think any of this is real," Jamie said, setting down her coffee. "Not at all. But *if* there was something to it . . ."

She walked into the living room and surveyed the bookshelf, which was overflowing with Drea's true-crime stuff and books about Area 51, then grabbed a thin blue binder from the bottom shelf.

"When I was pregnant with Andrea, there was this stretch of . . . five months or so where I was living here with John, going to school, and babysitting for the Micenmachers on Wednesdays and Sundays to make a little extra money," Jamie said. "Herschel was just a baby, and Rebekah was three years old, maybe? But Wednesdays and Sundays were the nights that the au pair had off. I would go over there at five, walk through Stepwood, and then take that path that leads to Northcott House. I felt so creeped out by Stepwood on all my walks, and so creeped out by Northcott House when I was babysitting, and so interested in their shared history that I started a scrapbook about the mansion and the cemetery. I fell off on it when I stopped babysitting, but for a while during my pregnancy I was quite into *macabre stuff*, Andrea. Probably why you're so obsessed with Mothman and Bigfoot and things like that."

"I don't care about Mothman," Drea said, making a move like she was going to grab the scrapbook away from her mom. Jamie deftly blocked her and opened the blue binder herself. "I only care about *real* stuff, like the Roswell Greys and unsolbed murders."

"Anyways," Jamie said, ignoring Drea, "I got pretty into it." She flipped through the scrapbook, and I caught a glimpse of charcoal grave rubbings kept safe in plastic sleeves. "I even researched Stepwood during my free periods at Regional. It has a crazy history, along with Northcott House. I had a story about Northcott House—and Stepwood Cemetery—in here that I xeroxed out of some book about the history of the Quabbin. It *almost* sounds like your story."

Jamie had definitely relaxed a little. I could see it in her face and posture: now that she wasn't freaked about whatever glimpse she had caught of us emerging from the Vision Thing, it was becoming less real to her. To her, Bastion wasn't a real person who had died . . . just a puzzle to be solved. We were just a bunch of kids telling a good story, not human beings in pain. We were like an episode of *Scooby-Doo* or something.

It sucked. I didn't realize how much of a relief it was to have an adult on our side until it was already over.

"Here we go," Jamie said, handing the binder to Drea. "Take a look at that article."

Drea laid the binder down on the table. There was indeed a xeroxed page from a book, carefully preserved. I could see the edges of the book page. Drea scanned the first few lines, and started to read:

"'The Swift River Balley area was resettled in the early seventeen hundreds. For the next two centuries, the modest townships of the balley would quietly thribe—'"

"Drea, you have a beautiful voice, an amazing voice, I'm so glad you're our Voice," Dove said. "But I literally cannot listen to you read a whole thing right now. You need to blow your nose."

"My nose is full of clotted blood!" Drea said, gesturing to the gauze on her face.

The phone rang, and Jamie went to answer it. After a minute she walked back into the living room, dragging the mint-colored phone cord with her.

"It's my aunt," Drea said after we all listened for a second to confirm Jamie wasn't ratting us out to any of our concerned parents who might've happened to call. "She's gonna be a while."

"You read it," Dove said, passing the book to me. Honestly, I am not a good "read-aloud" person. I passed it to Brandy.

"'The Swift River Valley area was resettled in the early 1700s. For the next two centuries, the modest townships of the valley would quietly thrive, until the growing population of eastern Massachusetts made it necessary to produce more water. The Quabbin, which slaked the thirst of Boston, was built on the land that once housed four towns, all of which were evacuated for the sake of the reservoir,'" Brandy read.

We all paid attention, even though we'd all heard the stories about how the Quabbin became the Quabbin like a billion times. Pretty standard stuff, living like we did on the edge of it.

"'When the Swift River Act was finalized in 1927, residents of the four towns slated to be flooded to make the Quabbin were given a hard deadline: the towns must be entirely evacuated by April 27, 1938,'" Brandy continued. "'On April 27, 1938, a farewell ball was held in North Dana, a town that itself was—just barely—saved from being disincorporated as part of the Quabbin project. Mr. and Mrs. Bernard Wellstone, who owned the grand mansion that had once belonged to the Northcott family, opened up their palatial home to the public for the occasion. Nearly everyone from the community attended. Northcott House filled up until the party overflowed onto the lawn, the grounds, and even into Stepwood Cemetery, the adjacent family graveyard of the Northcotts.'"

"I don't get how this is like what happened to Bastion at all," I said. But Brandy shushed me with a finger to her lips and kept reading.

"'When the clock struck midnight on April 28, the towns of Enfield, Greenwich, Dana, and Prescott ceased to exist. The former residents drank glasses of champagne . . . and at dawn, Stepwood Cemetery was home to a brutal murder.

"'No less than eleven people, all in prominent positions within the townships of the Swift River Valley, were convicted for participation in the execution-style slaying of Erica Agnes Skerritt, a twenty-five-year-old woman from North Dana. Skerritt was not a noted member of the community, and the fact that older and wealthier townsfolk readily accepted jail time for the opportunity to kill her was baffling to investigators. More baffling still was that none of the participants would give a clear reason for committing the murder. The only documented statement comes from a Mrs. Ellen Cook: "The Stepwood Specter is what I'm talking about. Its starless maw and boundless lust. And as for Erica . . . we had to kill her before she could run back to *it* and change the world some more," Cook said when speaking to law enforcement. "We knew there would be consequences . . . that's why we all shot at the same time. The little fool could have flown under the radar, we wouldn't even have known she had been to see that *thing*, that the dissolution of our homes was the fare for some *fancy* of hers. Instead, she got greedy. Blabbed it around town. But when she stole our lives away from us, it was really too much. You people, even the people in our towns—you all think that this plan has been in place for over a decade. But I . . . I had my home yesterday. She changed the world yesterday. I have no idea what she got in exchange for such a steep cost. Not an immunity to bullets, obviously. And the worst bit is that in the confusion, someone grabbed the key. Lord knows what *it* will do for the next fool who comes to it with a wish."'"

Brandy stopped reading. "That's the end of it," she said. "Any ideas on what it means?"

"I think it means that Mr. Nous has been here for a while," Dove said. "Which I don't like at *all*."

CHAPTER EIGHTEEN

Monday, November 22, 1999

For a minute we all contemplated Dove's statement in silence. But I was struck by something weird that Mrs. Ellen Cook had said.

"His *starless maw*," I said. "Isn't that what Jane Doe wrote on her arm?"

"Oh shit, yeah," Dove said.

Brandy dragged one neatly manicured finger up the side of the xeroxed page, then flipped it over. "Your mom wrote the book title and author down here. *Oral Histories of the Swift River Valley* by Professor Lenore Slocum-Cuthries and Jules Kermit Tethonius."

"Jules Tethonius . . . Oh shit. Old Tet," Drea said.

We were all confused. (But you weren't, right? I told you Old Tet was going to be important later.)

"Wait, what?" I asked. Dove and Brandy seemed equally bewildered.

"Bastion told me his real name," Drea said. "Jules Tethonius. You know he had a soft spot for Old Tet. He said Tet used to be a local historian before his alcoholism got out of hand. He even lectured at Amherst. The Prof apparently said he was brilliant."

"Um. If Old Tet wrote this, then we should definitely talk to him," I said.

"Yeah, let's go," Dove said, grabbing her little backpack.

"Wait!" Drea said. "Do you guys know where he is?"

"I mean, we can check that tent thing he has set up by the train tracks," I said.

You may not think this is as cool as I do, but I once read that Massachusetts has over a *thousand* miles of abandoned train tracks. One chunk of those abandoned miles is in North Dana, a relic of the old Rabbit line that used to run through the Swift River Valley. Now the tracks were mostly deep under the Quabbin, but the bit that ran into North Dana could still be found . . . and walked along if you wanted to go on a cool nature hike. Old Tet had a home base tarp-slash-tent deal in the ruins of the train station, which had just been a little Victorian house before 1935 when the train line was dismantled.

Growing up in New Haven, I met and interacted with many homeless people. Some of them were scary, but most of them were just drug addicts or mentally ill, people with no support system. Sometimes people with cool stories who had been forgotten by the world. In North Dana, which was like a hundred miles from any urban resources or shelters, there was basically no homeless population. It's hard to survive with nothing. Surviving with nothing in a place with no help for those who have nothing, surrounded by country people who don't want to acknowledge your existence . . . well, that seems pretty impossible.

Bastion felt the same way I did. He liked to walk out along the train tracks sometimes and listen to Old Tet's stories, maybe give Tet his lunch money. Bastion didn't care if the money went to booze. He just wanted to help someone else feel like they had personal autonomy for a minute, even if they used that autonomy to further trash their liver.

Because he had no personal autonomy. Because something else owned Bastion Attia's free will. I understand that now.

Brandy was absolutely freaked-out by Old Tet, probably from whatever crap her mom had fed her about homeless people being, like, monsters who were getting punished for their sins or something, but she made zero objections to our plan. I was proud of her.

We ducked out while Jamie was still caught up in her phone conversation and ran back through the woods toward my car. As we hit the edge of the cemetery, Drea paused, making a "wait" gesture with outstretched arms.

"I don't know if it's the magic mushrooms or what, but this place feels bery uncool to me right now," she said. "You know?"

"You feel something from the mushrooms?" Brandy asked, nervously.

"I don't feel anything, it was like the tiniest amount," Dove said.

I was suddenly weirded out by Stepwood, too. I thought about the fact that the Stepwood Specter and Mr. Nous were probably the same thing. Between that and Bastion's mausoleum key . . . it all implied that somehow the creature that had controlled Bastion was *right here*, in this cemetery. I thought about the haunted carnival, and the laughter that sounded like rotting silk. The thing in the darkness when we broke into the town hall.

I took Brandy's hand in my left and Dove's in my right. Then Drea held on to Brandy's other hand, and we stayed connected as we went into Stepwood. I did not look at the Northcott Faire mausoleum as we passed it. We ran through the cemetery linked like that, and no monster came snapping at our heels. But at the iron gates right before my car, I turned for a minute to take in the layered, sloping hills and the way the graves were hidden in pools of shadow in the middle of the day. A crow cawed from somewhere in the pine trees. Then I got behind the wheel and started the car, and we sped away from Stepwood.

We headed toward the edge of the Quabbin. I parked at Gate 18 and the four of us walked along the old train tracks. It was barely two in the afternoon, but I felt like weeks had passed since the morning. Eons since Bastion had been murdered. Eternities since things were normal and good.

Some things still felt real: the crunch of the brown leaves under our feet. The pine smell on the cold air came from both sides of the tracks, where the forest grew wild and deep. The girls. The three of them seemed vividly alive to me, realer than even the terrible things happening to us.

Old Tet's camp was visible from way off: surrounded by tiki torches, with tattered prayer flags hanging from the trees. A bonfire pit sat in the direct center of the old train station ruins, and the fire crackled and gave off a nice smoky smell that made me think of Halloween. Tet's old beagle Elizabeth sat up as we approached, let out one hooting bark, and then laid back down, her tail thumping on the dirt. Then Old Tet emerged from the tarp-covered tent to the right of the fire, waving his arms. Brandy flinched but carried on walking toward him with the rest of us.

"No! No sir, I want nothing more to do with it!" Tet hollered. In his long coat and knitted poncho, behind his massive beard with the little braids in it, he did look pretty imposing. Like a refugee from Bike Week that had set down his Harley at the edge of the woods one day and morphed into a forest troll.

"Hey," I said, waving. I figured he was probably drunk, but he was normally a chill enough dude. "Hey, Mr. T, I was hoping we could ask you about something!"

"I said no, kiddo!" Tet said, coming closer. I saw Brandy glance between Old Tet and the pump shotgun he had resting against his tent, and kind of shrink back. But Drea held her mom's blue binder up.

"Did you and a lady named Professor Lenore write a book called *Oral Histories of the Swift River Balley*?" Drea asked, flapping the binder in the air.

"I already got taken in for questioning and had to sit in a cell the size of my ass with that pissant Sheriff Andy—the jackass—watching me for three days! Lizzie getting picked up by animal control! Just because I'm *impoverished* and I sometimes like to walk in Stepwood, they think I'm a damned child-eater!"

"Um, Mr. T—"

"God, I hate this place. I'm not getting involved, kiddo, so just march your posse back to that ugly car of yours," Tet said, wagging a finger at me. "I'm not doing it anymore. I don't want to be involved."

"But, sir!" Drea said.

"You remember him," I said, taking a deep breath. "You remember Bastion."

"What? Course I do. The poor kid only got deep-sixed last week, for chrissakes."

"Nobody else does," Dove said. During the exchange, she had meandered over to the bonfire. She crouched in what I supposed was Old Tet's front yard, patting Elizabeth on the head thoughtfully.

"It's also last week. Again," Drea said.

"Hm? Well then, I don't remember any Bastion. And I think it's last week."

"Please," I said, reaching out and grabbing Old Tet's sleeve in one of my bruised hands. "Please. We are in so much trouble. The world is *wrong*. Please—if you wrote that book, if you know anything else about the Stepwood Specter, something called Mr. Nous, or *why* nobody can remember Bastion . . . please help us."

"Please," Dove said, from behind him.

"If you didn't want to talk about it, you shouldn't habe started off with flagrant denial," Drea said. "It comes off pretty suspicious, Mr. T."

Tet looked at Drea, and Dove, and at my hand. Then he sighed, and gently removed his sleeve from my grasp.

"Okay. But you all need to put your gloves on, pull down your sleeves, whatever. Cover up those *N*'s." Tet pointed at Drea's exposed wrist, where a Nexus cut we'd made for our investigation was visible. "It's bad enough you're walking around with its mark on you. I don't need it listening in. It's made my life a damned misery enough already."

"With *its* mark?" Brandy asked, her eyes going very wide.

"Yeah, what the hell do you mean?" Drea asked. "That's *our* mark, Old—I mean, *Mr.* Tet."

"It's for a Nexus," Dove added defensively. "For the times when we do a very important spell."

"It's a mark made so Mr. Nous can see and hear you," Tet said. He sat cross-legged in front of the fire, sighing heavily. I sat down on one side of him, Dove on the other, and Brandy and Drea opposite us. "Cover those, please. I don't think it will do any good, but cover them all the same. And if you little witches can do a healing spell to speed things along and get the mark off your skin, well, the sooner the better."

"I don't understand," Brandy murmured, tying her scarf around the scabby N on her wrist. "Why would Bastion make it so Mr. Nous could see and hear us?"

"He never would," Dove said.

"Absolutely he did," Tet declared. "But it wasn't a malicious act." He reached deep within the pocket of his poncho, brought out a half-empty bottle of the cheapest schnapps that Quabbin Liquors had to offer, and drank deeply from it. The wind sent the smoke from the bonfire up toward the treetops, sparks dancing in the wake of it like aimless stars.

"Maybe you should explain to us what Mr. Nous *is* first," Drea said. "We have exactly one Bision Thing and one book excerpt to go on right now."

"You really *do* know all about this," Dove pressed. "Don't you?"

Old Tet slid Dove a sidelong glance and then nodded, reluctantly. "I know more than I ever meant to. If I'd've known how dangerous it was to be a *historian*, I would've gone into something less dangerous, like logging or coal mining. Or skydiving instruction."

"We need to know about it," Brandy said very firmly. "Please, sir. Tell us what you know about the thing with the red hands . . . and what it was doing to our friend."

Old Tet sighed again, like something heavy sat on his chest.

"It's like this, kiddos," he said. "My research partner and I—she was another historian, and an excellent one—started working on collecting all the oral histories of the Swift River Valley that we could find in the mid-seventies. We thought it was a great project, and a great opportunity to catalog some history that was on the verge of being lost forever."

He closed his eyes for a second, remembering.

"But the project went on even after Amherst College published our little book. We'd found a strange pattern in the histories, you see? Lots of stories about the Northcotts, who were the richest family in the valley for hundreds of years. Lots of stories about Northcott House and the cemetery next to it. Lots of *dark* stories. Murders and trysts and bad blood. And this . . . thing kept coming up. This tale of a creature. A specter. It was something that had tagged along with the people who came to steal and colonize this land, maybe the Northcotts or maybe someone even earlier. Nobody knew for certain. All they knew was that it was something that lived in Stepwood Cemetery, underneath the Northcott family mausoleum, and it kept dominion there, hidden away by its own design. Hidden from everyone in the world—except for *one* person."

"Which person?" Drea asked.

Old Tet shrugged. "That changed. It was always only one person. I think it was always someone *in* the Northcott family at first.

But then . . . after a while, they lost track of the token—the key—and new Advocates kept turning up over the years."

"Advocates?" Dove asked.

"Uh-huh. We didn't know what that meant at first, either," Old Tet said. "It took us quite some time to piece the story together, but it went like this: Mr. Nous makes its home in a phantom bazaar under Stepwood—"

"Carnival," I said. "It was a carnival."

"I imagine it's been a *lot* of things," Old Tet said. "Mr. Nous can make that place into whatever it wants. So it has this bazaar—or den, or *carnival*—and it only opens shop for one individual at a time. For the Advocate: the one who bears the token."

"So if you wear its key, it can make your *wishes* come true?" Drea asked.

"If you wear the key, you *have* to make wishes," Old Tet said, and his voice got very deep and very stern. Another gust of wind spread fire-sparks around us. "There are *rules* the Advocate must follow. Nine rules, I believe. One of them is that they must make at least one wish a year, or else . . ."

"Or else what?" Drea asked, in a tone of voice that said she already had some idea that the *or else* was very bad.

"If you fail to follow its rules—or ever take the key off—you will meet a terrible fate," Old Tet said. "Brought about by its sharp teeth and starless maw."

"So if you fuck up, it eats you," Dove said. "That about right? "

Old Tet nodded. "And the wishes themselves are terrible things. Each *fancy* comes with a *fare*. Paid, of course, by those around you. And the price is always bad, and it is always taken from someone else, and it is always whatever will amuse Mr. Nous the most."

"Paid the fare?" I asked. I was thinking about the *Fare* and *Fancy* boards in the nightmare carnival. And child-Bastion in the Vision Thing, saying "—*nobody else can pay my fare but me.*"

"Yep," Old Tet said. "The more we looked into it, the more it seemed like every strange misfortune ever suffered by someone in the Swift River Valley was the *fare* for some *fancy.*"

"Bastion stopped it from taking its . . . *fares* from other people," I said. "He took it all on himself."

"Were you eber the Adbocate?" Drea asked. "Did you eber wear its key?"

"Oh no," Old Tet said. "Not me. It always *eats* the ones who wear the key . . . eventually. Eats them and drags their souls back down to its lair. I suppose it is a bit like an animal that way."

"But I thought that Mr. Nous took its *fares* from other people, not its Advocate," I said.

"Right," Old Tet said. "It does. There's nuance to how Mr. Nous operates. Like it's insidious, like it's *playing.* So the people it takes the fares from are victims for sure. But the *Advocate* is the real . . . meal. Mr. Nous likes to make folks regret their wishes, you see. Destroy the lives of everyone who ever mattered to the Advocate. Leave 'em empty and alone. Real monkey's paw kind of situation. Why, I bet more than half of those poor souls don't get eaten for breaking one of the rules of its game. I think they choose to take the token off. To die. Just to get away from it. Which is terrible, of course, because I don't believe they ever really get away, even in death."

I thought of the plywood people that dotted the carnival mid-way in Mr. Nous's realm. There were so many of them.

"Your research partner . . . Professor Lenore? She co-wrote the book with you, right? Is she around?" Drea asked.

"My poor, lost Lenore," Tet said, and took another long swig from the schnapps bottle. "No. I think you and your brother found her, huh, kiddo?"

He gestured at Dove, who looked up with dawning comprehension in her eyes.

"She was the Jane Doe," Dove said.

"Unfortunately for your brother, the key has a habit of . . . jumping. Whether the next Advocate wants it or not. Lenore got too deep into researching the Stepwood Specter. And she was *excellent* at her job, you know. I told her it was a bunch of hokum and to leave it be, but . . ." Old Tet shrugged. It was a casual gesture, but I could see the sadness in his creased eyes.

"She left you a message," I said. "She wrote it on her arm. *'I'm sorry, J. I love you.'* Did you know?"

I wasn't trying to add to Tet's misery, but my words clearly hurt him.

"I didn't know that," he admitted. "I hoped she was sorry."

"She knew it was going to kill her. And now it has her down there," Drea said. "In Northcott Faire."

"It has her down there and the wishes made can never be undone," Old Tet agreed, heavily. "So it has me up here, as well."

"What price did she make you pay for her wishes?" Brandy asked, making one of those intuitive leaps that came so easily to the Eyes of the coven.

"I can never leave," Tet said. "I mean *never*. At first, when Lenore disappeared, they suspected me. I was told to stay close for questioning. And I told Sheriff Andy that the Jane Doe they'd *just* found was Lenore. He agreed. He saw that it made sense. He was going to bring in the *real* police, to investigate. Until the next time I saw him. He'd forgotten by then . . . like the connection between Lenore and the *real world* was being erased. She just became one of the missing. And I . . . I was marooned. What she'd done to me . . . or what *it* had done to me, through her wishes, became clear. You think it's"—he gestured around himself, at his encampment—"normal for a hobo to live this way? I can do whatever I want, pretty much. They don't tell me to get off this government-owned land, which they surely should. Never have I been troubled by a park service person or a forest ranger. The cops always eventually let me go. I can do anything . . . except leave. Or better my situation. It's the same, always the same."

"What did she get in exchange?" Brandy pressed.

"That I do not know. She told me about it in the beginning, when she was first caught by it. When we were still historians. But later she stopped telling me anything."

"But you cared about each other, right?" I asked. "How could she leave you trapped like this?"

"You don't understand, kiddo," Tet said. He looked past us, into the darkness where the woods got closer together. "Mr. Nous is very clever. It starts the game with a set of nine rules. One of those rules is that the Advocate must bring it one fancy a year. You can make more wishes than that, of course, but once a year is *necessary*."

"Or else you get eaten," Drea chimed in, and Tet nodded.

"That's right," Tet said, with his eyes still trained on that dark and distant spot. "Of course, you don't have to pay your own fare. In the beginning, it might make you choose between paying your own fare and having someone you dislike—or are indifferent to—pay it for you. Obviously, most folks choose not to pay themselves. Then the wish goes agreeably. You get what you want. You ask for more and . . . your morals kind of erode. I think it has that effect on people. On *most* people. And later it might not offer you a choice. Then the fare gets paid by someone you love. And someone else. And then a wish will go wrong. Then another one. It *creeps*, you see. It has an eternity of time. Creeps up on you."

We were all quiet for a minute. Dove lit a cigarette, and Tet looked around at her. "Got one for an old vagrant, kiddo?"

"Yeah, of course," Dove muttered, handing off her menthol and bringing out the Dupont to light a second one. She sounded as rattled as I felt. Having an adult confirm all of this, so matter-of-factly . . . even if it was a somewhat unreliable adult . . . was a lot to take in.

Old Tet took a long drag of the cigarette and blew out three perfect smoke rings. "Sometimes an amoral person gets ahold of the key, like that girl who drowned the four towns back in 1938. Sometimes a good person gets it. The result has been the same—*bad*—for at least three hundred years."

"Why can we remember stuff nobody else can?" Drea asked.

"Same reason I can, I imagine," Tet said. "Your buddy made a wish to give you all an awareness of Mr. Nous's machinations. Lenore did the same for me, in the early days. Just to have some-one to talk about it with. She wanted me to remember."

"Something you said before," Drea said. "It doesn't make sense. You said our Nexus symbol is the mark of Mr. Nous, so it can see and hear us."

"That it is," Old Tet agreed.

"Why would Bastion do that?" I pressed. "He would never hurt any of us."

"Not to hurt you! You said he only had you carve that symbol into yourselves for *really important* things, right," Tet said. "I don't know if the kid had a magical bone in his body. But the four of you *do*. Maybe he was trying to help you fix your problems yourselves. Keeping that creature in the loop so it could tell him if your spells ever worked. If they didn't, well, I suppose then he paid the fare himself. Anyways, at this point having the mark on your skin is not going to do you a bit of good."

"Paid the fare himself," Brandy echoed, looking grim. "For the things *we* needed?"

"Look, did you actually talk to him about any of this, or are you just guessing?" Dove asked, sharply. I understood her tone. Dove usually sounded pissed when she was upset. I was thinking about Nic getting sober and what it had cost Bastion. I bet Dove was thinking about their unborn brother, the almost-baby Bastion traded away for Dove's health. And how it traumatized Bastion so much to do something bad that he had taken the entire burden on himself forever after.

"I talked to him about it a little," Tet said. "Not too much. The damned don't need to ask the damned if they're both in hell, you know."

"So there's nothing we can do?" I asked. "No way to get Bastion's existence back? No way to stop this thing?"

"No way that anyone has found yet," Tet agreed. "But for a while, I felt that if anyone ever could, it would be the kid. He was the only one I know of that ever thought to take all of the fares on himself, to ruin half the fun for the creature right out of the gate. Terribly brave stuff. He brought you all together. Helped you make your own magic . . . even if your magic didn't end up being quite sufficient for your own witchy ends. I do believe he was gearing up to fight it someday."

Suddenly my hands prickled sharply. I glanced around the fire, to see Brandy swiveling to look toward the dark part of the woods. The gray sky was still bright above us, but I felt as uneasy as if it were the dead of night.

"Can you tell us the nine rules of Mr. Nous?" Drea asked. "Do you know them?"

"No, not all of them. But a few," Tet said, with his gaze still fixed on a point beyond the treeline. "But you should go now . . . I don't mean to scare you kids, but sometimes I have a sense about things. I think right now it might be *listening* to us."

I shot to my feet, motioning to the others. The large swath of darkness in the woods suddenly felt like more than a trick of the light.

"Will you be okay?" Dove asked Old Tet.

"We need to go now," I said, tugging at the shoulder of her coat.

"I'll be fine, kiddo," Tet said, and Dove pressed her half-full pack of cigarettes into his hand.

"We'll be back," she vowed. "Thank you."

Then she let me drag her away.

"Do a spell to heal up those *N*'s! You kids have something real in your little coven!" Old Tet yelled after us. "And don't worry about *it*—it never acts alone! Worry about the new Advocate! I hope that they're predisposed to goodness!"

His voice faded away as we put distance between ourselves and the ruins of the North Dana train station. We were not attacked by anything, and nothing stirred in the forest. But I did feel like something was watching us. Listening to us. Following us. And *laughing* at us.

We made it back to the car. As I drove away, Drea leaned forward.

"Guys," she said, gravely. "We are totally fucked if we don't do something about the limitless wishes the ebil monster has granted to Cameron-dickbag-Winship."

I had to agree with her.

CHAPTER NINETEEN

Monday, November 22, 1999

It was three o'clock.

It felt like it should be midnight, or the next day, or the next *month* since that morning. I could see it in the tense expressions of the girls. They looked scared and tired and wired, all at the same time.

"Go to his house," Drea said, as we headed back toward the center of North Dana. "Maybe we can catch him there . . . and get that key away from him, or something."

"We can't do that," Brandy said, immediately. "Mr. Nous will eat him if he takes the token off, remember? Mr. Tethonius said so. If the Advocate takes the token off—"

"Yeah, anyone who takes the necklace *off* is definitely killed like . . . like Bastion was," Dove said. "Plus, way more importantly, whoever *gets* the key becomes the next Advocate. I am *not* letting it get its creepy red hands on any of you."

"Or you, Dove Bar," I said, touching her hand for a second. Dove looked over at me, and then flicked a bunch of cigarette ash—from the last remaining cigarette she hadn't gifted to Old Tet—out of the rolled-down window.

"Whatever," Dove said. "I'll be fine."

"I'm *serious*," I said. "You better not try some heroic bullshit. If anything happened to you, it would kill your mom."

I meant that it would kill Anna to lose two kids, but that wasn't *really* true. Anna Attia had no idea she'd lost one kid to begin with. But the sentiment was still the same, and I could see Dove absorb it.

"Yeah," she allowed, kind of grumbling. "I guess."

"And stop smoking in my car," I added.

"You let me smoke in here earlier!" Dove said.

"You were in shock then. Chuck it," I said.

Dove rolled her eyes gratuitously, but she ditched the cigarette.

"We can at least try to have a conversation with Cameron *not* at school," I added. "He might be more truthful without a crowd of witnesses."

"If we try that, we might just push him into wishing us out of existence," Drea said. "If he hasn't decided to already."

"Let's just *see* if he can be reasoned with," Brandy said. "I don't imagine that he is particularly ecstatic to be the Advocate, regardless of how much power he has. He's not stupid. He can probably tell he's in bad trouble."

"He's pretty stupid," Dove said, which made Drea laugh-wheeze through her bandaged nose.

Personally, I agreed with Brandy: Cameron *wasn't* stupid, and he probably wasn't happy about the deep dark monster that he was entangled with. But I didn't trust him. I thought of his stubbornness back in freshman year, when he was my nameless Gym Buddy. His almost insane persistence . . . and his *quiet desperation*. Someone with all that quiet desperation was not exactly the person I'd trust most with limitless power.

I headed toward the center of North Dana, and slowed to a roll on the road as we passed the Winship's big white Victorian with the black trim.

"Scope it out," I said, and the rest of North Coven craned their heads to the right, peering at the Winship's yard (still manicured in the cold months) and driveway.

I looked too: and lo and behold, there was Cameron climbing out of the driver's side of a newer Volvo. That was weird, because I was almost sure Cameron didn't have his license—

—and then we all gasped at the same time. The hair on my arms stood up.

Mayor Winship was getting out of the passenger side of the car.

I guess we should have probably figured out he was still alive . . . but knowing you're a week in the past and seeing a guy who died in front of you walking around totally alive are two very different things.

Cameron and his dad—you needed an adult to ride around with you while you were still on your learner's permit—walked toward the house together. For a second Cameron turned around, glancing toward the road, and I sped off in the world's most recognizable car.

"I don't think he saw us," Drea said, as we tore out of sight.

"It doesn't matter," Dove said. "He knows we know. I can't believe that little pukelord brought his horrible dad back."

"I can't either," Brandy said, with an echo of the pain I had heard in her voice years earlier, when we had first met. *Three and a half more years and I'll be free*, she'd said, the day we did the spell to change her mom's heart . . . the spell that apparently didn't work.

I opened my mouth to tell Brandy that Mayor Winship wasn't as bad as her mom, and then shut it. What did I know? Maybe he *was* that bad. Maybe Brandy had seen something in the situation that the rest of us couldn't.

There was a bleak silence for a minute. I contemplated the enormity of bringing someone back from the dead. I tried not to think about Bastion in the context of resurrection.

"We habe to do something about this right now," Drea said. "I need to research. I'm sure I can come up with something. Nez, can you bring me to the library?"

"Sure," I said.

"The rest of us should stake out Stepwood," Dove said. "Make sure Slime Man doesn't try to use the mausoleum key."

"Cameron won't be able to get over there. He's going right back to Regional. He has a game tonight," I said, feeling pretty bitter about it. The game that was supposed to be canceled because Bastion had been murdered.

"Okay," Dove said. "Let's all go together."

I didn't spend much time at the Leander Storey library (unlike Drea, who made it into basically a second home), but I *loved* looking at it when I drove by. It was a small concrete structure built in the 1950s with windows all over, and it looked like a robot mushroom and a ranch house had a really strange baby. It was the only example of brutalist architecture I had ever found on the Quabbin, and it was mostly hated by the locals. But I appreciated it, in all of its semi-hideous glory. It was so out of place on Main Street that it seemed like it had been transplanted there from some other world entirely.

We all went inside and spent over an hour waiting around for Drea while she pulled stacks and stacks of books and tore through them at lightning speed. Brandy at least tried to help, but Dove (after Drea told us to "get out of the way" for the third time) flipped her way through a bunch of back issues of *Vogue* while I read the October issue of *Popular Mechanics*.

Brandy came and got us like thirty minutes before the library closed, saving me from an article called "The Plane that Might Have Saved JFK, Jr." and led us back to the table where Drea had scattered her reference materials. She was such a regular here that this kind of disarray didn't even attract negative attention from Mrs. Kersh, who had been the librarian since the place opened and was roughly eight hundred thousand years old.

"Whatchu got?" Dove asked, sliding into a seat across from Drea.

"A couple of things. They didn't habe a copy of *Oral Histories of the Swift River Valley*, but there's another book by Professor Lenore. This one was put out by the unibersity press too, and it's all about the murders and biolent crimes committed in the Swift Riber Balley before the Quabbin was made. Didn't really go into anything about Mr. Nous that we haven't learned already, but check this out."

She rifled around on the desk and pulled out a slim cloth-bound book, titled *A Land Steeped in Blood: Crime and Punishment in the Swift River Valley.*

"She starts with the colonizers committing atrocities against the Nipmuc Tribe in the 1600s and ends it when the Quabbin was made. Guys, there were *so many* biolent crimes that happened around here. So many weird ones that I'be neber heard about, because the records are old or gone. Then it has this segment in the back where she talks about that Erica Skerritt murder again," Drea said. "It's really interesting. It's more like official accounts than the page from the other book. But I was looking through it and I found this part—"

She flipped to a page she had marked with a strip of paper and handed it to Brandy.

Brandy took it and read out loud: "'*Wishes*. Fragment found in Amherst College library archive, circa 1956. Author Unknown.

> *A lass went out to Northcott Faire*
> *and brought the Valley ruin there.*
> *They paid the fare she made below,*
> *and townsfolk wept on windswept land*
> *where water was to go.*
>
> *"For men of money do as money must,"*
> *and Boston's thirst reduced four towns to dust.*
> *Not all believed, nor memories negated,*
> *before her fancies cost them all the earth.*
> *For it delights in sowing fear and hatred.*

Then on that April Eve 'fore all was drowned,
A final farewell in North Dana town.
The secret caged in iron was discussed.
To call it up was to cast your soul down—
The Stepwood Specter and its boundless lust.'"

Drea nodded along to the poem until Brandy finished.

"You kids keep it down over there!" Mrs. Kersh said, in a reed-thin voice, even though Brandy was *way* quieter than Drea. "We close in twenty minutes!"

"There isn't even anyone else *in* here, you old bag," Dove muttered.

"What was that?" Mrs. Kersh asked.

"She said 'you won't eben know we're in here,' Mrs. Kersh!" Drea said, enunciating as much as she could with her busted nose.

"That's fine. Thank you, Andrea," Mrs. Kersh said.

"Anyways. The poem is weird. I don't think Professor Lenore would habe included it in her crime history if she wasn't already onto the Mr. Nous thing," Drea said. "In fact, I think she was kind of looking at the bloody-ass history of the balley because she *suspected* Mr. Nous was behind a lot of it. Some of those poem lines were written on her arm when she died, along with the *starless maw* thing. Nobody eber figured out anything about her, but . . . she was trying to leave a message about who did this to her."

"Anna would be so pissed about the rhyme scheme in the first stanza not going with the rest of it," Dove said.

"I liked it, I think it's a cool poem," Drea said. "And so did Professor Lenore, obbiously."

"Lenore was never identified even though Old Tet knows exactly who she is," Dove said. "The cops seemed to be willfully ignoring the obvious connections between her murder and Bastion's even before Bastion was erased. The hay on their clothes from the carnival, like, vanished. I don't think Nous *allows* people to figure out stuff about his victims."

"The chain of victims is unbroken forever," Brandy said, quietly. "No choice for the next Advocate. No chance to escape."

"I wish we could tell people that Lenore was the Jane Doe," I said. "Even if she did lousy things once she was the Advocate. She deserves to be remembered."

"There's a picture in the back of this book," Drea said, and flipped to the acknowledgments. I saw *Jules K. Tethonius* listed as one of the people she thanked before Drea turned the page to a grainy old picture. A smiling woman with long ironed seventies hair looked out into the world, forever captured by the camera.

"Her painted figure is down there somewhere," I said. "In his carnival."

"Jules thinks that's her *soul*," Dove said.

None of us said what we were all thinking: that a painting of Bastion was somewhere under Stepwood.

"Now for the urgent stuff," Drea said. "I habe a spell idea. I went through the *Nicodème Witchery Almanac* and found something that could buy us a bit of time, so Cameron Winship can't set his ebil genie on us while we try to come up with . . . a more long-term solution."

"Which is to destroy Nous," Dove clarified.

"Right. But in the meantime . . ." Drea laid the almanac in front of us and turned to a page in the middle. *Spell for Binding the Will of an Enemy* was written across the top.

"I'm gonna check the almanac out today and copy this spell down in our grimoire," Drea said. "I habe a good feeling about it."

"Makes me think of *The Craft*," Dove said, scanning the page. "I *bind* you, Nancy, from doing harm—"

"More complicated but kinda a similar idea," Drea said, tapping the pages. "You have to strike a fine line between binding the negatibe impulses and taking the free will entirely. You know, like what we were *trying* to do with Brandy's mom. But apparently didn't do."

"Yeah, and Mr. Nous did for us," Dove said.

"*Bastion* did it for us," Brandy said, and when I looked at her, I saw that her lovely face was very serious. She looked like a cemetery statue. "He paid the fare to save me from my mother."

"And to save Nic," I said. "And to save the house for Drea and Jamie. And to save Dove."

"Yeah," Drea said. "So like I said. We are going to destroy Mr. Nous. But we also need to bind Cameron, and we need to change our tactics. Because the last time we tried to bind someone's will, we didn't actually do shit to Mrs. Jackson. We need to make this work *without* getting help from Mr. Nous's powers. A *helping hand*, you could say."

"Terrible," Brandy said, while Drea snorted at her own joke.

"Right," Dove said, nodding along.

"Basically, we make an effigy and submerge it in wax, bind it really well with a thrice-repeated platonic spell of general compassion and kindness, split the effigy between the head and the heart, and bury the two pieces separately, with running water between them," Drea said.

"Okay, so then what?" I asked.

"So the idea is that we can recombine the pieces by melting the figure back together to release Cameron. Once we figure out a way to take care of Mr. Nous. But the thing I'm worried about . . ."

"Yeah?" Dove asked when Drea looked a little hesitant.

"The thing is that we need something really personal to Cameron, a cherished item," Drea said. "I think stealing his stupid expensibe cell phone is gonna be an issue, and I don't know what else he, like, *cherishes*."

"Right," Dove said. "What else?"

"We need his *hair*," Drea said. "We need something precious to Cameron and a decent clump of his bleached-ass hair. There are substitutions for those components, but they are *much* grosser and harder to get."

"Right," Dove said. "I doubt he's gonna be cool with a haircut."

"Yeah, exactly," Drea said. "So . . . we need to get into his house. I was thinking during the football game tonight. He's the quarterback now, so he'll play, and his parents will definitely go."

I was nodding along to all of this, caught up in the planning, when I realized all of the girls were looking at me. Brandy raised an eyebrow.

"What?" I asked. "Sounds good. What's up?"

"We need someone to break into the Winship's house and steal Cameron's hair and personal items," Drea said, still staring at me.

"Yes, I got that," I said.

"Someone who can pick locks. Someone, you could say, who is good with their *hands*."

"Oh," I said. "Wait. No *way*—"

But as you've probably already guessed, I ended up being the one who had to infiltrate the house of Cameron-dickbag-Winship.

CHAPTER TWENTY

Monday, November 22, 1999

We had two hours to work out our entire plan before the game started, and I dropped the three girls back at Drea's before heading home. They were going to gather all the materials necessary to do our spell, and then get Jamie to bring them to the football game. I was going to take my own car and meet them there, then bail once we were certain that the entire Winship family was not at home.

If someone from Cameron's family *didn't* attend, leaving his house occupied, I was . . . I was supposed to do something. We hadn't exactly worked out what. Infiltrate the locker rooms and steal his Nokia. Pull a clump of hair out of his head after the game. *Something*, before he wished us out of existence.

But there was a snag, of course. When I got home, Nic and my dad were waiting for me in the living room.

"Where have you been?" my dad said, the second I made it into the house. It was so unlike my dad to even *notice* my comings-and-goings, much less *question* them, that I knew I was in the shit pretty much immediately.

"Out," I said, which got a little indignant huffing sound out of Nic.

Nic and my mom were more similar than Nic and my dad. They shared a dramatic, passive-aggressive-and-sometimes-tantrum-throwing kind of flair, a thing which Nic probably would have *killed* me for pointing out. But I knew that huffing sound. It was a sound I'd heard my mom direct at my dad a lot before they'd gotten divorced. It was the sound that Mom and Nic both made when they were pissed but not saying anything yet, a "can you believe this asshole?" kind of sound.

It was a sound that made me know I was digging my own grave by being flippant.

"I was out with Dove and Brandy and Drea," I elaborated. "We went to the library."

"Then why did Coach Silva call and give him an earful about you attacking some kid on the school grounds and leaving school?" my dad asked, in a neutral tone that still conveyed disappointment.

"Not just any kid," Nic said. "The mayor's kid."

"*You* talked to Coach Silva?" I asked, looking at Nic. The rest of the sentence went unsaid: *And you ratted me out to Dad?*

"Uh-huh," Nic said, twirling a toothpick around in his mouth with not an ounce of visible remorse.

"You suck," I said. "And you're not my legal guardian. I don't think you can take calls about me from school administrators."

"Don't tell your brother he sucks," Dad said. "He's just looking out for you."

"Why are you flipping out at school?" Nic asked, narrowing his eyes.

If things had been the way they *really* were, I could have leveraged my grief to get my dad to leave me alone. He was pretty uncomfortable with grief. But as far as Dad and Nic knew, I wasn't grieving. There was no Bastion Attia to grieve for, and no pass for me to be on bad (or at least *weird*) behavior.

But I *also* couldn't be in trouble. I had a football game to pretend to go to, and a house to break into, and I couldn't get grounded and forced to sit at home while North Coven was in peril.

So I did a pretty crappy thing, fueled by my anger at Nic for being a stupid busybody and tattling on me to Dad like I was a baby.

I sighed deeply, like I was repentant. Then I looked directly at Dad, ignoring Nic.

"I'm sorry," I said. "I shouldn't have gotten into a fight. I just hate Cameron for what he's doing. All of us do."

"What is this Cameron kid doing?" my dad asked, still pretty even-keeled. I definitely had a chance of getting out of trouble if I played my cards right.

"He's selling Oxys at school," I said. I was still looking right at Dad, but I could see Nic flinch out of the corner of my eye. During his worst druggie phase, Nic had been supplementing his heroin habit with enough OxyContin to keep a small pharmacy in business. I'd been the one who found his painkiller stash before his overdose, prompting our worst fight of all time.

"It's stupid and it's dangerous," I went on, pressing my advantage. I could see from Dad's expression that I had played it right. Now he was empathizing with my anger and fear, thinking about that horrible time fourteen months earlier when Nic had almost died. "And he could literally be getting other kids killed. I know he won't get in trouble because he's *Mayor Winship's* kid. But I had to do something."

Cameron Winship would literally never have sold drugs in a thousand years. It might screw up his chances of getting into an Ivy League school, or something. But they didn't know that. Now I basically sounded like a hero. Dad believed my story. Nic did, too. When I glanced over at him, Nic was staring very hard at his hands.

Did I feel guilty? Yes. I felt like a real dickbag, actually. But I kept going.

"I won't do it again," I said to Dad. I am not normally a good liar, but my desperation made this into an award-worthy performance. I could almost *see* my punishment evaporating.

"Well, you're looking at five days of detention, according to Coach Silva," my dad said. "But I think that's enough of a lesson. You should try to tell your teachers about what that boy is doing."

Thank god for Dad and his pathological hatred of confrontation. If it had been Anna Attia—or even Jamie—who had been told about a kid selling painkillers at Regional, they would have been on the phone with the principal in *seconds*.

"I'll try," I said. "But it probably won't go anywhere."

This was pretty copacetic with my dad's (not inaccurate) worldview about powerful people avoiding punishment. He nodded.

"Are we good?" I asked, carefully, still trying to look remorseful.

"We're all set," my dad said. "You want some dinner? We're going to order from Crescent Moon."

"I ate already," I said. It was another lie, but I was too nervous about the breaking and entering I had to do that night to think about eating dinner, even from the good takeout place. Nic didn't look up at me as I left the room, and I pushed my guilt down as far as I could.

I tried to think about anything else, which led me to thinking about our magic. Mr. Nous had said it wasn't impressive *enough* to "remake the destinies of our world." But even *it* had agreed with Bastion that North Coven had real power. It seemed like a good idea to stack the odds in our favor in any way I could, and so I went to the bathroom and stopped up the sink, sprinkled a little salt into the water, and held my hands under it, whispering a made-up chant to myself.

"Unlock, open, pry apart, find the doors, eyes-*hands*-voice-heart. With my hands, I work my art. Give me strength to do my part."

Not the most creative spell, I'll grant you, but I felt my palms start to prickle in the way that normally meant something supernatural was happening after about ten repetitions. I hoped really, *really* strongly that I'd secured whatever I needed to in order to be successful that night.

Then it was time to go. I headed back to the kitchen/living room, where Nic and my dad were eating and watching TV.

"Going to the school football game," I said, and Nic looked up at me in utter disbelief.

"What are you really doing?" Nic asked.

"That." I grabbed my keys and waved.

"Have fun!" That was Dad.

Regional was on so much land that even though it was a rural school, it had this ridiculously huge football stadium. *Huge*, but not super updated. The benches were wooden, and the scoreboard was rusty, but the view—faraway black pine trees that fell into sloping forests—was awesome. I guess football people didn't care about the view, much like how I didn't care about the game.

Drea and Dove and Brandy were waiting for me in the parking lot, and I made my way over to them as groups of people known and unknown to me meandered toward the benches, trailing clouds of breath in the chilly air. Regional students were decked out in scarves and school colors, and the faint scent of pot and cigarettes mixed with a hint of hidden alcohol on the breeze.

"My mom's sitting in there already," Drea said. "She was so confused about why I wanted to go to the football game, but I said I'm thinking of doing an article on the bad behabior of sports parents for the school paper."

"You actually made your mom come?" I asked.

"We need her as an alibi for you just in case," Dove said.

"You're going to do fine," Brandy said. She touched my shoulder for a second, and I leaned into it, feeling just a tiny bit reassured.

"Can we just go over the plan again?" I asked, trying not to sound too pathetic. We had already done this once before I dropped them off.

"Yes," Drea said. "You come sit with us and then get up to switch seats right after the kickoff. Mom thinks you're here for the whole game. That way we also get firsthand confirmation that Cameron and his parents are actually definitely here."

"Right," I said.

"You go to the Winships' house. Park far away. Then you break in through the back door, which is the kitchen door. It's a screen door in front of a farmhouse-style wooden door. Probably standard, with a regular lock plus a chain latch."

"And if they have an alarm?"

"They probably don't. Nothing happens here. But if they do, just bail. There are some . . . other . . . ways that we can get what we need from Cameron."

"Okay," I said, nodding. "Then what?"

"Then you go straight to his room and get some hair off a brush and grab a few things that could be 'treasured items.' Don't take eberything from the same place."

"Where the hell do I look for his treasured items?" It was an honest question. I had no idea what Cameron Winship could possibly treasure.

"Top drawer of a bureau, or a nightstand, or a jewelry box, or under the bed," Dove said.

"So then after you grab the personal stuff, get out of there," Drea said. "It shouldn't take you long, but if it does for some reason then we'll call his house from that payphone right over there when the game ends and let the phone ring *three* times before we hang up. That's your signal to get the hell out. Got it?"

"Got it," I said. "And we meet at Gate 22, right?"

That had been my choice. Gate 22 led to a path that ran alongside Calisher Creek, which was a good and secluded place where we could bury the two halves of our Cameron effigy with running water in between them.

"Right," Dove said as we walked into the stadium and the noise of the crowd went from a rumble to a roar.

I did the bit with showing myself to Jamie and left through the farthest exit right after the game started. Seeing Cameron running out onto the field in a black-and-silver #9 WINSHIP jersey that had always been a #9 ATTIA jersey made me almost sick with anger.

I channeled that anger into productivity and drove to the center of town. My orange car was too distinctive, so I parked it at Hazy Dee's and snuck through a half mile of Main Street backyards until I reached the Winships' looming white Victorian.

There were actually four locks. The screen door had one, and the farmhouse door had a surprise dead bolt. But it didn't matter. I could do absolutely no wrong. Pin-and-tumbler locks opened before the pick-and-tension wrench in my hands like a paperback in a windstorm.

I thought I heard a faint noise, the end of some longer sound, when I got into the kitchen. But it was gone before I could register it.

Unfortunately, the thing I *almost* heard was the phone ringing for a third and final time. Drea's warning call had come too soon, before I'd even made it into Casa del Winship.

But I had no idea. I relocked the doors behind myself, feeling the magic in my hands. Feeling unstoppable. My confidence carried me up the stairs as the Winship family drove home.

CHAPTER TWENTY-ONE

Monday, November 22, 1999

The Winships' house was big. Not as big as Dove and Bastion's house (and not even *close* to as big as Northcott House, where the Micenmacher family lived), but much taller and narrower. It was decorated pretty much exactly how I expected it would be: lots of black-and-white family portraits, perfectly matted and framed. Lots of tasteful old Oriental rugs. The faint smell of cinnamon and floor polish. Everything was immaculate. By now you've probably noticed that I have a thing for cool architecture, but this standard Queen Anne–style Victorian house did not particularly thrill me the way something like a Frank Lloyd Wright house would, for example. The only thing about the mayor's house that really intrigued me was the enormous octagonal turret that jutted out from the left side of the roof. Which, as it turned out, is where Cameron's bedroom was.

The Winships hadn't left any lights on when they went out, and I wasn't about to turn any on myself and announce to the whole nosy neighborhood that I was there. But they did have a lot of those fake flicker candles that people sometimes put up in their windows as winter decorations. I could see well enough by their glow to make my way upstairs, checking every bedroom as I went. Finally, on the third floor, I opened the door to the big turret room, and under the dome of the sloping ceiling, I saw a setup that definitely belonged to Cameron. I turned my flashlight on and went in, carefully pushing the door closed behind me and keeping the beam of light close to the ground.

Cameron's octagonal room was painted deep blue, and his unmade bed had sheets in the same shade. Heavy toile curtains, definitely picked out by his mom (or his mom's interior decorator) hung on the windows, but the rest was all him.

Douchey striped sweater thrown on the bed. Cowrie shell necklace on the bureau. A motivational sailing poster that said P E R S I S T E N C E on the wall, and another one with more sailboats advertising the Cape Cod Cup. A 1995 New England Patriots poster signed by . . . someone, I have no idea who. A desk. A television. A Nintendo 64, a Dreamcast, *and* a PlayStation. Judging from the case, he was in the middle of playing *Soulcalibur*, which Drea had told me was excellent.

"Okay," I whispered, moving carefully through the room. "Dove said to check the nightstand, top bureau drawer, under the bed."

Under the bed was empty. Like suspiciously empty, like the Winships had a cleaning service or something. I rifled the closet next, but it just looked like the Gap's warehouse. Nothing seemed, you know, special.

The nightstand had a bunch of receipts, a mini spiral note-book with phone numbers written in it, three pens, one broken Disney World keychain with *Cameron* on it in big bubble letters, three empty inhalers, contact lens solution, and a pair of glasses in a case.

"Cameron Winship actually has asthma. And wears glasses, who knew," I said. The glasses part was kind of funny, and some-thing he definitely hid religiously. Then I realized I was talk-ing out loud, probably because of how nervous I was, and made myself shut up.

But I already felt like I wasn't going to find something secret and precious to Cameron in here. There was a vibe about the way the house was, the way he kept his things. Like he had no privacy and no room for secrets.

Still, I hadn't risked arrest just to give up. I went to the bureau and grabbed the hairbrush sitting on top of it. It was loaded up with a mat of blond hair, and I shoved the entire brush into the deep inner pocket of my jacket and contemplated the cowrie shell necklace. Was it special to him? The way it was kind of thrown against his deodorant and his bottle of Polo Sport (ugh) made me think *no*. So I opened the top drawer of his bureau and found nothing but socks, boxer briefs . . .

. . . and my red Toad's Place hoodie, given to me by my mom, and lost in the workout room at Regional on October 30, 1997.

"What the hell?" I said.

I contemplated the sweatshirt for a minute, feeling very odd about finding one of my belongings here, in this terrible austere place. *Why would he take this?* I wondered. *Is it for some weird reason, like—*

My hands suddenly started to ache, and then I heard something.

It was laughter. Laughter that flapped and whispered like a length of silk that time was shredding into rotted nothingness.

It was coming from inside Cameron's closet, from somewhere in the darkness behind the doors I had shut seconds before.

I stopped breathing when I heard it. Oh Jesus, it was *right there* with me, it had been *right there* when I put my hands inside the closet, oh Jesus Christ, I almost *touched* it—

And then I heard voices in the house.

Human voices. The laughter from the closet stopped as abruptly as it had started. The ache in my hands vanished. But now I had *other* problems.

Shit shit shit, my brain buzzed. My heart, already pounding from the interlude with the thing in the closet, hammered even harder. I hadn't gotten any three-ring warning. I hadn't heard the Winships come back, thick as the well-made plaster walls of the old house were. I hadn't seen car headlights because I was on the opposite side of the house from the driveway. *Shit shit shit.*

I darted for one of the windows and gauged the drop. I could make it. Maybe a broken arm, but better than dealing with the cops. I tried to pry the window open, but it was so large and so stuck that it immediately shrieked and groaned as I tried to force it up. I dropped my hands and backed away.

The voices were closer. A light came on in the hallway outside of Cameron's bedroom.

"—don't know your own strength, it's like you got your body *yesterday*" came a deep and very irritated voice. The voice of Mayor Winship, back from the grave. "Your brothers all played through college and none of them have ever had *anything* like this happen! You deserve to be suspended from the team for a move that idiotic, that absolutely goddamned idiotic. I swear, Cameron—"

"No, I didn't mean to! No, it was a mistake! No, Dad, I swear—"

I was out of options, and they were almost to the door. I slid under the bed, turned off my flashlight, and pulled the comforter down to the ground with shaking hands to create a cave of concealment. I tried to breathe as quietly as possible, even though my heart was beating so hard it made my temples pulse. The door slammed open, and two sets of footsteps made vibrations along the wooden floor I was sprawled on. Light flooded the room, creating a glow around the edges of the comforter.

"Now I swear it was an accident, they can't suspend me for an accident!" Cameron said. He was yelling at his father, but he sounded more panicked than angry.

"You *stomped* on the DT's leg in front of everybody, you little *moron*," Mayor Winship snapped. He slammed the door *hard* behind them. I was just grateful that they were making enough noise to cover up the sound of the shallow breaths I was taking.

"No, I just, I just—"

"And why do you keep talking like that? For days now, starting every goddamn sentence with 'No' or 'Now'? It's infuriating, Cameron, I feel like you're doing it to infuriate me—"

"No, I'm—not! No, I just—"

"There you go doing it again," Mayor Winship said. He took a deep breath, so audibly that I could clearly hear it from under the bed, while Cameron sputtered. When the mayor started talking again, his deep voice was much quieter. More controlled.

"You are more talented than any of your brothers. You have a God-given *gift* for the sport. I believe that if it weren't for your . . . personal failings, you could even play professionally."

"No," Cameron said, still sounding pretty defiant. "No, Dad, I *am* going to—"

"You are not. You were suspended tonight for unsportsman-like behavior, for *conduct unbecoming*. Now VanBerkum will play in your stead, and we will lose this evening's game. The recruiters will hear about your behavior. You will *fail*."

I forgot to breathe quietly because I was so caught up in the conflict happening above my head. I'd always had a nasty feeling about Mayor Winship, but the raw contempt in his voice was more than I'd ever expected in my life.

"No, I won't *fail*," Cameron said. He was talking more quietly now. But his *dad*—his dad sounded exactly the way Cameron had sounded the first time I'd ever heard him speak to Dove. The day he'd called her a *stupid bitch* and I thought he was going to hit her. Mayor Winship sounded, at that moment, like he actually hated his son.

"You will. You will always fail, even with *all* your talent, because you are a *failure*. If Chase had your skill, or even Chris, we would be in a completely different situation."

Mayor Winship's voice was even. Measured. Almost *relaxed*. But dripping with contempt.

"As it is, I have to watch every bit of excellence I could ever hope for squandered by a weak, pathetic person. A person with-out patience, without manners, without good judgment."

I heard Cameron take a shaky breath. "No, Dad, I—"

"Quiet. I have done my *very* best with you, Cameron, but you remain uncivil. Unsubtle. Unintelligent. I shouldn't have to talk to you this way, but you force my hand. As you have so many times. I ask myself, often—*why* are you like this? Why? What could possibly have made you turn out like this? How have I done so poorly with you, when your brothers are all exemplary? Have I slipped? Or are you somehow *lesser*? Regardless, I am about done with your behavior. It hurts me badly to say this, but it is true: you are my biggest disappointment."

There was a weird hitching sound as Mayor Winship fell silent, and then I realized that Cameron was crying.

"We will discuss your punishment later," the mayor said, after a silence that felt like it lasted forever. "When you are ready to stop pitying yourself and talk through things with me like a man. Stay up here until you're composed. I don't want your mother to see you acting this way."

His footsteps were heavy on the floor as he walked away. The bedroom door creaked open.

"N-n-now . . . ," Cameron whispered, in a teary voice.

"Yes?" Mayor Winship said, from the doorway.

"Now you have no idea what I did for you, asshole!" Cameron said. He was clearly trying to yell, but his voice was too choked up with tears. "No, no, you're—you're such a fucking asshole, Dad, you know that? Now that I have *everything*, it still isn't good enough for y—"

Slap. Mayor Winship had crossed back into the room at lightning speed and, as far as I could hear, smacked his son right across the face. I heard Cameron suck in a shocked breath.

This may sound strange since I had just punched Cameron in the face about seven hours earlier, but I . . . I saw red. I forgot about my terror at the laughter in the closet. I forgot about self-preservation entirely, and before I could help myself, I had hauled ass right out into the room.

I think that father and son were both extremely thrown off by an entire person crawling out from under the bed. Cameron let out a yelp when he saw me and dropped his hand away from his face. He had a handprint across his cheek.

And a cut on his lip, but that one was from me.

"What the *hell* is going on!" Mayor Winship growled, looking me up and down with his hands curling into fists. I think he recognized me but couldn't actually remember my name.

"Nothing much, Mayor Dickbag," I said. My anger carried me like wings, and I put one finger directly on the mayor's chest. "I just came over to steal your son's hair. But I feel honored to have been graced with a little halftime special, as you jocks would say, about the dangers of child abuse."

"Nesbit?" Cameron asked in a tiny voice. "Nesbit, what are you doing here?"

"Stealing your hair," I said, without taking my eyes off the mayor. "I don't think your, um, constituents or whatever would take super kindly to you verbally *and* physically abusing your kid."

"Get out of my house or I will call the police," Mayor Winship said. He had spots of tomato-red high up on both his cheeks, but his voice was even.

"You don't know why he's *like* this? You're a *scumbag*, huh?" I said, pressing my finger a little harder into his chest. "Call them.

Call them so I can tell them I was a guest who witnessed a domestic dispute with the fucking *child-abusing* dickbag mayor! Call them, asshole!"

I was shouting in his face. Maybe my reaction was overblown. But Cameron had changed the world, and probably a good part of why the person I loved most had been erased was to impress *this* guy? This lousy excuse for a human being?

"GET OUT OF MY HOUSE!" Mayor Winship shouted, little drops of spit spraying from his mouth. He hadn't put his hands on me yet. But I wanted him to. So I could hit him. My hands vibrated with wanting it, and with magic that could make every punch I threw perfect and true.

"WHY DO YOU THINK HE'S LIKE THIS? WHY?" I screamed, matching his volume. "BECAUSE YOU FUCKING MADE HIM LIKE THIS!"

"NESBIT!" Cameron yelled, and grabbed my arm. I whirled around—I think I was about to punch Cameron in my rage—but the expression on his teary, blotchy face stopped me dead.

"Nesbit, please stop," Cameron said, in a voice that was so quiet that I *almost* couldn't hear the fear in it. "Now. Now, you have to stop now. Nesbit—his *heart* . . ."

It was like ice water all over me. I glanced back at the mayor and realized that he was probably one good punch away from *another* massive and fatal coronary.

"Um," I said, as all the wind was taken out of my rage sails. "Okay. I'm gonna go. See you . . . later, Cameron. Maybe have him chew an aspirin or something."

Then I shoved my way out of the bedroom and ran down the three staircases, past Mrs. Winship, who was in the process of coming up the stairs (probably on account of all the screaming), ignoring her shriek when she saw me, and then I was out the door, and then I was at Hazy Dee's, and then I was in my car, and then I was driving away.

I went to Gate 22 and told the girls—who were very worried about me since I hadn't gotten their warning call—about the failure of the plan. About everything that had happened.

Well, almost everything. I didn't tell them about the Toad's Place sweatshirt. It felt like a thing that was so insignificant and yet so bizarre . . . I really wasn't sure what to make of it. Maybe Cameron liked my sweatshirt. Maybe he swiped it to piss me off. Maybe he got confused and thought it was his. Maybe it meant nothing.

I had an inkling in the back of my mind, of course. About my Gym Buddy and his quiet desperation. About the look on his face the day he caught me kissing Bastion backstage.

But I put it out of my head. I couldn't think about why. I didn't want to think about why. I decided I didn't know what to make of it and left it at that.

I mean, I didn't know what to make of it until the first time we heard Cameron talk to Mr. Nous. Then it all became clear.

CHAPTER TWENTY-TWO

Tuesday, November 23, 1999

I was *very* suspicious of reality when I got up on Tuesday, but after some careful newspaper-checking and television-watching, I concluded that nothing else too major had changed. So far. Actually, I was grateful that I still existed and had woken up at all.

Nic avoided me in the morning, which was unusual, and I felt crappy about my stupid "Cameron Winship deals OxyContin lie" for the entirety of my drive to school.

School itself was also going to be extra dispiriting. As Dad had mentioned the day before, I was looking at five days of detention. That meant I had to serve one detention that very afternoon after the end of our half day, with the rest waiting for me after my second Thanksgiving break. I thought my sentence was light compared to Drea's, probably because Coach Silva had always liked me, but I didn't point out the unfairness to any authority figures.

Dove sidled up next to me in the student parking lot and slipped me a jar of salve like we were two cons passing drugs through cell bars.

"That should heal up the Nexus mark by the end of today," she said. "Old Tet said Mr. Nous shouldn't be able to listen in on us after that. I hope. I *especially* hope after it was watching you at Winship's house. Anyways, I charged it with snowflake obsidian and a bunch of tears last night."

I didn't comment on the fact that Dove had been crying again. For a whopping *third* time. I spent the night sitting at home beating myself up mentally for missing every clue about what Bastion was going through, plus jumping at every shadow like Mr. Nous was going to spring out of it and devour me. And of course, waiting for my imminent erasure from the universe via one of Cameron's evil Advocate wishes. Or for the mayor to call our house and tell my dad I was a burglar. It was probably a rough night for all of North Coven.

"Thanks," I said, rubbing some of the salve into my hands and wrists. It stank like pepper and grass and burned like hell on the N, and almost as badly on the raw mess I'd made of all my knuckles with my attack on the mausoleum. Dove was looking at my hands when I pulled my mechanic's gloves back on.

"Dude," she said. "Be careful with those puppies. We need the Hands of North Coven to be like, functional and still attached at the wrist."

"We need the Heart of North Coven to not be a shriveled black hole, but we're making do with you," I said, and she laughed.

"What did you get, anyway? I got five days of detention," I said.

"Same thing," Dove answered. "I also lost senior courtyard privileges until January, for being the instigator."

"I was thinking. What if Cameron is having a bad time being the Advocate?" I asked, floating a theory I'd been working on. "He already gave Mr. Nous his voice. Plus, he is obviously *not* good at 'navigating within the linguistic boundaries' like Bastion."

"That's because Cameron is a brainless puke pile," Dove said. "I don't think he's chosen the path of kindness, Nez. He's got Kim Palmer, head cheerleader and all-around hottie, on his arm. And a primo spot on the football team. And his *dad*."

That was a good point. But I didn't have time to tell her so, because as we walked through the main doors of Regional, I saw Herschel Micenmacher standing in the concourse like a coat rack enchanted into life, and Dove all but shoved me away in her sudden discombobulation.

I know I told you this before, but I was not exaggerating when I said that Herschel was a weird kid. As a person who is considered to be one of the weird kids, I want you to appreciate that I would not label someone as "weird" without due cause. Seeing Herschel at Regional was a little like getting a surprise visit from Ichabod Crane, if Ichabod Crane were a goth science genius who only came to your school for remedial English classes.

Herschel had boots so big and so covered in buckles that they rivaled Dove's. He wobbled on stick legs at an incredible height. His jaw was angular, his nose Roman. His acne was prolific. His dark blue hair was long and hung over his face. His glasses were pure "old man": huge, squarish prescription jobs that seemed designed to completely obscure his eyes. Dove looked at him like he was a god walking among mortals, and (though I couldn't actually make out *what* Herschel was looking at behind his giant frames) it seemed that he viewed her the same way.

"Dove," Herschel mumbled, with a level of awkwardness that would have made more sense if he was addressing a stranger on the subway, "I was hoping to see you today."

Dove recovered her composure, sort of. She gave me a quick look that said "fuck off away from here" pretty clearly, which I chose to ignore. Life had been devoid of anything fun for a while, and seeing Dove interact with her one weakness was always highly entertaining.

"H-hey, Hersch, I—have you met my best friend Nesbit? He was just leaving," Dove said, glaring at me.

"I don't believe so," Herschel muttered, waving one spidery hand at me. "Nice to—"

"We've actually met like six times," I said, and fist-bumped him heartily. I instantly regretted it. My hands were not in great shape for fist bumps. "Your sister dated my brother for a little bit."

"Ah," Herschel said, in a manner that told me he had no idea who I was or what I was talking about.

"Did you catch the Gilliam retrospective?" Dove asked.

"I saw it. Gilliam is God. I knew you'd be happy that they showed the correct cut of *Brazil*."

"Yeah, I was. This isn't, like, a day you normally have class here, is it?"

"No, it is not," Herschel said. "I'm heading over to the Amherst campus now. Um. I did want to stop by and formally invite you to our pre-Y2K party this Friday."

In the reality where Bastion had died, the Micenmachers' annual late November party had been canceled out of respect. Now, of course, it was back on the menu.

"I thought all of junior and senior year got invited," I said, and Herschel looked over at me with his brows knitted, like he had erased all memories of my existence for the seventh time.

"That's right . . . Nesbit," Herschel agreed. I guess I'd interrupted him in the process of re-forgetting my name. "And the freshman and sophomore years at Amherst. I just . . . um . . . wanted to invite Dove personally."

And then, I kid you not, he pulled out an invitation on thick dark paper, with silvery writing, and handed it to Dove. The handwriting definitely supported the remedial English classes thing. It looked like a five-year-old serial killer wrote it. I stared at them as Dove took it, her cheeks turning extremely pink.

"Come over, it should be . . . it should have music and costumes and things that make you happy," Herschel said like he was describing the activities of an alien species. "You should bring a date. I have to take my telescope out on Friday—the Leonids meteor shower on the eighteenth sucked majorly for viewing outside of Europe and the Middle East, so I have some extra observations I gotta make over the weekend. Clear skies permitting. But I wanted you to come and have fun."

Dove stepped closer to Herschel, turning the invitation over in her hand like it was worth its weight in solid gold.

"I'll try," she vowed. "Thanks. I can't explain this to you, at least not right now, but trust me when I say that I am dealing with a very . . . intense . . . personal crisis. Converging and diverging realities and crap. If I can make it, I will."

"I understand," Herschel said. I'm going to admit my jaw dropped a little at his total acceptance of a statement that sounded pretty batshit insane if you took it at face value. "Please, um, tell me if I can be of any help."

"I will, if you can," Dove promised, and then Herschel seemed like he was gathering up his courage. He took a breath, grabbed her free hand, and brought it to his lips for the briefest kiss. Dove's pink cheeks turned flaming crimson, and I actually looked away out of respect at that point. And also to keep myself from laughing.

"Later, Dove," Herschel said, and headed out the main doors like a street performer on stilts. I waited until he was outside to raise an eyebrow at Dove.

"Shut up," she growled, still red and totally refusing to meet my eyes.

"You guys are *soooooo cuuuute*," I said. "Dove Bar and Herschel's—"

"I swear to god, say that Herschel's-kiss thing again and I will feed you to Mr. Nous," Dove hissed, stomping toward the main hallway.

"So do you guys have, like, an open relationship or what?" I asked, matching her pace. "Did he ask you to bring a date to his party because he'll be busy, or because he's kinky? Does he want to watch?"

"I am going to *murder* you," Dove said.

"No more murders, please," Brandy chimed in. She was waiting for us by the Round Theater and fell in line with us as we walked up. "Any more changes today?"

"Nothing I noticed," I said. "Dove and Herschel are still in *wuv*. The pre-Y2K party is back on."

"I am going to admit that I don't really understand the appeal of Herschel Micenmacher," Brandy said, somewhat diplomatically.

"Good," Dove said edgily. "I mean, you"—she lowered her voice—"you are a *lesbian*, so I wouldn't expect you to—"

"I don't understand it either," I chimed in. "He is a *weird* guy. I don't think Drea gets it either, and she's bisexual," I added. Brandy covered her mouth with one hand to hide a laugh.

"Well, I don't understand the appeal of Drea! Or my *brother*!"

"She really speaks ill of the dead like that when you give her a hard time about Herschel," I said to Brandy. "Must be love."

"I thought it was *wuv*," Brandy said, a smile barely gracing her lips.

"Both of you can fuck off," Dove said.

"Not before I tell you Drea's updated plan," Brandy countered. "I think it's a good one. She called me this morning and I made some notes. Meet at the greenhouse after school?"

"Dove and I have detention," I said. "Did you get in trouble at all?"

"Of course not," Brandy said, wryly. "I didn't do anything."

Dove gave Brandy the spelled salve, and we arranged to meet after detention and instead go straight to Galactic Video, where Drea had picked up some shifts during her suspension.

The short day ended at noon, and Mrs. Jonshade was so obviously dying to start her own vacation that detention hall was a total joke. We were released after twenty-eight minutes, met Brandy at the doors, and joined the tide of faculty members and late-leaving students that spilled out into the crisp day, ran to the late bus or their cars, and talked animatedly the way people always talk before a holiday break. There was such a sense of joviality in the wintry air. It made me feel far removed from everyone, from all of these people who had no idea that Bastion had ever lived.

Cameron had missed school.

"I wonder if he's sick," Brandy said as we climbed into the Hyundai. Dove and I shook our heads at the same time.

"No way," Dove said. "He's a scared little slime right now. He knows we know about him and Mr. Nous, or at least he knows we know *something*. After Nesbit showed up to freak him out, I bet he's terrified of what we'll do next."

Dove looked kind of gleeful about Cameron's imagined fear. But Brandy did not.

"Maybe when his father hit him it left a mark," Brandy said, "and that's why he had to stay home."

Brandy knew all about things like that.

Dove groaned and made a face in response. "Why do you have to say things that make me feel bad for *Winship*? You guys are not the same."

"We both have an abusive parent," Brandy said. "I'm just pointing it out."

"Yeah, but the quality of your character means that *you* broke that cycle of abuse and aren't a fucking bullying elitist puke to everyone you come into contact with," Dove said.

"I don't know if that has anything to do with character," Brandy said. "I have people who love me and helped me."

"Well, I agree that Cameron has nobody who loves him," Dove muttered. I couldn't help but laugh at her sullen face. She *really* didn't want to feel bad for Cameron.

"I'm really worried that he's going to make a wish that will seriously screw us over," I said.

"Me too," Dove said.

"That's what Drea has been thinking about," Brandy said. "I think she found an alternative way to do the binding spell."

Dove brought her binder of CDs (smaller than Drea's, but still impressive) and played L7 on the way to Galactic Video. We pulled up at the end of "Pretend We're Dead" and went inside. The screens at the back of the store were playing a Thanksgiving-themed *Garfield* special at a low volume, and Drea rang a couple out up front while explaining to someone on the phone that the tape of *Planes, Trains, and Automobiles* was definitely already rented out. As soon as she had a minute, we crowded around the counter.

"You look better," I said. It was even kind of true. The bandage was off, but Drea had a cut on the bridge of her swollen nose and yellow-blue bruises under both her eyes.

"Yeah. I can talk again, too," Drea said, in an almost normal voice. "I feel bad for yelling at Mrs. Bledsoe now. She's a sensitive soul."

Brandy glanced around to confirm we were alone and then stroked her fingertips against Drea's cheek. "Poor you," she said, and Drea sighed in a way that was definitely meant to evoke extra sympathy.

"I'll be okay, babe," Drea said, in a long-suffering-but-brave manner. Dove snorted, but Brandy was clearly totally taken in.

"You had some news?" Dove said, tearing open a box of Milk Duds.

She got quiet when the bells on the glass door tinkled, and Mr. Howard from Biology came in, totally ignored all of us, and made a beeline for the Red Room of Porn at the back of the shop.

"Oh, puke city," Dove whispered, which made me snicker.

"I gotta respect him, actually; it's always stuff with foxy older ladies and a decent plot. Never like barely legal shit," Drea said. "On the way out he'll get a new rom-com, too."

"Wow, what a guy," Dove said.

"Whatever. Like you've never looked up porn in your family's computer room."

"I can't, there isn't a *door* to that room, just a stupid arched entrance," Dove said, which made me snicker again.

"So there is another way that we can do the binding spell on Cameron. I copied down the main version of the spell and the version with substitutions into the book last night," Drea said, producing North Coven's grimoire from behind the counter. In lieu of—" Drea broke off as Mr. Howard came up with a tape I couldn't make out the title of, grabbed *The Wedding Singer*, and got rung out for both by Drea while pretending that the rest of us didn't exist.

"So we still need Cameron's hair, which we have," Drea continued, when Mr. Howard was gone. "Thanks to Nez's skills. But in lieu of a treasured item, we have to use saliva, blood, or semen."

"*His* semen?" Dove asked, wrinkling her nose. "Ew."

"Or his blood, or his saliva," Drea said. "We'll just get him to spit on you. Shouldn't be hard."

"We'll have to think of something," Brandy said. "The longer this goes on, the more damage he can do."

"I've been thinking about it all day, babe," Drea said. "When is the earliest we can see him again? Without more breaking and entering?"

"The Micenmachers' Y2K party?" I said. "Probably? So Friday."

"Oh, right. That's happening again," Drea said. "You think he'll go?"

"Everyone goes," Dove said. "Especially if they're shallow pukes who want to be seen at the cool party."

"Herschel stopped by Regional to give Dove her own *special* invitation today," I said.

"Shut *up*," Dove said, and dug the magic tear-infused salve out of her tiny backpack. Probably to change the subject. But once she explained the purpose, Drea held up her wrists to show that they were unblemished, with no sign of the Nexus mark anywhere.

"I did a charmed bath on it last night," Drea said. "Moonflower and tears."

"Good. Guys, check yours," Dove commanded, and Brandy and I rolled our sleeves up to reveal unblemished wrists.

"Jesus," I said, quietly, and all three of them looked at me.

"What?" Drea asked.

"Just like, you guys are really like . . . effective witches," I said.

"Um, you too, buddy," Drea said, raising an eyebrow. "Pretty sure that was already a known thing?"

"I know what he means," Brandy said. "We both started as skeptics. Then we believed that we were changing all kinds of things for the better. And then, in the Vision Thing, Mr. Nous told Bastion our power was *real*, but it just wasn't strong *enough*. And yet in the past few days—between actually *casting* the Vision Thing, and this—"

"Yeah. Somehow it went from 'I'm worried we have no powers without Bastion' to 'we have more powers than ever before,'" I said.

I thought of the nightmare I'd had after we found Bastion dead in Stepwood. His pleading voice, whispering to me through the grilles of shiny old hearses in an endless showroom.

"Nesbit, you have the power now. Not just you—it's for all five of you, of course—but you have the dreams—"

"Well, it's a good time to get proficient," Dove said, dismissing our speculation.

"I'm going to come up with a new plan," Drea said. "Centering around the acquisition of the alternate spell components."

"And I'm going to throw up!" Dove said, with a lot of fake enthusiasm.

"For real. Give me a day to think about it. We can meet up, like, tomorrow or—"

"Thanksgiving night," Dove said. "After family stuff. You know Anna loves to have all her writer friends over for their anti-Thanksgiving brunch. And she'll definitely host it this year, since she forgot that her kid was just eaten."

"Ugh," I said. "Your mom's parties sound so boring."

"Bastion loved them, because he was a dumbass," Dove said, with affectionate sadness. "Last year he was totally riveted by Doug Attaquin's mimosa-fueled lecture on the literary establishment's anti–Native American reactions to Longfellow's publication of *The Song of Hiawatha* in 1855. I mean, he was riveted for like the first thirty minutes, after that I think even *he* tuned out."

"Yeah," I said. I'd had to hear all about that particular lecture from Bastion. It was awful. But I would literally sit through a recap of it again, just to talk to him one more time.

"Anyways, I told Jules I would go visit him afterward and bring him some anti-Thanksgiving dinner. Let's meet up then and see if we can come up with a coherent plan."

"Deal," I said.

"Deal," Drea said.

"Agreed," Brandy said.

When I went home, Nic was already shut up in the Winnebago. The house felt lonely. Or maybe I was just lonely. So I took a drive to Gate 43 and sat in the dirt parking lot, thinking about my last fight with Bastion. After a while, I gave in and put the radio back on WJIN.

"Hey, Big Fun," I said to the empty car. "Why didn't you tell us what was happening to you?"

But of course Bastion didn't answer. Couldn't answer. And sitting there felt like wallowing. So I drove back home in the dark, and hoped that Cameron wouldn't wipe us out of the universe before we could acquire his bodily fluids and/or excretions. Which was the weirdest thing to worry about, probably, of all time.

CHAPTER TWENTY-THREE

Thursday, November 25,
& a few minutes of Friday, November 26, 1999

Thanksgiving was not so different in my house whether or not (as far as Nic and Dad knew) my boyfriend had died a few days earlier. The weather wasn't enchanted: it was still medium cold and sunny, with hardly a breeze stirring the dying brown landscape. My mom still called, and I still talked to her and to Ted and to my little sisters, and Nic still refused to talk to her at all. We still got takeout from Crescent Moon (for a magnificent *second* time in four days, and this time I actually ate some) because all three of us thought traditional Thanksgiving food was moderately gross. The major differences were in what *I* did. Instead of feeling only a numb emptiness, I felt all keyed up and hyperaware of time passing, until Dove finally called me and said she had extricated herself from her family's festivities. Then I headed out into the dark, to the place where Old Tet made camp.

When I got to the remains of the old train station, I found out that Dove had brought a ton of anti-Thanksgiving food for everyone. And a carton of smokes for Old Tet. We drank white wine she'd swiped from the brunch and filled in Old Tet on everything. And eventually we got down to discussing our new action plan.

"This is what we're gonna have to do," Drea said. She'd had a *lot* of wine by then and was slurring a little. She gestured elaborately with a cigarette she'd bummed off Dove that she kept forgetting about and having to relight.

"Enlighten us, dear," Brandy said.

"Not *you*. Dove. It's what Dove's gonna have to do to be able to bind him."

On the opposite side of the bonfire, Dove was sitting on a pine stump with her legs crossed. "Tell me, O Drunken Oracle," she commanded.

"You're gonna have to sleep with Cameron W-Winship and steal his cum," Drea said.

"Quite a way to talk, kiddo," Old Tet said. Dove snorted in what I can only imagine was disbelief.

"Semen, ejaculate, spunk, jizz, whatever," Drea said, flailing her cigarette-holding-arm even more wildly. "I need it for the spell. I need something besides hair."

"And why the hell do you think that Cameron and I would ever sleep together?" Dove asked. "We literally hate each other."

I nodded in agreement, patting Elizabeth the beagle in rhythm to my nods.

"I know *you* hate *him*," Drea said. "It's not about that."

"He is also dating Kim Palmer," Dove said. "So even if he didn't despise me, he has someone *very* gorgeous to screw."

"Kim gives off major virgin vibes," Drea said. "And while . . . while, um, you hate Cameron, I firmly think and have *alllllways* thought he was obsessed with you. Think about it, guys. He has insane hate-lust for Dove. And preps always want goth chicks, it's like a known fact."

"Hmmm. You may actually have a point," I conceded. "There could be some unresolved sexual tension there. He *really* goes after Dove at every opportunity."

"That's fucked," Dove said, stabbing a finger at the fire for emphasis. "That's not how you should treat someone you're attracted to."

"I literally swear to god that if you make a pass at him during the Y2K party he will go upstairs with you," Drea said. "Swear to god. Plus, it's not, like, all bad. He's so pretty."

"Pretty? Ew! What the *hell*, Drea?" Dove said.

"I also object to that sentiment," Brandy said, arching an eyebrow.

"Listen. Listen," Drea said, smiling at Brandy. "I am drawn to beauty like a moth to . . . beauty. And you and Cameron are the most beautiful things at Regional."

"Can't believe you forgot about Herschel Micenmacher like that," I said, and Dove reached down and flicked me on the shoulder.

"I know Cameron has the worst personality ever," Drea plowed on, ignoring us. "And is a thief of Bastion's accomplishments or whatever. It totally undermines his beauty. But I am a *connoisseur* of beauty. On the most shallow, uh, purely visual level . . . he's got the goods."

"Yuck," Dove said.

"Seconded," Brandy said.

"I don't think you should be offering your friend up as some kind of sexual sacrifice to the Advocate," Old Tet said, a bit admonishingly.

"Seconded," I said.

"Thirded," Dove said. "But . . . it is worth a shot. I could get him alone and seduce him, then either blow him and not swallow or scratch the fuck out of him and get some blood. Or steal that cell phone, which is apparently the only thing he *cherishes*."

"You kids really grow up a lot quicker than we did in my day," Old Tet said, looking a bit taken aback. Or at least I thought he looked taken aback under his giant beard.

"The thing is, Mr. T, is that Dove likes sex," Drea said, waving her hands around again. "And she doesn't, uh, attach a lot of . . . *importance* . . . importance to it. So it's a good bet that she would be down to do it with a guy she hates in order to save the . . . world?"

"The town," Brandy clarified. "Or maybe just our own lives. And Bastion's memory."

"I'm just saying," Old Tet said, addressing Dove. "You shouldn't feel pressured into this sex magic stuff, kiddo."

"I follow you, Jules," Dove said. "I don't capitulate to pressure that easily. But this might be a decent plan. He's probably been pining away for me."

"I just don't *see* it like that," Brandy said. "Sorry, Drea."

"I *do* see it like that, Miss Eyes," Drea said. "I know I'm right about this."

"I could see it," I agreed.

"I think I could too," Dove said. "I guess we're going to that party."

"*Herschel's party*," Drea and I said at almost the same moment in almost the same simpering tone, which made both of us laugh a lot.

"Anyways," Dove said. "I would do more than that. For Bastion, you know."

For a minute we all got quiet and looked at the fire.

So would I, I wanted to say. But they knew it. We were all on the same page. It wasn't just for us, to save ourselves. It was also for him.

So with the party-attending-and-seduction plan agreed upon, Dove bailed around eleven, taking Drea and Brandy with her. Then it was just me, Old Tet, Elizabeth, and Old Tet's half-finished bottle of Smirnoff.

Instead of leaving right when the girls did, I hung around for a few and contemplated the bonfire. Above our heads, the pines parted around what had once been train tracks. The sky was so bright with stars away from the fire glow that I thought I could almost make out the arm of the Milky Way, though not as vividly as I could when North Coven went to the Near-Depths.

"It's really peaceful out here," I said, after a minute. "What do you do in the snow, though?"

Old Tet shrugged and stubbed out his cigarette. "The same. As long as we keep the fire going, we're all right. A few times during the deep freezes I had Dolores—from the diner—take Elizabeth overnight. She's not bound to survive no matter the weather, unlike me."

"Do you . . . think you can't die?" I asked. "Are you cursed to live here forever?"

"I'm not sure, kiddo," Tet said. "I know that what I've lived through . . . and what I've put my goddamned body through . . . should've been enough to kill me. And I know for certain that I can't leave."

"What happens when you try to leave?" I asked.

"I can show you if you want. But don't you have to be heading home?" Tet said. "It's late, you know."

It was after eleven, and as you may recall, eleven was pretty much my standard curfew time. Until now I had always obeyed it. But I just . . . I couldn't bring myself to care about curfews or my dad being mad at me. What mattered at all, in a world where Mr. Nous existed and Bastion didn't?

It was so easy to see how Jules Kermit Tethonius, historian, had become Old Tet, homeless town drunk. Not just because he was forced to be by magic. Because nihilism felt like the appropriate response to a universe that let evil go unchecked this way. Where nothing had stability or permanence. Where not even entropy was guaranteed.

"Yeah. Show me, please," I said.

"We gotta walk a ways into the woods. If we follow the old Rabbit Line, we come to the place where North Dana ends. About a quarter-mile up that way."

"Okay," I said.

"You want to take my shotgun?" Tet asked, gesturing to the antique resting against the tent. "You'll be alone for the walk back."

I didn't like the sound of that, but I liked my chances with the grimy old gun even less.

"I'm good," I said.

Old Tet bent his massive body down to kiss Elizabeth on the head and she sighed contentedly and rolled over without waking up all the way. Then he led me away from the warmth of the fire.

"I do this pretty often," Tet said. "Just to check."

The woods, as we headed toward the Quabbin and away from civilization, were dark and unforgiving. It was cold, and my fingerless gloves were doing me no favors. I hunched deep into my Nuñez Auto Body coat, my hands shoved deep into my pockets, and followed Old Tet as he picked his way along the path, stepping over fallen branches and around stones and divots in the earth with the grace of a person who has walked the same road a thousand times. Then the moon came out again, and it lit the sky brilliantly. I felt like I was looking up from the bottom of an abyss, a crack in the trees my only glimpse out of the depths. The moon made the arm of the Milky Way disappear, but I could still see so many stars that it seemed like there were more points of light than patches of darkness. Somewhere to our left, an owl hooted every minute or so: *hoo-h'HOO-hoo-hoo.*

Neither of us talked, and the only sound besides our friend the owl was the crunching of dead leaves underfoot. I thought about how it reminded me of the walk I had seen twice now. The walk through Northcott Faire to the tent where Mr. Nous waited.

"Mr. T?" I asked, feeling thoroughly creeped out.

"Right up here, kiddo," Tet said, and pointed to a spot on the trail that had a line of little stones across it. "I marked that off ages ago. It's the town line. Well, one of 'em. We'll walk side by side across it, yeah?"

"Yeah, sure," I said. I didn't like the look of the little line of rocks in the moonlight. In fact, I was kind of wondering why I had wanted to do this in the first place.

"Meet me back at my camp," Tet said, right as we stepped over the stones. I turned my head to ask what he meant and saw nobody.

Old Tet was gone.

I was alone in the dark and quiet forest. The owl had gone silent. And the worst part was that I imagined . . . I imagined that I *almost* had an impression of some long, long arms and red-gloved hands dropping out of the treetops like spiders to lift old Tet away into the darkness. I swore under my breath about my own stupidity at leaving my flashlight in my car. Then I turned around and jogged back to the camp as quickly as I could in the moonlight, looking over my shoulder into the woods every few minutes.

When I saw the glow of the bonfire I felt better. Old Tet was sitting on the stump in front of the fire, and Elizabeth ran trotting over to greet me, bleating out one old-lady bark as she came up with her tail wagging.

"Good girl, Lizzie," I said, and reached down to scratch her ears.

"You see what I mean, kiddo?" Old Tet said, taking a long swig of Smirnoff. "I just can't leave."

"I get you," I said, rubbing my hands in front of the fire. "Thanks for showing me."

"You should go on home. I expect it's after midnight, and on a family holiday," Tet said. Then he looked up at me. Even behind the age and the hard living and the fog of liquor, I could see the intelligence in his eyes. Tet really took a minute to study me for maybe the first time ever, and I let him scrutinize me.

"Yeah, I'll head out," I said, after a pause. But he held up a hand.

"Good. Good kid. You're . . . Nez, right? Nesbit?"

"Yes sir," I said, slipping into addressing him like he was an authority figure. He seemed authoritative suddenly.

"He really cared for you, Nesbit. I think he would've done just about anything for you."

"Bastion?" I asked, trying not to give anything away with my tone.

"Yeah. Now, listen, kiddo, I'm gonna tell you something. You may not want to listen to me because I'm old. The young never want to listen to the old. But I think you might understand that I have a little perspective on your situation."

"I mean, yeah, of course."

"I don't understand *all* of your situation. It's gotta be tough to be . . . the world, even now, isn't really socially where it should be. I remember the Summer of Love, you know. That was thirty years ago. We were all starry-eyed hippies who thought everything was about to change."

"Right," I said, not sure at all where he was going.

"But social progress marches on, albeit slower than I'd like," Old Tet said, lighting another cigarette. He offered it to me, and I shook my head no. "It always does. You'll be an adult in a world that gets easier to live in all the time. You won't be so . . . persecuted. What I'm trying to say, kiddo, is that Bastion was a really special kid, but he wasn't your only shot at ever finding love. I'm sure in a small town like this it could feel that way."

"Um, okay," I said. I did *not* think Old Tet was going to talk to me about my sexuality. It was kind of mortifying. I definitely felt my face get hot.

"And," Old Tet went on, "I don't want you to get tangled up in this for love. Now, his sister, I wouldn't even try to say this to her. That girl is *iron*. She's gonna go after Mr. Nous until the bitter end and probably meet one of the many bad fates people meet by getting involved with it."

"I'm in it too," I said. "To the end."

"I respect that, I do," Old Tet said. And, to his credit, he sounded like he *did* respect it. "But I couldn't have a clear conscience if I didn't tell you this. I thought my love for Lenore was enough to fight it. That love made me strong. That I could . . . help or something. But I couldn't help. My love meant nothing. Mr. Nous is more powerful than love. It eats love. And it'll toy with you and wound you and maybe kill you if you stay in North Dana. If you were my kid, I'd make you leave town right now, tonight."

"Thank you for telling me," I said. "I can't go, though."

"Why not?"

"I . . ." I really thought about it. Tet looked me right in the eyes, and it felt like an important question to answer correctly. "I can't leave my brother and my dad in a town with this thing. And I can't leave my coven. And . . . I can't even leave Cameron, that dickbag who's the Advocate now. He doesn't deserve this either. And most of all, I guess—I guess I can't live in a world where Bastion never existed."

"Kiddo," Old Tet said. "You are living in that world right now. Whether or not you fight it, you're already here."

Then he got up and whistled to Elizabeth and they went into his tent. I waved good night and walked back to my car. I thought about Lenore's last message: *I'm sorry, J. I love you.*

I wondered what Bastion would've said to me if he'd had the chance.

I wondered what had happened after our fight. Between him and Mr. Nous.

And I wondered if, when I looked at Old Tet, I was looking at the kind of future I was doomed to have.

CHAPTER TWENTY-FOUR

Friday, November 26, 1999

Herschel was a totally bizarre dude, but his parties were unmatched by anything anywhere. Actually, that was probably his sister's doing.

So Mr. and Mrs. Micenmacher were the richest people in North Dana. Maybe in the whole county. I don't know how they got rich, I have no idea what they did for jobs or anything. But they lived in a mansion on the opposite side of Stepwood from Drea's trailer park, down a long driveway and through acres and acres of deep dark forest. Northcott House was so far out in the woods that it basically overlooked the Quabbin. It was the only estate around, connected to the rest of the town only by the path that led from the mansion's grounds into Stepwood Cemetery. The backyard was a long field that met super-tall pine trees in a severe line. When you walked all the way out to the trees, you realized that you were actually at the edge of a vast drop-off that fell straight into the still waters of the reservoir.

I knew this because I'd snuck off with Bastion to find a discreet outdoor place to have sex during the spring party of 1999, and we had almost gone plummeting into the water. (The spring party was Bacchanalia-themed, everyone wore togas. Bastion looked really good in a toga.)

The Micenmachers went on two vacations abroad every single year to visit family, and when Herschel's older sister Rebekah had turned eighteen the kids had opted out of vacationing and stayed home in Northcott House. That was how the Micenmacher parties came to be. They threw a late-spring party and a late-fall party every year like clockwork.

Everybody from Regional within the invited grade range came. Every invited student from Amherst College (where Herschel took most of his classes) and Smith (where Rebekah went) came, too. The parties could top four hundred people, and because Northcott House was so far away from everything, the cops never came to break it up, even though all kinds of illegal crap went down.

I picked up the girls at eight sharp. They were all at Dove's getting ready, and going past the Osiris statue and into the Attia house was one of the hardest things I had done so far.

There were no pictures of Bastion in the scattering of framed candids that the Attias had incorporated into their funky decor. No stupid black-and-silver letterman jacket hanging on the Eames coat rack. No mobiles adorning the stairwell from the Alexander Calder phase Bastion went through in the seventh grade. I knew his bedroom was gone, and I didn't want to think about that any more than was absolutely necessary, so I stayed downstairs and waited for the rest of my coven to meet me.

"Nez!" Dove called, and strutted down the stairwell like a runway model. In the spring we'd all gone to see *The Matrix* at the Evening Star Drive-In, and Drea and I liked it so much that we'd seen it three more times. So I instantly recognized that Dove was doing a "Trinity in the club" look: a black pleather corset top that bared her shoulders over an equally shiny and utterly microscopic miniskirt. Her boots were so tall that she was almost average height. Her hair was slicked back tightly to her skull, and she wore no jewelry at all—no accessories, in fact—except for her tiny, tinted sunglasses.

"What do the advance reviews say?" she asked me, twirling on the last step.

"They say you look extremely cool," I said. "Would you call Herschel your own personal Neo?"

"Oh my god, shut *up*," Dove said, with a highly dramatic groan. "You suck *so* badly and so intensely. Brandy! Do your reveal!"

Brandy came down the stairs with an expression that said she thought the fashion show was a little bit much, which was funny, because she was pretty brilliant when it came to making and altering her own clothes. She just wasn't so keen on being the center of attention.

Of course Brandy's outfit was the coolest one. Her hair was done up in Bantu knots with flecks of gold twined into the little buns. Her dress didn't really scream "Year 2000": it was just a typical black sheath dress that you could imagine someone wearing to a cocktail party. But as she got closer, I saw that she had little charms that looked like golden scarab beetles all over her. They were fixed onto her dress, tucked into her hair, and looped onto her bare arms with golden wire.

"I'm the Millennium Bug," Brandy said.

"You look awesome," I said.

"She spent like an hour hot-gluing those plastic beetles onto her dress," Dove said. "If Cameron doesn't go for me, he'll definitely go for her, she's a total dime."

"Oh, Lord. I would sooner be eaten by Mr. Nous. I will *never* touch Cameron Winship, not to save the universe and not if I lived a thousand years," Brandy said, and I could tell she meant it.

"Drea!" Dove said, and Drea came down the stairs in . . . her JNCO jeans and oversized black hoodie.

"Wow, a real departure for you fashion-wise," I said.

"Eat me, dude who is wearing the same jacket-and-hoodie-and-jeans combo he wears every day," Drea said.

"Okay, that's fair," I said.

"We had her in a cool bustier thing for like five minutes before she ripped it off," Dove said, sadly. "That one Brandy found for her at the Salvation Army, remember?"

I did not remember. I normally didn't go on thrift store trips with them unless I needed pieces for a woodworking project. Then it was sometimes cheaper to buy old crappy furniture than it was to just buy wood.

"I'm not putting my enormous tits out on display at a Micenmacher party. They are for Brandy's eyes only," Drea said, waggling her eyebrows suggestively.

"I am a lucky woman," Brandy said, with the slightest smile.

So I drove to the party with my beautiful friends. I guess we *could* have parked at Drea's and just walked the path that led from Stepwood over to Northcott House, but for obvious reasons none of us wanted to walk through Stepwood Cemetery if we could help it. When we got there, we were greeted by silver balloons tied to the mailbox, and a traffic jam a mile long going up to the estate. And when we finally rolled out of the tree-lined driveway and the house came into view, looming at the top of the field like a painting of darkness, it gave me a chill like it always did.

The architecture nerd in me was completely obsessed with Northcott House way before I knew it was connected to a monster. The estate grounds, with the sunken gardens and the free-standing statue-lined solarium, were cool enough. But the house itself was *awesome.*

I had read as much as I could about Northcott House after seeing it for the first time. The things I knew could probably fill a decent-sized book (about a haunted house, of course), but just to give you a sample:

When the Northcott family first settled on the edge of the Swift River Valley, all they built on this land was a humble farmhouse.

The mansion came later. It took six years to construct. It was stripped to beams twice, given a new layer of stones, turrets modified. Painted black as a void. Family fights during construction. Finally completed in 1847.

The plans were lost. The stables burned in 1859. Eleven horses and one stable boy, Alsey Coyle, perished in those flames. The stables rose again the year after. It was the final project overseen by the Northcott family.

1861. Alice Northcott, the last member of the family, disappeared.

And so on and so forth until the Micenmacher family bought it in the eighties to raise their weird-ass kids in. Actually, that's not fair. Rebekah seemed pretty cool.

Of course, in all my learning about Northcott House, I had never heard a whisper about Mr. Nous. Now it all seemed like a totally different picture. It wasn't just some funky old mansion plagued by misfortune and a miserable rich family. All the stories took on a new light. Old Tet had said that the Northcotts were always the Advocates, until they lost the mausoleum key. Had Mr. Nous haunted them for centuries? Longer? Did it *make* them build Stepwood, somehow? Were their misfortunes caused by wishes? Was their money gotten the same way? Was Alice Northcott down there in the carnival now—nothing but a painted person, her soul trapped forever?

I had to think yes, and yes, and yes.

So we pulled up onto the lawn of the creepiest mansion in New England, and I squeezed the Hyundai in between a minivan and an old wood-paneled station wagon that belonged to Rob Malone.

The massive main doors of the house were thrown open to the freezing night, and space heaters on extension cords, plus a bunch of hidden fog machines, created an opaque wall of warmth and mist that you had to walk through blind. It didn't break until we were inside the foyer, and then the party spread out all around us like a banquet.

The giant staircase that spiraled down into the center of the foyer was covered in silver balloons and paper streamers. The floor was a mess of glitter and party favors: noisemakers, plastic eyeglasses that were shaped like the year 2000, discarded Solo cups, and the detritus of a party that had been going on for days. In reality, it couldn't have been more than two hours since people started showing up, but Micenmacher parties were for partying *hard*.

"We should find Cameron ASAP," Dove yelled, over the music that filled every room, and I nodded and stayed close to her as she started weaving through the crowd.

The ballroom—yes, the *ballroom*—seemed to be the epicenter of the party. A DJ spun popular dance songs I hated into something faster and cooler-sounding at the back of the room. Glowsticks and blacklights gave the only illumination once you stepped through the arched entranceway. Silver balloons covered every inch of the floor that wasn't occupied by humans. People danced really close together in the almost-total darkness, wearing ridiculous "futuristic" outfits. I saw someone in a full-on alien costume vogueing with four Regional cheerleaders, and Brandy shook off the advances of a college dude in a silver jumpsuit without even slowing her stride. Drea had gotten booze from one of the overloaded tables of food and drinks and handed the cup off to Dove after having a sip.

"You're gonna need this for the Cameron Encounter," Drea yelled.

"I would never need alcohol to seduce a worthless man for my own purposes!" Dove yelled back, but then she grinned and chugged it anyway.

"I hope he's here and not out in Stepwood making more wishes," Brandy said.

"I agree," I told her.

"Let's split up and look for him," Drea said. "We meet in the kitchen in fifteen minutes, yes?"

It was a yes from all of us. I used the old servant's staircase to go up to the second floor. Up there the volume of the music was slightly quieter, and people were using the many, *many* bedrooms for a few different things—sex, drugs, or those intimate conversations that spring up between the unlikeliest groups of people at parties.

I didn't know what I would say if I found Cameron first. I'd avoided getting into more trouble since the detention debacle with Coach Silva. Mayor Winship hadn't called my dad to rat me out as a trespasser. I wondered if it was because I'd caught him smacking his son. Probably. And I hadn't been busted for coming in after curfew, either. Nic was in the Winnebago with the lights off by the time I got home and crept in through the back door, and my dad, who was used to me obeying the eleven p.m. rule, hadn't stayed up to make sure I did as I was told.

I walked along the corridor until I reached a balcony area where I could look down into the library. There was music in there, too, but much quieter, and guests talked and drank in little groups on the velvety chairs and extra-long couches. A projection screen was showing a movie on mute . . . it took me a minute to realize it was *2001: A Space Odyssey*.

Then I spotted Cameron. He was down in the corner with a posse of jocks and their girlfriends. Kim Palmer was next to him, which kind of cramped the seduction-via-Dove angle. I hurried down to the kitchen and waited for the girls.

"Okay," said Drea, when I told her where Cameron was. "Easy enough. Nez, you tell him to meet you in—"

"Herschel's room," Dove said. "He's out with his telescope. It's the third floor, third door to the right, with the wolf's-head door knocker."

"You want to have sex with Cameron in your boyfriend's *room*?" Drea asked.

"He's not my boyfriend," Dove said. "And I'm probably just going to make out with Cameron until he's distracted and then scratch the shit out of him. Or swipe his cell phone."

"Why will he agree to meet me, exactly?" I asked.

"Tell him you're sorry about what you did and that you want to give him back what you stole," Dove said.

"Why don't *you* ask him to meet you?" I countered.

"Uh, he's not going to meet me if I go up and ask him in front of his new girlfriend," Dove said.

"Okay," Drea said. "We'll wait right down the hall from Herschel's room and help you book it out of there once you get what you need."

"I don't feel like this is going to be a grand success," Brandy said.

"We *know*," Drea said. "Babe. Just relax."

They went up to the third floor and I went to the library. Cameron was still surrounded by people, and I waited until Kim Palmer looked up at me. I waved and pointed to Cameron, mouthing, *Can I talk to him?* Kim nodded and whispered something to Cameron while he bumped his Solo cup against Dylan Everett's.

Cameron looked over at me, and, to my surprise, got up immediately. He and his ironed cargo pants came over to the corner where I was leaning against the bookshelf. On the projection screen, the camera showed the ominous dome of HAL 9000's single eye . . . and the little bit of gold chain I could see around Cameron's neck glinted in the light.

"Nesbit, what is it?" Cameron asked, all businesslike.

Maybe it wasn't *all* businesslike, actually. That was a front. Cameron doing his Cameron Winship thing. Maybe there was some kind of layered emotion there. I almost thought I could see it a little, in his eyes.

On some level, despite whatever shitty decisions he'd made, Cameron had to be afraid. He'd seen what happened to Bastion— he'd gotten a better look than I had, even. And what I'd seen was bad enough that it was seared into my brain forever.

And he wasn't screaming and shouting at me about the fact that I had broken into his house. Which was weird.

"Nesbit, did you call me over so you could have a good long *think* to yourself?" Cameron asked, when I didn't say anything right away.

"Yeah, no, sorry," I said.

I was so used to hearing my name start off a sentence when . . . when someone's voice belonged to Mr. Nous. It felt familiar and weird at the same time.

We can help you, I wanted to say.

But it wasn't true. We couldn't even help Bastion.

"I think we should talk about the other night. Um, I wanted to apologize—apologize, and, uh, I stole your hairbrush—"

"No shit," Cameron said, which almost made me smile. That was one I'd never heard from Bastion.

"But not here," I said, which felt like the most stupidly contrived part of the whole gambit. It was a good thing that we were witches and not secret agents. "Upstairs. Meet me in Herschel's room in five minutes. Third floor, third doorway on the left with the wolf door knocker."

The library was pretty dim, but I could see Cameron nod slightly in the ambient glow from the projection screen.

"Cool. See you," I said, extremely relieved. I hadn't really expected him to agree so easily.

Then I raced upstairs and met the rest of North Coven in the corridor.

"Want to see Herschel's room? It's super weird," Drea said, holding the door open. I saw a flash of terrariums and a NIN poster on the wall before Dove yanked Drea out into the hallway.

"You guys wait around that corner," Dove said, pointing. "I'll come running out this way, and we can take the back stairwell down to the garden."

"Then we need to go to . . . Calisher Creek? I guess we need to figure out a new place to do spells," Drea said.

"We'll improvise," Brandy said. "Dove, if you're going to go through with this, you should get back in there."

"You didn't really get to show anyone your Millennium Bug costume," I whispered to Brandy as we ducked around the corner.

"I don't care," Brandy said. "As long as Drea likes it."

"I like it," Drea whispered, with a big goofy grin on her face. She and Brandy looked at each other with such pure love that it made my heart ache for a second. Then I heard the bedroom door open and close around the corner.

"Here we go," Drea said softly. "Get 'em, Dove."

We waited all of fifteen seconds before I heard yelling, and Herschel's door slammed open violently. I whipped my head around the corner and saw Cameron *booking* it away down the hall. Dove was standing in the doorway with her arms crossed.

"Sooooooo. No secret attraction on his end?" Drea asked, sheepishly.

"I told you so," Brandy said.

"No, you dumbass! I can't believe you talked me into believing that crap! The little slime hates my guts and he just said he was going to 'make us leave him alone *forever*'!" Dove said, raking a hand through her slick hair.

"Oh, shit," I said. "He's going to Stepwood."

"Well. We'd better stop him," Brandy said, with quiet determination.

Then we chased Cameron through the woods.

CHAPTER TWENTY-FIVE

Friday, November 26, 1999

It was pointless to get the car. The driveway was so tightly packed that it would take me an hour just to find the people who had blocked the Hyundai in and have them move *their* cars. So we had to chase Cameron on foot. By the time we got outside, I could barely make him out. He was just a silhouette, hurtling away from us toward the treeline. Whatever Cameron had changed about himself, he was still the fastest runner at our school.

It was a quarter-mile on the old path from the Micenmachers' house to Stepwood, and our lives depended on us beating Cameron to the Northcott Faire mausoleum. We ran as fast as we could across the vast lawn that lay between Northcott House and the woods that bordered it on one side (and Stepwood on the other). We ran until the mansion looked like a few points of glowing light on a night-black ocean. Dove fell behind as she unstrapped her boots and kept running through the forest in nothing but socks.

Drea was keeping pace with me, breathing heavily and crashing over little logs and around pine trees as our eyes slowly adjusted to the night. Brandy was ahead of us, moving so quietly that I kept losing her position.

"Magnolia Path is up here," Brandy called back, after an indeterminate amount of time. Then we were minutes from the cemetery. That thought urged me to go faster and faster once we reached the path. I felt myself grimacing with effort. I couldn't let him do this. Couldn't let him hurt my friends.

"Ahhhhh, huhhh," Drea moaned, clutching her side. But she kept running. I couldn't hear Dove behind us in her bare feet, but I could see her outline in the dark when I glanced over my shoulder.

We reached the western side of Stepwood, marked out only by a few ruined posts of iron where a fence had once been, and I went from a run to a sprint, tripping over familiar graves until I saw the Northcott Faire mausoleum.

And here is where we got very, very lucky. The door was a door again. And the door was *open*.

I'm actually not sure if Cameron just forgot to close the mausoleum up because he was so freaked-out by us chasing him, or if he might have done it on purpose, subconsciously, if you know what I mean.

The mausoleum was the only point of light in the whole nightscape of the cemetery, besides the moon overhead. The cracked-open door glowed red like a dark fire was burning just inside. Brandy was ahead of me, standing by the entrance with her hands to her face, her shoulders rising and falling from the effort of her run. Then Dove came pushing past me and dropped her boots next to the door.

"Come on, we need to go," Dove said, pointing toward the red glow. Of course we did. I'm not going to lie and say I wasn't scared at the idea of walking into Mr. Nous's realm. Or home. Whatever. But I *had* to.

"Uhhhhhh, augh. Okay," Drea said.

"No, I—I can't, I can't," Brandy said, looking back and forth between us. She'd lost a lot of her little gold scarabs during her run, and a branch had cut her along one of her cheeks, drawing a perfect thin line of blood.

"You have to," Dove told her. "North Coven sticks together."

"No no no, I can't go *in* there," Brandy said, into her hands. She looked terrified.

"You have to—"

"You *don't* have to," Drea said, glaring at Dove for a second. Then she looked at Brandy and her expression got much softer. "You stay right here, okay? Keep watch for us."

Drea took off her black hoodie, revealing her *X-Files* T-shirt underneath, and draped it around Brandy's shoulders in a tender kind of way that I had seen probably a thousand times. But right then it seemed extra important.

"Stay here and keep watch," Drea said. "Wear this, it's cold. Okay?"

"No. You can't go in there," Brandy said, grabbing at Drea's hand. "You can't go in there, Drea—"

"I gotta go, I'll be all right," Drea said, and kissed Brandy for a long minute. I could see Brandy shaking even as she brought her hands to Drea's shoulders.

"We need to *get in there before he does something*," Dove said, and Drea broke away from Brandy's grasp.

"I love you. I'll be right back," Drea said. Brandy nodded wordlessly, holding on to Drea's sweatshirt.

My hands burned, and I had to swallow back my own fear. Then three-fourths of North Coven walked into the place where Mr. Nous waited.

CHAPTER TWENTY-SIX

Friday, November 26, 1999

There were facts about Northcott Faire that dreams and Vision Things couldn't ever capture.

The *smell* was the first one I noticed. It smelled like a real fair, or like a carnival, but more. Popcorn and sugar wafted toward me on the same barely there breeze that stirred the hay under our feet. There was a faint stench of old oil, maybe from the unmoving rides. Apple-scented something. It smelled like shoes and bodies and hot autumn sun and a million other things that I didn't believe were actually there. Old Tet had called it *a phantom bazaar*. I wondered how many times this place had changed identities over the centuries. I wondered if I was even looking at what I was looking at, if you follow me.

There was music, too. Just faintly. It sounded like a calliope sometimes, then other times like a classical piano, a quartet, a lone saxophone bleating far away. Then silence again except for the breeze.

The sky over us was the dull red of my dream, and everything else was black and white. When I looked down, I saw that my skin had been rendered grayscale like everything else. Dove was a colorless and shoeless sprite in the world of towering Ferris wheels as she led us down the midway. Drea's blue eyes looked light gray.

"There are so many of them," Drea whispered, and flung her hand out in a wide gesture. Her rings threw back the monotonous red of the sky in tiny chips of light.

She was pointing at the painted people. They looked more sinister than I remembered. They were blurry, almost darkly featureless, like plywood vortexes in human silhouettes. But their *eyes* were brightly rendered. White eyes, wide open and staring, looked at us from every false attendant we passed on the dead midway.

"They can't all be from the county," Drea said, softly. I had an awful thought and looked at her to confirm that she was thinking the same thing. There were too many figures here for the collection of something that had eaten an Advocate once a decade or so for a few centuries. The scope of the carnival was *vast*. And the false attendants were everywhere.

I wondered if Mr. Nous crouched between many worlds. If he could go to the Near-Depths like we could when we worked our spells. If he plied his particular brand of misery across the multiverse, to victims from more places than I could imagine.

As if to confirm my suspicion, Dove brought us to an abrupt stop in front of a little caravan with a crystal ball painted on the side. The plywood figure here looked . . . distinctly inhuman.

Well, it was a humanoid, I guess. It had too many arms and no head that I could recognize. But it was vaguely, like, bipedal.

Or tripedal. It had eyes painted in the wrong spots, too . . . all up and down what I would have called arms.

The board displayed above it on the caravan was unreadable. I could make out where the Fancy and Fare columns were supposed to be, and the Fare was written in the same searing red color as the gloves Mr. Nous wore. But looking at the letters . . . if I could call them letters . . . hurt my eyes. The characters were nothing like any written language I had ever seen. Until, of course, the last box in the Fare column. Which said, in perfect English:

Revocation of the token. **Granted.**

Just like it had on the board above the girl who guarded Mandy's Menagerie in my long-ago nightmare.

"Keep moving," Dove said, and set off again at an even faster pace, almost jogging. I followed her and watched the painted figures as we went. Shapes blurred by me, some that looked human and some that did not. Aliens, or maybe humans from very different realities. People in ancient clothes and garments that looked different from anything I had ever seen in a history textbook. Boards in English and Spanish and what I thought was Arabic and many, many others, and sometimes languages that I was sure had never existed in our world.

I didn't see Bastion's figure anywhere.

Then the striped walls of the Big Top came into view, and I had to physically force myself to keep moving. It scared me, man, it scared me even more than I thought I could be scared—based on how scared I was already. Drea kept swallowing, over and over, like a nervous tic.

"My throat hurts," she muttered when I glanced at her.

"My hands, too," I said, flexing them. My fingers and my wrists ached like I was arthritic and eighty.

Dove marched toward the walls of the Big Top. Perspective made it look like the tent was so big it blotted out the red sky, disappearing up into nothingness. Everything I could see became a field of black and white lines.

Dove stopped right in front of the sign: *Fortunes Told and Fates Changed Within! See Mr. Nous! The One Who Knows!*

She lifted the tent flap just slightly, peering inside.

As I caught up to her, I realized that I could hear voices. The sickeningly sweet buzz of Mr. Nous. Rotting silk. And Cameron, who was much quieter but still audible.

I looked through the crack in the tent and saw Cameron, a faraway dot against the wall of velvet curtains. And behind him I thought I saw the briefest glimpse of a long red hand.

"—*told you before that a wish made can never be undone, fair child,*" Mr. Nous purred. It sounded amused, even pleased. It did not call Cameron "clever one" like it had with Bastion.

"No, I remember the rules. Nine rules," Cameron said. "No, but I'm *saying* that they won't leave me alone. No, these idiots remember everything! No one else, just the four of them, and that wasn't the deal!"

Cameron—okay, this was funny. Or maybe the very opposite of funny. Cameron talked to Mr. Nous the exact same way he'd talked to his dad the night I'd broken into their house. Same tone. Defiant but afraid, afraid but defiant.

"We gotta go in there now," Drea said, looking panicked. "He's about to wish us out of existence."

"Wait," I said. "I don't think so."

Because Bastion *was* clever, and I trusted him more, even dead, than anyone else alive. And Mr. Nous confirmed what I thought when its insectile voice flooded through the tent again.

*"I am so sorry, fair child. But I cannot make those four forget. They are protected from my enchantments by the previous Advocate. Even **my** eyes are blurred when I look for them, unless they make themselves known by marking their bodies with my sign. They are immune to my charms. I can grant you anything else. But nothing to do with those children."*

"N-n-n-now you think you might have fucking told me that when you said you could give me *everything* Bastion Attia ever had! Now you think you might have mentioned that you couldn't do anything about his gay lover or his crazy fucking sister!"

"I don't believe I ever lied," Mr. Nous said. It sounded so *happy.* This was what it had wanted all along, this pain and fear and frustration that Cameron was giving off. Bastion was a brick wall and Cameron was . . . a paper hat. A very scared paper hat, judging from how shrill his voice was.

I realized that Dove was shaking with rage—and maybe fear, though she would never admit it—and I put my arm across her chest to keep her from pushing her way into the tent.

"Hold on," I mouthed. "Listen."

"No, no, no, you did lie! Now, you already got my voice in exchange for one more week with my dad! No, it was *you* who came up with the trade, wasn't it? Now, wasn't it?"

*"Everything of clever Bastion's that I could give you while obeying the rules, I **have** given you,"* Mr. Nous said. Its voice had a hint of laughter in it. *"It was a fair exchange. You got to have everything Bastion had, for the simple cost of everyone's memories of him. You*

have his talent. His accolades. His academic record. The admiration that belonged to him. The girl who adored him. Even the physical strength he possessed."

"Now come *on*! No way did you not know what I wanted! Not some girl, not some grades," Cameron said. I had to admire his guts, honestly. He was totally outmatched by Mr. Nous. He could barely even figure out how to talk within his new parameters. He was clearly scared shitless. But he still fought back against it, with the same almost idiotic tenacity that had made him keep trying to land a blow on Bastion when Bastion was literally holding him up off the ground.

"Yes, you wanted two things, didn't you?" Mr. Nous said. It spoke sweetly, with a facsimile of concern. *"The boy. And your father's approval."*

"No . . . ," Cameron said. I could see his head moving all the way across the room. He was nodding *yes* as he said *no*, which would have been funny if it wasn't so creepy.

My Toad's Place hoodie in Cameron's drawer—carefully hidden away for years—came into my mind then, so vividly that I couldn't ignore it for a minute longer. I felt as sharply shocked as if I'd recreationally stuck a fork in an electrical socket. I *knew*.

"I can't give you the love of the boy," Mr. Nous said. An edge of impatience bled into its voice. *"I just told you. Wishes made cannot be undone. That boy is off-limits."*

"No, fine, it's fine, that's fine," Cameron said, like someone who was trying to convince themselves that it was cool that their house was burning down.

There was a long stretch of quiet, and the silence freaked me out. For a second I thought that Mr. Nous had seen us. Dove turned and gave me a loaded look, and I looked back at her, trying to put *I'm as shocked as you are* into an expression. I hadn't known. I hadn't wanted to know. Then Cameron spoke again.

"Nous, what if . . . now what if I wished for something about myself?" Cameron said, suddenly. "No . . . yeah, what if I wished to . . . to not be different anymore? Now if I could be, you know, *normal*, then I wouldn't have to think about him," Cameron said.

"I can grant you that fancy," Mr. Nous said. *"But I fear it will not help with your unrequited love. I cannot touch **him**, so your feelings for everyone else, everyone else in your whole little world, will be changed. But your feelings for him will remain steadfast. Troubling as they might be."*

Mr. Nous sounded close to laughing again, and it made the skin on my arms prickle.

"No, you're right, that was a stupid idea," Cameron muttered, so softly that I almost couldn't hear it. Then I saw another flicker of red from behind the black curtains under the *Novelties!* sign.

"In love, I cannot help you, fair child. But . . . ," Mr. Nous said, teasing out the edge of the word until the canvas walls of the Big Top vibrated with the sound of its voice. *"As for your father, I can give you time."*

"Now, what do you mean?" Cameron asked, suspiciously.

"It will be expensive. A hefty fare for a fancy so extravagant."

"Nous, are you saying you could, like . . . I could have my dad back for a long time? Not just a week?"

"Cameron, I regret that I cannot assist you with your painful and unreciprocated love for Nesbit North Nuñez," Mr. Nous said. *"It may come as some comfort to you to know that, in as far as I can see truths between people, I believe your love is pure and steadfast. But*

since I cannot help you ensnare the object of your heart's devotion, I propose to give you the only other thing you truly want. And . . . to demonstrate my kindness . . . I will ask for a fare that costs you nothing at all."

"Cameron Winship is in love with *him*, not me," Dove hissed, making it so I missed whatever Cameron said in response to Mr. Nous. "Drea, you dumbass! How can a bisexual have such crap-ass gaydar?"

"I didn't know!" Drea whispered back, looking totally chagrined.

"If we'd sent *Nesbit* into Herschel's room, we wouldn't be in *here* right now—"

"Shhh," I said.

"Nous, if I say yes, I don't have to do anything else? Nothing bad? Nothing bad, and then I get my dad back?" Cameron said, reiterating. I didn't believe the *nothing bad* part for a single second, whatever it told Cameron.

"That is correct, fair child."

"Now, I think that's . . . now, I think that's pretty good," Cameron said cautiously.

"Then we have a deal," Mr. Nous was saying, with all the delight of a starving man invited to a feast. *"The will of North Dana belongs to me, to do with as I see fit, for twenty-four hours, starting at midnight. And your father's heart keeps beating for another twenty-four years."*

"No!" I said, and whipped back the tent flap. "Cameron! WAIT!"

"Nous, I agree," Cameron said. I couldn't see what happened next, but I assume they shook hands because sparks of red light sprang out around Cameron's head like a terrible halo. Then he spun around, toward the sound of my voice, his eyes wide.

"*Hello, Nesbit,*" said Mr. Nous. Inside the circus tent, even all the way at the back, I could hear it speak with perfect clarity. Its voice filled the domed space with a buzzing sound that reverberated in every molecule of air and made my knees feel weak and watery. My hands burned like they were in an oven. I heard Drea make a choked sound, and Dove threw her left hand over her own heart like it pained her.

Cameron looked back and forth between us like he couldn't believe what he was seeing.

"*Hello, Andrea,*" Mr. Nous went on, almost pleasantly. And— Jesus Christ, I still have a hard time talking about this—I saw its *hands*. For the first time in real life. Its red-gloved hands that ended in razor points moved in front of the curtains in a gesture of greeting.

"*Hello, Dove,*" said the voice behind the curtain. "*I've been longing to meet you. If you can get my key away from Cameron, I'll kill him. Then **we** can bargain. I do love a challenge.*"

Then, to my horror, the red arms got *longer.* They stretched out from across the tent—now five feet long, now ten, now hurtling toward us.

"FUCK YOU!" Dove screamed, and tried to launch herself at the arms that rushed forward to embrace her. Drea and I grabbed her and dragged her backward, away from the reaching claws. Cameron, clearly deciding he'd seen enough, booked it past me, running out of the Big Top.

"Come *on,*" I grunted, shoving Dove as hard as I could toward the tent entrance. "RUN!"

Shouting directly in her ear seemed to shake Dove out of her blind rage. She started moving, and I grabbed her hand and Drea's hand and dragged them outside with me, into the dull, red-lit world. Behind us, a scratching sound came . . . like Mr. Nous was dragging its long nails against the inside of the tent.

I kept running and didn't let go of my friends.

The labyrinth of the carnival stretched away from me, and I followed Cameron as he ran, even though he was a decent way ahead of us. I trusted him to know how to find the exit, and I *didn't* trust him to not lock us up inside of Northcott Faire if he got out before we did.

As I ran, I thought I saw a flicker of movement. Not from Cameron, up ahead, but to the side of the midway. I slowed down for a second, peering into the empty food stands that clustered together to our right.

"What is it?" Drea asked.

"I saw something," I whispered. And then I saw it again.

One of the painted people was moving. It crept fluidly behind a rusty cotton-candy stand, inching around to cut us off farther up the midway. The details of its form were lost. It was just a shadowy shape with wide, staring white eyes.

"Uh," I said, my scalp prickling. "Keep moving. Now."

I squeezed their hands more firmly in mine and started running again, as fast as I could. As we ran, I saw more flickers of movement, and we passed empty boards with no figures underneath them. The former Advocates were following us, mirroring our movements just to the sides of the midway.

"Oh no oh shit oh no oh shit," Drea chanted as we ran. She'd seen them, too.

Then, up ahead, I saw it: a door in the wall of a ramshackle dark ride called Cemetery Scares. The view through the doorway looked different: it was *our* world, our nighttime world. I could even make out Brandy, peering into the opening. Cameron darted through the door, colliding with her.

I heard a noise from above me. A white-eyed figure crouched on the top of a carousel roof, looking down, and as I watched, it slipped to the ground in front of our path.

"Go go go!" I yelled, veering us sharply to the left. Something grabbed at the back of my jacket, and I wrenched away from it and kept moving. Drea made it through the door first, and as I turned around to pull Dove through with me, I caught a glimpse behind us.

The midway was *filled* with figures slinking toward us. They weren't plywood anymore at all. They had form and depth and substance. Bodies made of fluid darkness. Not all of them were shaped like human beings, and they were coming toward us, their eyes wide and staring. Then I fell back through the dark ride door, and down the mausoleum steps, dragging Dove with me. Brandy and Drea immediately slammed the door shut, and I watched as the keyhole vanished into a solid plane of brass.

CHAPTER TWENTY-SEVEN

Friday, November 26, 1999

Dove sat in the grass looking at the door with a dazed expression. Then she reached for her discarded platforms, fished her cigarettes out of the left boot, and lit one.

Brandy was touching Drea all over: her arms, her face, her hair.

"I thought you'd die in there, I'm so sorry I didn't come with you," Brandy said. "Oh Lord, are you all right?"

"I'm fine, babe," Drea said, stretching her hands out grandly. "Not a scratch, just uh, um . . ." She took a weird hitching breath, gulped, and then turned around and puked all over the mausoleum steps.

"Wimp," Dove said, in a hoarse voice.

"Uhhhhhh," Drea moaned. "Whatever. At least I didn't try to arm-wrestle that freaking monster like a total dumbass."

Then the four of us turned around and stared at Cameron Winship, who was sitting with his arms around his knees against the Dearest grave.

We had to talk to him. But I didn't want to be the one who talked to him. I had no idea how to approach Cameron now.

He wasn't just the preppy dickbag, he wasn't just the Advocate, he wasn't just the guy who always gave our coven shit, he wasn't just the thief who had stolen Bastion's abilities. He was also a kid whose dad slapped him around. A kid who desperately loved his dad anyways, enough to do something *very* stupid to get him back. He was a guy who had such intense feelings for *me* (this was the most uncomfortable part) that he'd actually tried to use Mr. Nous to wish me into loving him back. That attempted—or at least *discussed*—violation of my free will made me very angry. But it also made me feel *bad* for him. The same way I felt bad for Kim Palmer. Because, I guess, I understood what it was like to love someone and not be able to give them that love. In my case, it was because the person I loved was dead. But it was a shitty deal either way.

And above and beyond all of this, in my eyes, he'd reverted to the person I had originally known, way back in freshman year. My Gym Buddy. Filled to the brim with quiet desperation.

Brandy didn't know what had happened, and the other two were clearly waiting for me to do something. And, reluctantly, I decided on being *very* direct.

"So, Cameron," I said, walking over. I crouched down next to him, but he refused to meet my eyes. "Looks like we should all have a chat, huh?"

"No way," Cameron said, staring steadfastly at the mossy ground. "Nesbit, leave me alone. Now I want all of you stupid fucking homos to leave me alone—"

"Whoa," Drea said, wiping off her mouth and coming over to us. "I think you should close your kisser, closet case."

"No, fuck off," Cameron said, sticking out his chin. His ears were red.

"Drea, I don't think you should be saying that kind of thing," Brandy said anxiously.

"We need to catch you up," Dove told Brandy. She held out her hand, and Brandy pulled her up and steadied her while she put her boots back on.

"Come on, Cameron," I said. "I want my car. We have until midnight before Mr. Nous takes over the *will* of North Dana, whatever that means, and I don't think we should be in town when it happens."

"No, *you* shouldn't be in town," Cameron said, to the brown November grass. "Now me, I'll be fine." He made a gesture, almost touching the chain around his neck.

"You *so* don't deserve this, but Nez just offered you a chance to get the fuck out of here with us," Drea said. "You want in? Or do you want to stay around and see if your special status as the Advocate is good enough when Nous starts to get funky with North Dana?"

"Yeah. Are you in or are you out?" Dove said, from behind us.

Cameron shrugged, still folded in on himself.

"*Winship*," Dove said, sharply, and Cameron flinched without looking up. "I know you don't actually want to be involved in this, even if you are a literal tumor posing as a human being. No sane tumor would."

Cameron snorted a little. I glanced at Dove, who stood behind me, still slightly supported by Brandy. I wondered kind of absently how injured Dove's feet were, and how far she could walk, if we had to walk. Or *run*, if we had to run.

"Now I have to think about my dad," Cameron said quietly. "Now my dad—"

"Is going to live for another twenty-four years regardless," Dove said. "Right? That's what Mr. Nous said. *We* just have to stay away for twenty-four hours. Starting at midnight. We're going *now*. Are you in?"

"Nez will be there," Drea suggested, brightly. "Apparently you're a huge fan of him."

I barely had the presence of mind to give her a *Seriously?* look, but I managed it somehow.

Cameron finally lifted his head all the way to glare at me and Drea. But then he stood up, and meticulously dusted off his Tommy Hilfiger cargo pants.

"Now, I'll come with you for *one* day," Cameron said, like we had been begging him. Which, weirdly, I guess we kind of had. I don't know if that came from our empathy—when you got down to it, none of us really wanted Cameron to be eaten by Mr. Nous, no matter how tumorlike he was—or our group intuition telling us we might *need* him. I think both could be true. We did need him with us, later. And . . . we didn't actually want him to die.

"Cool," I said. "Let's go. I have no idea how long it will take to get my car out of the Micenmacher's driveway."

"Uh, speaking of that," Drea said. "Anybody got the time?"

After a second, Cameron pulled out his cell phone from his pants pocket and stared at the screen.

"N-n-n-n-*now*—goddammit, it is so hard to talk like this! Now it is eleven fifteen."

We all looked at each other. That was not very much time at all. It was *definitely* not enough time to get my car out of the

Micenmacher's driveway. I felt like I could hear Mr. Nous chuckle, somewhere just at the edge of audibility.

"Okay, change of plans," Drea said. "My house! Let's go!"

We went up the hill toward the trailer park, all five of us. Right before the end of the woods, I saw Dove, who was ahead of me, slip on a leaf-hidden rock, and Cameron threw out an arm to steady her. The gesture was quick and impersonal, but still.

I'd seen a lot of things since I moved to North Dana. A lot more than that since Bastion died. But that—that was the first time I ever saw a miracle.

CHAPTER TWENTY-EIGHT

Friday, November 26,
& Saturday, November 27, 1999

We all went into the double-wide, which was quiet and dark except for one yellowy light over the sink and the flicker of the television, which was playing *Unsolved Mysteries* on mute. Agent Scully came over to greet us, did a funny little stretch, and went back to sleep on the couch.

There was a note on the kitchen table:

I'm working a second shift for Chet,
but I'll probably be home before you anyway.
I love you SO MUCH!
Have fun at your party.

xoxoxoxo Mom

Drea read it and then looked over at us with relief.

"She'll be out at eleven thirty. Hopefully she'll get here by eleven forty-five."

"What about the rest of your families?" Brandy asked.

"Yeah, I need to call them," I said, and Dove nodded.

Cameron had been looking around the double-wide with something like fascination. I wondered if this was his first venture away from, like, the comfortable echelons of upper-middle-class living.

"Okay, so we tell our families . . . What do we tell them to get them to meet us outside of North Dana?" I asked.

"Car wreck," Dove said. "Nez, you crashed your car over by the Dunkin' Donuts in Gardner. We need them to come get us *right now*. You gotta be vague and hang up quick so they're panicking."

"What about you?" I asked. "Anna's not going to bring all your little siblings with her to pick you up from a car wreck."

"Fuck, you're right," Dove said. "Fuck, fuck!" She shook her head for a second. "Let me think. God, I wish Bastion was here. He would have come up with something."

I was watching Cameron over Dove's shoulder. He had walked into the kitchen, and now he was reading Jamie's note to Drea.

I watched him read it once, and then read it again, with an expression I couldn't quite define. Maybe it was surprise, or wistfulness.

"Now, my mom calls your mom trailer trash," Cameron said, setting the paper down. "Normally, or sometimes 'a good lesson on the dangers of teen pregnancy.'"

I heard Brandy exhale in what was probably horrified indignation, which was on par with a less mannered person screaming *You are an asshole!* at someone.

"Thank you, Cameron, that's very nice," Drea said. "Maybe we can discuss what a horrible snobby jerk you are later when *we're not all gonna die.*"

"No, I'm just saying," Cameron said. "Now my mom's never left me a note like this ever. Nice—it's a nice note."

"And that's why Drea is great and you suck, Winship," Dove said. "It's the *nurture* side of the nature-versus-nurture argument. Give me your cell phone."

Cameron handed it over with only a small grimace. "Now, be *careful*, that's expensive," he said worriedly.

"Oh, really? Guess I'll hold off on shoving it up my ass, then," Dove said. Then she took a deep breath and dialed home, walking off down the hallway as it rang.

"Your turn, Nez," Drea said, and handed me the mint-colored house phone. I called home, winding the cord through my hands anxiously as it rang. If I could make a Nexus at that very moment, I would've made one with any god or monster that would listen. *Please make sure Nic and my dad are okay.*

"Now, aren't you going to call your mom?" Cameron asked Brandy.

"No, I am not," Brandy said.

Cameron nodded, like that made total sense to him.

The phone rang out and our answering machine picked up. Nic's prerecorded voice spoke into my ear:

"Yo, you have reached the Nuñez household. Say something cool at the beep."

"Dad? Dad, you need to wake up Nic and come get me right now," I said. "I need *both* of you to come. I'm at the Dunkin' Donuts in Gardner. I . . . There was an accident and I need both of you there right now, you need to be in Gardner by midnight. *Both* of you, okay?"

I hung up and then dialed the garage, just in case Dad was working late.

"Do you want a muffin?" Drea asked from behind me.

"No," Brandy said.

"You sure, babe?" Drea asked. "It's lemon poppyseed."

"Don't call me that, please," Brandy said, and I turned around in time to see her indicate Cameron with her eyes. The message was pretty clear: *Don't call me that in front of him.*

"What? It's fine, he's gay," Drea said. "Or are you bi, Cameron?"

"No," Cameron said. The tips of his ears had gotten quite red. "No, that'd be easier, wouldn't it?"

"Actually, not really. That's a common misconception about bisexuality," Drea said. "We can talk about it more like, at some time in the future. You want a muffin?"

"Naturally," Cameron said, and took one. Despite my sweaty palms and growing fear for my family, I *almost* smiled.

There was no answer at the garage.

"I might have to go over and get them," I said.

"You're not going to make it there on time," Brandy said, pointing to the clock over the stove. It was 11:37.

"I can make it," I said.

"You don't have a car!" Drea said.

I kind of deflated. I had forgotten that my Hyundai was trapped in the driveway of Northcott House.

"When is your mom going to be here? We need at least ten minutes to get over the town line," I said. I dialed my house phone again.

"Maybe ten minutes," Drea said, clearly getting as nervous as I was.

"Nesbit, I think your family will be fine, won't they?" Cameron said, hesitantly (and through a mouthful of muffin). "Nous said it would only control the will of North Dana for twenty-four hours."

"I'm sure that seemed like a sweet deal to you," I said, trying to keep my cool. "To get so much more life for your dad. But that means that Mr. Nous can do *anything it wants* to our families for an entire day."

"It can make everyone in town drown themselves in the Quabbin, or all like cannibalize each other," Drea said. "It's a *monster.* Who knows what horrible shit it can come up with?"

This was, of course, something Bastion had probably considered at length. He would never have agreed to such an ambiguous deal. But Cameron was not Bastion. He looked pretty freaked out by what we were saying, like he'd only just realized how very *bad* the fare for his fancy could actually be.

The phone rang out onto the answering machine again, and I pressed the switch hook, listened for the dial tone, and punched in our number one more time.

Dove came back into the kitchen, walking gingerly on her beat-up feet. "The line is busy," she said. She said it calmly enough, but I could hear the pent-up emotion in her voice. She set Cameron's Nokia down on the table so carefully that I knew she wanted to chuck it at the wall, scream, freak out.

"Do you think Mr. Nous is doing it?" Brandy asked. Her forehead was making the V-shape of worry.

"*No,* I think that either Anna or Youssef is dicking around on the internet," Dove said, pushing her tiny sunglasses up onto her hair. "They're getting a second phone line installed next week, which doesn't help me at all right now."

Then I heard a distinct sound: the approach of Jamie's tired old Cadillac. We all waited in silence while the car pulled up and turned off.

"What do you guys want to do?" Drea asked.

The clock on the stove said 11:48. We were cutting it very close.

"Grab your mom and let's go," I said.

Drea met Jamie at the door. "Mom, give me your keys. We have to get out of town."

"Wha . . . Andrea?" Jamie asked, then looked at the rest of us in surprise. "I thought all of you were spending the night at the party."

"We left the party. Now we have to leave the town. Give me the keys, come on, Mom, we gotta *go!*" Drea said.

The clock on the stove said 11:51.

"We need to go now," I said, trying to stay calm.

"I'm not leaving my mom," Drea whispered. "Mom, I will *leave you here* if you don't come with us right now. *Give me the car keys.*"

Jamie, seeming totally lost, handed over the keys to her junky old Cadillac Cimarron. Her gaze wandered over all of us, probably checking to see if we'd all gone as insane as Drea. Then her eyes widened when she looked at Brandy. "Honey, what happened to your face? You're all cut up!"

"Car, car, car," Drea chanted.

"Jamie, we *gotta go*," I said. Dove and Drea started leading her to the car.

"Nesbit, you drive," Drea said, and tossed me the car keys. I caught them in the air and ran after them out of the trailer.

"Wait! Agent Scully!" Drea ran back into the trailer as I started the car and emerged ten agonizing seconds later with her cat blinking sleepily in her arms.

"Hello," Jamie said to Cameron. They were both in the back, with Dove squeezed between them into the middle seat. Drea got into the front, and Brandy slid over and pulled the seat belt over both of them.

"Nice to meet you," Cameron said, stiffly.

"Mom, I can't really get into it right now, but we have to get out of town immediately," Drea said. "What's the fastest way out?"

"North," I said. The Cadillac was a standard. I threw the stick shift into reverse, raised the clutch all the way, flew backward out of the trailer park onto the main road, and made the Cimarron *crank*.

Everyone was tense and silent as I pushed the speedometer over eighty. Even in fifth gear, the Caddy didn't want to give me the speed I needed, but I didn't care. I could repair any damage to the car. If we survived.

It was 11:58.

"We aren't going to make it," Brandy said, clutching Scully to her chest.

"What are we trying to *make*, exactly?" Jamie said tersely. She was starting to look more pissed than freaked out. "What the hell are we doing right now, guys?"

"Remember the Stepwood Specter? From your scrapbook? It's real, it's all real," Drea said, turning around.

"Oh, guys. Is this about that kid you think was erased from reality?"

"*Bastion*," Drea said. "He *was* erased from reality."

"Now, he really actually was," Cameron chimed in. "Not lying. No, I know because it was my fault."

"*You* erased him from reality?" Jamie asked. "Aren't you Laura Winship's little boy?"

I took the turn onto Lost Lake Road. After that, it was a clean two-mile shot up to the 202 intersection, and then we would be over the town line.

Then I saw red-and-blue lights in the rearview. One of Sheriff Andy's three-strong posse of deputies, who had nothing much better to do than hang out on empty North Dana roads at night.

"Cops," Dove said.

I flicked the hazards on and sped up. The car shuddered in protest.

"Nez, what are you doing? Pull over!" Jamie said.

"I will. As soon as I get over the town line," I said, gritting my teeth.

I saw the cop lights getting closer. Rapidly. I threw my right arm over Brandy and Scully and pulled the wheel sharply to the left, trying to avoid getting hit, but it was too late. The cruiser *rammed* into the back of the Cimarron, sending it spinning. The seat belt yanked against my shoulder hard, and Brandy flew forward against my arm. Dove shrieked from the back. Or maybe it was Cameron. Scully yowled, climbed onto the dashboard, and leaped into my lap, all her claws out.

"Ow!" I said, and Scully rubbed her striped head against my chin.

"Ahhh, what the hell?" Drea yelled. "Why did they hit us!?"

I tried to get the car moving again the second it stopped spinning. No dice. It stalled out.

The clock said 12:00.

The door of the police cruiser opened. I cranked down my window. The night—alternately lit up by flashes of red and blue—was very quiet suddenly. I could hear the purr of the cruiser's engine and the sound of the deputy's feet on the pavement as he walked toward us.

"I've *got them*!" Jamie screamed, suddenly, and she threw the back door open. Dove cried out, like a real cry of pain. I looked back, and Jamie was dragging Dove out of the car. She had the short, gelled hair on the top of Dove's head in an iron grip . . . and her *hands*—

Her hands were covered in red gloves that went all the way up, disappearing under her shirt.

"Oh no," I said. Then I scrambled out of the driver's-side door, leaving Scully on the seat.

"Jamie! JAMIE, STOP! This isn't you doing this!" I yelled. Jamie ignored me. Dove fought against her grip, trying to grab at Jamie's red-gloved hands, but Jamie seemed unnaturally strong.

"Mom! What are you doing?!" Drea shouted. She was also out of the car, running to us as Jamie dragged Dove to the police cruiser with jerky, unnatural movements. Then the deputy slammed me hard against the side of the Cadillac.

"Hands up," he said. He had gloves on his hands, too, and his red right hand hovered over his gun.

No way in hell was I putting my hands up. I felt around in my pocket for my box cutter.

"Hands up, *Nesbit*," the deputy said, sliding up close to me and speaking in a voice that sounded like the faintest echo of rotting silk moving over broken glass. "Can't have you using those magic fingers, my boy."

Suddenly the back door slammed open, directly into the deputy. He went over with a grunt of pain, and Cameron jumped out and kicked him right in the nuts with every ounce of Bastion's strength. The deputy moaned and curled in on himself, holding his stomach with two red arms.

"Nesbit, you okay?" Cameron asked. His expression was completely open, for once, and full of fear for me. It made me feel weirdly uncomfortable, him checking on my well-being the way Drea checked on Brandy.

I didn't answer him. Brandy was out of the car now, too, and she and Drea were grappling with Jamie.

"Mom, stop, Mom, stop!" Drea shouted, slapping at her mother's red hands. Dove screamed again, trying to buck Jamie off. I bolted directly for them, getting low and grabbing at Jamie's legs in the closest approximation of a slide tackle that I could manage. We all went over in a big pile, but Jamie released Dove for a second, and I stood up and dragged Dove to her feet.

"We gotta run," I said. "For the town line."

"But my mom!" Drea said, her eyes bugging out. "Mom, what's *wrong* with you?"

Jamie didn't answer. She just started to get up from the pavement, her blond hair falling all around her face.

"Nous has her! Come on, *move!*" I said.

Brandy skidded back to the Cadillac and scooped Scully into her arms.

"Nesbit, the cruiser!" Cameron said, indicating it.

"I can't jack a cop car! We need to run!"

"No, you don't need to *hot-wire* it," Cameron said, and pointed again. Then I saw it: the cruiser was still running, with the driver's-side door flung wide open.

"This way! Get in, get in!" I said.

All five of us, plus Agent Scully, got into the car. I slid into the passenger seat without thinking about it, and the girls took the criminal spot in the back seat, separated from us by a grate. It was an older Crown Victoria, which meant we had plenty of room.

Cameron got in the driver's seat. Then someone *slammed* up against the side of the car, making us all recoil. It was Jamie, who immediately started to open the door on the driver's side.

"Lock it!" I said, and Cameron did. Then he hit the gas, pulling away from Jamie and her red-gloved hands as she clawed at the car.

Drea reached up and tapped me through the mesh grate that separated the front seat from the back. "I don't want to leave her," she said, with tears in her eyes.

"We have to," I said. I probably sounded harsh, but I felt awful about it. I was leaving Nic and my dad, too. It was terrible, but not as terrible as whatever Mr. Nous had planned for us if we stuck around.

"Okay, we've got this," I said. "Nice and steady. Just take us right up the road to the 202 intersection. We can get out and ditch the car."

"Go *faster*," Dove urged, looking over her shoulder at the dark road. She had one hand to her head where Jamie had gotten her by the hair.

Cameron sped up a tiny bit, still looking highly freaked out.

"Not like my mom's car," he said nervously. I wanted to jerk the steering wheel away from him and slam on the gas, but I resisted the urge.

"We're going to make it," Drea said. Her voice still sounded like she was about to cry.

"Don't say that! People never make it when they say that!" Dove said.

"No, we *are* going to make it," Cameron said, as seriously as I'd ever heard him say anything. He sped up to an almost acceptable speed.

Then the curve in the road straightened out, and beyond the wall of winter-bare trees I could see the 202 intersection. My heart, which had been hanging out somewhere in my throat, sank.

Cameron slowed the car to a crawl.

The only other two cop cars in North Dana were parked sideways along the road with their lights on. And a line of people—not just cops, ordinary townspeople—stretched from one side of the intersection to the other, extending all the way into the woods with flashlights in their hands. They were all still. They were all wearing red gloves. I was too far from them to pick out individuals, but I thought that even from a distance I could make out uncanny smiles on their faces.

"It's a blockade," Dove said.

"We have to turn around," Brandy whispered. Her voice was shaking. Agent Scully, still in her lap, let out a low growl as we surveyed the scene.

"Cameron, reverse it," I said.

"No, I can't," Cameron said, and when I glanced in the rearview, I saw that red-gloved people had crept behind us there, too. A pickup truck—maybe even my *dad's* pickup truck, though I couldn't tell for sure with all the people blocking my view—pulled sideways across the road behind all the people, cutting off our path of retreat. The people of our town advanced on the car from both sides.

"Nesbit, what do I do?" Cameron asked, his voice thin with panic.

"Run them over," Dove said.

"Do not run them over," Brandy said.

"No, I'm not running anyone over!" Cameron said.

"We might *have* to," Drea said, sounding horrified by her own suggestion. "How the hell else are we going to get out?"

Nobody said anything for about three seconds as we contemplated that terrible option. The possessed people of North Dana got closer to us. Now, they were maybe five yards away, in front of and behind the cop car.

"Nous, it sounds like a deal Mr. Nous would make," Cameron said.

"Hurt them to save yourselves," Dove said. "You're right. We can't."

"No guardrails right here. Now, you better hold on to the cat. Now, when I stop the car, you all need to run, okay?" Cameron said.

I tore my eyes away from the approaching crowd to look at him questioningly. "What?"

Then Cameron hit the gas and *threw* the wheel, turning the car entirely sideways, filling up the air with the smell of hot rubber. The cruiser whipped around, literally inches away from people on either end, and drove straight off the road into the woods. Brandy, who had her arms wrapped around Agent Scully, screamed as we careened over the edge of the road. Branches slapped at the side of the car and rocks made us bounce furiously, until the cruiser hit something big (boulder or log) and we were stopped dead at the bottom of a low hill.

"That was genius, Cameron. Now, everybody RUN!" Drea said, and she and Brandy, still holding Agent Scully, jumped out of the car. Dove and I threw open our doors and got out. I could already see the silhouettes of red-gloved people appearing at the top of the incline. They started moving toward us, coming down the hill in a brisk and creepily mechanical way.

"If we get separated, we should meet at Old Tet's," I said to Dove. "The North Dana town line is up by his camp. We can get out that way."

"We're not getting *separated*," Dove hissed. "Come on!" Then she started to run, too, although with the amount of barefoot running she had done already she was limping really bad.

Cameron was slower to get out of the car. I turned around and waited for him as the girls headed deeper into the woods.

"Cameron!" I said, waving at him to *hurry up*.

"Nesbit, you go," Cameron said. In the alternating red-and-blue lights of the cop car he looked very composed. Almost brave. Then, still standing against the door of the cruiser, he took a deep breath and shouted at the tide of people rolling down toward us:

"No need to go after them! Not going to bother you! Now you can just go about your business! No, really, all of you should listen to me—I'm the Advocate! Nous's Advocate!"

"CAMERON, they can't be *reasoned with*," I said, and grabbed him by the arm. "Stop the heroics and let's go!"

Cameron hesitated, practically fighting against the hold I had on him. But the crowd of people, almost upon us, decided him in favor of what I was saying. He turned around with me at the last second, and we bolted straight into the woods. He could have easily passed me—he was still the fastest runner at Regional, after all—but he stayed even with me as we ran through the trees and darkness, turning back every few seconds to see if they were gaining.

We caught up to the girls.

"Where *were* you?" Drea asked, and I just breathlessly motioned for her to *keep moving*. We ran over trees, crashing through underbrush, getting smacked in the face by branches. We were making a ton of sound, but I didn't care. As long as we could stay ahead of them.

The woods spit us out into a clearing by one of the many little streams that ran into the Quabbin.

"Which way?" I asked.

"That way," Drea said. "We might be able to get over the town line up there."

But we never got a chance. Mr. Nous must have known all the shortcuts through the woods, with his command of our part of the world. Because suddenly people—impossibly quiet people with red-gloved hands—crept out from behind the trees. They surrounded us in the woods.

"Oh SHIT!" Drea screamed. I heard Scully hiss and grabbed my box cutter as many red arms surrounded me, and blank-faced North Dana citizens leaned in close. I recognized Dolores from Hazy Dee's, Mrs. Winship, Manny, who worked with my dad, and

Erin Ashby from the funeral home. But none of them recognized me. Nothing familiar played out on those smiling faces.

"No, Mom! No, Mom, stop!" Cameron was saying, in a horrible echo of Drea pleading with Jamie not long before.

Someone was shouting. A flashlight went rolling away, and I heard the crack of branches. I fought against the tide of bodies around me, but my box cutter was thrown to the ground.

"Help! Get *off* me!" Drea screamed, her Voice unnaturally loud, as brilliant as a meteor in the dark. And I tried to find her so I could kick the shit out of whoever was hurting her, but a dozen bodies pushed me down, and something hit the front of my head. I felt the world slipping away from me, like the time I fell off a ladder as a kid and got a concussion.

I lost consciousness for a while then. And dreamed of the last fight I ever had with Bastion.

CHAPTER TWENTY-NINE

Saturday, November 20, 1999

Bastion's size made it kind of hard for us to have full-on sex in my car. His *height*, I mean, and his broadness, though he wasn't exactly lacking in other areas, either. But we managed to get each other off regularly even when we couldn't share a bed. And Bastion, of course, was the kind of person who got all chatty and contemplative after he had an orgasm.

I was still breathing hard and trying to pull my Cro-Mags shirt back on over my head when Bastion turned up WJIN and glanced over at me with a big goofy grin on his face. He had the passenger seat cranked all the way back, and he put his hands under his head and looked up at the Hyundai's roof like he could see straight through it to the stars.

The radio spit out some intensely ominous-sounding classical music, and Bastion conducted along with it lazily, moving one hand in the air while I finished getting dressed. The car reeked of sex, and I cracked my fogged-up window a little, letting in the night smell of autumn on the Quabbin.

"There is no way in hell that you know what this music is, Sporty Spice," I said, as Bastion waved his conducting hand like the sleepiest version of Leonard Bernstein.

"Nono, Luigi Nono," Bastion said, smirking at me. "Nono was a staunchly socialist avant-garde composer, died about ten years ago."

"Bullshit."

"*Nostalgica Utopica Futura* is the piece," he added smugly, ruffling my hair. "Now you may be asking yourself something like 'how did I end up with the most sophisticated man in the world?' Nesbit, it's a simple matter of attraction. Never forget, it's your good fortune that I find you so irresistible."

"I think you are the biggest dork in the universe, and by that, I mean in both volume and degree."

"No matter, I'm chalking that up to simple jealousy over my intellectual prowess."

"Mmm. Well, you do have some prowess," I said, and bent over him. We kissed for a long minute, and then I leaned back and ran a fingertip over his eyebrow, on the point of vitiligo where the hairs turned white. Bastion blinked his long eyelashes open and looked directly into my face, his brown eyes catching a gold halo from the little overhead light. The gold chain gleamed around his neck. His hand pressed against the small of my back, not insistently, but like an anchor.

"I love you," I said when I sat back. I said it because it was true, and not because I was looking for reciprocity. It wasn't the first time I'd said it.

"Nesbit, I appreciate that," Bastion said, and he reached up to draw a heart on my foggy passenger-side window. He meant it, I could tell. He did appreciate it. He liked hearing it. But his glib response kind of irritated me.

Why? I guess because I was thinking about that stupid list. The list of *Things Bastion Attia Cannot Do (That we know of, so far)*. I would've let it go, though, and spared us everything that happened after, if Bastion hadn't, in his post-orgasmic motormouth way, started talking about what he started talking about next. I swear I was going to let it go.

"Nesbit, have you decided what you want to do after school? Now I know that the great college-versus-family-business debate rages on."

"Um. I still don't know," I said. I'd told Bastion—and only Bastion—that I was thinking about possibly enrolling at UMass Amherst to study architecture. I didn't have the grades or the money for MIT or RISD, but I could swing tuition at a state school if I worked full-time. On the other hand, I really did enjoy working at my dad's shop. And I had the aptitude for it.

"Noncommittal? No problem," Bastion said, putting one large hand on my chest. "Nail down your preferences when you feel ready, and I'll make my plans based on that. Nesbit, I was thinking we could use my trust fund to get an apartment near whatever town you want to live in after you decide what you want to do. North Dana or Amherst or even out-of-state, it doesn't matter. Now personally I want to take a gap year and learn how to work for a living, but afterward, I'll just pick the best school near wherever we end up."

He looked up at the ceiling again, his expression soft, like he was imagining our future. "Nonprofit work really appeals to me. Nice and noble. Nothing can compare to how much I'd like to get an entry-level job working at a reputable not-for-profit organization."

I tried not to get upset. I really did. I've told you before that I hate arguing with people. But . . . it just made me mad.

"Dude. Sometimes I don't know how somebody so smart can be so in denial," I said, shaking off his touch.

Bastion looked over at me sharply, his brows drawing together for a second. "Nesbit, what's wrong?"

"I just . . . I want to be with you too, obviously," I said, trying to temper my anger. "But I don't know how you can, like, rhapsodize about this big, beautiful future for us when you aren't willing to even face the *present*. Are you ever going to . . . you know . . . work on your problems? At *all*?"

Bastion flinched like I'd struck him. It probably felt like I had. I'd never brought up his issues in a negative context before. Or in almost any context, really. I don't think we'd talked about his N speaking thing since that first day at Stepwood.

"N-n-n-n-not sure what you mean, Nesbit," Bastion said. I'd shaken him up enough that he was stuttering over his words.

"Not sure what I mean," I repeated. "Yes, you are. You know exactly what I mean. Your issues. Your obsessive-compulsive disorder, that's what I mean."

"Nesbit, I think I've made this clear," Bastion said, sitting up all the way. "Neurologically, there's nothing atypical about me. Not only that, but I consider it a disservice to people who *do* live with neurological issues to even imply that I—"

"Don't try to railroad me, Susie Soapbox," I snapped. "I'm not everybody else. You can't just bamboozle me into submission with your big brain."

"Nesbit, I'm just saying that I *don't have a disorder*," Bastion said. He was the closest to angry I'd ever seen him, putting his hands to his temples in frustration. But I was frustrated too.

"Oh yeah? So what, you just can't apologize because you've never been sorry? And you just can't say your name because what, you don't like it?"

"Nobody lives without *some* limitations," Bastion said. "Nobody. Not my name, either."

You have to understand, we *never* fought. Because we never fought, I was so worked up that I missed some stuff. I think I just discarded the *Not my name* thing as a sentence fragment. But now I'm pretty sure that Bastion was saying Bastion wasn't his actual name.

Bastion scrubbed off the heart on my passenger window with one big palm, clearing all the condensation in a single swipe.

"Some limitations, sure," I said. "But healthy people—or people who *want* to be healthy someday—are willing to talk about their limitations. I read about this medication, clomipramine, that can really help with compulsions. If you were willing to go to a psychiatrist—"

"Nice, very thoughtful of you," Bastion said sarcastically. "Never had anyone try applied treatments for the disorder I *do not have* before—"

"Then what the hell is *wrong* with you?!" I shouted, surprising myself with how loud I was.

"Nothing! Nothing you could ever understand!" Bastion shouted back.

"Why don't you *try* me?"

"No need to try, Nesbit," Bastion said, suddenly very cold. "Negotiation on this subject is over. Not going to talk about it. Nor would you comprehend it even if I could."

My hands were clenched into fists. Bastion was glaring at me while he scrubbed his wrists together. I felt bad about what I was doing to him. But I just wanted him to admit something—*anything*—for once. I wanted to break through the relentlessly optimistic facade he always showed the world and see a real person behind it, the person in pain that I knew was there. I'd seen a glimpse of that person just twice. Once when he talked about football as a battle against an enemy. Once backstage at the rehearsal of *Oliver!* when he asked me how he'd given away the fact that he wished he could be in the play. That wistfulness bordering on desperation. But I'd never seen it again.

"Why are you like this?" I asked him. "Why? *Why the fuck are you like this?*"

Yes. Before you say anything, I'm aware that this is also what Mayor Winship said to Cameron the night I broke into their house.

Bastion turned away from me, still scrubbing his wrists. His jaw was set in the picture of stubborn refusal.

"Please," I said. "I don't need you to be perfect, Bastion. I just want you to be able to admit that you can't do everything you want to do."

"Nesbit, I am fine with my life as it is," Bastion said, deliberately. "Now, if you are not happy with *me*, maybe you should be looking elsewhere for a relationship."

"You're gonna threaten to break up with me if I push this?" I asked.

"No, I'm just saying—"

"Don't just *say* shit like that, Jesus Christ," I said shakily. Then I tried to compose myself. I knew Bastion couldn't cry, but he looked like he wanted to. His eyes were . . . sad.

"Listen," I said. "I think I'm pretty relaxed about a lot of stuff. I just want to know this one thing. Can you tell me this one thing, please?"

"Not sure, but I'll try," Bastion said, refusing to meet my gaze.

"Thank you," I said, nodding. "Bastion. At any point, for the rest of our lives . . . are you ever . . . I mean *ever* . . . going to say 'I love you' back?"

It was very quiet in the car. Even the scratchy, doom-filled music by Luigi Nono, socialist composer, seemed to fade out.

Then, after what felt like a hundred years, Bastion looked up at me. He was as handsome as I'd ever seen him, so handsome that it hurt my heart. His eyes were big and luminous. The expression on his face was so sharp—barely a Bastion expression at all—that it made him look cruel.

He locked eyes with me deliberately, making sure I was watching him like he was watching me, and parted his perfect lips.

"No," said Bastion, holding my gaze. "Never."

I saw red.

"Get out," I said. "Get the hell out of my car."

"Nesbit, I—"

"I don't give a shit," I said. "Get out now. It's three miles to your house from here. Nice night to *get a run in*, right?"

Bastion climbed out. Whatever he had been trying to do with the "*No, never*" thing, it was clear he regretted it now.

"Nesbit," he said, standing just outside the car door. "Nesbit, when I was a child, I did something very bad once. Now, I think if you knew, you could never forgi—"

"Bastion, I honestly no longer give a fuck," I said, and leaned over. I slammed the passenger-side door and pulled out onto Red-wick Road with sad classical music thrumming through my car.

My last glimpse of Bastion was in the mirror as I drove away. He stood alone in the dirt lot of Gate 43, hands at his sides as if he didn't know what else to do with them. The pines loomed behind him in a line. He looked very small in front of the trees. Like a little kid. He watched my car, and I watched him in the rearview, until we lost sight of each other.

CHAPTER THIRTY

Saturday, November 27, 1999

It was still dark out when I woke up, but it was clear that hours had passed. The black sky had that gray-light quality at the edges, and the stars were blurry in a way that told me it was getting close to dawn.

The first thing I noticed was that my arms hurt. Then I came back to myself and realized my *head* hurt even worse.

"Help," I whispered. "I think somebody hit me with a flashlight."

Someone had taken my mechanic's gloves. My hands were bare, and I was sitting up with my arms behind my back. When I tried to move them, I realized I was handcuffed. And in the back of a squad car. Parked just outside the front gates of Stepwood.

"Uh-uh. No way," I said, and started thrashing around.

"Nesbit, stop, *stop*," came a voice from the front seat. I shuffled myself forward to look through the mesh cage and saw Cameron.

"Cameron, are you okay?" I asked.

Cameron tried to say *yes* (I think) and got stuck. It was *eerily* similar to Bastion getting stuck.

"N-n-n-n-n-n—" Cameron stuttered, like he was choking.

"Just say *no*. If you can say something, it will break it," I said. "Hey. Cameron. Say *no* and take a deep breath."

"N-n-n-*no*," Cameron said, and coughed.

"Okay?" I asked.

Cameron's eyes were kind of watery, but he nodded.

"Good," I said. "Now. Can you get out of the cruiser?"

"Nope," Cameron said immediately, and raised his arms as much as he could to show me why. He was handcuffed too.

"Shit," I said, and sat there in silence for a minute, trying to think of how I was going to get us out of this.

"Nesbit, you really *know* about this," Cameron said into the quiet car.

"Huh? Oh, the tricks for talking? Or like, about Mr. Nous?" I asked, and Cameron nodded *yes* to both.

"Well . . . yeah," I said. "I mean, no, I never knew about Mr. Nous before all of this. But Bastion and I have been spending like five days a week together since freshman year. I'm used to the talking thing."

"Nesbit, that sounds annoying to deal with," Cameron said.

"He wasn't *annoying*," I said, sharply. "There was nothing *annoying* about him. I'd watch my mouth before I call anyone *annoying*, Winship."

Cameron recoiled from my anger, his eyes getting all wide. I couldn't blame him. I sounded pissed.

"Nesbit, I wasn't *referring* to *him*," Cameron said, in his trademark prissy dickbag tone. "No, I simply meant the *way* it forces us to speak. Now, there's no need to get mad."

"Well, I am kind of mad, actually," I said. "We are pretty screwed, in case you didn't notice. We are *fucked*, actually. And this wouldn't even be *happening* if you weren't so worried about your stupid abusive father!"

"Not just *worried* about him," Cameron snapped. "Nous told me when he was going to die, you know. Nesbit, it told me the exact *minute* my dad was going to die. Now, you know I checked the *minute* on my cell phone at the funeral. No, I thought. No such thing as magic. No—this has got to be a hallucination or a scam. Nope, he died *right in front of me* right when Nous said he would, remember?!"

"Okay, okay," I said. "You're right. I'm sorry for getting mad. It's pointless for us to sit here yelling at each other. And . . . I bet it was pretty hard to take. But your dad *is* an asshole."

"Not all the time," Cameron said.

"Yeah, I'm sure. But you have to know that, like, nothing you'll ever do will be good enough for him, right? That's clearly the kind of guy he is."

"Now, my brothers—"

"Probably also feel like they've never been able to please him," I said. "This is an obvious one, Cameron. I know you're not stupid."

Cameron was quiet for a minute. "Not so obvious from the inside," he said.

"I guess from the inside things never are," I said. I was thinking about Bastion drawing the heart on my car window.

"Nesbit. Now, I am sorry, you know," Cameron said. He wasn't looking at me. His eyes were fixed somewhere far outside the window, and he looked pretty sorry. And sad. "Not just saying it to sound good. Nesbit, I am very sorry for bringing my dad back. Not just sorry about this wish. No, the first wish, too. Not an excuse, but I don't . . . no, I *know* I wasn't strong enough to resist seeing him again. Nous offered. Nous offered to bring him back, *and* to give me everything I needed so that he would actually *love* me. Nesbit, I didn't even think about it, I just said *yes, please.*"

I had tried not to think about Bastion in the context of resurrection. I had tried not to think about what fare *I* would be willing to pay . . . just to see him again.

"First of all, I think your dad loves you. Badly and abusively. But I think he does," I said. "Secondly, I accept your apology. If I was in your position, I probably would have done the same thing."

It was quiet again for a minute. In that quiet I realized that what I had said was true. I really *did* forgive Cameron. Some part of me had always been waiting to forgive him, I think, because I alone out of all of North Coven could see his quiet desperation.

"Nesbit, thank you," Cameron said.

"Don't worry about it," I said. "Cameron . . . can you see anything up there like . . . a paper clip or a bobby pin? A small piece of metal?"

"Need to look," Cameron said.

"Hey," I said after a minute of him rattling around. "You're getting better at talking. You'll be as good as Bastion soon."

"No lying, please," Cameron said, without looking back at me. "Never going to be as good as Bastion at *anything*."

"That's not true. You're already better at getting the town involved in your wishes," I said.

Cameron huffed out an involuntary-sounding laugh from the front seat. "Not seeing anything up here," he said.

"Keep looking." Then I had a thought that made me feel cold all over. "Do you know what happened to the others?"

"No, they got away. Not Drea, she's in another cruiser."

"Shit," I said. "At least Dove and Brandy are safe." I was worried that Brandy might come back for Drea . . . and that Dove might come back to fight.

"North Coven, right?" Cameron asked, turning back to me for a second. "Now can you guys actually do magic?"

"We can. It didn't turn out to exactly be the magic we *thought* we were doing. Like our big spells never worked. But yeah, we definitely can. Lately more than ever."

"Nesbit . . . that's probably why it's afraid of you."

"What, Mr. Nous? It's not afraid of us. It's, like, out devouring people from across the multiverse."

"No, it seems like an awful lot of effort to go through. Needing to control the whole town just to catch some high schoolers."

Cameron had a point.

"Well, even if it is afraid of us," I said, "I have no idea why. So that makes me kind of a useless foe."

"Nesbit, I found a ballpoint pen," Cameron said.

"I might be able to use the metal clip as a shim," I said. "Pass it back here."

Cameron wasn't cuffed behind his back, so he was able to lift the pen up to the mesh by twisting his body around and raising his arms. I had to take the pen from him with my teeth. Then I dropped it onto the seat next to me and crab-walked sideways on the bench so I could get my hands on it.

"You know the nine rules of Mr. Nous, right?" I asked.

"Nesbit, *obviously*," Cameron said, rolling his eyes.

I laughed a little. "Okay, right. Well, I haven't been filled in on all nine of the rules. So let me ask you: Is there any rule that says you can't tell *other* people about Mr. Nous?"

"No," Cameron said. "Nothing like that."

"Huh. Bastion never told me," I said. I didn't mean to say it out loud, but Cameron looked at me through the cage without judgment.

"Never told anyone, I bet," Cameron said. "Neither would I. Not after the ball starts rolling and you make some . . . questionable choices."

"Can I ask you another question?" I said, trying to get a grip on the pen.

"No, I'm way too busy right now," Cameron said sarcastically.

"Hah. Right. So why didn't you ever out us at Regional?" I asked. Cameron instantly turned red. It was funny. In an extreme enough situation, you'd think people would move beyond embarrassment. But it never seemed to entirely go away.

"Seriously," I pressed. "You could have. It would have ruined Bastion's football stuff. Or did you try to and you couldn't? Bastion said he made a Nexus . . . which I'm pretty sure was code for 'a wish.'"

"Never tried to tell," Cameron said.

"Why?" I pressed. "Even if you're gay, too—you still could've really screwed up our lives. If you'd wanted to."

Cameron looked completely overwhelmed by me even *saying* "gay." It was strange. It kind of reminded me of how touchy I'd been about discussing it, back when I had first joined the coven. I managed to get a decent grip on the pen and started trying to work the metal clip off of it.

"Nesbit, you *know* why," Cameron said. He almost sounded bitter about it.

I don't know what I had been expecting. Some declaration of morality or altruism, maybe. But the look on Cameron's face said that the reason was more in line with why he kept my stolen sweatshirt folded up in his underwear drawer.

"Sorry," I said, feeling embarrassed myself. And bad about pushing him for an answer.

"Not as sorry as I am," Cameron muttered.

"You don't need to feel so bad," I said, after a minute. I kept working at the metal clip on the pen while I talked, my words kind of fitting the rhythm. This was my big moment of gay activism, by the way: a heartfelt attempt to comfort another gay kid before we both got murdered by an incomprehensible monster. "If we somehow don't die in the next couple of hours? You can go to college somewhere with an actual gay community and then you'll be drowning in dates. You'll be so popular. You're a major twink. I'm just . . . I . . . first of all, I don't even know why you like me. And I just kind of have other stuff going on right now. With my dead boyfriend and everything. It's really not personal."

"Nesbit, a *twink*?!" Cameron sputtered. His red-faced embarrassment had just started to fade, but now he was beet red again. "No—I have no clue what that even means!"

"You do know what that means," I said, hiding my smile. I almost had the metal clip off the pen. "You wouldn't be reacting like that if you didn't know what it *meant*."

"Nope, I have no idea," Cameron said. He was laughing a little, too. "Nesbit, do you think—"

Suddenly, the back of the cruiser opened. I flinched—I hadn't seen anybody coming—and then I was being pulled out by one of the deputies. Cameron was saying something from inside the cruiser, but the door slammed shut and his voice got cut off mid-sentence.

"Hey, Nez," said a voice that I knew better than anyone else's. I looked up, and my heart dropped. Nic was walking toward me, flanked by about sixty townspeople. I saw Jamie standing behind him. Red gloves peeked out from the sleeves of Nic's oversized drug rug.

"Nic," I said. "Hey. Nic, I know you can fight this. This isn't you, this is Mr. Nous."

"Mr. Nous says I owe it my *life*," Nic said. His words buzzed slightly. "Would you say that's true?"

"No," I said. "You don't owe that fucker anything."

But Nic wasn't listening to my answer. He grabbed my shoulders and spun me around, then pried open my fingers.

"I *told* you guys to keep an eye on his hands," Nic said, ripping the pen out of my grip. He tossed it to Jay from Galactic Video, who pocketed it.

"Nic, *please*, please, I *love* you, please, man, just fight it," I said. I didn't care if I sounded stupid. I couldn't stand seeing Nic controlled like that. It was like the drugs had been but worse.

Then there was a slight commotion, and Drea was frog-marched through the crowd. She had duct tape over her mouth, but I could hear her trying to scream behind it. She was taking in big, painful-sounding breaths through her (still kind of messed-up) nose.

Tape over her mouth. So nobody could hear her voice. And they had to watch my hands. It made me think of what Cameron had said. That Nous was afraid of us.

"Come on, bring them up," Nic shouted, and suddenly many arms were guiding us through the gates of Stepwood. I glanced back and saw Cameron pounding on the window of the cruiser with his handcuffs.

I tried to dig my heels into the dirt, but there were too many people pushing me. "Leave us alone! Just let us leave! Please! We'll never come back! At least let Drea go!"

"It's too late," Jamie said, to my left.

We were half dragged and half carried up the series of little hills toward Northcott Faire. The mausoleum door was flung wide open again. The red light fell out of it in an elongated rectangle, and I was pushed down to the ground in the path of that other-worldly light. Two of the deputies held me against the ground, coating my head in ash from the coven's makeshift firepit. Jay and a guy who worked at the bank grabbed my legs. I didn't stop trying to fight for a second, but I couldn't get any momentum with my arms behind my back and my legs pinned.

"Take his hands," Nic said from above me. "And her tongue."

I heard Drea scream through the duct tape, and I started thrashing even harder.

Someone unlocked my cuffs. I tried to get my hands under me and scramble away, but I was flipped over. My arms were pulled up over my head.

"No, no, Nic, please stop them," I begged. Someone else had a knife. I think it was one of Dolores's big kitchen cleavers. I just saw the edge of it gleaming in my peripheral vision, held by an anonymous red hand.

Then I heard a disgusting ripping sound. The duct tape was coming off Drea, probably taking skin with it.

"AaaaaAAAHHHH!" she shrieked.

"Keep your mouth shut," I yelled at her. "Don't let them—"

But Drea did not keep her mouth shut. She took a deep breath and started screaming the spell she had written for the Vision Thing.

"*WITH OUR BOUND HANDS!*

OUR STRONG ENCHANTMENTS!

OUR SHARP EYES,

OUR CUNNING HEARTS—"

"Stop her," Nic said. But Drea's voice was so thunderous that he was almost entirely drowned out. Drea sounded louder than any one person could possibly be, like a megaphone, like a firecracker in a cathedral. And the wind, which hadn't put in an appearance at all that night, suddenly kicked up. A tornado of dead leaves spun around us.

Drea's voice, which the red-handed people had tried so hard to silence, was actually *doing* something. She had figured out what Cameron had implied already: that we had some power attached to our places in North Coven, something that Nous didn't want us using. I imagined that my magic was there, too, in my hands. But I was being pinned down. I couldn't use my hands to help Drea—so I started screaming along to the spell, though my voice could never have matched her volume.

Three people, including Jamie, were covering Drea's mouth with their gloved hands, but somehow her words were crystal clear:

"WITH OUR ONE VOICE!
OUR DARKENED ALTAR!
OUR STRONG BONDS,
OUR BETTER SELVES."

As I chanted along with her, I felt something in my hands. It was like a cramp at first, or a very light static shock. But then it got stronger until my fingers were almost vibrating with it.

"WITH YOUR KIND BLESSING!" Drea howled into the dark. I shouted the lines too, and my voice blended with hers and with the wind in a way that almost sounded, at least to my terrified ears, like music.

"YOUR ONE EXCEPTION!
YOUR MANY WORLDS,
YOUR SACRED VISIONS!"

The wind blew so hard that it pushed back everyone around us. Jay was blown over in a flurry of branches and graveyard dirt, and Jamie fell against the Dearest grave. Nic was knocked to the earth. The deputies staggered back down the hill. The crowd was driven away, and then the wind blew through my fingers, and for a second the tattoos on my left hand glowed the exact green of the ribbon we used for rituals. Just for an instant, my North Coven symbols were illuminated. But then it was gone, so quick I almost thought I'd made it up.

"Ahahahahhhhhhhh," Drea said, half laughing and half screaming, and staggered over to me. Her lips were torn and bleeding. I held on to her in the narrow frame of light from the Northcott Faire mausoleum.

Whatever Drea had done to drive Mr. Nous's minions away, it only worked for a second. The red-handed people of North Dana started creeping back, circling us. I spun around, to keep Nic in my view as he got up.

Then a shotgun blast went off, so close to us that I jumped about a foot in the air. Nic and the other encroaching townspeople slunk back again.

"You'll want to leave them alone," called a voice from the bottom of the closest hill.

I peered down and saw Old Tet, brandishing his pump shotgun. His hands were totally normal. Brandy was behind him, and Dove came jogging up with Cameron, still handcuffed.

"Jesus Christ," I said. Drea slumped against me in relief.

"You okay, kiddos?" Old Tet called up.

"Um, no, we are *not* okay," Drea said.

"Then you'd best come along with me," Tet said, indicating the gates. I grabbed Drea by the shoulder of her *X-Files* T-shirt and started down to meet them when I heard something.

A *lot* of somethings. It was the sound of engines. A long line of cars, more cars than I thought there could be in North Dana, started pulling up at the Stepwood gates.

"Out the back way," I said, and turned around to go up the hill.

But people appeared there, too. More people than trees, in fact. Smiling red-gloved partygoers from Northcott House flanked us on one side, and residents of the trailer park approached us on the other.

They came toward us so quietly. I heard car doors slamming from the base of the hill.

"No way out," Cameron said.

"We can fight our way out," Dove said.

"There are too many of them," Brandy whispered.

"You kids make a run for it," Old Tet said, and raised his shotgun. "I'll clear a path for you."

"We're not leaving you here, Jules," Dove said.

"No! No, wait," Cameron said. He looked at all of us, and then pointed toward the square of light that fell out of the open door of Northcott Faire.

"What? No *way* are we going in there," Drea said.

"No, we need to," Cameron said. "Nous is in there. Nous will grant any wish I make, it *has* to. Nous will even grant a wish to keep all of you safe until its control of North Dana is over."

"That's . . . actually *brilliant*," Dove said.

"No surprise, coming from me," Cameron said.

Drea laughed. It was weak and scared and raspy, but it was a real laugh.

The townspeople were closing in on us again, and that made Cameron move.

"Now we need to go," he said.

He pushed ahead of all of us, hands cuffed in front of him like a jailbreaker, and walked into the red glow of Northcott Faire. After a second we followed him.

CHAPTER THIRTY-ONE

Saturday, November 27, 1999

We passed through the mausoleum like we had hours before. When we walked out into the world of the dead carnival, Dove immediately slammed the door behind us. I had no idea if the door would turn into a brass wall back in our world, or if it would be enough to keep out the people of North Dana. But it didn't matter. It wasn't like we were any safer inside Mr. Nous's domain.

"Where is Agent Scully?" Drea asked, grabbing Brandy's hand.

"Curled up in my tent with Elizabeth," Old Tet said, still holding the shotgun. "Dolores comes to visit me every Sunday after work. She'll find them, once she gets un-possessed." *If we don't make it back alive*, he didn't say.

"God, you guys look so messed up," Dove said, touching my arm. "I'm so sorry. I tried to get you."

"It's fine," Drea said, off to my right. "Kinda sweet, actually. Now we all get to die together."

"Don't say that," Brandy whispered. It was her first time inside the carnival. Tet's too, I think. I could see them taking everything in. Brandy held out her arm in front of her like I'd done to myself, staring at her own body, leached of all color.

There were no attendants that I could see anywhere, which gave me a creeping feeling of dread. And something else was happening.

The carnival was coming alive around us. The flat red sky had turned dark maroon like the nonexistent sun was setting overhead. The endless cascading lines of Ferris wheels started blinking on, turning against the dim sky. The carousel to my left sprang to life in a discordant jangle of calliope music. Empty benches and riderless horses revolved by us slowly. Old Tet swung around, pointing his shotgun at the carousel, which kept spinning merrily.

"You remember how to get to the Big Top?" Drea asked Cameron.

"Not something I could forget," Cameron said. I had walked this path enough, in dreams and Vision Things and real life, that I felt like I had it memorized, too.

"Now let's go, *quick*," Cameron went on. "Nous probably isn't going to be happy that I'm messing up its plan with a wish."

We started in the direction of the Big Top, moving as quickly as our various injuries would allow.

"I never thought I'd say this," Dove said. "But—thanks. We owe you."

"No, you don't," Cameron said. "Not when this is my fault."

"Don't overstate your importance," Dove said. "Mr. Nous doesn't need *you* to play mastermind. *It* is doing this, Winship."

That was about as close to absolving Cameron as I ever expected Dove to get in a million years. Closer, maybe.

"I still don't get why it's trying so hard to kill us, though," I said. "Cameron said it seemed afraid of us. Like suddenly it's desperate enough to make a workaround to the 'my magic can't touch them' thing by getting townspeople to hunt us?"

"Maybe because we like, know all about it?" Drea volunteered, wiping a hand across her bleeding mouth.

"There's no rule that people can't know about Mr. Nous," I said. "According to Cameron, anyway. I still don't know the rules, but I know that *isn't* one. I even think it *likes* to be known about because it makes people have less trust in each other."

"*For it delights in sowing fear and hatred,*" Brandy said, quoting the poem from Professor Lenore's book.

"It was trying to make them cut out my tongue," Drea said, looking at the smear of mouth-blood that came away on her hand.

"And cut my hands off," I added. I realized then that I actually felt really weak and messed up. I was shaking, probably coming down from an adrenaline high.

"Nesbit, can you get these off me?" Cameron asked, waving his cuffed hands out in front of him.

"Yeah," I said, and stopped in front of an empty popcorn stand. "Let me see."

Cameron refused to look at me as I grabbed his hands, instead staring at a patch of hay-covered ground right to the left of us. But there was no awkward moment where we had to be in close proximity—I touched the handcuffs, thinking that I wanted to take them off, and then the tattoos on my left hand lit up with green light again. It was the only color besides red in all of

Mr. Nous's world, for a second. The green glow vanished as quick as a camera flash, and the handcuffs fell from Cameron's wrists onto the ground. Cameron looked up at me then, in candid shock.

"Holy crap," Drea said.

"Um . . . I feel pretty powerful right now," I said. It seemed like our powers had been stronger by a mile ever since Bastion had died. That was becoming more obvious as we were tested under major duress. "You must too. That was a crazy move you pulled back in the cemetery."

"You ready, kiddo?" Old Tet said to Cameron. Cameron looked . . . well, he looked *terrified*, honestly. I could understand. I didn't like the idea of going back to the Big Top, either.

"No, but we should go anyway," Cameron said.

Suddenly, there was a crash and a shrieking sound behind us.

I looked back. A hundred yards away, the door on the wall of the Cemetery Scares dark ride—the door that led back into the Northcott Mausoleum, and from there into our world—flew open. And red-gloved arms started pushing through it.

"Go!" Old Tet yelled, lifting up his shotgun. We all ran deeper into the carnival, sprinting toward the dark heart that was the Big Top, with Old Tet bringing up the rear.

The red sky overhead had turned completely black. It was starless, a total void, a cup of darkness. Not at all like the many layers of stars in the Near-Depths. We ran through the midway as I'd never seen it before. During all of the other journeys I had taken through the carnival to the Big Top at the center, it had been a quiet, dead place. But now it was *active*.

Pearly black-and-white strings of lights blinked on above ancient rotting tents as we passed them. A sudden wind moved the rug-covered doorways on caravans that were going back to the earth. Popcorn makers started popping, and bouquets of cotton candy wound from nothing on rusted spools. A ride called the Devil's Wheel spun idly through the dark with a whirring sound. A Ferris wheel so tall I didn't believe it ever could have existed in reality rotated to our distant left, playing *Nostalgica Utopica Futura* from all the gondolas.

We ran so fast that everything started to blur together, and I thought I saw flashes of other scenery in between the carnival things as I ran. A glimpse of a forest, all the trees too big for it to be anything but primordial. A path that turned into an ancient bazaar, complete with an arched ceiling and tiled floor. A city made of mud and clay. A craterous moonlike landscape. A white pond with black shores. Then it was just the labyrinthine carnival again, but bigger and louder and more *alive* with every second.

The noise drowned everything out, even my labored breathing. I had my hand around Dove's arm, dragging her along with me, but I couldn't hear her footsteps over the cacophony of sound. Bells and buzzers and beeping and clanging alarms and whistles to start off squirt-gun races mixed with music, every kind of music, and the creak of machinery that had sat for a long time without being used starting up again.

And then, underneath all the noise, I could hear people coming closer. It was faint at first, washed away by all the other insane sounds. Then it was easily audible. Then loud. Then earthshaking. I glanced back and saw the people of North Dana running toward us. *Hundreds* of people, moving shoulder-to-shoulder without speaking. They ran at almost-impossible speeds, like Olympic sprinters, all of them with smiles on their faces and their red hands extended and clawlike. And they were gaining. I thought I saw Nic near the front, but the throng was so close to us that I couldn't waste any more precious microseconds by looking at them. I faced forward and put on an extra burst of speed, holding Dove's arm so tightly that my fingers ached.

Then the rides and games gave way to the clearing at the center of the carnival, the spot where the Big Top squatted like an endless monster.

We were at the place where Mr. Nous lived. But the *scope* of it had changed.

It looked like the center of the carnival had expanded, turning a space that was eerily large into something unfathomable.

Where before the clearing had been maybe thirty feet across, it was suddenly five hundred feet wide, a thousand feet, a mile. It stretched so far, so insanely far in both directions, that I lost sight of the carnival on either side.

And at the distant end of the clearing was the Big Top. It filled the space—it had *grown* to fill the space around us. It was so long that I couldn't hope to see where it began or stopped. So tall that the flag-topped peaks sat all the way up in the dark basin of the sky. One side of the world had been walled off entirely by endless black-and-white stripes, moving in the weird wind.

I knew we had to get Cameron to the Big Top. But between us and the tent was another new sight to behold.

An abyss.

The abyss yawned away, slashing across the whole clearing. It was as endless as the midway, as interminable as the Big Top. There was no way to tell how deep it went, only that a strong wind howled out of it, the source of all the air that now blew through the carnival. It looked like a crack in the universe. And it was guarded.

Between us and the Big Top lay the abyss. Between us and the abyss stood the white-eyed souls that were locked forever in Mr. Nous's carnival.

The false attendants—at least, the ones that had once been human—no longer looked human, or even like their painted selves. They were just voids, almost as black as the yawning chasm they stood in front of.

The abyss was *sharp*—the edges so cracked and crystalline where they met the packed dirt of the midway that it almost hurt to look at. Sharp like my lost box cutter. And the attendants—the *souls*—were blurry. Their outlines rippled and faded and took strange, warped shapes, flowing like ink from one posture to another. They formed a wall of moving bodies, a line as long as the abyss.

"Nous isn't going to let us get to it!" Cameron said, his face pallid and frightened.

"It wants to stop Cameron from making his wish," Drea said. "Oh, shit. It's stopping us from *reaching* it!"

"That's not fair, you fucking puke!" Dove screamed at the abyss and the distant Big Top and the flat darkness of the sky. "That's FUCKING CHEATING!"

We had all slowed down. But not stopped moving toward the attendants entirely. We couldn't stop, because up behind us rushed the people of North Dana, red hands ready to tear us apart.

Brandy shrieked as we approached the abyss, and I saw one of the creatures crouched in front of her. It was down on its hands and knees, almost doglike, white eyes staring. It had the corner of Brandy's dress in its mouth, and it yanked at the sheath, head tossing back and forth in quick animal movements.

"Let her GO, creep!" Drea said, and—at the sound of her voice—the thing that had once been a person dropped Brandy's dress and skittered away, sending a shower of hot-glued golden scarabs in all directions.

Skip Ullman, a sweet old retired dude who lived two streets away from me on Annabel Lane, slunk up behind us and grabbed Dove by the shoulders with his gloved hands. Dove bared her teeth at him and wrenched herself away, knocking into me.

We were trapped between the abyss and the possessed townspeople.

"No, I don't want to be like that," someone moaned. I didn't want to take my eyes off the crowd of people from North Dana, but I looked over quickly and saw Cameron staring at the false attendants. He seemed totally transfixed with horror.

"Gotta get you to that circus tent, Cameron," I said. "Keep it together."

"Nesbit," Cameron said, in a cracked voice. "Nesbit—*they*—they—they are what's *going to happen to me*—"

He was right. I couldn't tell who any of those people were. For all I knew, any of the dark things guarding the abyss could be all that was left of Tet's lost Lenore, or Erica Skerritt, or even Bastion.

Please no, I thought. *Not Bastion.*

I couldn't stand thinking he had ended up like this, with all these warped and inhuman creatures.

Old Tet fired off a round from his shotgun high into the air, buying us about two seconds as the crowd of people from North Dana scattered back.

"Stay away or I *will* kill you," Tet growled.

"You can't kill us all, man," came a voice. Then Nic pushed his way to the front of the crowd and looked straight at me.

"Nez," he said—he almost sounded like himself, except for the way his voice buzzed slightly on every word. "We only really need one of you. I'll even let you pick. If we take your buddy Brandy's eyes, she might even survive."

He took a step closer to me. Tet brought his shotgun level with Nic's chest.

"Hey, hey," Nic said, almost amiably, holding his hands up. Then he looked at me again. "It doesn't even have to be your friends, Nez. One of you can take the key from the Advocate and—well, Mr. Nous will take care of it. Then the four of you can be free."

"Don't listen to him," Dove said, glancing at me. But I *was* listening. Not to the deal Nic was offering, but . . . something about the way he was offering it. Mr. Nous had said before that it couldn't lie. I believed that. That truth was one of the arcane rules of the game it and its victims were bound to. So whatever it was making Nic say had to be, on some level, the truth.

We only need one of you. It could even be Cameron.

"You should listen, honey," Jamie said. She was standing up with Nic now, looking at Drea. "Andrea. You don't all have to die, sweetheart."

The crowd pressed a little closer. The attendants made a smoky wall behind us—but they were too insubstantial to attack us. They were just there, like the canyon in the ground, to force us toward the people Mr. Nous was going to make into our killers.

I glanced over at my friends. Brandy was totally surrounded by the false attendants, teetering on the edge of the abyss. The wind blowing up from the black chasm got stronger by the second, almost drowning her out as she spoke.

"I think we might have to jump," she said.

"Shut up, oh you stupid bitch, what do *you* know?" Nic snapped, and leaped forward. Tet pulled the trigger on his shotgun, squeezing off a round.

"No!" I shouted, knocking the barrel to the side. It just grazed Nic's shoulder, sending him flying back into the crowd instead of killing him. The sound of the shot became a wall of silence, deafening me for a second and leaving behind a ringing in both my ears.

From somewhere in the back of the crowd of townspeople came an answering sound, the sound of another shotgun. Or a hunting rifle. It didn't hit any of us, but someone had definitely fired a gun. I felt very cold. Nic and Dolores and Jay and Skip might not have guns, but *some* people in North Dana surely did. It was only a matter of time before Mr. Nous dragged up the people with weapons and sent them after us.

"We're gonna die if we stay here!" I yelled. The false attendants were all around us now, crawling around our legs and straightening up to tug insubstantially at our hands. I felt revulsion; I didn't want them *touching* me.

"Drea? Dove? Nez? I know what we need to do. We need to jump," Brandy said again, and looked out at us. Her face looked so beautiful, like a sculpture, and a single tear—from fear, I think, or maybe from the wind that howled up from the chasm—fell across the cut on her cheek.

"That is *insane*, babe," Drea said. "We're not throwing ourselves into that void!"

"The void . . . I can see it. it's just a place where Mr. Nous pulled back the skin of his world. To trick us. To stop us from reaching him. To pen us in. It doesn't think we'll jump. But I think . . . I think we can reach the Near-Depths from there," Brandy said. "If we all go together."

"Good enough for me," Dove said.

"Near-Depths?" Cameron asked.

"We need to jump," Brandy said, again. "Drea. I can *see* the Near-Depths in there. Between this world and all the others. It underestimated us. This is the one magic we've *always* been able to do."

"You heard her," Dove said, and grabbed my arm the way I had held hers. "Come on! We've gotta jump! Jules! Let's go!"

Dove pulled me to the edge of the drop and then let go of me. The attendants crowded around us. They almost seemed to be shielding us from the people of North Dana.

I looked into the abyss, but nothing looked back. I wasn't the Eyes of North Coven. I didn't see the Near-Depths. It was only darkness below. No walls. No light. No sound except the wind that blew up from beneath.

"Come on, Drea," Brandy said. Drea looked half-insane with her bruised eyes and bleeding mouth, and black shapes swirling around her ankles like white-eyed tumbleweeds.

I turned around for a second, to see if I could get another glimpse of Nic in the crowd. I had a weird thought that I should tell him I loved him again before I jumped. Maybe he would remember, even if he was possessed.

"You gonna be a party to this madness, kiddo?" Old Tet said, still watching the people of North Dana.

"I think so," I said. "Cameron, come on." I held out my hand to him.

"No way," Cameron said, white as a sheet. "No fucking way!"

"I think we have to stick together," I said. "We go on three. Give me your hand."

The crowd surged forward suddenly, arms outstretched. I heard more gunfire, like distant claps of thunder. Drea and Brandy fell forward into the void holding hands. Dove took a breath like she was about to dive into a pool, and then she jumped too.

"Come on!" I said to Cameron, who was still paralyzed with terror.

"Don't have time to debate this, kiddo!" Old Tet said, and he grabbed Cameron and fell forward. The weight of his body sent them over the edge. The shotgun flew away from his hand, disappearing. I felt the air and darkness rushing up around my face as I leaned over the edge.

Cameron was screaming: a stammered *n-n-n-n-n-n-n* sound that became *n-n-n-n-n-n-n-n-n-noooooooooooooooooooo* after a second and then faded into silence.

Then I took a big breath, like Dove had done, and jumped. But as I fell out over the side, I felt a hand around my right wrist. It held on to me with terrifying, red-gloved strength, even as I plunged into the abyss. My fall was stopped abruptly by my shoulder dislocating.

I screamed in agony as I was lifted up over the edge of the abyss by my dislocated arm. Then I was dumped on the ground. People were crowded all around me. I opened my eyes and tried to move my arms, to crawl back to the chasm, but I was trapped in a tight circle of bodies. Then someone—or several someones—covered my mouth and nose. I don't know if Nic was one of them or not.

The panic was immediate and overwhelming. I fought as my air supply dwindled, trying to bite, trying to punch, to kick, trying to escape. *I don't want to die this way*, I thought.

It was my last clear thought. Then I felt consciousness slip away from me entirely.

I lost myself. There was no sensation of heat or cold. There was no color, no light. No pain. Not even fear. After a minute there wasn't even any sense of concern. I floated like a feather on the breeze into the underworld.

I was in a void as black and endless as the abyss that three of the remaining fourths of North Coven had jumped into. In the void of my unconsciousness, I did, for just a second, rally myself enough to speak. Or to try to speak.

"If anyone is out there," I said, "I would really appreciate some help."

My words drifted away from my mouth one by one and were silenced before they could travel through the dark.

Then, after I have no *idea* how long, I heard Bastion.

CHAPTER THIRTY-TWO

Sunday, November 21, 1999

"—nothing further to do with me. Now the . . . particular thing you stole from me the day I met him has cost me my future."

*"That you **paid** with. I cannot steal."*

"No. No. No, you know your own game perfectly well—you forced your token on me. Nearly every poor Advocate down here knew better than to take your key without you guiding their hand. Nothing you remove from me will alter my conviction—you've destroyed my life from the moment we met, for no other reason than . . . no other reason than that it gives you pleasure . . ."

"Your bright—and imaginary—future was over long before you ever knew your precious boyfriend. Was it not you who willingly traded your brother's life for your sister's health?"

"N-n-n-n-now, when I made that bargain I was a child. Not something I would do again."

"Nevertheless. Your brother would have lived for eighty years and died surrounded by his family. Generations were wiped out by your

*decision. The course of your little world changed forever, in ways that even **I** cannot guess at. If I am a monster, so are you."*

I came to rest very gently on my feet in the Near-Depths.

This wasn't like the theater space we had conjured during the Vision Thing. A cone of illumination, like a spotlight, showed Bastion talking to the thing behind the curtains. Around this narrow circle of visible space shone the layered stars and ever-moving nebulae of the Deep. The curtains where Mr. Nous waited hung across one side of the lit circle.

One red hand traced the split in the black velvet. Even that little glimpse of Nous made me shiver in revulsion.

I stood on the dusty floor, invisible to their exchange, just feet away from where Bastion sat.

Sat is the wrong word. He was kneeling in the dust. Bastion always lived within his limitations in a way that made them almost unnoticeable. He was the master of it. But now . . .

I could see that he was trying to cry but couldn't. Instead, his face twisted and worked like he was sobbing without tears. His eyes fell shut and opened again soundlessly. He raked his hands through his hair until it stood strangely on end.

His voice, though. None of the sadness crept into his voice. Bastion spoke like a person who had moved beyond all lighter emotions, into the great flat colorless plains of despair. I imagined that *despair* looked a lot like the gray world of the broken carnival.

"Never could tell you how sorry I am for it," Bastion whispered. It seemed like he was talking to himself. "Nesbit and the others . . . they would never understand."

"I do understand!" I said, stepping in front of him. "Bastion, I do understand. There's nothing to be sorry for—it *tricked* you.

It used your good nature against you. Tet said it eats love. Eats it and shits out suffering! Please, please, I'm sorry I fought with you, please, just don't give up—"

But Bastion was just an echo. Or else I was. He couldn't hear or see me, and when I tried to touch him, my hands went through him like smoke.

I don't think he could feel that I was there. I think we were separated by space and time. But suddenly, Bastion seemed to come back to himself a little. His eyes focused, and he got slowly to his feet.

"Nous, I want you to know something," Bastion said. "Now, I feel that this is important to say once."

Mr. Nous sounded gently bemused when it answered, and the softness of its tone made it even more unpleasant. Two red hands slid all the way out from the curtains, and red fingers tapped together expectantly.

"*Tell me, clever one. What is it you wish to say to me?*"

"Nous—I've seen a lot of things on my quest to best you, to break the hold you have over me. Nocturnes of surpassing beauty, in those people I might not have brought together if it weren't for you. Nobility and selflessness and friendship. North Coven has allowed me to bear witness to moments most people could never hope to see. Nuances of the multiverse that I would never have imagined existed otherwise. Nothing that ever made me feel that the cosmos was anything but far-flung and beautiful and terribly strange."

"*Very poetic.*"

"Necklaces of pretty words are the one thing I can string together," Bastion said hollowly. "Not the point. No, the point is that I want to tell you that I . . . at times I was almost grateful to you for the course you set my life on. Not . . . *often*, but I had moments where I appreciated my life for what it was. Nature does as nature will, and though you seem cruel and unnatural to me, and your playground is a graveyard of horrors, I believe that you are only acting upon your own nature. Not only that—but I forgive you."

There was a low buzzing sound, and for a minute I thought the spotlight-construct I was inside of was collapsing. Even the glittering stars around us seemed to shiver at the vibrations. Then it grew louder and louder until I had to put my hands to my ears, and I realized that Mr. Nous was laughing.

Laughing. Not chuckling softly in the dark but laughing like Bastion had told the finest joke in the world. Each wave of laughter hurt like a needle to my temples.

After a million years of agony, the sound subsided.

"So amusing, my clever one. I must admit, you never bore me."

Bastion was not deterred. He turned his handsome face and his dry eyes toward the curtains and squared his shoulders.

"Nous, I forgive you. Nous, I *forgive* you. Not that you will ever understand, but—I'm sorry it had to be this way."

Bastion paused and took a deep breath.

"Nevertheless . . . all of our enchantments have always failed. Now, I thought *now*, now this time for sure North Coven has altered the course of their own destiny. Now we have seen the Near-Depths. Now we have broken the laws of physics. Now we *must* be strong enough. Not this time, maybe, but *next* time for certain. Next time, or the time after that. Never quite managed it, though. Not even with all of their earthly talents."

*"And you never will. Despite the fragments of inborn magic in them, despite their chemistry . . . they are still only human beings. It was selfish and foolish of you to think that they could ever help you extricate yourself from **our** bargain. Human beings can do so little against the cosmos."*

"Never wanted to believe that," Bastion said. Then he smiled. It was a heartbreaking smile, so full of pain that it hurt me down to my bones. "Now I think I have to. Now . . . I'm so *tired*."

"Are you giving up?" Mr. Nous asked, with what I think in a human voice would have been disbelief. *"All these years of battling one another, and you're giving up at long last because you cannot speak of **love**? I took words of love from you years ago, my clever one. Certainly you can live without them."*

I would have expected only malevolent glee from Mr. Nous at Bastion's admission of misery. But even *it* sounded like it thought he should reconsider. I wonder if maybe it hadn't ever had a victim it considered a worthy challenge before he'd come along.

"No longer able to wish for anything—and in the second, all wishes for power and greatness would die within him," Bastion muttered. But just to himself. He said it quietly, under his breath. Then he raised his voice.

"Not ever giving up," Bastion said. "Never. Nous, I'll fight you until my last breath."

But Bastion was afraid. I saw it on him as clearly as I saw his despair. He hid it better than he had when he'd visited Mr. Nous as a child, but he was afraid. And I was afraid that this moment in time—what I was witnessing—was the *last* time.

Bastion had come to Northcott Faire for the last time in despair. Tired of fighting, and alone and in despair.

He was always alone, I thought. *Always.*

But I had made the despair more profound. I saw the pain of it on his face. I'd dug his grave the minute I pulled away from Gate 43. Left him with nothing at all. For what? A fucking *sentence*? Because I thought he needed to be more in touch with his *problems*?

He'd tried to tell me about his brother at the end. The one great secret that someone like Bastion would've always carried around, thinking it made them the worst person in the world.

He'd tried to trust me enough to reveal his deepest shame. Maybe even to tell me *everything*. And I had said—

Bastion, I honestly no longer give a fuck.

That was the last thing I ever said to him.

I know it was stupid, but I couldn't help myself. I stood in front of Bastion and screamed, beating my hands against his chest without making contact at all.

"I don't care about your mom's stupid unborn *fetus*! I don't care what you can't do, what you can't say! You have nothing to be *sorry* for! None of the people it trapped in this game have ever had anything to be sorry for! It was this thing, it was Mr. Nous! All Mr. Nous! Bastion, we can fix this . . . there's still time. I can still *help* you! LISTEN TO ME!"

But my words and my fists did nothing. I was a ghost, looking at a rerun on an old television.

"Interesting. So tell me, clever one. How will you fight me today?"

There was nothing left for me to do except watch. I watched as Bastion took a shaky breath and touched the gold chain around his neck. I watched as he straightened his shoulders. I watched as he scrubbed his wrists together—just for a second—before making himself stop.

I watched his mouth fall out of the brave smile he'd fixed there and twist like he was trying one last time to cry. I loved him so much, you know. Jesus Christ, I loved him more than anything.

"Nous, I've come with a fancy," Bastion said. He even bowed a little, before the velvet curtains.

"*Tell me your fancy*," Nous said. *"And I will tell you the fare."*

"Now," Bastion said, looking forward into the darkness with his eyes wide open—

"Now give me the power to defeat you."

CHAPTER THIRTY-THREE

Saturday, November 27, 1999

The final showdown between Bastion and Mr. Nous did not fade
out of view, shatter, or dissipate into something else. Instead, I
opened my eyes and realized I had been dreaming.

I was on my back at an angle. My arms and legs were bound
to something . . . I tried to look below myself and concluded that
it was an ancient Ten-Cent-Win game board at least as big as I was.

I was still in Northcott Faire. My right arm was still dislocated, and being tied had stretched my joints to a terrible angle. It
felt like my whole right side was on fire. My head throbbed, and
the rest of me was miserably cold. But those discomforts were
really secondary to the pain in my arm.

My view of the world above me was only black velvet. Velvet-
shaped like a cavern ceiling, with dripping cloth stalactites falling down so far that I was almost pinned under them. The floor
around me was dusted in snow and scattered with plush velvet

stalagmites. Flakes of white hung motionless in the air. I could see my breath.

In front of me was Mayor Winship, standing with Nic and Jamie and Dylan Everett and Kim Palmer and Dolores and Jay from Galactic Video. And a bunch of other people, some I knew and some I didn't. I looked for my dad and was happy when I didn't find him. I didn't want him to see whatever was going to happen to me, even if he was possessed. It was bad enough that Nic was there.

I didn't see the Attias or Mrs. Jackson. Anyone too far away from me I couldn't make out, because my vision was still blurry from when I'd been smothered into unconsciousness. Jay looked at me with nothing behind his eyes. A stare so blank that I could almost see Mr. Nous squatting inside his brain, puppeting him. The shoulder of Nic's drug rug was soaked in blood, but he didn't act like it hurt him.

I was too tired to plead with them anymore. In fact . . . at that moment, after everything, what I really wanted to do was give up.

Let them cut my hands off or something. Bleed out. Die. Stay down here in Northcott Faire forever. Maybe whatever was left of me would find whatever was left of Bastion.

"Okay, let's get this over with," Mayor Winship said, in his low voice. He leaned in toward me, a grim look on his unsmiling face. "Are you ready for this, you little punk?"

"Go to town, Captain Coronary," I said. My voice came out sounding like ungreased door hinges. "Super excited to be here."

I saw a flicker on the mayor's face. He was a piece of shit, for sure, but he was a strong-willed piece of shit—probably where Cameron got *his* stubbornness from. And shitty as he was, the mayor definitely did not have "murdering teenagers" on his usual agenda. I could almost see his reluctance. Almost. But it wasn't enough to defeat something as powerful as the force that controlled him. He gestured to Dolores, who came forward with one of her enormous kitchen cleavers.

I looked up at the ceiling again and saw that it was just the black-and-white stripes of the Big Top. I didn't know how I could have mistaken it for a cave before. I was bound up in the Big Top, facing the black velvet curtains and the *Novelties!* sign.

"Are you guys going to do it, or what?" I asked. I was very proud of myself. I hardly even sounded afraid.

But Dolores didn't move to cut me. She seemed to be waiting for something. Then I heard a soft rustling from far away. Like a slithering or a scratching deep within the distance.

The red-handed citizens of North Dana turned as one, toward the black velvet curtains in front of me.

The sound got louder and louder and louder until I wished to be untied just to cover my ears. And then it stopped all at once. Dust fell from the canvas walls of the Big Top, dust that I had mistaken, earlier, for suspended snow.

Two red hands gently pushed through the slit in the curtains. In the visions I'd seen—and the one time I had visited the Big Top before—Nous's hands looked just a *little* too large and just a tiny bit too long. Now, though—the hands were each easily as big as I was. They folded together like enormous birds, attached to forearms as big as old stone columns.

"*Nesbit North Nuñez,*" came the voice behind the curtains. "*Hello again.*"

I wanted to say something back to it, something smartass before I died. But the voice was so *big* this time, so loud and earthquaking in its vibrations, that I could only choke and gasp and hope that I lost my hearing soon. It was still sticky-sweet even as it hurt me. I saw Nic and Dolores and Mayor Winship get spontaneous nosebleeds and felt blood trickle down over my own lip.

I realized, then, that Mr. Nous had always been restrained before. Even when it was threatening us in the Big Top on our first visit. Even when it was about to eat Bastion. But now it wasn't playing. Things were serious now. Why were things serious now?

I hoped the rest of North Coven had escaped. I hoped Tet was okay. I hoped Cameron made it out safe.

But why *were* things serious now? What could make this monster, so much more powerful than human beings could ever hope to be, put down the toys and really *fight* us?

"You don't seem so remarkable, save for one . . . or **two** *things about you,"* Mr. Nous went on. *"I must admit, I always wondered at the appeal. You have been quite popular with my last two Advocates. But . . ."* Then it chuckled, and the brief quiet around the breaks in its laughter made me realize I was screaming. Wordlessly screaming, little scream-hiccups of pain each time the voice spoke. It hurt like nothing I had ever felt, like screws in my brain. My hands burned like they were being cooked over a flame.

"But I suppose there aren't many people to choose from. Small towns, and all that," Mr. Nous went on. I think it was still talking, but it hurt too much to listen. The meaning of its words started to slip away from me.

"Now give me the power to defeat you," Bastion said, in my head.

I could guess at the fare for that fancy. The same thing that killed everyone else down here. *Revocation of the token.* **Granted.**

He'd seemed so afraid, like he *knew* that making that wish would cost him his life. So why make it? What was the use of that power if Bastion was dead?

"*Personally, I find his sister very interesting,*" Mr. Nous was saying. "*I will have her as my next Advocate. My current one has already begun to bore me. But the Attia girl . . . the ways that she will torture herself over the mistakes she'll make— mouthwatering.*"

Behind the curtains, I could almost hear it . . . slobbering, despite the refinement of its agonizing speech. Drooling from its starless maw. I did find the strength to struggle a little then. It could get fucked if it thought it was going to get Dove.

In the back of my mind came another noise. Not the buzzing of Nous and the sound of its terrible voice.

Nesbit, can you hear me?

I rolled my head back and forth. "What?" I whispered.

"*Take his hands now, please,*" Mr. Nous said. One clawed hand made a grasping motion. "*And bring them to me.*"

We're in the Near-Depths! I can see you. Can you hear me?

Mayor Winship started to untie my right hand. I couldn't move my dislocated arm at all. Dolores came closer, brandishing her meat cleaver.

Nic touched my other shoulder. "Only gonna hurt for a minute, Nez," he said.

Nesbit, can you hear me?

Suddenly there were words that made sense.

Nesbit, can you hear me? We're in the Near-Depths! I can see you. Can you hear me?

At least I wouldn't die alone like Bastion did.

"Drea," I said. "I can hear you. I love you guys."

I closed my eyes as the mayor finished untying my wrist. And with my eyes closed, I figured out how to defeat Mr. Nous.

"WAIT!" I screamed, opening my eyes. I tried to crane my neck around. Dolores was above me, raising her knife. My scream actually startled her into taking a step back—which meant it had startled Mr. Nous.

Cameron had said Nous was afraid of us when we were alone in the cop car. And things were serious, now. Why would a creature with such unfathomable power be afraid?

I remembered my dream from the night Bastion had died. What his ghost had told me in the long hall of hearses.

Nesbit, you have the power now. Not just *you—it's for all five of you, of course—*

"The coven! The coven! It needs to break the coven! He *gave* it to us, oh shit! Jesus Christ, Bastion made Nous give it to us! The power to defeat it! It said 'even Cameron will do,' Cameron is the *will*! It needs to divide us to win! That's why it needed to kill one of us before we reached it, that's why it separated us, oh shit, *HELP ME YOU GUYS I NEED YOU TO COME HERE NOW*," I yelled.

I didn't know if they could get to me from the Near-Depths, and I didn't have time to wait and find out.

I needed a spell. I couldn't think of anything for a minute—I wasn't the Voice, after all. I was just the *grip*. But I could remember the first spell we had ever done together.

The day Bastion gave up his words of love. The spell to reshape the heart of Brandy's mom. It hadn't worked then. But it could work now.

"North Coven, we stand together," I said. My voice was almost totally blown out, but I managed to speak firmly and clearly. "Northcott Faire before us. Nearest grave behind us. Necropolis around us. Nexus compels us."

It was all true. Each word was true. And my hands stopped burning and started to buzz. The dust in the tent looked like snow again, and the veneer of the Big Top started to warp and melt into stalactites of velvet.

Nic tried to hold me down and Dolores swung her cleaver at my wrist, but I suddenly had control of my right arm again. It was like it had never been dislocated. My whole body vibrated with the magic of the coven, healing my wounds, making me strong.

I reached my untied hand up and grabbed the knife as it swung down. Instead of splitting my bones, the blade bounced off of me like my fingers were made of diamond. Dolores lost her grip on the cleaver, and it flew away into the cavern. I touched my right hand to the ties on my left and they melted away. The tattoos on my left hand were glowing again, the pure green color of our binding ribbon. The hand, the heart, the mouth, the eye. Even the sword of *will*.

Then the *cavern* started to shift. It was dark velvet and then it was starry void. The looping, eternally recurring beauty of the Milky Way. The Near-Depths were merging with the space around us. I saw Nic and Mayor Winship and thirty other people fall to the ground as the space *flexed* with the power of its sudden transformation.

And the girls appeared, standing with Cameron and Old Tet. They had all been right around me the whole time. Intangible to me, and invisible—but there. My words and their words, spoken together, had bridged the gap between Northcott Faire and the Near-Depths. Velvet particles of rock and white snow and stars began to fall around us, burning and freezing and scorching the earth. But we remained untouched as the many worlds became one.

"Nexus compels us," echoed the girls.

"Name your places and name yourselves and *Nous* will hear our voice like bells," I said.

I could still see Mr. Nous's hands as the world spun around us. Now its hands were peeking out from a dark cave, surrounded by a snowy forest. Now from an alley at the end of an unlit street in a city I had never seen. Now from the shadowy corner of a cloth tent at a black-and-white bazaar. Now rising from the inky water of a crack in the seafloor. Now at the bottom of a crater. Now in the old coop at the back of a dusty farm. I saw doors and doors and doors and black holes—and the red arms held sway over all, a fixed point in a spinning universe.

"*This should not be permitted, children,*" it said, in a tone that shattered the rest of the stone above us. The board I sat on broke apart into a million splinters of wood, freeing my legs. I fell to the starry ground in a cloud of debris. The girls made a circle around me, with Cameron to my left and Tet in front. Glossy rocks rained down over our heads without reaching any of us, creating a whirlwind.

"It *shouldn't be* permitted, but it *is*! You permitted it, asshole!" I shouted. "Now, conjurers, follow my words! North Coven! I am your hands! I build and tear apart! I give you all that I can create! Send this fucker away!"

"North Coven, I am your heart," Dove said. Her sunglasses were gone—probably lost in the abyss—and she looked straight at the black point that held the red hands, eyes wide open. "I feel the wrong and right of things. I bring my love and hate. Now. Take Mr. Nous *away*—"

Then Mr. Nous shot its massive arms out and grabbed at Tet, who stood in front of all of us protectively, his huge coat flapping in the maelstrom. Tet's arms and legs were speared by its clawed hands.

"JULES!" Dove screamed, reaching after him.

Tet let out a grunt of shocked pain, and then Nous lifted him away and flung him from us, through the whirlwind and out of our sight.

"No, *no!*" Dove shrieked, but the winds only intensified. I saw cave walls flicker into tent walls and into gravestones-nebulas-corpses-fires, the fires of all creation, a white light that was so vast I could barely see it, like the beginning of the universe, a green rope binding us, a world lost in snow—

"North Coven, I am your eyes," Brandy said, clinging to Drea. Her eyes shone with the same brilliant green light as my tattoos. "I see *all* with my sight! Please, oh Lord, please see us victorious—"

"NORTH COVEN, I AM YOUR VOICE, I WANT THIS FUCKER TO GO BACK TO WHERE IT CAME FROM," Drea shouted. Everything in the entire multiverse rippled as she spoke.

Then Mr. Nous darted forward again and seized me, pulling me out of the center of the circle with one red hand. I felt Drea and Dove and Brandy grabbing at my legs, but it was too vast. I was held by a hand the size of an oak tree, with an arm that was longer than I could see, that went back all the way to the end of everything, bleeding out into nothingness at the edge of my vision, with only blackness behind it.

"Cameron," I called back. "Finish it! You are our will-be-done! *Cameron!*"

"*Do it and your father will perish, fair child,*" Nous murmured, as it carried me away.

I turned my head and saw Cameron gaping. His eyes were as wide and shocked as they had been the day his father died in front of him.

"Cameron!" Dove said, but then I couldn't hear her anymore. I was pulled out of the winds and the moving worlds into pure flat darkness. I struggled in the iron grip of the hand that held me. Claws the size of scythes tore through my clothing and knifed along my skin.

Bastion, I thought. *I am experiencing some really crazy shit. Wish you were here.*

The hurricane surrounding the coven turned into a microscopic point in the distance. Everything was soft blackness. I could make out the velvet curtains again. They were all around me. I thought of the enclosed space between the stage curtains where I had kissed Bastion once, against my better judgment.

"*This is the end of you, little grip,*" Mr. Nous said. The black curtains hurtled toward me. Soon I would see what lay behind them. "*I normally allow some last words before I eat. Anything to say?*"

All I could think of was the sign in front of its lair. "Novelties," I said, and almost laughed.

Then I heard it. The faintest sound. Cameron was almost whispering. But it shook the foundations of the starless space I was in. Maybe of the entire multiverse.

"North Coven, I am your will-be-done.

Now, please, I just want to get rid of Mr. Nous."

A bolt of green light flew out in all directions, like footage I'd seen in class during our World War Two unit. The Manhattan Project. Oppenheimer saying: *"Now I am become Death, the destroyer of worlds."*

This was like that—an atomic blast. A wide ring of the purest green I had ever seen whipped out around us in a circle, followed by a pillar of light and cloudy fog.

At first, the blast seemed to spread out through entire galaxies. But as it expanded, the space around it collapsed. I was a thousand miles from the coven. Then only the length of, say, a football field. Then I could almost make out their faces.

Mr. Nous *howled* into the green-and-black void, shaking my body.

"No no no nononono no nononono no NOT ACCEPTABLE I WILL NOT BE BESTED BY HUMAN BEINGS—"

It was much smaller. The hand dropped me to the ground, and it was only a red hand. Too big to be a human hand, and too long, but not large enough to cup me in its palm like a bug. We were back in the Big Top, with the people of North Dana around us.

Then the sound of the green blast reached us, thirty seconds after the light, just like an A-bomb. It drowned out Mr. Nous. The sound rolled through the tent and *collapsed* the striped walls. The people who had been getting to their feet fell again. Dove slammed into me from the force of the sound and grabbed my arm, trying to tear me away from the black velvet curtains. Canvas and steel poles and pennants crashed to the ground around us.

Some impulse made me reach out, then, and grab Mr. Nous's retreating left hand in my own. My tattoos still glowed.

"Don't ever come back," I said, squeezing our palms together.

I felt the slickness of the glove and the movement of whatever lay *under* the glove, concealed. Mr. Nous shrieked again, and as it shrieked the rest of the tent fell, leaving the black curtains afloat in space. I could see the dead carnival behind it.

Maybe if I could have forgiven it—or *loved* it—I could have killed Mr. Nous right then, with our hands connected. But I wasn't Bastion. I couldn't forgive it. And I wasn't Dove, who could certainly have never loved it but who was, after all, our Heart.

Plus, the pacifist who had given up his life for this had explicitly said *defeat* and not *destroy*. Which was so like him.

I felt Nous shrink from me, trying to extricate its hand from my grip. And then—the final wave of green-colored sound slammed through what had once been the Big Top of Northcott Faire.

For an instant, the curtains blew back, and I caught a glimpse of *something*. Something vast and hungry and—even in the moment of defeat—something that smiled forever and ever, with more teeth than God.

Then the curtains flapped shut again and pulled themselves into a single round point of darkness. There was a shattering sound, and Cameron cried out as the chain around his neck snapped. The gold necklace, with the key still attached, flew into the ribbon of darkness, and vanished.

I staggered back to stand with North Coven as the dark spot flashed red, hanging in nothing, before winking out.

Our friends and families and all the other hostages from North Dana disappeared. Mayor Winship grabbed at his own chest for a second before vanishing, like his heart had stopped the moment that Mr. Nous made its exit. Cameron gasped. He reached toward the space where his dad had been for a second before dropping his hands.

I saw Dove glance between Cameron and the empty air, and then put one hand gently on his arm. The look on her face was kind.

The sky over the carnival was the color of November dawn. In the distance, I saw a Ferris wheel topple over, making a colossal sound as it crashed to the earth. The wind had started blowing again.

Dove and Drea and Brandy and I turned to each other.

"Wow," Dove said, looking us all up and down. She still had one hand on Cameron's arm. "You guys look really bad."

"You too," Drea said, and started to cry. She looped an arm around me, and one around Brandy. I held on to Dove with my right arm, which had started to dully throb. We pressed our foreheads together and hugged, a single unit for a second. I know, I know, it sounds pretty cheesy. But—we fucking *earned* it.

Cameron had extricated himself from Dove's grasp, and he sat down on the ground, blond hair blowing into his face, and fought with his bloody, muddy, shredded cargo pants until he got a pocket open. He was breathing kind of quickly, almost gasping. Then he checked his phone, which was completely smashed. That made him gasp harder. Then he opened his *other* cargo pocket and pulled out an inhaler, which he shook for a minute and then sucked on.

Dove wiped her eyes and bent down in front of him as he shoved his inhaler back into one destroyed pocket. "Winship?" she said.

Cameron looked up at her. His expression told me that he was still reeling from his dad's second death.

"Hey. You with us?" Dove asked.

"I just needed my inhaler," Cameron said, in a breathless rush. He didn't seem to notice that he could talk normally again. "Oh god. My dad. I killed him. Mr. Nous said I would kill him if I finished that spell. It was a spell, wasn't it? Oh god—"

"It wasn't your fault," Dove said, simply, and offered him her hand. He took it and got unsteadily to his feet, gray pieces of hay falling from his clothing.

"It wasn't your fault," Drea said. "Your old man was already a goner. Member of the walking dead."

"*Drea*," Brandy said.

"You didn't kill your dad. And you *did* save me," I said, catching Cameron's eye. His eyes flicked over to mine for a second, and then away, out at the crumbling world of the carnival. "Actually," I added, "you kind of saved all of us."

Cameron seemed a little more with it. Like he was processing some of what we were saying. He took a deep breath and looked around at the four of us.

"I could feel it in my head," Cameron said, pushing his hair back. "The . . . *magic*? Do you guys feel that?"

"Yeah," I said. "We feel it."

"Oh. Weird," Cameron said, faintly.

"North Coven welcomes you," Drea said, and pulled Cameron in by the shoulders. She hugged him with one arm, and then Dove put her arm around Cameron's other side. After an instant, Cameron put his arms around them in return.

For a second, the five of us made a single unit—a connected circle—with our arms around one another. It was just as cheesy as the first time. But it felt strangely right, too. When we dropped our arms, it seemed significant . . . almost like we had made a vow without words.

"I didn't know you really had asthma until like three days ago," Dove said.

"Well, I do," Cameron said. "But . . . I also played up that attack in Mock Trial freshman year—and when we were doing the spring play last year—hey! I can talk again!"

"That's great, asthma-faker," Dove said.

"It's all coming down," Brandy said, as a Tilt-A-Whirl far away from us crumbled into nothing. I saw a white light, a silhouette of a glowing *person*, ascend toward the brightening sky as the ride shuddered out of existence. "We have to get out."

We struggled down the midway as fast as we could. Dove was hobbling a little, and Cameron stopped to take another puff on his inhaler. But I kept looking at the *people*.

The former Advocates were no longer black formless voids with staring white eyes or painted plywood. They were fully human beings, glowing with an unearthly brilliance. We walked by Mandy's Menagerie, and I saw that her *Fancy* and *Fare* sign had disappeared. The little girl stood in front of it, looking very tiny in her nightgown, with a soft expression on her face. When she saw us, she gave a shy little wave.

"Are you okay?" I asked. "Um . . . Mandy? Do you need us to help you leave?"

"I *am* leaving, sir," Mandy said, in a peculiar accent. "See?"

She extended one little hand, pointing up, the way the hand tattoo on my finger did. As she pointed, the Menagerie started to crumble into dust.

I watched it blow away in the wind. Mandy seemed to follow it. She grew brighter and brighter and became translucent and *ascended*, straight up into the sky until I lost sight of her.

"Oh, wow, okay," I said, looking up. As I looked toward the sky, I heard a groan coming from the other side of the midway.

"Jules!" Dove said, hobbling toward the sound. I could see Old Tet out in front of us, closer to the Cemetery Scares dark ride. He was bleeding from his legs and arms, but very much alive.

"Mr. T, I thought you were lost in space," Drea said, hustling over. Cameron and Brandy followed her, but I turned back for a second, to look at the space where Mandy's Menagerie had been.

In the empty spot it had left behind, I could see clearly into another row of games, running parallel to ours. Another path in this endless place, where all roads led to the blasted circle that had once been the Big Top.

I was the only one looking back as the other four-fifths of North Coven crowded around Old Tet, the only one who saw the antique Wheel of Fortune game down that other aisle.

Bastion's Misfortune, the sign above it said. I took a step toward it. Then another. Then I was running, even though I thought I had no strength inside me left for running.

So, yeah. I told you right at the beginning that I saw Bastion one last time, and I know you *know* I didn't mean in dreams or visions . . .

CHAPTER THIRTY-FOUR

Saturday, November 27, 1999

He was standing by the far side of the painted wheel with his hands behind his back, like a really polite businessman waiting for a bus. His clothes were the clothes he'd died in, stupid letterman jacket and all. His face was whole and unblemished, from his perfect star-white spot to his angular jaw.

"Nesbit!" Bastion said when he saw me. He looked almost shocked, and held out his arms.

"Bastion, Bastion, Jesus Christ," I said, choking on my own words, and wrapped myself in his embrace. He squeezed me tightly to his chest, and for the first time since that more-than-a-week-ago night of November 20, I felt happy. His arms were perfect around me. He smelled like himself. My chest hurt from how much I wanted to be there pressed against him, like a knot that had been tied at the center of my being had come undone all at once.

"I'm so sorry," I said. My voice was shaking. I took my hands away from his back and reached up to touch his face. "I didn't know, I didn't know."

"Nesbit, I was too ashamed to tell you," Bastion said, looking down at me with his brow creased. "No way your attraction to me wasn't at least partially because you thought I was a *decent* person. Nous—if I told you about the things I'd done, the wishes—I always thought you'd stop caring about me—"

"Shhh, stop, stop," I said, touching his mouth. I was crying. I was crying a *lot*, actually, tears falling down my face until Bastion was shimmering in the pre-dawn light. In the distance, I could hear the smashing and splintering of more carnival attractions breaking apart in the powerful wind, but I didn't think about it.

"You're okay now, we did what you wanted, we defeated Mr. Nous. He can't hurt you anymore," I said. "You don't have to talk like that anymore, Bastion, it's okay now. It's okay now."

"Nesbit," Bastion said. He looked at me for a second, and then leaned down and kissed me. I kissed him back, tangling my fingers in his hair. My hands buzzed just from touching him.

Then he pulled back. "Nesbit, I have to tell you something," he said, and I took a second to wipe at my teary face.

"Cool, yeah," I said, sniffling. "What is it?"

"Now I couldn't tell you before," Bastion said, holding me by the shoulders. "Nesbit, I know this sounds crazy, but, well. Nous wouldn't even let me *say* it—but I felt it anyway. Nesbit, I love you."

"I know," I said. "You're so obvious, Big Fun."

"I hoped you knew," Bastion said, in a tiny voice. He looked shocked again. Probably because he'd started a sentence without *N*.

Then *he* was crying. I'd never seen it. He'd given his tears away to Mr. Nous before we'd ever met, in exchange for what I don't know. I brushed teardrops away from his cheeks as they fell.

"Nesbit, I love you," Bastion said like he was praying. He pressed a kiss to my mouth after every sentence. "Nesbit, I love you so very much. Nesbit, Nesbit, I love you. Nesbit, if people are ever made for one another, then I was made for you."

"Okay, okay," I said, leaning back. "I love you, too. We can talk about it later. We have to get you out of here. Come on."

But you already know what he was going to say, don't you? I didn't. I was only thinking about how glad I was to see him. How it was like sunshine after a thousand years of cold and darkness.

"Nesbit, I can't come with you," Bastion said, shaking his head.

"Yeah, you can, of course you can," I said. "Come on." I tried to steer him back toward the midway, but he was as solid and immovable as always.

"No," Bastion said, and the simple sorrow in his voice stopped me cold.

"Don't tell me *no* right now," I said, pulling at his arms. "Don't do this to me."

"Nesbit, I'm already dead."

"No, don't *do* this to me," I said, trying to drag him with all my strength. It wasn't enough: he stayed firmly put. "Come on, come on, Bastion, please, we have to go!"

"Nesbit," Bastion said, looking at me. He looked so sad. "I'm already gone. Now I'm just a ghost . . . waiting for a ride."

"Please come with me," I begged. "Just *try*. Please."

A sound like wind chimes came from all around us. It started in the center of the painted old wheel, like glass vibrating against glass. I looked behind us and saw that the wooden pieces of Bastion's Misfortune were crumbling into dust and being borne up in the wind.

"Now I think I have to go," Bastion said, watching as the last of the Wheel of Fortune was reduced to shining particles. The dust seemed to catch on him as it flew, making him shine with his own light.

"No," I said, as the air glittered around us, making another little whirlwind. "Don't leave. I'm not ready."

"Nobody is ever ready," Bastion said, seriously. "Now *listen*—even though the multiverse is vast and strange . . . and I'm afraid that I do not understand it at all, even in death . . . I promise to try and find you again someday."

"Please stop," I begged. "Just come on, let's just go—"

"Nesbit," Bastion said, over my protests. "Never once will I forget who you are, the person that you *really* are. Never will I let go of . . . w-what you *meant* to me, which was everything, Nesbit, everything in the whole world."

"I won't forget you either," I said. I was crying again. "I'll try to find you, too. Someday."

Bastion held my shoulders and looked straight into my eyes, and I realized that his touch was less substantial. I could see the light behind him. He pressed a feather-soft kiss to my forehead.

"Nesbit. Nesbit—I think I have to leave now," Bastion said. Even his tears were vanishing, and the light that shone from him had gotten so bright that it hurt my eyes to look at. His feet left the earth, and he started to move upwards and away from me.

"Wait!" I said, reaching up through the cloud of glitter and fog. "What was your name? Your *real* name?"

The last expression he made before I couldn't really *see* him anymore was a smile. Bastion smiled at my question, as he was pulled away from me.

"Nesbit," he said faintly, "it's—"

I know he was trying to answer—but before he could speak again, the wind took the boy who'd once given up his name to fight a monster and made him *so* bright, so bright he hurt to look at, and pushed him *up up up*, upward into the sky until he was lost to me.

I never saw him again, awake or dreaming.

CHAPTER THIRTY-FIVE

Saturday, November 27, 1999

For a minute, or maybe longer, I knelt on the empty ground where Bastion had been.

"Nez," someone said, and I turned around and saw Brandy. I stood up on unsteady legs. She looped her arm around my arm, and if she'd witnessed anything she didn't say so. "We have to leave. Everything is almost gone."

Northcott Faire was falling into emptiness around us. Almost nothing remained except for a scorched field on the gray earth.

The others were waiting just outside the Cemetery Scares door. Brandy and I went out of it to meet them, and in the real world, I saw that Stepwood itself had collapsed into the earth.

Somehow it was night, even though it had been dawn when we went in. The stars illuminated a barren landscape. The townspeople who had surrounded us were gone. There was nothing there for them to be *at*, if you follow me. The cemetery itself had crumbled. The stones had sunk into the mossy dirt. The Dearest grave was just a little pile of dusty sandstone at the edge of a blank space. The impressive iron gate was in ruins. The plots that graves had overlooked were reduced to a single scorched clearing in the thick woods around the Quabbin. If there were ever any bodies buried there—whether they were the corpses of Advocates gone by, or the cursed souls of the Northcott family, or something else entirely—they were unmarked now, except by the simple fact that no trees grew over them.

Someday the trees *would* grow up in the clearing, and it would be impossible to distinguish from the rest of the forest around it. Except for one thing.

Where the Northcott Faire mausoleum stood there was now only a hole in the earth. It was too narrow to climb into, too tight for a person to get more than an arm inside. I have no clue how we managed to walk out of it and back into our world at all.

It was small and dark and innocuous in the mound of earth at the top of the hill, next to the thin beginning of the woods. Small enough to easily miss, or twist your ankle in if you stepped into it without noticing.

No. It was smaller even than that. In fact, it was so small that it seemed like nothing could fit into it at all.

Except maybe a key.

CHAPTER THIRTY-SIX

Sunday, November 28, 1999

As soon as we were out, we left Old Tet resting against a tree with his wounds bound in ripped-up pieces of Drea's T-shirt. Drea put her sweatshirt over her bra, and Brandy stayed behind, watching guard over Tet while we ran back to Woodland Estates trailer park.

Actually, it was more like we *dragged* ourselves there. We elected Brandy to stay because she and Cameron were the least injured, and Cameron had to help Dove walk. Dove was limping with every step she took. Drea's mouth was torn up, and her wrists were rope burned to hell.

I was in no shape to help anyone. In fact, I kind of wished that there was someone available to support *me* while I tried to get up the hill. My dislocated and magically relocated shoulder ached. My face still had grime on it from the nosebleed I'd gotten when I heard Nous speak with its full voice. My wrists and ankles burned from a bunch of possessed people handcuffing me and tying me up. My clothing and a good amount of skin underneath was completely shredded to hell from my time spent in Mr. Nous's claws.

And I felt *sad*. Terribly sad, deeply sad. Something lost forever sad. That was actually the worst of my injuries.

Agent Scully, who definitely had no idea she'd been on a wild adventure, greeted us as we went into the purple double-wide. Drea picked her up and kissed her all over her striped face until Scully got annoyed and wriggled away.

The clock in Drea's house said it was just after midnight. I wasn't immediately sure of the actual date, with everything that had happened. I called the ambulance, quietly, so Jamie wouldn't wake up. Then Drea went and woke her mom up anyway so she could make sure she wasn't possessed. She wasn't.

"What *happened* to you?!" Jamie said, totally freaking out when she saw the state we were in. I peered out the window to check that the junky Cadillac was parked in the driveway—it was, like we'd never taken it on a high-speed chase.

Behind me, Jamie stopped short when she saw Cameron.

"Nice to meet you," Cameron said, just as stiff as he had been the first time.

"Jamie," Dove said, sitting in one of the kitchen chairs with her bare feet propped up. The soles of her feet were almost black with dirt and blood. "Does the name Bastion Attia mean anything to you?"

"Oh, honey," Jamie said, her expression going from startled to sad all at once. "Is that what this is about? Is this something to do with his murder?"

"No," Dove said, looking away. "But I'm really, really glad you know what I'm talking about."

We had to direct the EMTs to Tet and Brandy when they reached us, because nobody had any idea what we meant when we said he was at Stepwood Cemetery. To everyone else in North Dana, Stepwood had never existed at all.

Everything, it seemed, had been erased. My car wasn't at Northcott House, because the Y2K party had never happened. I hoped that my round of detentions from Coach Silva had been erased, too.

The only thing left from the week we'd just lived through was the very messed-up clothing on our bodies. And our injuries. Oh, and Cameron's Nokia was still smashed.

"This is really bad," Cameron said, looking at his cell phone for the tenth time like it was going to magically repair itself.

"Must've gotten broken when we iced Mr. Nous," Dove said.

"When you iced what and who?" Jamie said, coming back into the kitchen with her regular clothes on.

"I think I need to ice my feet for a minute or two," Dove said, smoothly.

"I think you should have the EMTs take a look first," Jamie said.

"My dad got me this cell phone. Do you know how much it cost?"

"Fifty million dollars," I guessed.

"Two-fifty mil," Drea said.

Cameron glared at both of us, cradling his smashed Nokia. Suddenly I felt bad. The EMTs had reappeared with Tet on a stretcher, and everyone else went outside to meet them and Brandy, but I stayed inside with Cameron for a second. Mostly because it hurt too much to move.

"Hey," I said. "I meant it when I said that you saved us. You did the right thing."

"Tell that to my dad," Cameron said, still staring at his ruined cell phone.

"Come on," I said. "I don't think the Nokia was like the repository of all his love for you."

"He didn't love me," Cameron said. He'd said that before, when we were in the cop car together. He said it again now, not like he was looking for pity—but just like it was a fact, totally inarguable in his mind.

"I'm pretty sure he loved you, Cameron," I said. "He seemed like the kind of guy who only abused people he was *invested* in. Which is super fucked up."

"He *was* fucked up," Cameron said really quietly. "He was. But I . . . even if he didn't love me. Or even if he did, but he was fucked up—I loved *him*."

"I'm sorry he died," I said. I was, too, even though Mayor Winship's life didn't really mean anything to me. At that moment I felt like I couldn't take any more sadness. Or any more death. "But—it was his time to die, Cameron. It really was. He had a bad heart. And beating Mr. Nous was the only way for you to ever have any chance at a life. Being its Advocate wasn't any sort of life."

Cameron looked over at me then. His eyes were glinting in the half-light of the kitchen.

"Then how come," he said, "Bastion Attia managed to live more of a life than I ever have?"

"Jesus," I said. "He *didn't*, Cameron, that's the point. Whatever you were jealous of him for, whatever you've always felt like he

365

had over you, it . . . it didn't mean anything to him. He was lonely. He was trapped."

"I know you're right," Cameron said. His face lit up in red for brief intervals as the ambulance lights flashed in through the window. "But I didn't know that *then*. I only saw Bastion. I wanted to be like him. To me, he was . . . perfect."

"He wasn't perfect," I said. My voice broke a little. I was trying to smile, to be zen about it all, but . . . my grief was fresh again, and it hurt like a raw thing. "That would be so boring."

But it was as if admitting that he had wanted to be *like* Bastion opened some floodgate that connected directly from Cameron's brain to his mouth.

"I've wanted to be *him* since we were five. He always had the best grades. He always hit the home run in Little League. He always was the best at *everything*. The smartest. The coolest family. The coolest friends. Even when it seemed like he had developed some kind of weird *brain* disorder, everyone still liked him. He was *still* the best! I couldn't even make it onto the fucking football team. If I had been like him maybe my dad—"

Cameron's hands clenched tightly around his smashed cell phone as he talked.

"Your dad would have definitely still found something to be disappointed about, I promise," I said.

"And then he got to have *you*," Cameron said, not really listening to me. "He literally even managed to pull off being like— like how *I* am—"

"I'm *also* gay," I said mildly. "Very gay. I know what a twink is, remember?"

I was trying to crack a joke, because Cameron was starting to make me worried. His face was really flushed. With everything we had gone through, I didn't want him having a full nervous breakdown to end the night.

"I should have known you would be with him. You remember when we worked out together in freshman year? You remember?"

"Um, yeah of course," I said, aiming for soothing.

"You said you didn't care about organized sports at all. You—you weren't in there lifting weights to prove anything to anyone. You were just doing it because you *liked* to. And I thought about how you didn't care about the stupid things I spent my whole stupid *life* caring about. And I liked it. I couldn't *be* like that, but I liked it. And then you—when I saw you with him, I thought, *of course*. Because someone like you would never care about someone like me. You'd care about someone like *him*. And I was just *trapped*, Nesbit, trying to be as good as someone who was better than me in *every way*—"

I was trying to follow this stream-of-consciousness rant attentively (but still soothingly), and I put my hands up in the air in a *slow down* gesture.

"You don't have to do that anymore, though," I said. "You're *not* trapped. Not by your dad. And not like Bastion was, either."

"Bastion, Bastion, fucking *Bastion*!" Cameron said. "How did he deal with Mr. Nous without going *insane*? How was he still *everywhere* being good at *everything*? I don't understand it, and—and—and—and—you know what?!" Cameron said, and got to his feet in the flickering red light.

"No, what?" I asked, trying to project calm.

Cameron looked down at the Nokia still clenched in his hand, and then with one deliberate movement he hurled it against the wall.

"Whoa! This is not your house!" I said. Jamie's wall looked mostly unscathed, but pieces of Cameron's phone littered the floor.

Cameron sank back down in the chair and met my eyes. "You know what the worst part is?" he asked, like he hadn't just had a total freak-out.

"Um. What is the worst part?" I asked.

"The worst part is that I'm actually pretty fucking sorry that he's dead," Cameron said, and then he put his face in his hands and started to cry.

It was so surprising to hear him express sadness over Bastion that for a split second I thought Cameron had to be referring to the mayor. But he honestly *was* talking about Bastion.

I thought about how they had known each other since they were five. All those years of Cameron measuring himself up against someone. And then that someone was *gone*.

"I get it," I said. I was suddenly fighting back tears of my own, even though I had already shed enough tears that night to easily last for the next decade or so. I put my left hand on Cameron's knee while he cried, and after a second, he took his own left hand away from his eyes and rested his tear-damp palm on top of my fingers. I could feel the buzz of coven magic connecting us.

"I get it," I said again, and Cameron used his free hand to wipe at his face.

"You don't get it," he said. "You loved him. And he loved you. Even *I* know that. And that . . . that's . . . it's *clean*. It's a clean sadness. I feel gross. Like a gross, conflicted piece of shit. I feel like the fucking *bad guy*, Nesbit."

"You are not the bad guy," I said, thinking of Mr. Nous. "Relax with that. You'd be the lamest bad guy ever."

"I do feel like the bad guy," Cameron said, insistently.

"Well, you're not," I said. "You're just kind of a dickbag sometimes."

That stopped Cameron cold. He actually laughed. When he laughed, he kind of snorted through his tears, so that he was weirdly cry-laughing. Which made me laugh, too.

I looked up and realized Dove had limped back in while we were both basically crying and laughing and holding hands. I wasn't sure how long she'd been standing there, or how much she'd heard. Cameron startled when he saw that she was in there with us, and snatched his hand away from mine.

"The EMTs want to take a look at you guys," Dove said, circling us like a tiny one-legged vulture. "If you're done sniveling sometime in the near future."

"Fuck off," Cameron said, still wiping his eyes. But there was no real malice in his voice. And then Dove put her hand on his arm and squeezed, just for a second, like she did when one of us was upset.

We all ended up getting dropped off at the urgent care, while Tet was brought over to the bigger hospital in Amherst. Brandy— who had been scared of Tet a few days ago but now seemed to really like him—called the hospital while we were all getting looked over at the clinic. She'd gotten Dolores from Hazy Dee's, who was Tet's emergency contact, and Dolores said that Tet was going to make a full recovery.

That was interesting, actually. Tet *had* been able to leave North Dana, unlike the night when he'd given me the demonstration of what happened when he tried to cross the town line. It seemed like Mr. Nous's *fares* had been erased.

As for my recovery, well . . . my arm was going to be okay, but I had two very nasty lumps on my head and a mild concussion, plus an exciting variety of flesh wounds.

Just like the day that we'd found Bastion dead, our parents were called. Brandy's mom showed up first. The fact that Mrs. Jackson didn't seem particularly evil when she picked Brandy up gave me hope that the *fancies* hadn't gone away when the fares did.

In my case, Nic was called. Nobody could get in touch with Cameron's mom.

"She's in a Valium coma," Cameron said. He seemed a lot more normal after his meltdown in Jamie's kitchen. "My dad just died, remember? She's heavily sedated right now. No one is going to answer that phone."

"I can take you home," I said.

Anna Attia showed up second. She looked *so* freaked out, probably scared about losing a second kid, but Dove soothed her and then demanded that they go to Old Tet's camp to check on Elizabeth.

Before Dove left, she stopped in front of the room where I was getting the worst of my gashes stitched up.

"I'm taking the week off from school," she said, standing in the doorway. "But . . . Friday around eight. Hersh said we can use the Northcott House solarium for our coven stuff, at least until we find a better location."

"You called Herschel? It's like two in the morning on a Monday."

"I have his cell phone number and he *never* sleeps."

"Are you going to tell him about any of this?" I asked, honestly curious.

"Of course," Dove said. "He'll understand."

"Okay," I said. "Very cute, actually. Such a profound understanding between my favorite maybe-couple, Dove Bar and—"

"Shut *up*, oh my god! You are so lucky I'm too tired to kill you right now!" Dove said. "But for real, we're having a coven meeting. It will feel good to have five people again." She gave me a sad little smile. "Even if our fifth is a sentient pile of living puke."

"You actually invited Cameron?" I asked.

"Had to," Dove said, shrugging. "He's the Will."

When Nic showed up, sleepy and confused and definitely not possessed or shot, I felt my throat get tight like I was going to cry *again*. I wanted to apologize, to promise I would never again do anything as crappy and underhanded to him as I had with the whole OxyContin story. But Nic didn't even know I'd ever done that. So instead, I just hugged him when I slid into the passenger seat.

"Um, yo," Nic said, patting my back. "You okay? What the hell happened? Who's the little yuppie?"

"That's my friend," I said as Cameron got in the back. "Cameron Winship."

"The mayor's kid? I thought you guys hated him," Nic said, with absolutely no regard for the fact that Cameron was two feet behind him.

I caught Cameron's eyes in the rearview mirror. "He's pretty cool, actually," I said.

Cameron turned red enough that I could see it in the dark car, and looked away. "Thanks," he said. But he sounded like he meant it.

The flags in the center of North Dana were at half-mast for Mayor Winship. At the Winship's white Victorian (with the four locks) in the center of town, I did something I considered to be a pretty amazing gesture, given the condition of my body, and walked Cameron up to his back door.

"You have keys?" I asked, when Cameron was in front of the farmhouse door. He didn't say anything for a minute, just reached up and felt around on the top of the doorframe. Then he brought down a silver set of spare house keys.

"Wow, that could have saved me a lot of trouble during my break-in," I said, feeling kind of dumb. Cameron smirked at me from behind a curtain of extremely grimy blond hair and jingled the keys together a little.

"Seeing someone come crawling out from under my bed like a giant human spider was the *actual* scariest thing that's ever happened to me," Cameron said.

"Even considering everything that's actually happened to you?" I asked, smiling.

"Yup," Cameron said, and he smiled back—a real smile. For a second we stood there in silence, and then Nic beeped the horn. Not loud, just a tiny little honk to let me know to hurry up so he could crawl back into his Winnebago.

"I gotta go," I said. "Are you going to be okay?"

I didn't know exactly what I meant, even as I asked. But I felt like I should ask.

Cameron nodded. "Yeah. I think so. Are *you* going to be okay?"

I thought about Bastion disappearing into shimmering light and fog.

Nesbit, I love you.

I love you so very much.

"Yeah," I said. "I will. Eventually."

Then Cameron let himself into his house and I dragged myself back to the car and climbed in like a ninety-year-old man.

Once I was sitting down, Nic looked over at me for a second. I could hear him moving his gross toothpick around in his mouth.

"Nez," he said, after a beat. "The doctors spent like three full minutes listing off all your injuries. You gonna tell me what happened?"

"Landslide by the Quabbin," I said, sticking to our planned—but incredibly lame—story.

"Yeah? Did the landslide stab the old homeless guy numerous times in the limbs?" Nic asked.

"He's not an old homeless guy," I said, leaning back and closing my eyes. "He's a historian. His name is Jules."

I hoped that Jules would get to make the most out of his new life. That we all would. For Bastion's sake . . . and as a tribute to what he sacrificed.

"I mean, okay," Nic allowed. "That's . . . rad, but . . . how concerned should I be right now? For your well-being?"

I thought about how Nic had sworn that Dad *made* him come with me to Bastion's funeral. At the time I'd believed it. Now I thought it was probably Nic's idea all along.

I hoped that Nic was still protected from relapsing into addiction by the wish Bastion had made for him. I hoped that Dove wouldn't suddenly get sick, and that Brandy's mom wouldn't go back to the abuser she'd been before. Mr. Nous had said that wishes made could not be undone. But now Mr. Nous was gone. What did that *mean*? I just didn't know. I *hoped*, but I didn't know. All I knew was that from now on we would have to help each other with whatever life kicked our way. With drugs. With abuse and pain and sadness and sickness. With our magic. And, of course, with the empty place that Bastion had left behind.

It seemed terribly hard. Like a long span of mourning and pain. Like a lot of things that only time would help or tell or heal. And it seemed frightening.

But not as frightening as what we'd been through together. And like I said—I had *hope*.

"Just be a regular amount of concerned," I said, my eyes still closed. I was more tired than I could ever remember being.

"Will do," Nic said, and drove us home.

I dozed in the car, even though it was a short ride. When Nic woke me up we were in the driveway, and the little ranch house was lit up and waiting for me.

The night was cold when I stepped out into it. The universe above me was vast. And the stars were so bright that I could almost make out the arm of the Milky Way.

ACKNOWLEDGMENTS

I owe many thanks to my editors, Laura Schreiber and Sarah Levison, who improved this story more than I thought possible, and to my matchless agents, Martha Perotto-Wills and Molly Ker Hawn, as well as Diane João, Marinda Valenti, Renee Yewdaev, Grace House, Colin Verdi, Liam Donnelly, Erin Ashby, Codie Crowley, and Alex Russell. And to the many historians—amateur and otherwise—of the lost towns of the Swift River Valley.

ABOUT THE AUTHOR

Freddie Kölsch is a connoisseur and crafter of frightful fiction (with a dash of hope) for teens and former teens. She lives in Salem, Massachusetts, with her high school sweetheart-turned-wife, a handful of cats, a houseful of art, and a mind's eye full of ghosts. *Now, Conjurers* is her first novel.